ALSO BY ROSE SZABO

We All Fall Down
(River City duology #1)

WHAT
TE

BIG ETH

ROSE SZABO

SQUARE
FISH

FARRAR STRAUS GIROUX

NEW YORK

To my grandmother, Kathleen.
She says she does not like books about werewolves,
but she is proud of me anyway.

WHAT BIG TEETH

WHAT BIG TEETH

(A MENAGERIE)

"This he afterwards explained by saying that to a boyar the pride of his house and name is his own pride, that their glory is his glory, that their fate is his fate."

  —*Dracula*

Here, said she,
Is your card, the drowned Phoenician Sailor,
(Those are the pearls that were his eyes. Look!)
Here is Belladonna, the Lady of the Rocks,
The lady of situations.
Here is the man with three staves, and here the Wheel,
And here is the one-eyed merchant, and this card,
Which is blank, is something he carries on his back,
Which I am forbidden to see.

  —T. S. Eliot, *The Waste Land*

PROLOGUE

SOMEWHERE IN THE NIGHT FOREST, THE BOY IS running.

I cannot smell him, like my sister Luma and our cousin Rhys can, his sweat and his fear. But I can hear him, as well as the creak of branches, the rustle of the leaves that stir underfoot. He's moving from the birch stands onto the pine needles. I can hear the pounding of his blood, the frustrated sob he tries to keep in his mouth as his legs struggle on the unfamiliar ground.

Our other cousin Charlie is here too, clattering through the streambed below on new shoes. He's clumsy and young, but he has other talents. So do Rhys and Luma, who changed as soon as we left the house and now run on all fours, so silent that even my ears can't pick them up. I left my shoes on the porch, and my bare feet are whispers on the pine needles, but I'm sure that they can hear my heart beating wild excitement.

It's spring dusk. A thin crescent moon slices upward through the sky.

The boy bursts out into a clearing, full of tall grass and the burrows of small animals. This is the choke point. The boy puts his foot in a rabbit hole and falls. I glance past him, across the clearing, until I spot a pair of luminescent eyes. Rhys tilts his head up and rumbles. *Now.*

We all converge at once: Rhys from the right, me from the left, and Luma pounces from behind with both forepaws. The boy goes sprawling onto his stomach under her weight, rolling as we let him get up, scrabbling through the wet grass and trying to get his feet under him again.

Charlie stumbles out of the dark and plants his hands on his knees, wheezing a little. The boy crawls for Charlie. He is saying *run.* And then he looks at us and notices that Charlie is showing no fear. He begs him for help.

Rhys and Luma nip at the boy's ankles while I climb onto his back, riding him as they drag him backward into the dark. The boy is still yelling at our cousin. Charlie finally gets a breath into his lungs, straightens up. He pushes his glasses up his nose and trots along after us as we recede toward the tree line.

"Don't you all ever get tired of this?" Charlie asks us while the boy cries for us to let him go. "Don't you want to play something else?"

Rhys lets go of the boy's ankle for a moment, cocks his head up at Charlie, panting, grinning now from a human face. "No," he says.

We drag the boy back into the shadow of one of the big pine trees. Someone's yelling for us back at the house. It sounds like the visiting banker has realized his son is missing.

"What should we do with him?" Rhys asks.

"Boil him up into soup," Luma says. She hates soup, but the joke is lost on the boy, who sobs harder.

Charlie is restless, looking around. "I'm gonna make him forget. We'll get in trouble if we don't."

"Wait." I hold up a hand. I feel something that's new, some hungry hollow little place inside me. "I think . . . I want to eat him."

Rhys slaps me on the back, and Luma squeals with delight. I've never wanted to eat anybody before, and they're proud.

"You can't, though," Rhys says quickly.

"We promised Grandma," says Luma.

"Alright." I plant my hands on the boy's shoulders and start to climb down off of him. As I do, my mouth stretches wide like a yawn, although I don't feel tired. "Let's go—"

And then something happens that I do not understand. I'm sitting on the pine needles, my jaw aches unbearably, and the boy is gone.

ONE

I OPENED MY EYES, AND I WAS ON THE TRAIN.

I was the only passenger left. How long had I been asleep? I looked down to make sure I still had my things: my straw hat, my suitcase stamped with the letter *Z*. I'd hung on to them this whole way, through sleeping on a bench in Penn Station and sprinting to catch a train in Boston, ever since I'd left Saint Brigid's School for Young Ladies this time yesterday. Thinking about it, I ran my tongue over my teeth again. No matter how many times I did it, I could still taste copper.

The door at the far end of the car clattered open, and I jumped. Just the conductor, coming down the aisle to check on me. He looked nervously down at me, and I felt guilty, wondering if he could tell I was on the run.

"You the stop in Winterport?" he said. I nodded. His eyes had wandered down to my suitcase.

"You got people there?" he asked. "I'm kin of the Hannafins, myself."

People up here were like this, I remembered suddenly. Always wanting to know about your family. "The Zarrins," I offered.

He twitched like a rabbit before settling himself back down. "I thought you might be," he said. "They don't leave Winterport much, do they?"

"I did," I said. "I haven't been back in eight years."

Once I said it I froze, terrified he'd ask me why I was coming back now. I rummaged frantically in my mind for a convincing lie. But he just smiled at me tightly and touched his hat.

"We'll just be slowing down, not a full stop," he said. "Don't worry, people do it all the time. When the whistle blows the first time, get ready."

He disappeared, and I stared out the window and watched the landscape for a while. It had been almost summer in Maryland, but as we rumbled across the bridge that divides New Hampshire from Maine, I saw a few stubborn patches of snow clinging on beneath the pine trees. I'd been angry when I'd gotten on the train, and that had kept me in motion. But the weather chilled my anger and crystallized it into fear. Maybe there were good reasons I wasn't supposed to be at home. I had a vague, half-remembered feeling that it wasn't exactly safe. It all felt faded and vaguely ridiculous. None of it seemed plausible when I held it up to the light. But if it was true, if I was right, then I needed to be home again.

After all, there was no other place for me in the world. Not after what I'd done.

Lucy Spencer flashed in my mind for a moment then. Her red hair coming out of its braid, her face twisted in that expression people make right before they start screaming—

And then the whistle was blowing. Get ready, he'd said. I hefted my suitcase, clapped my hat on my head. Time to go visit my family.

The conductor came back to open the door for me as the train slowed. He couldn't even look me in the eye. He mumbled something that sounded like "Be careful," and then we were rumbling slowly past a platform, and I was stepping out into the air.

I felt a jarring, sickening sensation of the world rising up to meet me. I staggered, let go of the suitcase, and hit one knee on the wood of the platform, the train still trundling behind me. I crawled away from it, feeling like I'd been in an accident. It was moving faster than I'd thought, when I was on it.

I told myself not to be weak. I made sure I hadn't scraped my knee; I didn't want anyone around here to see my blood. I got to my feet, checked to make sure my suitcase hadn't popped open in the fall, and took a moment to get my bearings.

The platform was deserted. Beyond it the single cobbled street of the town bent like an elbow out into the ocean, with houses lining the crook. Along the water were docks where fishing boats bobbed up and down at their moorings. The sun was going down behind the tree-covered hills, bathing the town in alternating stripes of red light and shadow. Three young boys knelt in the street, their hand-me-down coats straining threadbare over their backs.

I found myself watching them closely, my eyes locked on them. They were using a stick to try to loosen one of the cobblestones. One of them looked up and saw me, and froze. I watched him reach down as though he thought if he moved slowly enough I wouldn't see him. His dirty fingers scrabbled at the edges of the stone until he held it in his hand. I saw his fingers clamp shut around it, and I saw the muscles in his shoulder begin to tense. I tensed, too, sinking down lower, ready to duck or run forward. It was like he knew me. Like he knew what I'd done.

"You there!"

An old man hobbled out of a store, waving a walking stick. The boys scattered, tearing off across the cobbles.

I shuddered like someone being woken up from a dream. The man brandished the stick halfheartedly after the boys, but it seemed like he'd already forgotten them as he turned to look at me up on the platform, shielding his eyes to see me more clearly. I clambered down to meet him. He was bent at the shoulder, his blue eyes cloudy with age, and he wore a clerical collar.

"Ah, young Eleanor," he said.

"I . . . I'm sorry," I said. "I don't think I know you."

"Father Thomas," he said. "Your grandmother didn't want to introduce you to me until you were older." He had the same sharp, staccato accent as the man on the train. "But I know about all of you." He winked. I blushed, not quite knowing why, wondering what it was exactly that he knew.

"Well, thank you for . . . chasing them off."

"My job. Pastor of Saint Anthony in Winterport. Here to help the lost." He chuckled a little to himself. "Do you need directions up to the house?"

"I think I remember. Who were they?"

"Oh, them? Kids from town," he said. "They don't understand that you're safe enough. I suspect there's something instinctual that makes 'em want to throw rocks at Zarrins."

His matter-of-factness chilled me. But I'd known my family was dangerous, so why was I surprised that other people knew it, too?

"I don't think they're expecting me," I said. "Will that be a problem?"

"The Zarrins have never much liked unexpected company," he said. "But they are expecting you. Your grandma sent Margaret down this morning with a note, asked me to greet you."

I hadn't seen that coming.

"I'll walk you as far as the church," he said.

He offered to take my suitcase, but I said I'd manage. He hitched along beside me, leaning on his cane. The whole way I thought I spotted people watching us—a twitch of lace curtains at a window, a rustle as though someone had just ducked behind a hedge. It was almost funny. But then when we got to the weathered clapboard church, and he went away up the path and in through the door, nothing about it seemed funny anymore. I was alone.

At the edge of town, the road went nearly straight up a steep incline into a copse of silver birch. The climb was hard; my suitcase banged against my already bruised leg, and I started carrying it in my arms. The wind curled through the trees, blowing through my uniform until I couldn't stop shivering.

A car crawled along behind me for a while, and then passed me at a crest when the road widened. At school, cars would honk at us as we walked in groups; boys would lean out and ask us if we wanted a ride and the nuns would yell at them to leave us alone. Not here. I wondered if the driver recognized me, or just the direction I was walking.

I came to the place where the road forked. To the right, it became a bridge that spanned a narrow sound and traveled onward up the coast. To the left, a dirt road that darted directly up the steep slope into the deep woods. Trees made a tunnel overhead. It was beautiful up there, in the darkening forest, but

I sensed that it was not a place to be caught alone at night. I bent my knees and adjusted my gait to move silently, then crept forward.

Birds sang here, and wild creatures rustled in the bushes. My ears pricked at the small sounds. The geography settled into place around me. To my right down the tree-lined slope: a streambed that carried a torrent of meltwater every spring, eventually pouring off a cliff into the sea. A little to one side of that, there was a line in the woods where it transitioned from birch to aspen. And a little farther up the path, visible in glimpses as I climbed steadily, was the front lawn. I rounded a bend, and the trees fell away, and all that remained was the house.

It loomed over the landscape. Towers and porches and balconies and bay windows. Story after story of decorative gingerbreading, crown molding, sunburst emblems, recessed niches, and high gables, and all of it covered in gray scalloped shingles, like scales, and at the very top of the highest tower, the creaking weathervane in the shape of a running rabbit. It was hard to look at: not all of it fit in my view at once, even after I took a few steps back. I realized that now, it scared me. It was too much. It felt oppressive, a giant squatting at the top of the world.

I stared the house down, willing it to blink its windows first. And then I took a few quick steps across the narrow band of lawn, planted my foot deliberately on the first step, and launched myself up to the door.

It was black. Not painted: black wood, with twisted carvings and a brass horsehead with a ring clenched in its teeth. I lifted the ring and let it fall.

No answer for a long moment. Behind me the wind ran up my spine and made me shiver. I reached for the knob and threw the door open.

A moan filled the air, a window open somewhere that pulled the air from the door through the house, turning the front hall into a throat. As soon as I stepped forward into the house, suction yanked the door shut behind me and the sound of the ocean sloughing against the cliffs on the far side of the house faded to a whisper. Other than that, there was no sound, except for somewhere down the hall, a heavy clock ticking.

I looked around with heart pumping, my hands locked around my suitcase. The entry hall soared two and a half stories, the ceiling lost in darkness somewhere overhead, the rails of the second floor lined with unlit post lamps. The central staircase snaked down in two streams from the upper floors, joining in the middle and unfurling into the front hall, covered in carpet the faded red of a tongue. The walnut wainscoting gleamed, but the baseboards were scratched and scarred, and the wallpaper, printed with scenes of men hunting stags, lay tattered in places. An age-spotted mirror stood propped on a narrow hall table that also held a cut glass dish of desiccated peppermints. The walls were lined with portraits of dim figures, paintings of sprawling landscapes, lovingly rendered still lifes of animal haunches and goblets overflowing with wine. Things I remembered but didn't recognize, as though I'd seen them in a movie, or a dream.

I felt suddenly dizzy. I wanted to sit down, but what should I sit on—the chair carved in the shape of a grinning devil? A long bench lined with a dozen briefcases with deep gouges in the leather? A pile of twine-tied packages all stamped with FRAGILE and a picture of a skull? Maybe I should just keep moving forward. There were the stairs. Somewhere, two stories up, was my childhood bedroom, and maybe if I could make it in there, shut the door, I would be transformed back into someone who belonged here. But that seemed like a long way to go on legs that were longing to carry me down—to the floor, or ideally back to town, to the train, to safety. But there was no train.

I couldn't leave now, I told myself. Where would I even go?

The front hall was lined with portraits. I got close to them and studied them in turn, trying to see who I could remember. The largest was an oil painting of a squat, grinning young man with impressive sideburns, holding a team of white horses by their reins while they reared and foamed and rolled their eyes. My grandfather, I thought, but not the doting, laughing man I remembered—he looked fiendish. Next to him, an array of men who looked like him but with varying expressions: a skittish man in a red sweater who must have been my father. A sleek boy with a jagged smile in the same sweater as my father's picture, but faded and frayed. And there were women here, too, all with sharp cheekbones, olive skin, dark eyes, nothing like my flat, wide-mouthed face. I scanned the whole room and could not find a single photograph of me.

I closed my eyes and steadied myself on the newel post at the base of the stairs. And then from farther back into the house, I heard a voice call out, "Eleanor! Is that you?"

I'd know that voice anywhere: it was clear and gentle, like the bell on a buoy. It cut through my fear and touched me. Mother. She used to sing to me, when I was little. And she was here.

"Where are you?" I called.

"The back garden, dear." She sounded happy. "Come through the kitchen, it's fastest!"

Mother. She had soft hands and she'd let me braid her long hair when I was a child. Suddenly my reservations left me, and all I wanted to do was see her again.

I quickly followed the hallway to the door that led to the kitchen. I was about to be back with my mother, and then everything would be alright. I opened the door, and as it swung open, I realized someone was standing there, waiting for me to open it.

I'd forgotten about Aunt Margaret.

She stared straight at me from under her ragged tangle of hair. She looked like the women in the portraits, but wilder: sallow skin, bags under her eyes, her clothes covered in grease stains. She frowned at me and muttered something I couldn't make out. She didn't like to be stared at, I remembered, and she didn't like to be spoken to. I could work around this. I averted my eyes and held very still. Slowly, she shuffled back a few paces from the door. "Mother?" I called out again, more tentatively.

"Just follow my voice, dear!"

I edged around Margaret. In my childhood memories she was somehow lovable, always humming a tune. She muttered to herself as I skirted around her through the dark kitchen, across its brick floor and past the big stone oven blackened with years of soot, to the old farmhouse-style back door. The top half was already propped open. I slipped out through the bottom half and shut it behind me, penning Margaret in the kitchen.

My eyes had adjusted to the darkness of the house, so I was blinded at first when I stepped out into the sun. Mother gasped, then said, "My little girl!"

As my eyes adjusted, I saw the shapes in the back garden more clearly. A tall, narrow old woman in a faded black dress, a man in a suit, a woman sitting in what looked like a large iron washtub. And behind them, a table set with plates and glassware and trimmed with faded bunting. A party?

"Hullo, Eleanor," said the man. He was older than in his portrait, but I knew he must be my father. I stepped closer, but he didn't reach out to hug me, just looked at me curiously for a long while. Finally, I put out a hand, and he shook it dazedly.

"Eleanor," Grandma Persephone said. I was already looking past her, looking for the voice that had called to me earlier. But when I really saw my mother, I gasped.

She was wearing a thin robe, drenched with water. Half of

her face was just like mine. I recognized my high forehead, my profile. But as she turned to look at me I saw her other side: an eyeless, earless mass of red polyps that ran all the way down her body until they disappeared into the water of the tub. All of them were straining toward me, as though they could see me, as though they wanted to reach out and grasp me and suck me into the mass. I stumbled back and caught myself on the porch railing.

Her one eyebrow shot up, her half of a mouth opening in dismay. I forced myself to smile, but she reached out her good hand and took a damp towel from the edge of the tub and smoothed it protectively over the inhuman side of her face.

I knew I should go and hug her. I knew that I used to. That when I was little, I'd loved her. But now all I could think about was the feeling of those things squirming across my face.

"Hello, Mother," I said, trying to sound breezy, like the girls at school. But they always said *mummy*, or *mama*. I couldn't imagine what that would sound like in my mouth.

"I told them we should throw you a little party," Mother said. "It's been so long."

"How did you know I was coming?"

"I saw you," said Grandma Persephone. And when she spoke, I realized that my eye had been avoiding her in the way that it was still avoiding Mother. I forced myself to turn and take in the woman who had sent me away from home all those years ago.

Her hair was milk-white, like mine, and had been since she was young—a family trait. She towered over me, taller than a woman ought to be by her age. Hers was the original face that had spawned all the women in the portraits: her features bonier, crueler, her nose more hooked, her eyes more sunken. I swallowed hard.

"Grandmother," I said. In my mind it sounded dignified. But it came out softer than I'd expected. Like a question.

"You made it here, I see."

I wondered if she was angry at me. She'd told me, in letter after letter over the years, to stay put, and I hadn't. *Well, I'd better get this over with.* I cleared my throat.

"I need to talk to you," I said. "Something happened."

Her eyebrows shot up, and she looked angry for a moment. "Not now." She glanced out across the fields. "The others are coming. They want to say hello to you."

As if in answer, from the woods came a long howl.

"That will be your grandfather," she said.

But it wasn't just him—it was three voices, mingling on the breeze. I was surprised to realize I recognized them. The long vowels of Grandpa Miklos, the sharp yips of Luma, Rhys's guttural bark. But a part of them felt different now. I used to hear that sound and run to the door. Now I stood frozen in place like a rabbit, my eyes scanning the tree line, dreading what might come out.

"Quite alright?" Grandma Persephone asked. My throat was too dry to speak.

It was spring dusk. They were nothing more than smears of light and shadow among the trees. If they came for my throat there would be no way I could stop them. The sound of their voices made my chest ache with longing, but my legs wanted to run. A dangerous combination, to want something so badly and also be so afraid. I felt that hunger open up inside me again, the same one I'd felt gripping Lucy Spencer by the hair—

I realized I'd shut my eyes, and when I forced them open again, three shapes had broken free of the tree line, ambling along upright, laughing and joking and straightening clothing. One of the shapes, a young man tugging on a red sweater, saw me and started into a run across the lawn. He vaulted the low stone wall, rushed me, grabbed me, and heaved me high into the air. Against my will my body went limp, preparing for death.

"Ellie!"

He caught me up and held me out to look at me. My feet dangled in empty air. I still couldn't draw breath.

"Rhys, put her down." Grandma Persephone's lips were pursed, but I could see the smile twitching around the edges. She thought this was funny. I couldn't believe it.

"She likes it," Rhys said. "Don't you?"

"Please put me down."

He looked wounded, but he lowered me to the ground. As soon as my feet touched down I backed away. My ribs ached where he'd held me.

"Eleanor," Grandma Persephone said, "this is your cousin Rhys. A college man, when he bothers to show up to his classes. Popular with the ladies, or so I've heard." Rhys's chest puffed up. "And clearly, as you can see, a brute with no manners." She said it affectionately, but I didn't think it was funny at all.

"She knows me." He grinned at me. "Don't you, Ellie?"

"Of course." I tried to infuse my voice with warmth. He felt dangerous.

"I knew it!" He moved forward as though he wanted to scoop me up again, but stopped himself short. "Every time I'm home I ask *Where's Ellie,* and Grandma says—"

"She's been at boarding school," Grandma Persephone said.

"I know *that,* Grandma. Where's she been at Christmas?"

"Rhys, who's got the meat?" she asked.

"Grandpa."

"Why don't you go help him with that?"

Rhys nodded, then sprinted back toward the other two figures making their way across the lawn. One was an old man who tottered slowly, the other a blond girl who kept pace.

"If he's my cousin," I said, "who's his mother?"

"Margaret. And that's your sister there, and your Grandpa Miklos," Grandma Persephone said, behind me. She said it quietly, like a stage manager feeding me my lines.

"I know *that,*" I said. I watched Rhys catch up to them. He took the sack from the old man, leaped back over the wall, and opened the gate for him. The sack dropped to the ground with a leaden thud. As she stepped through the gate, the girl glanced up, and although I knew it was her, I recognized my sister for the first time. And she was the first thing I saw that didn't frighten me. She'd grown up, but she still looked like a movie actress, with her wide, bright eyes, cherubic face, and soft hair the color of a star. She ran toward me and wrapped her arms around me, and from her clothes came the familiar smell of pine forest and mail-ordered perfume. Luma. My sister, my best friend. I'd written her probably a hundred letters and she'd never written me back, but now I was here, and she had me.

"Eleanor!" she said into my cheek. I let her hug me, and for a moment, things felt normal. Then she pulled back and grinned cheerily at me with her mouthful of sharp teeth. Strands of bloody flesh still clung between them, and her breath smelled gamey. I kept my smile fixed as she stroked my cheek with a fingernail caked in blood.

"Luma," I said. "I've missed you."

"And you!"

"I have so much to tell you," I said. "I—"

"Mother," Luma said, "what's in your bath? It smells incredible."

"Sage."

"Heaven." Luma sat down on the edge of Mother's tub with a sigh, stroked the water, and splashed some of it across her face. I couldn't quite believe that after eight years away, she hadn't even let me finish my sentence.

All around me were little domestic scenes: Luma sitting on the edge of the garden tub, Father listening sheepishly while Rhys talked about the hunting they'd done, Grandma Persephone tapping Grandpa Miklos on the chest with one bony finger. "You forgot your cane," she said.

"I don't need it on four legs."

"You need it coming back."

"Ehhhh . . ." He waved a hand. "I don't like it. It makes me feel old."

"You are old."

He slung an arm around her shoulders, and she bent her knees to take his weight. As she moved to his side I got a look at his face. It was the face I remembered most vividly from childhood: those kind, dark eyes, those soft lines in his skin, his bushy eyebrows, his broad nose. But I didn't feel the way I used to when I looked at him. I was afraid.

"Miklos," Grandma Persephone said. "Don't you want to say hello to Eleanor? She's home."

He grinned as he turned toward me. But then he sniffed the air, his grin faded, and his head snapped up to lock onto his target. His eyes focused on mine, and as they did, his shoulders dropped down, relaxing but also . . . preparing.

I felt suddenly cold. Grandpa wasn't like Rhys or Luma or Father. He was older and came from somewhere less civilized. He wasn't seeing Eleanor, his granddaughter. He was seeing a young woman named Eleanor who had suddenly found herself at an isolated manor house. Someone no one would miss if she disappeared on a spring evening.

He took a step toward me. I took half a step back, praying my foot wouldn't catch on a stone, praying I wouldn't falter or fall.

Grandma Persephone saw it, too. She snapped her fingers under his nose. "Miklos. Miklos!"

He shook his head and looked a little dreamy.

"It is good to see you, my . . . darling," he said. "It has been too long."

I nodded, waiting for my heart to stop racing.

Grandma Persephone had him by one arm. I could see her fingernails digging into his jacket. "Let's toast," she said.

They all turned toward the table and took up flutes of champagne. Someone put one into my hand.

"To our Eleanor," Grandma Persephone said, and they clinked glasses and drank. I sipped.

I'd pictured a time like this every night for years, until the image got threadbare and worn. My family, welcoming me back, thrilled to see me, as though I had never left. And now that I had it, it was wrong. Or I was wrong.

The rest of them quickly fell to chatting, and I let myself sidle out of the way. At school, the easiest way to get out of things was just to stop existing. I watched them for a while, and then Grandma Persephone detached herself and drifted back to stand near me.

"You'll want to apologize to your mother once you've settled in," she said. "You were a little rude, but I'm sure she'll understand that you're just nervous. Which, by the way, is not something you should show your grandfather, either. If something runs, he has to chase."

"I wouldn't have been afraid if you hadn't sent me away."

It was out of my mouth before I could stop it, and after I said it, I glowed hot with indignation. She studied me, and I studied her back, looking all over her face for any trace of remorse for what she'd done to me, for sending me away, for letting me be afraid. Nothing. I realized she was curious about me, that she might have known I'd come back, but now that I was here, she didn't know exactly what I'd do next.

"I felt like that, once," she said at last.

"I'm sorry?"

"After my son died," she said. "The first Rhys. I looked at your grandfather, and I forgot everything that made him my family. I just saw a monster."

I looked around at the gathering. How could she see anything else?

"Give yourself time," she said, "to let your eyes adjust."

I glanced around at my family. They'd clumped together, laughing, drinking champagne. Aside from a few glances at me, they looked like they'd already forgotten I was here, that I was the reason for the party. Evening fell across the lawn as my sister still perched on the edge of the tub. Her long, sharp teeth, the ones that couldn't retract like everyone else's, glinted in the light of the rising moon. Father and Grandpa Miklos were looking conspiratorially at the bag on the ground.

"What's for dinner?" Father asked Rhys. "Show me what you caught."

Rhys grabbed the sack and pulled out a brace of young rabbits by the ears. Their bodies swung limply from their broken necks. Their white throats were pink with blood.

Maybe my eyes were adjusting, I thought, since everything seemed to be getting darker around me. And then I fainted.

TWO

I WOKE UP IN A DIM ROOM. FOR A MOMENT I thought I was back at Saint Brigid's, and I was relieved. Everything that had happened had been a terrible dream. Now I would wake up for morning Mass. I'd eat toast in the dining hall alone. Maybe I'd spend the morning reading with Sister Katherine. It was June, and everyone but me would be gone on summer vacations at last, so there would be no one to bother me.

But the bed underneath me was too soft, almost saggy. And there was a weight on me, pressing down, heavier than a blanket.

I glanced down, then screamed, instantly awake. Sprawled across my legs was a dead—something, big and covered in brown fur. I scrambled backward until I hit the headboard, and I stayed there, breathing hard, until I could bring myself to look more closely. A groundhog. No blood on it, just dead. A prank,

I guessed. Probably Rhys. And I remembered all at once where I was.

Rhys was a beast. Was he trying to frighten me away? He could try his best. This wasn't the first time someone had put something horrible in my bed.

I slithered out from under the covers, stumbled around the room until I found the curtains, and tugged them open.

Light flooded the room, and I blinked for a moment, stunned. My window overlooked the high cliffs and beyond that the ocean, sunlit and deep blue. I opened the window and felt an ache under my ribs. The smell of the sea called to me. I shut my eyes and sighed. I loved it here, in this place. I couldn't let Rhys scare me away.

I went to the bed and picked up the top sheet by the corners. I heaved the groundhog to the window and rolled it out. It hit the lawn with a thud.

There, that was a little better. I shook out the sheet and risked a look around.

My room at school had been austere: white walls, two narrow beds, one perpetually empty because no one would room with me. This room was its opposite, so packed with things and life that it was almost hard to look at. It had wallpaper printed with tiny flowers, an enormous black wardrobe carved with grinning faces buried in sprays of oak leaves, a cheery pink-and-red rag rug, a chandelier hanging from the high ceiling, heavy curtains of faded pink velvet with gold tassels, a spindly-legged desk crouched in one corner, and a dollhouse in the shape of the house itself, the roof caved in, as though someone had stepped on it. My suitcase was propped up by the wardrobe. There was a little armchair with a rabbit sitting in it, and my heart raced until I realized it was a stuffed toy. There were sheets of paper pinned to the walls, page-sized pieces that flapped a little in the breeze from the open window. Some had come unpinned and fluttered to the floor.

They were poems, their edges showing the rough scissorwork of a young child. They must have been cut out of a book. I leaned forward to read one.

O you who turn the wheel and look to windward,
Consider Phlebas, who was once handsome and tall as you.

My poem, the one I knew most of the lines to, the one I mouthed to myself late at night in my dormitory room at Saint Brigid's. I thought that I'd read it for the first time at thirteen, behind a shelf in our school's little library. I checked it out so many times that Sister Katherine had finally let me keep it. It was the only book I'd grabbed when I hastily packed my suitcase and ran for the train station. But here it was, something a much younger me had loved, too. How could I have forgotten?

Downstairs, plates clattered and people spoke in hushed voices. I should go down there and say something. I should try again. They were all I had, after all. I stopped in front of the mirror; they'd put me to bed fully dressed, so I was still in my school uniform. I smoothed my collar down. Close enough.

When I descended the stairs and came to the dining room, I hesitated at the door. Then Mother saw me. She was sitting in a barrel, a gauzy robe draped over her and trailing in the water. She turned toward me and smiled winningly with the side of her face that had teeth.

"Eleanor!" she said. "You're awake. We were so worried after last night."

"I feel much better now."

"Come have some breakfast!"

I tried not to look tentative as I stepped across the threshold. I remembered Persephone's words: If you run, he has to chase. So I tried to look confident as I turned toward Miklos, but he didn't see me. His face was a snout, buried in his breakfast, licking it up from the plate. Bits of meat and egg flew in all directions. At his elbow, Rhys and Luma were fighting over a last slice of thick undercooked bacon, until finally it ripped apart between them and Luma fell backward into Father, jostling his elbow while he cut his meat into little squares. Rhys looked up at me with an expectant grin. Determined that he wouldn't scare me, I stared impassively until the grin vanished. After his eyes dropped to his plate I let my gaze wander, and realized that there was someone else at the table, someone whose back was turned to me.

"Arthur," said Grandma Persephone. "You remember Eleanor?"

And the man whose back was turned stood up, unfolding himself from the chair in front of me.

He was not astoundingly tall, but his thinness accentuated his height. He looked neither young nor old—he had no hair on his head, but also no wrinkles, aside from deep pleats in his lips that made him look stern. He wore a black suit in an old style with a celluloid collar and a pair of old-fashioned dark glasses, the kind with lenses on the sides, obscuring his eyes. His skin looked almost bloodless, but he didn't seem sick. I noticed he kept one hand on the back of his chair, and a silver-handled cane was resting not far from his feet.

He smiled without opening his mouth. "I suppose the real question is: Do you remember me?"

". . . Mr. Knox?" I ventured.

"Please, call me Arthur."

I remembered someone of about his shape from my childhood. A dinner guest for the adults who had little to say to children. He drove an old Model T and sometimes parked it in our carriage house. At the time he'd seemed to me to be impossibly old and fusty, except when he'd—

"You used to play piano," I said, realization dawning. "I think you might have taught me how to play."

Grandma Persephone glanced over at him sharply, suddenly. His back was to her, so he didn't see it. I remembered sitting next to him on the bench, learning scales on a sunny afternoon.

WHAT BIG TEETH • 31

"I might have," he said. "It's been a while."

How was he so young? He didn't look like he'd aged a day since I'd left. But maybe I'd been wrong back then; maybe he was just one of those young people who seemed old.

He pulled out my chair for me, and when I sat in it, he settled me in closer to the table. I felt less afraid with him here. Not because he would protect me, but because he'd survived so long in the company of my family. That meant it was possible.

I liked him instantly. There was something delicate about him that made me want to hold him too tightly, dig fingernails into him, bite into him to test his firmness. At the same time, he felt cool, self-contained, like my favorite teachers at Saint Brigid's. I wanted to impress him.

"What brings you by today?" I asked, hoping it sounded natural, the kind of question that adult people ask one another.

"Your grandma didn't get her taxes done on time."

Grandma Persephone rolled her eyes. "I pay them enough that you'd think they could wait."

"And, of course, you'll stay for dinner," Father said.

Mr. Knox—Arthur—smiled tightly. "Of course."

I tried to concentrate on my breakfast, but I was aware of him in a way that reminded me of the feeling of someone standing just behind you. But every time I turned to try to talk to him, someone else already had his attention. Luma asked him about his car; Rhys wanted to show him how he could throw his spoon as high as the ceiling and then catch it in his teeth. Even Margaret, on her trips back and forth from the table to the kitchen, stopped muttering and looked at him fondly. Every time someone talked to him, he was courteous, charming. He didn't eat, but sipped at a cup of coffee with a wry smile flickering around the corners of his mouth. At one point he saw me looking at him and, for a second, turned that smile on me, and I felt like someone had held a match up to the edge of me and lit me on fire. But when I started to open my mouth, Father was already asking him when they could play billiards.

Finally, Grandpa Miklos pushed back his chair. "I am ready for some hunting."

"Father, you hunted yesterday," my father said. "Don't you think you'll wear yourself out?"

"The day I can't hunt, I am not Miklos. Who's coming?" Grandpa glanced hopefully at me.

"I can't," I said. In the woods he'd kill me for sure.

"You still can't become the wolf? I hoped you would grow into it."

"Miklos, hush," Grandma Persephone said. He shrugged and made a face at her. She giggled like a girl.

"I'm going to stay in today," Luma said. "You go, Daddy. Keep Grandpa company."

"Any requests?"

"Postman?" Luma said, and everyone but me laughed. "But really, anything. You know I don't mind."

"I'll come." Rhys stood up and stretched, flexing his shoulders until his sweater strained across his chest and pulled up to show his flat belly downed in dark hair. "See you later, Arthur."

"Luma, why don't you want to go with your cousin?" Grandma Persephone asked.

Luma laughed and combed her hair behind her ear with a long-taloned hand.

"I want to spend time with Eleanor," she said.

The hunters—Father, Grandpa Miklos, and Rhys—left, jostling their way out of the dining room. Persephone half waved at them before turning to Arthur. "Let's get this over with," she said.

Arthur picked up his cane and rested his weight on it while he waited for her. I looked at his legs, wondering what ailed him, or if he was simply older than I'd thought. He saw me looking and gave me a covert smile. How had I not remembered him? Maybe I'd been too young to notice someone so subtle. Now, he was all I could see.

"I'm going upstairs to play," Luma said. "Do you want to come with me?"

"Aren't you a little old for that?" I said without thinking, wanting to sound mature in front of Arthur. But Luma scowled at me, and I instantly felt sorry.

"If you think so, you don't have to come," she said. She turned and flounced up the stairs.

"We'll see you later, Eleanor," Grandma Persephone said. And then she and Arthur were gone, and I was alone.

I thought about going up and apologizing to Luma. But what would I say? That I'd snapped at her to impress our grandmother's accountant? It sounded silly, even to me. And she barely knew me now. What would she even say, if I tried to apologize? What if she didn't care?

I tried to forget the whole conversation, and looked around the house for things to amuse myself. But as the morning turned into afternoon in the big empty house, I realized I was bored. I sat and read a book in the front parlor for a while, a dark red room with a big fireplace and heavy rugs, and played chess with myself until I realized I couldn't remember all the rules. I pulled the dust cloth off of the piano and tried out some scales.

I could still smell the sea on the breeze and a part of me wanted to go to the water, but I was afraid of it—I hadn't swum in eight years. Maybe the ocean was now just another thing that wanted to kill me. And once from the woods I heard a series of quick barks, and then a wild creature screamed in a way that reminded me it wasn't safe to leave the house.

Finally, I went up to my room, where I squinted at myself in the fly-specked mirror and tried to make myself change my shape, like Rhys and Luma did. What did it feel like, to change? How would I know if I was close?

I thought of a way of making up with Luma. I crept down

the hall and knocked on her door. "Hello?" I called out. I opened the door a crack and saw her sitting on a low chair with her back to the door. "Luma, I have an important question and I really need your help."

She didn't turn around from her vanity, where she sat brushing her hair. But she nodded at herself in the mirror, and I knew she was pleased.

"Well," she said. "Don't stand in the door. Come in."

While my room seemed like storage for old furniture, hers was all matched: white bed, white dresser, white vanity with an enormous mirror. That whole wall was lined with mirrors of all shapes and sizes. There was a copy of *Rebecca* tented open on her bed, and a smattering of lipsticks around it, and *Jane Eyre* bookmarked with a sheet of false eyelashes on the bedside table on top of a tattered book that said *Birds of North America*. At Saint Brigid's you weren't supposed to read more than one book at a time. It was considered lax. I sat down carefully on the edge of the bed and tried to figure out how to ask her what it felt like to change your shape.

"It's a bit like turning yourself inside out," Luma said, after I tried asking three or four different ways. "Or like turning your insides into a disguise, and then tucking your disguise into your insides."

"It's like a disguise?" I said. "It seems a little more complicated than that."

"It's . . ." She left the brushing and rummaged in the toy box she still kept beside her bed. I felt embarrassed for her. She came out with a cloth doll in a long dress.

"Flip up her skirt," she ordered, and, still not understanding, I did. Underneath was another head and torso of a doll. The skirt, turned inside out, was a different color. The doll, upside down, a different woman.

"It's like that," she said. "Only faster."

I looked at Luma, in her white slip with her layers of blotted pink and red lipsticks staining her sharp teeth. I tried to imagine where the other creature was.

"Why does it bother you?" she asked. "It didn't used to. You could always keep up anyway." She pulled up the sleeve of her robe and showed me a ring of white scars on her forearm. "You bit harder than any of us, too."

The scars stared at me accusingly, as pearly as a set of baby teeth. I wanted to put my own teeth up against them, to prove by size and angle that they weren't mine.

"Oh, Luma," I said. "I'm so sorry."

"I'm fine!" she said, and I felt even worse. What kind of sister had I been? "It wasn't so bad. At least you don't have teeth like us."

"I guess I take after Mother."

She laughed. "But she's so quiet!" she said. "You know, I think she said something once about you being a bit like her mother. And then I asked her what she meant and she said she couldn't tell me."

"Her mother?"

"Our other grandmother, silly. She lives in France, I think. Mother writes a letter every year at Christmas."

"Have you seen her?" I felt a little kindling of hope. "Maybe I am like her."

"I always imagined she'd be like Mother, only all over," Luma said. I winced.

From downstairs I heard a door creak open. Grandma Persephone's voice filtered up through the front hall, and Arthur's, too. I'd forgotten he was going to eat with us.

"Can I borrow something pretty to wear?" I asked. "And maybe you could do my hair?"

She looked at me strangely then. "Why?"

"I just want to try something different," I said. "I've worn a uniform for a long time now."

She tilted her head. "That's sad," she said. "Sit down."

She arranged me in front of her mirror and began taking down my hair. It was nearly the same color as hers, but somehow hers was lustrous, and mine a faded grayish white that made me look old.

"What's this?" she asked, touching the back of my neck. It stung.

"Ow!" I said.

"It looks like someone pulled out a chunk of your hair back here." She looked me over. "And you're bruised, too. What happened to you?"

I thought of Lucy Spencer gripping my hair, yanking on it,

trying to hold me back. My face burned. "It's nothing," I said. "I got in a fight at school."

She tutted.

"Well, you're home now," she said. "If anyone comes after you, I'll eat them up." And then she giggled and hummed as she began brushing my hair. In her own room, she seemed wise, knowing. She was a few years older than me, but we'd always switched like this, taking turns being the older sister. I used to like it, but now I was suddenly unsure of my footing.

"Let's make you lovely," she said.

I didn't feel lovely, even in the frilly dress I borrowed from her. On her, I'm sure it looked elegant, voluptuous; it sagged on me like a sack, so that I looked like a little girl in a nightgown, and I ended up putting my school uniform back on. But my hair was nice the way she'd done it, in braids coiled around my head. She made me turn around and started dabbing creams onto her wrist, and then smudging them onto my cheeks and eyes. As she worked, a savory smell drifted up the stairs from the kitchen. They'd caught something, then.

"Why didn't you come home sooner?" she asked, tilting my mouth open and swiping a little lipstick on with her pinky finger. She frowned at it and reached for a handkerchief to wipe it off. "No. You're such a strange color. Almost green."

"They wouldn't let me come home," I said.

"Funny," she said. "Grandma told me you were too busy."

She licked her hand and used the spit to smooth back the flyaways at my hairline. I winced. "She lied. I wasn't busy."

She shrugged. "I don't see why she had to be lying. Maybe you were too busy and you just didn't know it."

"Busy eating plain toast for breakfast? Busy trying to make friends so the other girls wouldn't pour water on my bed while I was sleeping? I learned Latin, I suppose, but I could have done that here." I sighed. "I don't know."

Luma's eyes went wide. "That sounds awful. Why didn't you kill them?"

I started. "Because that's wrong!" I said, and then thought of Lucy, and felt a sick guilt in my stomach. "They were terrible, but not that terrible."

She cocked her head to one side and seemed about to say something, when Grandma Persephone called from downstairs that it was time for dinner.

"She should get a bell," I said, as we made our way to the staircase. "There's no way everyone heard that."

From behind us I heard a clattering of toenails on bare wood, and in a blur, Rhys came rocketing down the stairs past us on four legs, his black pelt glistening as he leaped clear over the last several steps. He skidded around a corner into the hall closet below, and emerged a few moments later on two legs, pulling a sweater on over his head and then reaching down to button his pants.

And then he did something strange. He stopped in front of the speckled mirror in the front hall and licked his palm. Carefully, he smoothed his gleaming black hair back from his forehead, the way Luma had just done to me. He turned left and right, watching his own reflection, rolling his shoulders back and sticking his hands in his pockets just so before he crossed the threshold into the dining room.

As soon as he was out of sight, I turned to Luma. "I don't remember him ever caring what he looked like," I said. It wasn't in his character. Rhys was a predator, sleek and unstoppable. It was strange to see him pouting at himself.

"I don't know who he's fooling," Luma said. "He's been trying to impress Arthur ever since he came home for the summer."

"Impress him? Why?"

"If you ask me, it's very childish," she said, and she flounced down after him. But I noticed that when she came to the hall mirror, she stopped, too. I hung back, watching as she curled a strand of hair around the tip of her finger, and then unspooled it so that it hung down alongside her face.

I was the last one in, and everyone else had already taken seats: Grandma Persephone at the head, with Miklos next to her, which surprised me since I'd assumed they'd sit in the same place every time. Mother was again in her barrel at the foot of the table. Luma and Rhys jostled for a seat opposite Arthur, and in the chaos I slipped into the seat beside him, unnoticed. Margaret came in bearing an enormous tray loaded with cuts of rare venison: loins, steaks, something I couldn't identify. Grandpa Miklos speared it with the carving fork and brandished it at me. "Little one, you should have the heart."

I froze. The heart on the fork quivered, and Grandpa Miklos looked confused, then sad. Finally, Rhys snatched it off the end of the fork with both hands. Grandpa grunted indulgently. And with that, dinnertime descended.

The air filled with the gnashing of teeth and the clink of fork tines on china. Grandpa Miklos shoved his whole face into the dish, scarfing up the tender bits and licking the plate clean with a tongue that seemed too big for his mouth. I ate slowly, the way they'd taught me in school, and watched the carnage from the corner of my eye. It was a little easier than breakfast had been, but I still felt that I could be next.

I glanced sideways at Arthur. He seemed to be smiling a little. I realized that he wasn't eating, just pushing food around his plate and occasionally slipping pieces of it into a napkin in his lap. I felt mortified.

"I'm sorry they're like this," I whispered to him over the chomps and satisfied snarls. "This would put anyone off eating."

He turned his head to me, looking perplexed.

"I've dined enough times with the Zarrins to know what to expect," he said. "You can't sit down to table with the wolf and not see a mauling."

"But you aren't eating," I said. "I'll ask them to use some table manners."

He snorted, and then composed himself. "You're very kind," he said. "But believe me when I say that this has nothing to do with the Zarrins' table manners."

I kept eating, bringing small forkfuls of venison to my mouth, but I watched Arthur out of the corner of my eye. I watched the way he tilted his head at the family, in . . . affection? Concern? It was hard to say.

"You seem to like them," I said. The cloud of noise made me feel like we were alone at the table, the only ones not scarfing down food with wild abandon. "Or you seem amused by them, maybe. Aren't you afraid?"

He raised his eyebrows, and I was happy to think that maybe I'd surprised him.

"Afraid?" he said. "No, not for a long time now, anyway. There have been times I've been furious with them. Or not wanted to see them at all. But I think I will miss them, when it's all said and done."

I felt my heartbeat accelerate wildly. "You're not planning to leave? Stop working for us?"

"Not anytime soon," he said. "But I work for Persephone, and she's getting on in years. Things will change when she dies. I suspect your grandfather will leave the public affairs to Rhys, and something tells me he won't have your grandmother's interest in business."

We both looked over at Rhys. He was pointing to something out the window to get Luma to turn her head, and when she did, he lunged forward and grabbed a joint of venison off her plate with his teeth. She looked back and swatted him and they both laughed, juices trickling down their chins. I glanced back at Arthur and saw him looking at me—or at least, I saw my own half smile, half grimace reflected in his mirrored lenses. But he was smiling, just a little.

"Why would they ever leave it to him?" I asked, feeling bitter. I tried to correct myself: "I mean, why not to my father? He's older."

"Because Rhys is their favorite. Because he reminds them of their long-lost firstborn son. They half believe Rhys is him." He clicked his tongue. "And because they think your father is missing the patriarchal quality. The Zarrins are a surprisingly traditional people."

I looked around at them: covered in blood and sauce, eating with forks, hands, and faces indiscriminately. He must have seen my shock, because he leaned in toward me, not touching me, but close enough that I could feel the electricity of it.

"You've been gone a long time," he said. "I know you think that's a bad thing, but you might be able to see things more clearly from your vantage point."

They ate until the platters were empty. A silence descended slowly over the table, except for a few sounds of lapping. Arthur leaned forward.

"That was a fine dinner," he said. "Persephone, can I trouble you for a cup of coffee?"

"I'll get it," Luma said. Rhys shoved her. She shoved him back. They began growling at each other, shoulders tensing.

"Eleanor," Grandma Persephone said, "why don't you get it? I'm sure Margaret's got the tray ready."

"Wish me luck," I said to Arthur. He laughed a little, under his breath.

"Luck with what?" Grandma Persephone was tilting her head at me again, in that way she did when she wanted me to stop being rude. I was going to start hating that soon.

"Never mind."

The coffee tray was already on the counter by the door. Aunt Margaret stood scrubbing dishes with her back turned to me. I picked up the tray as silently as I could, but a rogue spoon leaped off and hit the stone floor with a clatter. She turned and stared at me.

"Just a spoon," I muttered, setting the tray down and scooping it back up. I wiped it off on the edge of my skirt. "Sorry."

"Mmmmmmmmmm . . ." She was humming to herself, or it seemed that way at first. "Mmm . . . traitor." Margaret hadn't said a clear word to me that I could remember, but now she was making herself understood perfectly.

"Excuse me?" I said.

"Hm." And she turned her back on me, and returned to scrubbing a roasting pan.

I told myself I wasn't upset. She was just a madwoman, just a very strange aunt who would rather cook and clean than sit down to dinner with her family. I'd never seen her even speak to her own son; of course she didn't like me. I was a disruption in her routine.

But I was rattled. And the rattling spread from my mind down my arms and rattled the tray I carried, the cup of bone china ticking away in the socket of its saucer, the silver coffee-pot brimming over, the cream and sugar spoons chiming. When I stepped back over the threshold, Arthur looked at me, and all went silent. I glided across the floor to him. This must be Luma's job sometimes. I could picture how she would do it: her long hair draped over one shoulder, her steps light as they were when she walked the forest. I did it like that, tilting my head at a soft angle, pointing my toes, turning myself into someone else. I set the tray down in front of him and a stray lock of my hair brushed against his suit jacket. He glanced up at me, his face only inches from my ear.

"Thank you," he said.

I nodded and let go of the tray. My wrist brushed the hot coffeepot and I yanked it back, but I didn't even feel the pain. Not really.

"You've hurt yourself," he said.

"No, I'm fine."

"You're quite the stoic."

I found myself smiling. When I'd first gotten to school, I'd been a crybaby, someone who lost fights. But I'd learned.

"There's a salve for that in the kitchen," Grandma Persephone said. "Get it from Marg—"

"I'm *fine*," I said, a little too sharply.

She eyed me as I settled back into my chair. The noise in the room soon resumed, talking instead of gnashing, and the tension between us slackened a little.

But now my father was watching me. He had a perplexed look on his face, and he kept looking back and forth between Arthur and me. I looked at him closely for the first time since I'd gotten here. He looked like a young Grandpa Miklos, or an old Rhys: the thick dark hair, the heavy brows and jaw. But Arthur was right: my father was missing some essential quality that Rhys and Grandpa Miklos both had. He was timid and watery inside that solid body, like he was always embarrassed. I felt like I knew something else, too, but I wasn't sure exactly what that was yet. When he saw me watching him, he asked, "So, Eleanor. How are you getting settled in?"

"I feel like I've lost so much time," I said. "I only half remember how it is to be here. I don't feel like it's real."

"Oh, no," said Miklos, from the far end of the table. I glanced up at him. He looked genuinely sorrowful. Maybe he was the grandfather I remembered, when he wasn't eyeing me like I was a wounded deer. Maybe I could help him see me differently.

"I remember you used to tell the best stories, Grandpa," I added. "Maybe you can help me understand."

"That sounds like a wonderful idea," Arthur said.

My father glanced askance at Arthur again, but Grandpa smiled. The rest of him was human now, but his teeth were still the wolf's, so his grin was too big for his mouth. I forced myself to regard him, to breathe deeply through the darkness that swam at the edges of my vision. This would only work if I could be strong.

"What do you want to hear?" he asked.

"I want to hear how you first became like you are now," I said. "How you started"—I fumbled for the phrase he'd used at breakfast—"becoming the wolf."

Grandma Persephone looked shocked. "Eleanor!"

"Easy, my love." Grandpa Miklos put a hand on her shoulder. "That's a hard story," he said to me. "Too hard for right after a big meal. Another time, I promise. Let me tell you instead . . ." He thought. "Another story about our family. The story about my name."

Grandpa Miklos leaned forward in his chair and propped his elbows on the table.

"When I was young," Miklos said, "I was not Miklos. I was not Zarrin. I was a boy with no name."

I glanced around the table. Rhys and Luma had leaned forward, ears pricked, dutifully attentive. Mother had stretched her arm across the table to stroke Father's hand, Father was watching Arthur, and Arthur was watching me. I wondered what each of them saw, or thought they saw.

"You were an orphan?" I asked.

"No," Miklos said. "I had a family, a mother and a father and two sisters who were older. They had no names. None of us had names. Because none of us had any words.

"We lived like this."

He shifted in his chair, raised both hands, and began to pantomime like a silent movie star. His gestures created invisible objects: A wooden bowl worn smooth by generations of hands. A pitchfork that he used to stab at mounds of hay. A soft hat that his mother sewed for him and placed on his head.

I watched, transfixed.

Grandpa Miklos made a gesture that seemed to embody transition, the passage of time. "And so when I walked across the land—"

"Europe," said Grandma Persephone.

"—Europe, to the water, and got in the boat, that was almost the first time I heard people talking. I knew maybe people talked, but only the nobles, royalty. And on the boat, everyone was talking all the time. Such a waste! I loved it."

"But why did you leave the old country?" I asked.

The focus of the table shifted to me. Grandma Persephone raised an eyebrow. I stared her down. What did she want from me? How was I supposed to let my eyes adjust if I wasn't allowed to see anything at all?

Grandpa Miklos looked a little proud. "Ah, trying to get me to tell, I see. Clever," he said. "Not today."

"The boat," Grandma Persephone prompted.

"But the boat! I loved the boat. The men there, they taught me so many words. The ones who taught me good words, like hello, and share, and blanket, they lived and came to America, and the ones I could find later when I was rich, I made them rich. But the ones who taught me bad words . . ." He shrugged, and in the candle flicker, he let his face slip shape. One moment he was Grandpa Miklos. The next he was just a snarling mouthful of teeth.

It was over in an instant. I didn't have time to faint, so I just clung to the table for dear life while my heart thundered in my chest.

"Miklos!" Grandma Persephone said. "She's not ready for those kinds of theatrics."

"She used to love it," Grandpa Miklos said. *"Grandpa, Grandpa, show me the wolf—"*

"I'm fine," I said. He nodded at me approvingly. He could like me. He would like me. I'd make sure of it.

"And then I came to New York," he said. "And it was so *busy!* I didn't know there was more than one language; they taught me Polish on the boat, I think. And here, Spanish and Greek and Italian and English. I tried to get food, but I had no money. I tried to go in a house to sleep, but they chased me out. I fell asleep in a—a hole between houses."

"An alley," Grandma Persephone supplied.

"With trash cans and dead birds. And then when I woke up it was dark, and a drunk man was pissing near me!"

My face flushed hot. This was not a good story.

"And I was hungry," Miklos said. "And, well . . ." He bared his teeth and clacked them together. "And then I saw he had these fine clothes, so I put them on. And then I felt something in the pocket."

He reached into the pocket of his own vest and pulled out a cheap gold-plated watch on a chain much finer than the watch itself. He flipped it open and showed me the inside of the lid. It was stamped with the name MIKLOS ZARRIN.

For a moment I thought, absurdly, *This creature has eaten my grandfather.*

"And so that was my name," the man with the pocket watch in front of me said. "Two whole words that belonged just to me. My first week in America, and I was rich."

"Do you ever think about the man whose name you stole?" I asked.

When I said it, everyone got very quiet. Grandma Persephone's head swiveled to stare me down. Beside me, I heard Arthur give an amused cough.

Grandpa, though, looked thoughtful.

"Sometimes," he said. "Sometimes I think about him."

"And what do you think?"

"I thank him," Grandpa said. "He gave me everything."

And he did a little flick of his wrist and spreading of the fingers that encompassed the candle-bright dining room with its chinoiserie wallpaper and imported dishes, the cavernous dark of the foyer beyond, the zigzagging staircase. His gesture traveled up a winding path through pipes and ladders to the attic and burst forth from the lightning rod atop the tallest tower, arcing into the sky to rain like fireworks over our house, our land, the fishing village beneath where people whispered when they said the name Zarrin.

"And everything I have," he said, "I will someday give to *you*."

And just for a moment, I felt home.

Until I realized that when he'd said *you*, his gaze had shifted to Rhys, who sat there grinning like a king but not surprised. He had perfect teeth, Rhys. And Grandpa's face. And the absolute certainty of someone who has never had a troubled thought in his life. I realized that this must not be the first time Grandpa had promised him the house and everything in it.

"Well," Grandma Persephone said, "should we go sit in the parlor?"

I felt my stomach growl, and when I looked down, I realized I hadn't touched my dinner. Arthur glanced up at Grandma.

"She hasn't finished yet," he said. "Eleanor, are you still hungry?"

"I'm fine."

"Nonsense," Grandma Persephone said. "Take your time."

"I'll sit with her," said Arthur.

Grandma nodded, then left. The rest of the family followed her in a ragged train.

"Why did you do that?" I asked.

"You were hungry," he said. "And you weren't going to say anything."

He was still sipping his coffee. I looked into the cup when he set it down. It was blacker than any coffee I'd seen, and an oily sheen hung around its surface. It didn't look good to me, but it was the only thing he seemed to like.

"So," he said, "no one has told me much. What brings you home all of a sudden?"

I glanced up at him. "I ran away from boarding school."

"You must have used the money she sent you." He smiled at my confusion. "Don't look so surprised; I do all her books."

"Do you know why she's kept me away?"

He pursed his lips and shook his head. "If you think she tells me anything," he said, "you don't know your grandmother very well."

"What do you mean?"

He looked a little surprised. "You ask a lot of questions, for a Zarrin."

"What does *that* mean?"

He laughed. I found myself laughing, too, a little.

"I mean that you're curious," he said. "I like that. And you should know I'm not exactly your grandmother's most trusted friend, more an ally of necessity. I protect her assets, and she— well, she makes me coffee." He took another sip. "But I'm sure that whatever she's up to, she doesn't mean to harm you."

"It doesn't feel that way. Sometimes—" I thought about stopping myself, and then I plunged forward. "Sometimes it feels like she hates me."

I told him about boarding school, about the girls who had teased me for years, saying my family had given me away because I was too ugly to keep. How I'd written to Grandma Persephone begging to come home at first, and she'd sent me vague news and ignored my question. How I'd run away a few times and been picked up by the police and driven back to the school while they lectured me. How Lucy Spencer had made friends with me when I was twelve, and for a while I'd felt alright, but then she'd spread rumors about me later, told people things about me that made them hate me. How the fact that I used to care about her only made me hate her more. At that last part, Arthur raised his eyebrows.

"Tell me about her," he said.

"I mean," I said, "we used to be friends. Good friends. And then we just weren't. And it wasn't like anything happened."

"As though she'd outgrown you."

"Exactly!" I said, and I wondered if he'd ever felt that way about someone. I realized I'd said more to him than I had to anyone in years. And he had listened silently while I shared almost as much as I knew about myself. And so I told him about Lucy Spencer pushing me down the stairs.

We'd been the last people at school, her and her new best friend and me. They were waiting for one of their mothers to come pick them up and take them to New York. At breakfast, they'd caught my eye, hummed some little song, and then crossed their hands across their chests and snapped their fingers and dissolved into giggles. I was used to ignoring them, so I did. But then later that morning, I'd been carrying a box of files for Sister Katherine from a second floor storage room, and I'd heard footsteps, and then I'd been shoved hard, from behind. As I stumbled, spilling the box, I saw Lucy standing at the top of the stairs, smiling at a job well done.

Arthur shook his head. "People are so amused by cruelty. I've never been able to understand it."

He slipped his hand on top of mine for a moment. It was like the marble thigh of Saint Cecilia I'd touched in the cathedral one day when no one was looking: cool, and heavy, and smooth. I felt a chill run from the arches of my feet to the base of my brain. He had long fingers, hands good for piano, weighted like ivory keys. It felt like a weight that could carry me to the bottom of the sea. I almost felt as though I could tell him what I'd done next. But I didn't. I was too afraid that if I did, he'd look at me like he looked at the rest of the Zarrins.

"I've been alone for so long that I can't remember what it feels like to belong," I said. "And I'm worried that I won't belong here, and that if it doesn't end with Grandpa killing me, it will with Grandma telling me I have to leave."

He sighed deeply. "It was a cruel thing your grandmother did," he said. "You might never forgive her for it. But I don't think she's going to send you away. Not after you've come looking for her."

"Why not?" I asked.

"She admires it," he said. "It's obvious she's proud of you."

"Then why didn't she want me to be here?"

His hand slipped off of mine, and he shrugged. "She's inscrutable," he said. And then he laughed, as though to himself.

"I will say this about her," he said. "Whatever Persephone does, she does for her family."

But wasn't I her family?

We talked in the dining room for a long time before we went across the hall to the parlor. Mother sat in a copper tub by the fire reading a crumbling issue of *LIFE*, and Grandpa Miklos had sprawled out on the hearth and was dozing—not as the wolf but as a human, the vest of his three-piece suit unbuttoned to let his after-dinner belly expand. My father and Grandma Persephone sat playing chess, but when we came in Father stood up abruptly.

"Here," he said, and helped Arthur to a chair. He was courteous with him in a way that surprised me, and I wondered if it was because Arthur had a bad leg. It was definitely a little stiff, especially when he walked, but it was hard to imagine him needing help. I thought about how gracefully he'd helped me into my own chair.

Arthur got caught up in a conversation with Mother. Father's chess game with Grandma Persephone ended, and Arthur climbed out of his chair, the two of them switching places as though they'd done it a hundred times—Father to Arthur's chair, Arthur to chess table. Luma sat down next to me and talked to me about hunting bears and this new color of lipstick she liked, but my mind wasn't there. I kept thinking about my conversation in the dining room—what Grandma Persephone would do for her family, what to do about the new electric feeling in my core when I thought about Arthur touching my hand. I ignored her and half listened to the chess game. Eventually Luma stood up and left.

". . . had some luck with the plants this year," Grandma Persephone was saying. "The heated floor is working out well."

"I wouldn't say that taking my advice counts as luck," Arthur said.

"I was just tired of dealing with that odd little woodstove in there. A disaster." Persephone frowned at the board. "Check."

"You distracted me," Arthur said. I couldn't tell where his eyes were. I felt like a child, perched on the edge of the sofa, my hands folded in my lap. Mother was trying to show Father something in the magazine, but Father was watching the game, too. I realized that both of us were trying not to look too obvious about it.

"How did you meet my father?" I called to Arthur.

He turned from the board, but Grandma Persephone spoke first.

"He's been a family friend for some time," she said.

"So you and Father grew up together?"

"In a way," Arthur said.

I studied him. He didn't look nearly as old as my father. His eyes would have told me how old he was, but he'd kept those smoked glasses on all evening. I wondered if he was blind. Maybe that was why my father tried to hold his arm. Why he watched him so attentively. But then how did Arthur play chess if he was blind, or pull my chair out for me, or drive his Model T?

"Checkmate," Arthur said at last.

"Ah," said Grandma Persephone. "I didn't see that."

His lips peeled back into a smile. "I know."

I studied him. In the warm light of the parlor, he looked less pale than he had in the dining room, the fire casting a glow on his almost translucent skin. What kind of thing was he? Just a man, or something less or more? If he was my father's friend, where had they even met? Generally, no one from the family left town until they'd grown up. I tried to imagine Arthur as one of the ruddy children of Winterport, a wool scarf around his face clotted with frozen snot. It didn't seem possible.

Arthur must have noticed me staring, because he shifted in his chair to face me.

"Did you . . . want something?" he asked. It had no malice in it, but I flushed.

"I was just wondering where you were from," I said.

He smiled with his lips sealed shut. Grandma Persephone shot me a look. Something else I wasn't supposed to ask about.

"Arthur," she said, "will you play piano for Eleanor, since she's home?"

He glanced up from the board. "If that's what you want."

I knew, somehow, that that meant he didn't want to.

"Please do," she said. He began to stand up.

"You don't have to," I said from my place on the sofa. "You've been working all day. Please, *don't do anything you don't want to do right now.*"

I was surprised by how vehement I was. A glance around the room told me that everyone else was, too.

Arthur pushed in his chair. "Excuse me for a moment."

As he left the room, I saw Grandma Persephone's eyes follow him, and then look at me. I was starting to get annoyed with her constantly studying me. Even the nuns hadn't paid this much attention to every little thing I said and did.

"Let's play, Mother," Father said as he began to set up the board. Grandma Persephone humored him for a few minutes, but I could see her mulling something over.

"Eleanor," she said, when a few minutes had passed. "Would you go see if your aunt needs any help with the dishes?"

I stood up and left the room without saying anything. I wanted to scream at her, but I knew that would do no good. You couldn't let people see you were angry; they'd only use it against you. It was better to hold it in and wait for your moment to retaliate. I'd done it at boarding school more than once. Like with the girl who held me down while her friends rummaged through my trunk and took turns reading parts of my diary in an imitation of my voice. Back when I still kept a diary, with little bits of poems stuck in it, little notes to myself about things I wanted or dreams I'd had. I'd waited until that girl was shopping in town and cut the quilt her mother had sewn her to ribbons. I'd heard the scream from my dormitory room.

Of course, her mother had just sewn her a new one at Christmas. That was what it was like to have a family that wanted you.

I was so wrapped up in my own thoughts that I was halfway down the hall to the kitchen when I heard a scrabbling inside the wall.

I stopped under the portrait of Grandpa Miklos with the horses and listened, my ears pricked. It was coming from the opposite wall, the one under the staircase. What was making the noise? Rats? Ghosts? If there were such a thing, they'd be here. And when I looked at that wall more closely, I could see a crack, a seam, where I had thought there was solid wall. A door,

I realized. For a moment, it rattled in its frame. And then it exploded open, and Rhys came flying out.

He hit the wall opposite, and I saw his head snap back. His lips were so red they looked bitten, and there were red marks like handprints on either side of his neck. When he lowered his head again, his eyes were wild, his grin wide, and I saw his teeth grow sharp. He started to lunge back toward the doorway, but then he saw me and stopped in his tracks, stumbling forward. He caught himself on the wall, glowering at me.

"What did you see?" he asked.

I shook my head. "Nothing," I said. Out of the corner of my eye, I saw the door moving—being pulled shut from inside. What *had* I seen?

I forced myself to look at Rhys instead. He was angry. And something else, too. He was worried. About what I'd seen, or what I'd say. To whom? Who had pulled the door shut?

"What are you looking at?" he snarled.

"Calm down," I said. "I don't know what you're talking about." I looked right into his eyes. That was the trick, when you were lying. Stare them down. It worked on nuns, so I prayed it would work on Rhys.

He became the wolf all at once, his body stretching and snapping, and my head swam with the impossibility of it as he sprang away into the shadows of the kitchen. The back door slammed. After a minute, Margaret came out and gathered his clothes, which had fallen to the floor. She hung them up in the real closet, the one whose door wasn't just a crack in the wall. Glowering and muttering, she backed away from me and vanished into the kitchen.

When she'd gone, I ran my fingers along the crack—it looked like little more than a seam in the wallpaper. If I got my fingernails under it just right, I could pry it up a little ways. But after the first inch I could move it no farther. There was something on the inside, a latch or a chain, holding it shut. A secret passage? I didn't remember anything like that from when I was a child. Someone had latched it from the inside.

Luma wandered around the corner, and I turned on her.

"What's this?" I demanded, pointing at the wall.

She frowned. "I don't know," she said breezily.

"Were you just in there?" I asked. "Were you and Rhys fighting in the closet? Is he bullying you?"

"No," she said. "I just came from upstairs."

"Well, someone was in there with Rhys. And then shut the door again."

Luma's eyes narrowed. "I'm going to kill him," she said. "Which way did he go?"

"Luma, what's going on?"

She looked at me like I was stupid. "Rhys is trying to be with him," she said.

"With who?"

"With *Arthur*," she said.

I felt a little ringing in my ears. "What?"

"Oh, you know. Wanting to spend all his time with him. Wanting to be alone with him. Grandma told Rhys to stop playing with him, but he won't listen. He does whatever he wants," she said, tossing her head.

My mind reeled. It explained a lot—the preening in the hall, the mad attempts to impress him. And it was clear to me that Rhys was dangerous. I could see him cornering Arthur in the closet, shoving him against the wall. I imagined the look on Arthur's face, cool and reticent, in the face of my cousin's raw malice, and felt a little shiver that I liked. Maybe I'd like to shove Arthur against a wall.

And of course, that made me think of Lucy Spencer. What I'd done. What I was running from.

"We can't let this go on," I said. "What if Rhys hurts him?"

Luma grabbed my hands.

"You're right," she said. "And anyway, it's not fair for him to be keeping Arthur to himself like this. Arthur is the family friend, not his. And I hardly see Rhys anymore."

My thoughts were racing. This didn't seem right, somehow. Some piece was missing. I thought of the red marks on Rhys's neck, and imagined Arthur grabbing at Rhys, trying to push him away. I had to protect Arthur, I thought. Rhys was determined, and whatever he wanted with Arthur, he'd get his way.

"You can't make Rhys stop doing anything by force," I said. "He's too strong."

"Oh, I could fight him," Luma said. "He's a bigger person, but I'm a bigger wolf."

"No, we can't just attack him," I said. Why was this always her first answer to a problem? "He's family. But maybe he'd leave Arthur alone if he was with someone else." I could spend all my time with him, I thought. Whenever Arthur was here, I could be with him. Rhys didn't want me to tell anyone, so he wouldn't do anything in front of me. Probably. It scared me, but I was excited, too, to think I could help Arthur. After all, he'd already helped me. I thought of his laugh as Luma clasped my hands in hers.

"Of course!" she said. "You're so smart, Ellie."

Behind us, the front door opened. Arthur stepped inside, straightening his collar. For a moment, I doubted myself. Maybe I'd been wrong. Maybe he'd just been outside. He stepped lightly toward the parlor. My brain itched. Was I imagining things?

"I'll do it," Luma said. "For Arthur."

She strode toward the archway to the parlor. I followed along behind, more slowly, not sure what she was doing. By the time I got there, Luma was already taking Arthur by the hand and pulling him to his feet.

"I want you to take me on a romantic walk," she said. "In the moonlight."

For a moment I saw a ripple of anger pass across Arthur's face. He turned it, somehow, into a smile.

"Miles," Arthur said to my father, "Luma's told me she wants me to take her on a romantic walk. In the moonlight, apparently."

From her chair by the fire, Grandma Persephone gave a small irritated sigh. Father stood, looking worried. "Arthur, really?"

"What the lady asks for, I must obey."

He took her by the arm. As they passed me, Luma flashed me a radiant smile and a shoulder shimmy. Arthur gave me a smaller, conspiratorial smile, one that turned my guts to spiders. And then they left through the front door, disappearing into the night.

"Mother," Father said to Grandma Persephone. "Are you really going to let this happen?"

"She's a woman, Miles," Grandma said mildly.

"I think it's nice," Mother said from her washtub. No one responded.

They didn't come back for a long time. I sat and watched my father nervously try to converse with my mother while Grandma Persephone stroked Grandpa Miklos's belly with one foot. Someone put the record player on. Still they didn't come back. Father stood up and began pacing, but everyone else ignored him. Grandma Persephone asked Mother if she wanted a game of chess. Mother said no. Father sat back down and huffily pretended to read a book. Finally, I couldn't stand it anymore, and I stood up and made for the hall.

Margaret was in the dining room. She had the silver coffee service spread out and was polishing the pieces before putting them back in the cabinet. I looked to the room of warm idleness I'd left, and back at her, angrily scrubbing tarnish off of a pointless pile of junk used by one person who would have probably been fine with just a single cup. And that was the moment I couldn't stand it anymore.

"Why do you let them treat you this way?" I asked.

Her eyes narrowed, her brow furrowing over them.

"I know you can understand me," I said. "I know you can talk. You called me a traitor, remember? So what here did I betray? Did I ask too many questions, like about why you let them sit and relax and laugh and talk while you get nothing? Don't you get that? All your work is for nothing!"

She opened her mouth, and for a moment nothing happened. I knew that silence, though. It was the long silence of a child who's fallen down and hurt themselves. And then from deep in her throat came the groan.

At first, I thought she was just trying to scare me. But as the noise went on longer it got louder and climbed in pitch, until the silver on the table was rattling and the pictures jostling on the walls, and still it climbed. I felt frozen to the spot. The sound was going to rattle my bones out of my body, shatter me and turn me to jelly, bring down the rickety rafters of the high towers and then nothing would—

The sound stopped. I looked up to see Margaret slumped over. Grandma Persephone was kneeling on the floor beside her, cradling Margaret's head in her arms.

"You know you're not supposed to talk to her," she said evenly. "Now you've upset her."

"That's crazy," I said. "Don't you see how crazy that is?"

"Eleanor," Grandma Persephone said, her voice full of warning.

"What are you going to do?" I asked. "Abandon me again? Make me cook and clean for you?" I laughed, a little drunk on my own stupidity. "You can't just tell me to stop. After everything you did to me, I don't care what you think of me anymore."

Persephone straightened up and squinted at me. I felt suddenly cold. She studied me for a long moment.

"I don't think that's true," she said.

I'd had a thousand things to say lined up, but when she said that, they fled. I wanted to get away from her, so I started walking quickly toward the stairs. That was a mistake.

In the parlor, Miklos's head shot up. He clambered to his feet and started for me, stumbling toward me, his long wolf teeth already sliding into place. His shoulders had dropped, his eyes fixed on me.

I looked at the front door, but on open ground he'd catch me almost immediately. So I bolted left up the stairs, as behind me Grandma Persephone yelled, "Miklos! Stop it!"

I didn't dare glance behind me. I heard his claws clacking on the stairs, and then I felt something swipe the back of my ankle, stinging hot. I ran until I reached my room, then slammed the door shut, locked it, and shoved the rocking chair under the door handle. From the hall came the clicking of toenails on the parquet, and then shoes, and Grandma Persephone chastising Miklos softly. I held still until the sounds receded.

I looked down at my leg. He'd only scratched it, but blood was welling up along the back of my calf in bright beads, oddly yellowish, not red the way blood should be. Stupid. I wanted to cry every time I looked at my own weird blood. No matter how strange the rest of the family was, I bet even Miklos bled red.

I couldn't go get a bandage, not now. I went to my old wardrobe and got down a nightgown that was far too small for me now, then wrapped it around my leg, pressing it against the bleeding. Let Margaret clean this useless thing, if she wanted.

I was angry, but once that subsided, I was terrified. I climbed into my bed and sat listening for any sound of a tread on the stairs, any scratching at the window. This door between us couldn't keep me safe, I realized, if Grandma Persephone decided I wasn't welcome.

Eventually I heard footsteps in the hall outside, light and fast, and then a knock at my door. I sat up in bed. Was it Miklos, come to kill me? I'd shunned his family, and now I was like the men on the boat. I'd treated my grandmother with unkindness, and he was there to—

"Ellie?" Luma's voice sounded tentative. I breathed out, my heart still racing.

"One second." I scrambled to un-wedge the rocking chair and unlock the door, and climbed back into bed. "Come in."

She slipped in through the door and crawled under the blankets with me. I could smell the lavender water she splashed on her hair, the rank stink of meat on her breath. Her body was warm and downed in hair, like a cat's. I felt snug with her here. She sighed.

"It was so hard," she said. "Rhys saw us out walking and he looked so unhappy. I thought he was going to start a fight, but he just ran off into the forest."

"Luma, what I said earlier—I didn't mean *you* had to do it."

"Oh, I wanted to," she said. "There's something about him. It feels like I want to rip him to pieces, but I don't. I don't know, I kind of like it. Do you know what I mean?"

I did. And now I felt sick.

"You're in love with him?" I asked, not sure I wanted the answer.

"I don't think so," she said. "But I don't want Rhys to have him, so maybe I do love him?"

I'd never been good at talking to boys—even when we'd had school dances, I'd hid in a corner in a borrowed dress. But I knew about boys from watching them with other girls, and from listening to the gossip afterward. So I knew that no matter what you were like, or who you preferred, boys liked you best if you were beautiful. My chances weren't good here. Fish-face, the other girls had called me. I was funny looking, with protruding, heavy-lidded eyes and a wide mouth, to say nothing of the ugly web of skin between my thumbs and forefingers. Luma was beautiful. Even if I did say something to Arthur, he would choose Luma anyway.

Well, I shouldn't be upset about it, if it kept Rhys away from him. Rhys frightened me. I hadn't liked that look in his eyes in the hall earlier. It reminded me of Grandpa Miklos's eyes when he'd sprung at me, all raw intention.

"Did he like you?" I asked. "Did he kiss you?" It was like picking at a scab. I'd barely spoken to him, I told myself. Anything I thought I knew about him was wrong, so why was I so upset?

"He didn't try," she said. "He wanted to talk."

"What did he want to talk about?"

"Funny stuff," she said. "Poetry. He wanted me to tell him what all the noises in the forest meant, all the ones he couldn't hear. It was nice."

"I'm tired," I said.

She leaned over and kissed me on the forehead.

"Thank you," she said. "I never could have done this without you. I'm so glad you're home."

She slipped out. Her side of the bed cooled rapidly without her.

Maybe it wasn't too late to leave. I could ask for some more money, go to another school in another town where no one knew me. I could start over. But the thought of doing that chilled me, too. There was the thing I'd nearly done to Lucy Spencer to consider. I thought about how elastic and soft her neck had felt, and about Luma's ringed scar.

I fell asleep with racing thoughts, wishing I had any kind of clue of what to do next. When I finally drifted off, I dreamed about the greenhouse.

THREE

IT DIDN'T REALLY FEEL LIKE A DREAM. IT FELT like getting up sleepy for a glass of water, that shambling feeling. I drifted across the upper gallery that overlooked the ground floor to the back staircase, the one old houses have for servants. The stairs led down to the laundry, and to a rickety porch that had been walled in to make a hallway. It led across the yard to Grandma Persephone's greenhouse.

I was heading there to meet with the other children, Luma, Rhys, and Charlie. We were going to play a game. We'd often meet up there to play, the four of us. Rhys and Charlie were the biggest and the smallest so we always put them on a team together. It balanced it out. I think that was my idea.

Moving along the corridor, I could already half see in my

mind's eye the greenhouse, packed with rows of orchids and other exotic plants, the battered wingback chair where Grandma Persephone liked to sit and drink tea while she contemplated her deck of cards. It was a bright place, a daytime place. I was happy when I could get there.

Thunder rolled somewhere in the distance. When had a storm come in?

I opened the door and found the greenhouse shattered.

Shards lay everywhere, the ceiling and walls still raining down in places onto the bodies of crushed plants, intermixed with smashed pottery. Overhead the sky was red and thick as blood. Dim shapes stirred in that heaven. I didn't like it. I opened my mouth to speak and found that I could not make a sound. I woke up choking on words.

A loud crash of thunder came, and I screamed.

I sat up in bed and looked out the window. Nothing but a heat storm. Dim lightning flashed on the horizon over the water, no specific strokes, just an illumination of the sky. The sea below looked calm, but I could tell it churned beneath the surface, gathering force.

Someone knocked on my door. I went and opened it. Grandma Persephone stood outside, carrying a candelabra that threw her face into sharp shadows. It took me a few seconds to realize I wasn't still dreaming.

"The lights could go out any minute," she said.

"It's not raining here."

"Somewhere down the coast, the storm's breaking. Winter-port's electricity has a long way to travel." She tipped her head back, and for a moment I could see the mysterious smile I'd loved and feared when I was little. For a moment I felt eight again, like she'd never sent me away and no time had passed at all.

"It's the perfect weather for what we will do," she said.

She moved on down the corridor, the light receding with her. I ran after.

The house with its vast open spaces had the feel of a jungle. I felt safe from ambush in her circle of light and nowhere else. Around any corner could be Miklos, or Rhys. I realized I wasn't certain if Grandma Persephone had any power of her own, or if she was just a mad old woman who played at magic to make herself feel better about being surrounded by beasts. To make herself less afraid.

"How did you know I was coming home?"

"I read the cards yesterday, early in the morning," she said. "I saw you traveling and knew you'd come here."

"Not because you got a call from Saint Brigid's?" I asked, both skeptical and afraid of the answer.

"Have you seen a telephone in this house?"

She took me down the route I had followed in the dream. Down the back stairs, through the laundry, across the long crude corridor. I had a terror of what we would find at the end.

"We added this room and refitted the upstairs for a bathroom when your mother moved in," Grandma said. "After the War."

I nodded. I didn't know what any of this had to do with the middle of the night, or if she was just making conversation.

It was almost too dark to see in the hall, but when Grandma Persephone threw open the door to the greenhouse, a bolt of lightning split the dark and illuminated the room: the forest of palms and hydrangeas, the hothouse roses and African violets and so much of this one strange plant, a black orchid.

"*Draconis vulgaris*," Grandma Persephone said. "On Crete we called it *drakondia*, snake lily. Prepared one way it's a love potion; another way, it's poison. It's the backbone of our fortune, but it mostly takes care of itself. It's very hardy, under the right conditions."

"Why are you telling me this?"

"Sit," she said, waving me toward one of the armchairs, the velvet streaked with droppings from the birds that sometimes got trapped in the greenhouse. I remembered Rhys and Luma trying to catch them, when we were young. But I'd always been more interested in these chairs, and in the little table where Grandma Persephone laid out her cards.

The tarot deck was there now, in the middle of the table.

I perched on the edge of the chair, not wanting to lean back, resting my hands on the clean spots on the table in front of me.

"Eleanor," she said, "why did you come back?"

"This is my home."

"You barely remember it. You barely remember us."

"I had nowhere else to go."

"What did you do?"

That stung. "What makes you think I did anything?"

"Because I know you," Grandma Persephone said. "You were always doing something. Always up to something."

It sounded like she was talking about someone else. "I'm not like that. I'm a good student. I never get in trouble." Except that wasn't true anymore.

"I suppose that might be so," she said. "You've lived outside of the family. You have some sense of what the world is like, and you haven't killed anyone, which says good things about your character. Sister Katherine even says you look after people. Younger girls at school. She says you're never cruel, even to people who mistreat you."

That definitely wasn't true anymore. I cringed. I hadn't known I was being tested, all those years. I'd just been trying to survive. I thought about all the things I'd done because I hadn't known I was being watched.

I thought of Lucy Spencer's neck.

"Was Sister Katherine spying on me?" I asked. She'd been my favorite of the nuns, quiet and bookish like me. She used to let me read in her office.

"I wouldn't call it that. She just told me how you were doing."

This all felt so unfair. If I'd known, I might have behaved better.

"And now you've seen us again," Grandma Persephone said. "Have we satisfied your morbid curiosity? You certainly don't seem happy here."

"I don't want to leave," I said. I didn't. There was so much I still wanted to know. And I didn't want to let go of Luma. And I needed to keep Arthur safe from Rhys. And I—

"I can't go back, Grandma."

"And why not?" she asked. She sat up a little straighter in her chair, her body angling toward me like a knife. "I told you to stay put, and you still came back here. Why? Why are you here, Eleanor?"

I could barely breathe. I told myself I would say it on the count of three. I counted down twice before I managed to say, "Because I did something bad."

I told her, as best I could. I told her what I'd told Arthur: about Lucy Spencer, our friendship, her hating me. I told Grandma Persephone about the other day, when Lucy had pushed me down the stairs. And then I told her the rest of it. How her shoving me wasn't a surprise, or it shouldn't have been. Lucy had always bullied me, pinching me and taunting me about my strange webbed thumbs and my buggy eyes, my worn-out clothes and how I had no family. I'd learned to avoid her. I should have seen this coming, I thought, and that made me angry.

And so instead of catching myself on the railing, I'd tucked my head into the cradle of my shoulder and rolled headfirst all the way down. It hurt a lot, but I let myself go limp and knock about until I sprawled at the bottom in a heap among the books. I made it look worse than it was, letting one leg jut out oddly as though I'd broken it. I held very still until I could see Lucy's feet in front of my face through slitted eyes. And then I lunged.

I grabbed her ankles, and she let out a startled gasp and sat down hard on the floor of the stairwell. I sank in my nails and dragged myself up and over her by her legs, and pinned her arms to the floor. She started kicking at me, so I dropped my weight onto her so she couldn't move. I used my forehead to bash her face to one side, and then I bit into the soft skin where her neck met her shoulder. I bit until it snapped like a rubber band, and warm blood gushed into my mouth while she screamed, while she pulled at handfuls of my hair, while she kicked her legs under me, trying desperately to get me off of her—

"Stop," Grandma Persephone said. I stopped. "Did you kill her?"

I shut my eyes. "I don't think so," I said. When I'd fled the room, she'd been sitting upright, hands pressed to her neck, screaming. "No. I didn't."

She sat back in her chair, still gripping the arms.

"So you're dangerous," she said. "I knew that already. What I need to know is: Are you dangerous to my family?"

I wanted to cry. I realized that I had been hoping she'd like me better after I told her. That she'd see me and think of Luma, of Rhys, of the others. That I'd be one of them. Instead, she seemed unmoved. What was she so afraid of?

"No!" I said. "I don't want to hurt anyone. It all just happened so fast. And I didn't know where else to go. I don't have anyone else."

And at last, she softened.

"I want to be sure," she said gently. "Will you let me read for you?"

"Why?"

"So I know whether you're here to help us or to hurt us."

"Why would I hurt you?"

"Will you let me do it?"

I nodded.

She shuffled the deck, and the cards leaped between her hands. She'd drawn them all herself, I knew, years ago. The cards were soft with wear, edges blurred. She handed the deck to me and had me cut it, and then she laid out an elaborate spread. She turned over the first card, at the center.

"This is you," she said.

My heart leaped when I recognized that first card: the Page of Bones, the card that had always come up first when she read for me when I was younger. A young scholar, not clearly a man or a woman, peering at the skull of a bird with a magnifying glass. Maybe I hadn't changed as much as I thought, if this was still the card that meant *me*.

I watched Persephone, too. Her eyes unfocused as she worked, as though she were seeing something near and far at the same time.

"A young person of great intelligence who relies on their wit," she said.

She turned over the rest of the cards, following the old pattern, narrating as she went.

"Covering you—doubts and fears. Are you good enough? Strong enough? Crossing you—a great crowd of people, yammering different things in your ears. Who do you listen to?"

She looked up at me. "Well," she said, "you're not much of anything yet, it seems. Not this or that. Not sure what you're going to become. You could be anything right now. You could be like me. Or you could be something . . . very different."

"I could be like you?" I asked. "You mean, read cards and do magic?"

"That's only some of what I do. Mostly I manage the family."

"How?"

She sighed.

"I keep them from killing people, mostly," she said, "and deal with the damage when they inevitably do. I keep them healthy, and make sure they understand right from wrong as much as they can. I tend to the plants and distill the extracts and sell them to distributors. And I keep Winterport happy, as much as I can, so they don't turn on us and burn the house to the ground while we sleep."

"I could do that," I said. "You could teach me, and then I could help you."

She frowned.

"Eleanor," she said, "you already have enough talents. I'm not sure it would be a good idea for me to teach you anything."

I didn't feel talented. I had no sharp teeth or secret second body hiding under my skin. The least I could do was learn how to make myself useful. And maybe, I thought with a little hope, I could learn how to see the future.

"Please," I said. "I really want to learn."

"I'm not giving you an answer tonight. Let me finish reading for you, and I'll think about it."

She flipped over the next card. "Behind you: imprisonment, restriction, restraint. Just before you: freedom, but a kind that makes you nervous." She paused here to smile at me. "You're perched on the brink of a decision. Mine, or yours, I suppose. Still want to stay?"

I looked down at the cards, trying to puzzle them out. My card appeared to have vanished, until I realized it was under the card she'd said covered it. Oh, it was that simple. And then across it, a card with a group of people crowded around a heap of bones, stretching like they were getting ready for a dance. And a picture of a woman kneeling in a barren cell, holding a viper to her breast, and a picture of a great wheel with a blindfolded girl in spangled tights strapped to it and the word FORTUNE printed on it in large type. I wondered how she could see the future in all this chaos.

"How do you know what the cards mean?" I asked.

"Metaphors."

"Metaphors?" I was stunned. I'd only ever heard the word *metaphor* used in class, and never heard of one doing anything useful.

"You triangulate," she said. "Between your own knowledge, the images, and the words. And for a moment you can escape your own perspective, and leave the present, and you can see a little more widely."

My eyes went wide. "*I want to learn that!*"

She shuddered as though trying to shake something loose.

"Stop that," she said. "I can't make a decision tonight. Let's finish this."

I found myself excited at the prospect of learning to read the cards. It was one of those things that was easy to learn but would take a lifetime to master. I wasn't like Rhys or Luma because I wasn't supposed to be. I'd be something else, something just as good. And it wasn't something I'd gotten through dumb luck. I was going to earn it.

Persephone turned over the next card. I paid attention to the way her hand flicked the card, the way she slapped it down on the table.

"Above you," she said, "your best possible future."

It was a card that read Ace of Blood. It showed a chalice

pouring red out over a landscape, splashing over a horde of dancing figures below. It frightened me the way Grandpa Miklos's teeth did, the way Rhys's embrace did. It was a feral card. It didn't seem best to me.

"This card tells me that you might save our family," she said. "Save us, restore us, put us right—I don't know what it thinks it means," she said, giving the card a little tap, as though chastising it. I felt a twinge of fear. Fear would pass, I told myself. I had to hold steady. She said she wanted to know what I was. I wanted the same thing.

She flipped the next card. It was a rough drawing of the Chrysler Building in New York. People leaped from the windows, their faces contorted with pain and fear. "And this card tells me that you might ruin us."

"Grandmother," I said, "I'll do my best, I promise. Whatever it takes. I won't let them get hurt."

"You can't make promises like that," she snapped, and then took a breath and softened her voice. "I believe that you'll try. But it's important that you not take this lightly. You're at a crossroads. There are two ways that things can go, if you stay. And one is ruin. Do you understand me? This is not a game, Eleanor."

I felt like the worst creature ever to have lived. Everyone knew there was something wrong with me. Lucy'd known it, and look what I'd done to her. Margaret knew it. Grandma Persephone and every single card in her whole deck seemed to know it.

This wasn't what I remembered from my childhood. We used to play in the greenhouse while Grandma Persephone called us over one at a time to read for us, any question we asked. She'd lay out the spread and talk us through the problem, and then she'd turn over one last card and tell us how it was supposed to go.

"You haven't done the last card yet," I said. "The one that gives us a clue about the outcome."

She glanced up. "You're correct."

She reached for the top card of the deck. Her hand hovered, hesitating. The sky flashed.

She flipped it over and onto the table, but withdrew her hand quickly as though she'd been stung.

"Ahh," she said, her voice faint.

It was a card I had never seen in a reading before. It was a mass of dim shapes, hard to discern—spewing, spiraling outward from a central mass, where lurked a pair of glowing yellow eyes with slit pupils. When I looked at it, I was entranced. It was ugly, but I wanted to stare into it forever.

"Grandma," I said. "What does it mean?"

I looked up and realized she was clutching her arm. She slumped back in her chair, her white hair streaming back from her rigid face.

"I didn't draw this," she said. She could barely open her mouth.

"What do you mean? Where did it come from?"

"This is very bad," she said, through clenched teeth, shuddering as she fought to speak. "Listen carefully. I'm dying. You have to take over for me. Don't let any strangers in this house after I'm gone."

"But I can't. I don't know—"

"Shut up. You know what you can do. Make them listen to you. Keep them safe. Promise me!"

"I—"

Her whole body stiffened, and then sagged back against the chair.

"Grandma?" I said. And then again, louder. She wasn't breathing. Her eyes looked empty.

And then lightning split the sky and struck some point almost directly overhead. Saint Elmo's Fire sizzled down the glass walls, green and flickering. It was like the light under the ocean, filtered through water, and in it Grandma Persephone looked like a drowned creature.

I killed her, I thought. She read my fortune, and whatever she saw was so bad that it killed her.

I didn't know where I would go, as I sprinted down the wooden corridor that led from the greenhouse. I would have kept running if I hadn't bumped into Margaret in the scullery. She took one look at my face, grabbed me by the arm, and yanked me back the way I had come, into the greenhouse. When she saw Grandma Persephone in the chair she lifted her and put her on the floor, and then got down on her knees. She pinched Grandma Persephone's nose shut and started taking big breaths and breathing out into her mouth. She turned up to me and gave me a wild-eyed look, which I thought at first was hatred, and then realized was some kind of order. She jerked her head toward the door, and I nodded. Get the others. I forced my legs into a run, took the back stairs through the scullery up to the second floor, and started pounding on doors.

My mother came dripping from her bathtub, Rhys shirtless and matted from his room. He grabbed my mother up in her towel and carried her down the back stairs. I went to Grandpa Miklos's room, Father's, Luma's. When I told them what had happened they all took off running without saying a word to me. And so running around, I was the only one who didn't go to see her last moments alive.

Eventually I was alone on the stairs, the thunder outside the only sound. One by one the lights in the hall fizzled, flared, and went out.

FOUR

STANDING ALONE IN THE HALLWAY, I WAITED
for a long time, shivering. And then the noise began: screaming,
crying, howling—laughing? It washed over me like a wave, filling the house, echoing into every quiet corner and reverberating
back at me. So I fled, down the great front staircase and out
onto the lawn.

It was early morning, the sky gray and thick overhead, and
I felt cold to my core. I stuck close to the house until I reached
the back garden. The greenhouse jutted out on the garden's far
side, but the windows were so fogged over that I doubted they'd
see me. Still, I kept low until I got to the rickety staircase that
led down to the beach. It shook under me as I scrambled down.
When I got to the water, I let myself take a deep breath.

The red haze of the sun was just beginning to spread across

the horizon, making a thin line between the dark water and the dark sky. The wind blew off the water in gusts that sent a sticky salt spray over everything. I sat down in the sand with my back to the cliff, huddled up between two boulders, and watched the water. It rolled in large, blue-green waves.

I cried ugly sobs that the water blotted out for me. It had all happened so fast. For a long time I didn't think, didn't feel anything, just cried like I was trying to feed the sea.

The waves were dark in the early morning, and layers of water made strange colors and shapes just beneath the surface. It reminded me of the card. What had that thing been, in the image? And the light had been dim, but I could have sworn I saw it moving. It had been an omen of something bad coming. Something bad enough that Grandma Persephone had died seeing it, and had tried to warn me. What had she said? Don't let any strangers in the house? And more frightening still: make them listen to you. And now they were all up there together, and of course, I'd run away. What were they going to think? Maybe that I'd done something to her. Not that I could have. I wasn't like them: strong or powerful. I was just me. Just Eleanor, who was supposed to protect them.

That got me to my feet at last. A gust of wind off the water hit me as I stood up, and I shivered in it. I'd fled the house without any shoes on, I realized; my feet were almost blue from the cold, although I hadn't felt a thing.

I climbed the stairs, my feet so numb and clumsy that I

nearly slipped a few times. At the top, I stared at the back door of the greenhouse, listening for the noise that had sent me running earlier. It was gone now, but from inside, I could hear soft voices. I steeled myself and opened the door.

Everyone had clustered around Grandma Persephone's rigid body, but no one had closed her eyes or loosened the grip of her hand on her own arm, so she still looked stiffly awake and terrified. Margaret had collapsed, and Rhys lay half sprawled on top of her, bawling. Father had moved into a corner far from the body, and Mother sat on the floor beside him, the hem of her dressing gown sodden, trying to coax him toward her. Grandpa Miklos lay curled up in a ball, clutching at the hem of Grandma Persephone's dress. And Luma sat cross-legged on the floor with Grandma's head in her lap, braiding her hair. She was the only one who glanced up when I came in.

"Where did you go?" she asked.

"I went to think," I said. Grandma Persephone's dead eyes were looking at me. "Can you close her eyes?"

"They keep popping open," Luma said. "So we stopped trying."

"Well, what are we going to do?" I asked.

"We'll need to get some wood for a box," Mother said. "And then we'll bury her. In a few days or so."

"What are we going to do with her until then?" I asked.

Luma sighed. "What did they teach you at school? We've got to clean up the body, of course." Father turned white, and

Grandpa Miklos started howling in a pitch that made my blood run cold. "We'll keep it in the laundry where it's cool and dark so it doesn't go off, and then we'll bury her when Grandpa says it's alright."

"But what about a funeral?"

Luma looked confused. "Like in books? Don't be silly."

She stood up, and Grandma Persephone's braided head slid from her lap and thudded sickeningly on the floor of the greenhouse. "Alright, enough sitting around," she said. "Rhys, Father, help me, please? Mother, we'd better show Eleanor how it's done. We've helped Grandma do it for old people," she said to me. "It's not so bad; you just have to get used to it."

Father listened to her, I realized. He unwound himself from the corner, and he and Grandpa Miklos picked up Grandma Persephone's body and carried it into the house. Luma trotted after them. Mother crawled along the ground toward me until she got to the chair, and then used it to drag herself to her feet.

"Are you alright?" she asked, when everyone else had left the room.

"I'm fine," I said, trying not to look too closely at Mother's face.

"What happened?" she asked. "You know . . . I won't tell the others. Not if you don't want me to."

"She was reading my cards," I said. "And she saw something that frightened her. And she told me . . ." I thought about how to say this, how not to sound bizarre. "She told me that she wanted me to look after the house and keep it safe. And then she died."

"She had a heart attack last year," Mother said. "Margaret caught it in time. We thought she was doing better. I suppose it was the shock of it all."

"Of what all?" I asked.

"Well, you coming home," she said, and then hurried to add, "I mean, with the cards, too. I wonder what she saw. Did she tell you?"

I didn't want to tell Mother about what I'd seen. She seemed so fragile, clinging to Grandma Persephone's chair to even stay upright. I was supposed to protect them, wasn't I?

"Are we really just going to bury her in the yard?" I asked. "Shouldn't we get a priest at least?"

"I suppose we could," Mother said. "Can you help me back inside?"

She was my mother, I reminded myself, as she slipped an arm around my shoulders that was slick and covered in little polyps. I put a hand around her waist to help her walk—her whole body was clammy, pressed up against me.

"Shouldn't we invite people?" I asked. "Why shouldn't they know? I know she did work for some of them. She said a big part of her job was to keep them happy."

"She did dirty work for them," Mother said. "Dressing the

dead and doing secret things. Here, the dining room." I led her in and helped her step into the barrel at her place at the table. "They don't want to mourn her if they don't have to."

"That's not fair," I said. "She was a good person. I'm sure they'd be sad. And besides, they'll notice she isn't around. It'll be better if we tell them."

"You don't understand," she said. "We don't socialize. It's not our way."

"Mother, I'm serious. *We need to do this.*"

Mother looked at me strangely then. But she nodded.

"I can write some invitations," she said. "Can you get my stationery from the trunk in my room? It's next to the . . . bed, I think."

I nodded and then climbed the stairs and went into her and Father's room.

I hadn't been in it since I was little. It was neatly kept, but dust floated through the air, caught on beams of sunlight, and the room smelled strongly of Father's aftershave, not of her sage or rosewater. There was no washtub propped up by the fire or filled next to the bed, no indent in the carpet where one had been. She'd never slept here, I realized.

The trunk she'd mentioned was so dusty that when I opened it I left handprints on the lid.

The inside of the trunk was divided into compartments, and the compartments held mostly different types of stationery. I pulled out some black-edged cards with black envelopes that looked right, and underneath was an old cigarette box stamped with CIGARETTES GITANES, REGIE FRANCAISE. Didn't our other grandmother live in France? I fetched it out, then went to the door and pulled it shut behind me before returning to open the box.

The letters inside were still in envelopes and addressed in strange, loopy handwriting. The return address and the stamp were French. I opened one of them. My French was a little elementary, but I could read most of the letter:

> My dear Aurora,
> After having heard so much about your family over the years I would love to come and visit. I know that you have previously denied me, but your daughters are growing up, and I would welcome an opportunity to meet them. I hope that you and your husband are very happy. Please write me again soon even if it is only to tell me no again. I love to hear how you are, my darling.
>
> > Best,
> > Mere

I sat on the floor for a moment in silence. So this was my other grandmother. She was French. She sounded gentle. She wanted to meet me.

I folded the letter back up, and then on impulse, I sniffed it. It smelled like lavender. Why had Mother never let her come and visit?

"Eleanor?" Mother called from somewhere downstairs. "Did you find the stationery? Check the trunk!"

"Coming!" I tucked the letter back in its envelope and returned it to the cigarette box. I hurried downstairs with the black-edged stationery and found Mother at the dining room table in her barrel. She took the invitations from me with a sigh.

"We've never had a funeral before," she said.

"Grandma Persephone meant a lot to the people in town," I said. "Father Thomas can come and say a few words." I keep the town happy, she'd said. "And if we don't tell them, they might think something happened to her."

Mother looked up at me.

"Are you sure there's nothing you want to tell me?" she said. "Eleanor, you know I'd love you no matter what, right?"

I tried to figure out what she was saying. "Of course."

"So . . ." Oh. That was what she was wondering. My own mother.

"She got really scared," I said. "And she died."

"Did you—"

"I didn't *do* anything!" I said, startled by the force of my own words. "What could I even do?"

She shook her head and looked away.

"Alright," she said. "Who should I invite then?"

"Anyone in the village who Grandma Persephone helped."

"That will be a long list."

"Then they should all come," I said.

I went in search of Luma, but when I found her, she was going from the kitchen into the laundry, helping Margaret carry a huge cauldron of water. I glanced past them for a second into the laundry, and saw Grandma Persephone laid out on the floor before Margaret slammed the door in my face. I should be in there, I thought, helping with . . . whatever it was that happened with dead people. But my stomach was already turning, just thinking about it. Margaret must have heard me hesitating at the door, because she thumped her hand against it: *bangbangbang*. I jumped back and scurried away.

I was in charge. She'd left me in charge. What came next? I wandered out into the hall in a daze. I'd barely slept last night, and now my grandmother was dead. I found myself standing in front of the wall of pictures. I stared for a long time at the portrait of Grandpa Miklos looking devilish, holding the pair of horses by the reins. The artist had painted flecks of foam flying from their open mouths. He'd captured the wet gleam of Grandpa Miklos's canine teeth. All of these pictures, and not a single one of me, at any age. It was like she'd tried to erase me.

Behind me, someone coughed. I turned around. Arthur stood by the door, hanging an umbrella on the stand. I hadn't heard the door open.

"Oh," I said. "Have you heard?"

"I have." He looked at me. "I spoke to your father outside."

"I'm sorry for your loss," I said.

"It's more yours than mine."

He crossed the floor toward me and stood beside me, looking up at the portrait of Miklos. "Hm," he said. "Not my best work."

I turned to him, a little astonished. "You did this?"

"He didn't like other portraitists' work on him," he said. "He said they never got his eyes right."

I looked at Miklos's eyes. They were stunning: filled with animosity and glee. I glanced back at Arthur, who had his hands tucked behind his back, as though he were at a museum.

"Miles said you were with her when she died," he said. "That must have been a shock. Are you alright?"

"I'm . . . trying to be," I said. "She told me to look after things, actually. I thought she wanted me gone, but when she was dying she grabbed my hand and told me to take care of everyone. And to make them listen to me. I wish I knew what that meant."

"Did she, now?" He turned slightly. "What did she say you had to . . . do?"

"She didn't tell me much of anything," I said. "She said . . . she said that she runs the extracts business, tries to make the town happy, keeps the family safe."

He turned and looked down to face me. I couldn't see his eyes, so it was maddening to have him staring into mine. "Just because a dying woman told you to do something doesn't mean you have to. You can refuse."

I shook my head. "You don't just refuse someone's last request."

"This house isn't a nice place, Eleanor. If you can leave it, you should."

"What does that mean?"

There it was again: that set in his jaw, that little click that told me he wasn't going to tell me anything. I shook my head. "I'm sorry if that was rude," I said. "But I can't really think about leaving. There's too much to do, with the business, and the funeral—"

"You're planning a funeral?"

"She left me in charge, didn't she?"

I grinned at him, hoping he would smile. His eyebrows furrowed.

"I don't expect she said anything about me?" he asked.

"No. Is there something I should know?"

He opened his mouth but didn't speak. His jaw clenched, and he looked away.

"I suppose not," he said.

"Well, I'm taking it seriously," I said. "So if you have any problems, you bring them to me."

He nodded slowly. "Maybe I will."

My mother called to me from the dining room. "Eleanor?"

"I have to go," I said. "Lots to do now."

"I can see that."

I ducked into the dining room. I was still thinking about all the things he hadn't said when Mother plunked a stack of invitations into my hands.

"Here you go," she said. "Are you sure about this?"

"It's the right thing to do." I glanced out into the hall to see if Arthur was still there, but he'd vanished. And I could see our old farm truck idling on the front lawn already. Not Arthur's car, though; strange. "I'd better go," I said, and ran outside.

The truck had wood-slat sides. Margaret had been sitting in it for several minutes by the time I went outside to meet her, but she didn't even look at me when I got in. She drove us in silence down the hill, along the dirt track that led through the birch forest. I thought for a second I saw Grandpa Miklos between the trees, but then we rounded a corner and I could see nothing at all.

We rumbled down the main street of the town, and Aunt Margaret brought us to a halt outside the general store. She turned the car off, leaving the keys in the ignition. I waved my hand and pointed to them. She shrugged, then stomped off with the shopping list, leaving me alone.

The first invitation was made out to Father Thomas. Mother had told me to give them all to Mrs. Hannafin at the post office, but I decided I'd give that one to him directly. I dropped the rest off with her first.

"Oh, old Mrs. Zarrin's passed?" she said. "Set my leg one winter, the roads were out."

"She was a good woman," I said.

"Ayuh," she said, although she looked uncertain. "An ill wind that blows no good."

My face flushed. "That's a strange thing to say about a woman who just died."

"I'm sorry," she said. "You must be the granddaughter. I'll be sad to see her go, though."

"Just . . . please see that people show up," I said.

"I heard that grandson was standing to inherit," she said. "Hope Mr. Zarrin's keeping well."

"You must have heard wrong," I said. "Actually, I'm the heir." She squinted.

"No," she said. "Doesn't sound like what I heard."

The church was only a few houses down from the post office. It had lost some of its shingles in the storm last night, and outside Father Thomas was bent over a wheelbarrow, picking them up and tossing them in. He glanced up and started to raise his hand in benediction, and when he realized who it was, let it fall.

"Father Thomas," I said. "I'm confirmed; you can bless me."

"Your grandmother did say she sent you to the nuns," he said. "I doubt she thought you'd convert. Does she know you're here?"

I took a step forward and held out the envelope. "My mother asked me to bring this to you. Unfortunately, my grandmother has passed on."

The old priest doubled over as though he'd been shot.

"Oh God," he said. And he began to weep. He shook and sobbed, almost silently, his whole body shuddering.

"It's alright." I reached out, more to steady his shoulder

against the shaking than to comfort him. "She was at home with her family."

He nodded, sobbing. I'd never seen a man cry this much. He shook his head, tears pouring down his withered face, following the lines of the wrinkles. He gently moved my hand away from his shoulder and kept crying, turning from me to keep picking up the shingles that had fallen onto the lawn. I could see his hands shaking, so badly that when he caught hold of one he dropped it almost immediately. He picked it up again.

"Father," I said. I reached out to grab the shingle. "Please, let me help."

He shook his head. The tears were falling hard now. He looked up at me. I could see he wanted something. To do something, maybe, to make him feel better. Keep the town happy.

"It would mean a lot if you'd say a few words at her funeral," I said.

"I don't think I could," he sighed. "You see, I don't expect she was Catholic."

"She was . . ." I paused, thinking. "She was very devoted."

He half laughed at that, wiping his nose on his sleeve.

"You are so much like her," he said, still crying.

I didn't feel like her, as I let him take the shingle from me. He turned away from me, looking down at it as though he could read something in it, as though I weren't there at all. I watched him and wondered if I was ever going to feel like I knew what I was doing.

When I turned to leave, I noticed some boys hanging around the yard of the next house down. They looked like the boys from a few days before, the ones who had watched me so intently at the train station. They were snot-streaked and wind-chapped, dressed in torn sweaters and wool hats, their fingers lost in their oversized sleeves. The legs of their blue jeans were pressed, ironed into pleats in the front by some proud mother. I wondered what they saw in front of them. They looked too young to be boys I would have chased through the woods, but maybe their older brothers had told them about me.

As I headed back toward the post office, leaving Father Thomas behind, they started to follow me at a distance. I turned around once to glare and they broke into a run, tearing past me up the street. I thought everything would be alright, until I saw Margaret come out of the hardware store, carrying a stack of lumber over one shoulder.

As the boys saw her, their heads swiveled to follow her almost in unison. One of them pointed and said something I couldn't hear. The other boys shook their heads, but he bent down. I watched in horror as he picked up a rock and hurled it.

Everything slowed down for me. I felt calm, I realized as I pushed away from the ground and sprinted at the boy full tilt. About halfway there the rock touched down—fell short, skittering across the cobbled street. I registered that, coolly, but didn't care. It wasn't going to stop me as I plunged toward the boy, arms raised. I realized my mouth was open, that I was showing my teeth. Some small part of me was frightened, but most of me was ready to taste blood—

And then Margaret was there, between me and the boy. She grabbed me around the waist with one arm as I barreled past and my feet left the ground and kicked the air. Behind Margaret's back, the bad boy was picking up another rock when one of his friends punched him hard enough that he dropped it. "Idiot," his friend said. "She's gonna kill you!" And they took off running down the street.

I felt suddenly weak. They were just kids. I sagged, and Margaret lowered me to my feet. I glanced up. She hadn't even let go of the wooden planks; they were still balanced across her shoulder. I marveled at how strong she was, and wondered that she hadn't taught those boys a lesson herself, years ago. I had thought I was afraid of her. Now I realized I probably wasn't afraid enough. I tried meeting her eyes, to see if she was pleased, or angry, or frightened. But she grunted and turned back toward the car, walking so fast that I had to run a few steps to catch up with her.

As we jostled uphill in the old truck, I started to come back to myself, and the horror of what I'd done seeped in. I hadn't thought twice about it. I'd nearly ripped into that boy. I thought about Luma's ring of bite marks. Lucy Spencer with one hand clamped over her neck while blood seeped out between her fingers, her eyes wide in terror. The night—

I shook my head and looked down at my trembling hands.

I glared at them until they stopped shaking. My panic became determination. No one could find out about this. I would be more careful next time. Have more self-control. The family needed that from me. They needed me to be the normal one.

I glanced over at Margaret, about to ask her if we could keep this between ourselves. Her eyes were locked on the road and she was droning a low tone under her breath. She wouldn't tell them. Which meant the only one who had to keep their mouth shut here was me.

Back at the house, I tried to explain to everyone how I imagined the funeral would go. The priest would say a few words. The villagers would say they were sorry for our loss, and we'd say thank you. Everyone would wear black.

"I look terrible in black," Luma said.

"It's one day," I said. "And your grandmother is dead."

"She never cared if I wore black."

I gave up on convincing her, because I needed her help. I wanted to talk to Grandpa Miklos, who had slipped back into the house after a full day in the woods, but I was afraid to approach him alone. Luma stood behind me with her hands on my shoulders while I knocked on his door. He stuck his head out, his face scratched from running through thorns. I looked at the beads of blood that lined the scratches, but his blood was the right red. Not like mine.

"We're having a funeral," I said. "And it's going to be in four days, and I need you to be there for it. And I need you to promise me that you *won't hurt anyone who comes to the house*. Do you understand?"

He nodded hazily.

"I want you to be very gentle with them," I said. "They're not here to see you, they're here to pay their respects to Grandma."

He nodded. Tears had already sprung to his eyes when I mentioned Grandma Persephone. He scrubbed at them with the back of his hand.

"I will do this thing you ask of me," he said. "They should say good-bye without fear."

"Did you make him agree?" Luma asked when he'd shut the door in our faces.

I was confused by her question. "I guess we'll find out."

"You see the worst in everyone," she said. "Why are you so mad?"

"I'm not mad," I said.

"You are so! You smell of it all the time. I just don't know who you're so angry with."

"With whom I'm so angry," I said automatically, and then felt stupid. In the scale of things, grammar wasn't the worst thing Saint Brigid's had done to me, but it was infuriating none-theless.

"Ugh!" Luma's lip curled up, showing her row of jagged sharp teeth. "Why'd you come home if you can't stand us? Grandma was right, you really did forget about us."

My head swam and my vision narrowed in on Luma. Here

came that feeling again. Remember Lucy Spencer, I thought, and dug my fingernails into my palms, trying to keep myself conscious.

"Forgot you?" I said. "I wrote to you every day for the first month. I wrote you letters every month after that. Until I got to a hundred. And then I gave up. Because who gets a hundred letters and doesn't answer any of them?"

Luma scoffed at me. "You're such a liar," she said. "You didn't even send me one."

I stared at her in disbelief. I wanted to tell her that she was the liar, not me, but she stormed off into her room and slammed the door. I knocked for a while, but she growled at me from behind it.

Luma wasn't likely to make things up. Which meant she'd never gotten any of my letters. Who could have taken them? I could think of only one person.

Grandma Persephone had always kept her papers in the library, in an enormous glass-fronted cabinet behind her desk. I was sure that if I could get in there I'd find evidence. Or something.

I headed for the stairs but stopped when I heard voices coming from the front hall below.

"I don't know what you expect me to do about it," my father was saying. "I never understood any of that. It wasn't men's business."

They stood close together, but tensed, as though they were

connected by a wire drawn taut. Arthur was still in his coat and hat. My father was shorter than Arthur, but planted firmly with his feet apart. I'd seen too many girls stand this way at school, whisper intensely for minutes, and then erupt suddenly into violence. What did they have to fight over?

"Not men's business?" Arthur said. "Is that the excuse you want to reach for?"

My father twitched. Arthur relaxed but took a step forward. They were almost touching now.

"It was supposed to end with her," Arthur said. "That was the arrangement."

"I—I don't . . . ," my father stammered. He'd seemed many things to me before, but never a stammerer, never someone who would babble. "—don't want you to leave. You're not allowed to hurt me. Leaving would hurt me."

"What do you want from me?"

"I want you to stay here," my father said. And then his voice softened. "I want you to be happy here with us."

"Well, Miles," Arthur said, "you can't have everything, can you?"

The wire broke. My father turned and walked out of the room, double time. I was terrified for a moment that he would come into the parlor and see me, but he changed shape as he disappeared around a corner, and then he was gone. He was gone, leaving a pile of clothes behind.

Arthur stood alone in the empty hall. He took off his hat,

held it in his hands, and bowed his head. And then he glanced up, as though someone had come in.

"Why isn't it over?" His voice sounded small, and for a moment I wondered if I'd heard him correctly. "You promised."

For a moment I thought he was talking to me, that he'd seen me. What promise? Grandma Persephone had asked me to promise to take care of the family, but surely it couldn't be that. I hoped he'd say more, but he turned and left the room, in the same direction my father had gone.

I slipped down the stairs and around the corner, to the library door. I managed to get my hand on the doorknob and jiggle it just enough to know that it was locked before I heard footsteps behind me.

Aunt Margaret stood watching me. She had my father's clothes draped over one arm and was holding a fish-boning knife in one hand. I wondered what terrible thing she'd say to me this time. Would she call me a traitor again? Or let out her unearthly scream? I watched her mouth fall open, as though in one of those dreams where you can't move your feet, or talk, or do anything but wait for the inevitable.

"Lunch," she said.

Lunch was a sullen affair. Grandpa Miklos sat at the head of the table looking stunned and ashen. Even in their grief, with Arthur at the table, my family seemed to jockey for his attention.

Rhys stared at him openly, and Luma watched him from under her hair. Father kept passing him things, nudging them toward him, and trying to bring him in on jokes. Arthur ignored it all. Again, he didn't really eat, just pushed his food around the plate.

Eventually, Rhys stood up.

"Arthur," he said. "Can I show you something outside?"

"Maybe later," Arthur said.

Rhys stalked out of the room, and Luma sprang up and chased after him. From the hallway came the sound of clicking toenails skittering around a corner and then a bang as the back door flew open. I looked at Mother, and then at Father, expecting them to do or say something about it, but both of them were intent on their plates.

Eventually, everyone else finished eating and left. I lingered in the room, watching Arthur stir his cup of tarry black coffee and wondering how I could bring up the conversation in the hall. He might not eat our food, but he did drink the coffee; he sipped at it, swallowed, stared at nothing.

"You seem upset," I said.

"Sorry?"

"You didn't eat again today."

He turned to look at me, somewhere between perplexed and amused.

"I am upset," he said. "But perhaps not for the reasons you'd imagine."

"So why don't you tell me?"

He cocked his head and furrowed his brow at me, but it was impossible to see his eyes. His smoked glasses made conversation feel silly and fruitless, like talking to a mirror.

"Arthur," I said. "I don't mean to pry, but Grandma told me I had to look after everyone. And I think that means you, too. So I want to know if you're alright. Because you're one of us, and I think you're not alright."

It was hard to tell if the light in the room had changed, or if his expression had softened.

"I wish I could tell you," he said. "Do you have things like that? Things you wish you could talk about?"

"I bit Lucy," I said, without meaning to.

He tilted his head. "You did what, now?"

"When she pushed me down the stairs," I said, scurrying to explain myself. "I'd been afraid of her for so long, and suddenly I'd just had enough, and I . . . bit her." I left out the blood. The screaming. The smell of it, how hard it had been to tear myself away.

I heard a low creaking sound. The sound of his cheeks stretching back into a smile.

"It's not funny," I said. "I hurt her really badly."

"You're a Zarrin," he said. "If you didn't kill her, you were being gentle."

"It didn't feel like I was being gentle."

"What did it feel like?"

I thought for a moment. Trying to think of a way to say it

without sounding awful. "Like a relief," I said. That wasn't true, though. Or, that was only half of it.

His smile broke into a grin, and for a moment the light in the room seemed different, like the sun had slanted through the curtains and struck his teeth. "You devil."

From the kitchen came a skittering that changed into the pad of footsteps, and a cabinet door opened and slammed shut.

"Luma's in," I said. I watched his face, looking for a reaction.

"So I hear."

Luma burst through the door and into the dining room. She swept around Arthur and draped her arms around his shoulders. She had a large red scratch on her forehead near her hairline.

"I just fought my cousin for you," she said to Arthur.

"I'm flattered," he said. The smile, and the light, were both gone.

"Come for a walk with me."

"If that's what you desire." He stood up and offered her his arm. "Eleanor," he said, "you've cheered me up immensely."

Through the dining room window, I watched them follow the worn dirt track toward the woods. He glanced back toward the house, saw me watching, and gave a little wave over his shoulder.

I sat for a while at the table, not knowing how to feel. Sometimes it seemed like Arthur was treating me differently, specially. Like we were in a conspiracy together. That wave had felt private. But it wasn't me he was walking the grounds of our estate with. With whom he was walking, said the nun lodged in my brain.

I was all alone again. The house, which often seemed too full when even a few of the family were around, suddenly felt vast and empty. Something about the sudden stillness made me freeze like a rabbit, conscious of the passage of time, but with no sense of what I was supposed to do next. It was almost like panic, but slower, as I tried not to think too hard about Luma and Arthur walking together in the woods.

It wasn't important how I felt about him. There was too much to be done, I told myself, now that I was the head of the household. I set out to prove it by finding something to do.

I decided to check on the snake lilies in the greenhouse. But when I opened the door, I was surprised to find Father already there. He stood at one of the panels of glass beside the long trays of purple-black drakondia, his back to me. His reflection in the glass looked—worried. And I could see why as I glanced through the shadow of his face. He was looking at Luma and Arthur, standing at the edge of the woods.

"Father," I said, and he jumped.

"Oh, yes," he said. "Eleanor." He looked guilty, like I'd caught him doing something.

"Are you alright?" I asked. "I heard you and Arthur talking earlier, and he said something about wanting to leave. Is there something he's upset about?" I heard Grandma Persephone's voice in my head saying *manage the family*. Surely, that meant keeping Arthur.

"It's not really anything you should be worried about," my father said. But he wouldn't meet my eyes.

"I can help," I said. "Grandma Persephone asked me to, you know, when she was dying. She asked me to take care of you all."

My father furrowed his brow.

"I don't know why she'd say that," he said. "We have everything handled. Nothing for you to do, really."

He was lying about something. I could feel it.

"Well, she said to. So if there's anything I can do, please just—"

"You know what you can do?" he said. "Maybe you can explain to Luma that Arthur's not really a good choice for her. Maybe you could, I don't know, persuade her of this."

Suddenly, what I'd seen in the hall made sense. Father was worried about Luma. And there was something I could do, at least. I could comfort him.

"I know he's a little older," I said. "But I don't think she's in any trouble. He's a gentleman."

He shook his head. "He's not interested in her."

"What do you mean?"

"He won't make her happy."

"Look at them," I said, and pointed at Luma throwing back her head to laugh. As if on cue the clouds parted, and for a moment her hair floated in a beam of sunlight. As long as Luma was with him, I thought, Arthur would never have reason to look at me again.

Beside me, my father began to growl. I glanced over at him, and he stifled it, turning it into a cough. And my small moment of triumph vanished, as I realized that I still didn't know what it was that I was seeing.

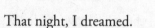

That night, I dreamed.

I was a girl who lived on a white island in the middle of a blindingly blue sky that bled into a dark and frightening sea. I had a battered journal that I carried under my arm that was full of the handwriting of my father, but I couldn't picture or remember his face. I walked down the street of white plaster houses on that dry white island, and old women in black shawls shuddered and spat on the ground as I went by. I climbed a hill to what I knew was my house, although I'd never seen it before, and I didn't want to go inside, but my feet propelled me in, and a drunk woman slurred something at me in a language I couldn't understand. My mother, I thought, but she wasn't the bath-bound mother I knew: she was a stranger.

This strange mother reached out, clawing for the journal in my hands. I tried to back away from her and she slapped me across the face, and I realized that it stung the way a real slap would. This wasn't exactly a dream. This woman could hurt me.

She grabbed for me and I ducked around her, trying to get away. We knocked a heavy bottle off of the table and it went rolling, spilling something that looked like water but stank like medicine. Tsikoudia, I thought, without knowing why. This woman wanted to kill me.

At last, she caught me by the throat. My hands scrabbled to pull her off of me, but hers were fastened around me like claws. Her breath was rank with alcohol as she spat in my face words I didn't recognize but somehow knew meant *damn witch*. Her eyes were wild and dark. She looked, I thought dimly, as I faded, a little bit like Grandma Persephone.

I jolted awake, my hands loosening from my throat. Had I been strangling myself? My throat was dry. I stumbled to my feet. Water, I needed water.

Through the crack in the bathroom door, I could see Mother sleeping in her bathtub. I didn't want to wake her, so I crept down the back staircase and past the closed laundry door, trying not to think about Grandma Persephone's body laid out on the flagstones. I slipped into the kitchen and was halfway to the sink when I realized I wasn't alone.

Margaret stood in the middle of the room with her back to me. She was working at the long low table, her hands doing something I couldn't see, something that squelched. I held very still at the sink, not sure what to do. She would notice me if I tried to leave, or if I turned on the faucet.

I had to be brave, I told myself. This was my family. Margaret used to stand me on a stool and let me help her in the kitchen, I remembered. Help with what, I wasn't quite sure.

I shifted so that I could see what she was doing, and had to stifle a gasp.

There was a vulture spread out on the butcher block, its naked neck and head hanging down. Its wings were as long as the table. Its belly was slit open, the knife she'd used was stuck point-first into the wood, and she was rummaging around inside its body, mumbling to herself as though she were looking for something in a handbag. Slick guts caught the moonlight. She combed through them for what felt like an eternity while I was frozen on the spot, not able to move. And then she looked up and turned to me. She held up a length of gut in bloody hands. She seemed to look at me and past me at the same time.

"Mother!" she said.

The back of my neck went cold. I squeezed my eyes shut, hoping I was still dreaming, that if I shut my eyes I'd wake up back in bed, and if I shut my eyes again I'd wake up in my room at Saint Brigid's, and from there I could shut my eyes and wake up a child again, somewhere in some house just like this one, but where I'd been happy.

Margaret's feet scuffed on the floor as she padded over to me. One hand, wet and sticky, touched my wrist. She pulled on it. Eyes shut still, I let her lead me, until my fingers brushed feathers, and I realized all at once what was about to happen.

I struggled, but she was stronger than me. She plunged my

hand into the guts. I thrashed, silently, afraid of what would happen if I screamed, afraid to open my eyes and see what was happening to me. And then all at once, I felt it. It was as if there were words, in there, in the guts. I relaxed my hand. I felt. The smell of dead meat and guano was almost unbearable, but somewhere in there was the truth. I just had to fight my way through to it.

But no matter how hard I tried, I couldn't make sense of it.

At last, I opened my eyes. I shook my head at Margaret. She let go of my wrist, flinging it away from her like some useless thing. And I fled into the predawn garden and desperately pumped water from the spigot to wash the smell of blood from my hands.

FIVE

IN THE GREENHOUSE, THE SNAKE LILIES WERE dying.

I'd watered them the day Grandma Persephone died, and the day after, but their leaves had quickly turned a sick yellow. Whenever I looked at them I felt panicky. And I wasn't sure how many I'd need to keep alive to fill our orders, mostly because no one would show me the finances. I'd asked Father, told him that Grandma Persephone had asked me to look after the business, and he'd just stared at me and told me not to worry about it.

And on top of all of that, Grandpa Miklos was getting worse with every passing day.

I'd heard from girls at school that often, grandparents died within a few months of each other. The human part of him seemed to feel that way; indoors he picked at his food, he talked less and less, and he stopped reading entirely. The wolf thrived, though; every day he went out into the woods, and sometimes he didn't come back until well after dark.

Things were falling apart, and Rhys, heir to the family fortune, was doing absolutely nothing differently than before. Grandpa Miklos still sometimes looked at him and said "All this will be yours," but Rhys seemed to be totally untroubled by it. Rhys didn't stare at the wilting plants and wonder what could possibly be going so wrong. He didn't worry about money, or if he did, he never said it to me. The house could probably have fallen down, and he would have just moved into the woods. He alternated between stalking around the house looking for Arthur and frolicking outside with Grandpa Miklos, seemingly without a care in the world. Why on Earth did Grandpa think Rhys should inherit the house? He certainly wasn't doing anything for it now.

"It makes sense," Luma said. "He's always been the one they worried about. Ever since he was born they treated him differently. I think they were afraid he was going to die."

We were in Luma's room. It was more of a mess than usual, with dresses and lingerie draped everywhere, over chairs and the old rocking horse and the knobs of the dresser, which she'd now shoved in front of the hole that she and Rhys had chewed through the wall between their rooms when they were younger. A few times when I'd come in to visit her, I'd heard him scratching at the back of the dresser to be let in.

"Rhys keeps asking me about Arthur," I said. "Yesterday he asked me if he ever came to see you when everyone else is out."

"He doesn't," Luma said. She tried to sound airy, but her voice was bitter. She brushed her hair back from her shoulders and turned this way and that in the mirror to look at her cut-glass earrings. "He's such a gentleman."

I began to feel it again, that longing I was trying to pretend I didn't have. I just wanted to talk to Arthur, instead of hearing Luma talk about him. Or—something. My throat was tight and itchy. I looked up at Luma and hoped she didn't know what I was thinking.

I also felt a little sorry for her. There was no way she'd be able to keep up with someone like Arthur, someone who always had something witty to say.

"Oh, speaking of Arthur," Luma said. "I can smell him on the landing. I wonder what he's here for?"

There was a knock on my door, down the hall. "Eleanor?"

"She's with me, one minute," Luma called out. She put on a silk robe, and then pulled the robe down to show off her shoulders. The silliness of it made me angry. "Come in."

Arthur opened the door. He looked at me.

"Do you still want to take over?" he asked.

"Yes," I said. I was already rising to my feet. "Why?"

"Your father and I are sitting down to look over some finances," he said. "I think he intends to close the extracts business and sell off related assets. If you're going to say something, the moment is now."

"I've got to handle this," I said to Luma. I hoped it would make me sound important, but she just shrugged, waved at Arthur, and then flopped down on her bed to read *Wuthering Heights*. I pulled her door shut as I left.

"Thank you for telling me," I said. "Do you think Father will be upset?"

"Does that bother you?"

"No," I said. "This is important."

"Good."

I followed him down to the library. The door had been locked the other day, and it now stood open, a key still in the lock. It was dark, but in the light of a single lamp I could see my father sitting at Grandma Persephone's desk. He had her reading glasses perched awkwardly on his nose. Spread out around him were various forms. He glanced up when I came in.

"Eleanor," he said. "What can I do for you, darling?"

He never called me darling. He was trying to appease me. I wouldn't have it.

"You can't sell off all the business assets," I said. "We're keeping the extracts business."

"No one around here plans to manage it." He looked back at the papers, and it took me a moment to realize that he had said all he intended to say.

"I want to manage it," I said. "Grandma Persephone left me instructions."

"The plants didn't look well the last time I saw them," Father said mildly. "And besides, you need to focus on your studies."

"I'm not going back to school."

"Your grandmother was clear about what she wanted."

"I just told you what she said!"

He shuffled the papers into a pile, then glanced at them and turned them the other way up. "The estate belongs to Rhys. So I talked to Rhys, and he said to sell the business because he doesn't intend to 'mess with plants.' I think that's accurate."

"You just can't tell him no," I said. "Why not?"

"Eleanor, this is men's business."

"Like the business in the hall the other day?"

I was warm with the fire of my own bravado, but even I could feel the chill that descended. Arthur smirked. Father stared at me in horror. And I realized suddenly that my father didn't like me. Not even a little bit.

"No one was with the two of you the night my mother died," Father said. "Every day for nineteen years, my father has said that he intended for Rhys to be the heir of his estate. I never heard my mother say otherwise. Now she is dead, and you say that she left everything up to you. I have a copy of the will in front of me that says everything belongs to Rhys. Do you have an alternative will? Or anything other than a very strange lie about my mother, who died recently, and whom you did not know very well?"

"I'm not lying," I said. "Father, I think it would be—"

"Miles," Arthur said. He crossed to my father's side and put a hand on his back, and Father's face flared with something I didn't quite recognize. "I think you should look at the will again."

Father glanced down at the will. "It says . . . wait."

"What?" I asked.

"Arthur, what's this?"

Arthur leaned in close.

"It seems to be saying that the estate belongs to Rhys," Arthur said. "Saving the materials and capital that pertain directly to the extracts business, which are left to Eleanor."

"I could have sworn it said that she was to receive Persephone's library books and the pearl-inlay vanity set . . ." He glanced up at Arthur. "How did this happen?"

"I don't know what you mean, Miles."

My father stared at me across the desk, angry beyond words. He looked like Margaret had when she'd called me a traitor. I hadn't even done anything, but that was how he saw me.

"Fine," my father said. "I was planning to channel that money into investments, so if you can't keep the business running, we will lose most of our income. Since most of us do not work, we would probably have to leave this town and sell this house, which has kept your grandfather safe and happy for most of his life. Are you sure you want to go against my judgment?"

Maybe this was what that card had meant, the tower, all of those people falling. I imagined us driving a FOR SALE sign into the turf of the front lawn. I imagined us packing up the wooden-slatted truck and moving away. It made me want to die. But she had told me to take care of the plants and the people. And what did my father know?

I looked at Arthur. His expression was neutral, but I wanted to believe there was something encouraging in it. He'd come and gotten me, hadn't he?

"I can do it," I said. "Please, believe in me."

Father stood up.

"Well, this is your desk now," he said. "And your meeting, with your accountant. I hope you know what you've gotten yourself into."

He left, shutting the door behind him.

"He hates me," I said, sitting down in the chair.

"That may be a bit much," Arthur said. "I think he fears you."

"Isn't that worse?"

"Relationships have been built on fear. Not all terrible."

I stared at the pile of papers in front of me.

"The plants are dying," I said. "But I promised her, at the end, that I'd take care of them and everything else. What do I do?"

"Your grandmother had a talent for resurrection," he said. "Perhaps it runs in the family."

He was trying to tell me something, I could feel it. I looked up at him, studied his face. There was nothing there to read. I still couldn't see his eyes behind those glasses. But it felt beyond me to solve it now. I had the business. That was enough to worry about.

"Alright," I said. "Help me figure out the finances, and then I'll see if I can find her notes about the plants."

We spent hours looking over the paperwork. Arthur had taken down a ledger the size of an encyclopedia volume that had income and expenses going back fifty years, the pages brittle and yellow. For the first time I was grateful for Sister Katherine's endless lectures about compound interest. Finally, Arthur tapped a stack of papers together and held them up.

"I am going to post these," he said. "Good-bye, Eleanor."

"Wait," I said. He stopped.

"Why did you back me up?" I asked. "And you changed the will, too, before I even got down here. Why?"

"You said it was what you wanted."

"Do you always give everyone what they want?"

He looked serious then. "Always."

"You're trying to tell me something," I said. "You've been trying to tell me something. Why won't you just say what you mean?"

He leaned toward me over the desk until our faces were very close together. He smelled strange, not like a person, but like things did: like wool, like cedarwood, like mothballs. Shoe leather, pennies. I wanted to lunge across the table and rip his throat out, or something like it. He opened his mouth, as though he were going to kiss me, or speak. I wondered if he was holding his breath: he didn't seem to exhale, but air drifted out, smelling somehow both clean and stale, like a big, empty house.

"You can't trust anyone in this house," he said. "It would be better if you remembered that."

He lingered near me for a moment, and then straightened up. As he left, he flicked dust from the shoulder of his jacket.

I realized at once that I was alone in Grandma Persephone's office for the first time. A day ago, I couldn't get in here, and now it was mine. I knew what I wanted to do. If I couldn't trust anyone, I might as well start by not trusting Grandma Persephone.

I opened up the big glass-fronted cabinet behind the desk. It was lined with wooden boxes, smooth from years of handling; she'd saved everything. They each had little placards on them with what they were. BILLS, TAXES. PERSONAL MAIL, one said.

As I dragged the box out of the cabinet, a cold breeze blew through the library, making me look up. None of the windows was open—there must be a crack somewhere. I set the box down on the floor and dug through it until I found what I was looking for: a stack of mail, all addressed to Saint Brigid's. None of it postmarked.

The air seemed to get colder as I riffled through the letters. All of them were from various family members. None looked like they had been unsealed—just gathered from the mail and bundled up. The one on top was from Mother, from a year ago. I opened it.

Dear Eleanor, I know that you've been quite busy and maybe it's foolish to ask but I do hope you'll come home this summer at last.

The next one, a few years prior, Luma. *I can't believe you. You're so selfish. Don't you miss me?*

There were maybe twenty of them, spread out over the eight years I had been away. Eleven from Mother, none from Father. Six from Luma, all angry. Two from Rhys, badly spelled. One from Grandpa Miklos, just a single sentence that took up the whole page: *I miss you my beloved.*

I stared at the pile of mail that had never gone out. For years, she'd stolen my only glimpses of home. Had they noticed that their letters weren't getting through? If they had, why hadn't they done something about it? Why had they left me to suffer alone? All they would have had to do to get past Persephone was go to the post office themselves, and they hadn't even bothered to do that.

The stack of letters immediately underneath was much larger. It was all of the letters that I had written to everyone in the house, every month for years and years. These were all slit open. The one on top was the last one I'd sent to Luma, when I was twelve. That was when I'd finally given up on them all.

I wanted to talk to Arthur. I wanted to show him what I'd found, and ask why my family was like this, why they were so craven or so lazy when they had more power than I would ever have.

I scrubbed my sleeve across my face and bundled the letters back into their wooden box, and on shaking legs I went and looked for him around the house. But he wasn't anywhere, and when I glanced outside, his car was gone from the driveway. Where had he gone in such a hurry?

It had been raining off and on, and the ground was soft. I could see two lines turning off of the driveway and onto the dirt track that led to our carriage house, where Margaret kept the truck.

I ran outside and followed the track. Something felt strange to me about this, and familiar. He'd left but not left. He was always doing that, now that I thought about it, pretending to do things. Not lying exactly, because it was so obvious if you were paying any attention at all. Eating but not eating. Smiling but not smiling.

When I got to the shed, he was just stepping out of it. He looked out of place outdoors, under the slightly overcast sky. Threadbare.

"You didn't really leave," I said.

"I wanted to put the car in the shed before it rained."

"What aren't you telling me?"

"That is an enormous question," he said.

We stared at each other for a long moment. I couldn't see his eyes. I knew if I could see them, he would open like a book and I would read him and he would be so relieved, so grateful to be read, as I had been when he had read me.

"Arthur!"

My father came jogging around the side of the house, his face red, his tie askew. I took a step back.

"Arthur," Father said again. "Glad I could catch you. Come have a brandy with me."

"Of course."

Still thinking about the leaving, the eating, the smiling, I asked, "Are you really going to drink it?"

My father slapped me. It happened so fast that I didn't have time to duck; I hadn't even known it was coming. It caught me across the cheek. Tears sprang to my eyes, time slowed down for me, and I thought about boarding school.

When we were younger, a little after Lucy and I stopped being friends, she used to get a group of girls to help her back me into a corner to scare me. One day instead of letting myself be herded by her friends, I stepped toward her and punched her in the stomach. I didn't know how to hit, and I hurt my hand badly, bending it back from the wrist so hard that my eyes filled up with the pain. But she had stood mesmerized, her body wrapped around my hand, with a glazed look of shock and shame. I imagined that was how I must look now. I knew it was what I'd said, but I had no idea why.

Then time contracted, as Arthur picked up my father by the collar and whipped him around with incredible strength. He held him out in the air as though he weighed nothing. Now my father and I were both staring dumbfounded: me at him, him at Arthur.

"I can't let anything happen to your family," Arthur said. "Do you understand?"

My father nodded, silent. Arthur set him back on his feet, let him go, dusted off his jacket.

"Miles," Arthur said, "let's have that drink."

They walked off together, all seemingly well. I stood by the car, under the awning of the shed, while it started to drizzle.

I was shocked. Father had never hit me, not that I could remember. I was close to something that he didn't want me to know, the same something that had upset him so much in the library. But what was stranger was that when Arthur had said "Do you understand?" he hadn't looked at my father, but at me.

For the rest of the day, Father ignored me. When I came into a room, he left it, except at dinner, when he just talked to everyone but me. He seemed embarrassed, but then why didn't he apologize?

I thought about talking to him, trying to apologize myself, but it was hard when I couldn't quite figure out what I'd done. I'd just asked a question. Arthur had been right: I couldn't trust anyone here.

The storm that had swept up the coast the night of Grandma Persephone's death hadn't really gone away. It hovered over us, gray and chilly and oppressive, occasionally spitting rain at us in dribs and drabs. On the day of her funeral, though, the sky broke open at last and it rained and rained.

Waking up that morning, I looked out at the mud running in rivulets down the driveway and thought no one would come. But at noon, a ragtag group came trudging up through the tree line. No car would have gotten up the slope in this weather, so they'd come on foot, huddled together, warily watching the woods.

It was mostly women, with a small handful of petrified-looking men. Almost everyone had a walking stick of some kind, or an umbrella with a beveled point. One old man clutched a fireplace poker. When they saw us, they lifted their black-ribboned envelopes like talismans.

Father met them on the porch and redirected them around the side of the house, toward the back garden. We, the family, went out through the kitchen and met them there. Grandpa Miklos and Father and Margaret and Rhys carried the coffin out through the back door, and all of us followed the pine box and its bearers down a narrow path into the birches.

The rain poured, surprisingly warm. Mother looked pleased. She'd put on some clothes, a dress of thin black cotton and a hat with a veil. She clung to Father's arm to support herself on her weak legs, letting herself get soaked. I realized I wanted to do the same, but the people from the village were watching me, and I couldn't bring myself to seem strange in front of them. I could hear them whispering about me. "Back from school," I heard. And "Not like the rest of them." I already knew that.

I scanned the crowd anxiously. Grandma Persephone had said not to let any strangers in the house, and I realized that a funeral might be just the moment when someone might sneak in. I started matching faces to names and invitations, and spotted someone I didn't know at first: a skinny boy in black, his hair cut into a bowl shape. He had no umbrella or raincoat, but the rain didn't seem to be hitting him. Beside him in a dark wide-brimmed hat was—*Grandma Persephone?*

No, I realized, as I hurried to catch up to her. It was my aunt Lusitania, all the way from Syracuse. And the boy was her son, my cousin Charlie. I remembered him. I'd had dreams with him in them, I realized. *Somewhere in the night forest—*

"Aunt Lusitania," I said. She turned, and flinched when she saw me. No water hit her either—it spattered off of her hat and seemed to shun her body. "We're so glad you could make it."

She furrowed her brow. "What?"

"I said, we're glad you could come."

She stared at me like I'd said something stupid. I looked to Charlie for help, or for something else to say. He was about thirteen, I guessed. I hadn't seen him since he was small.

"How are you doing, Charlie?" I asked.

"My grandmother just died."

They both looked so much like Grandma Persephone that it made me embarrassed to be here at all. And they moved in concert, without touching, exchanging quick glances now and then that erased some of the tension from Lusitania's face. Charlie was younger than me, and he knew how to do that for his mother, how to make her feel at ease just by being. My own mother was on the fringes of the group with Father, drenched, talking through her sodden veil to a stout fishwife with a yellow slicker on over her funeral black. The woman was edging away from the pair of them, and I didn't blame her; up that close, she could probably see some of what was under the veil.

The path wound and zigzagged through the birches. Up ahead in the crowd I could see Luma sniffing the air and looking uneasy. It was her other body that knew this path. She kept starting forward, as though wanting to drop to all fours. Straining against herself.

Finally we came to a clearing, and a high stone wall with an iron gate. Father helped Mother to the front of the procession, and she took out a big ring of brass keys and unlocked the gate to the plot. The mourners funneled through after the coffin. I was jostled to the back of the procession. The funeral was starting somewhere up ahead of me—the pallbearers bringing Grandma Persephone's coffin to the grave and lowering it in. Aside from the black-gated tomb that Grandma Persephone and Grandpa Miklos had bought for themselves, there were a handful of small graves here, some with names and some without, and sunken patches of scrub grass in front of them. Most of these were infant brothers and sisters of mine. A memory came back to me of a baby whose whole body was like my mother's, just a mass of polyps, with no eyes and no mouth. Nothing to be done about her strange little body but wait. I knew that Mother had named that one Junia.

My mother had kept trying to have children all throughout my childhood, even though for every living child she'd had, two had to be buried. I wondered why anyone ever had children.

My eyes lit on another headstone, a black marble obelisk that stood in the shadow of the tomb. It was for another Rhys, Persephone and Miklos's firstborn son. And there was our Rhys, beside the grave with his name on it, helping the others lower Grandma Persephone's coffin into the ground. I wondered why they'd bothered to have a mausoleum, if they were just going to put the bodies in the dirt. It seemed like a waste of money. Maybe neither of them had known what a tomb was for when they bought it. Did they even have tombs in Grandpa Miklos's silent country?

The coffin thudded into the grave, jarring me from my thoughts. After some shuffling, Father stepped to the head of the grave and started reading the selection he'd promised me he'd pick out. I couldn't hear over the rain and the shifting of bodies. But a flicker of movement caught my eye—Rhys was moving quickly and deliberately from the grave to some destination. Following his gaze I found Arthur, with Luma leaning on his arm. Rain dripped from the brim of Arthur's hat; his face, in profile, seemed hard and soft to me at once, and I wanted to touch his cheek and tell him that everything would be alright. Luma wore a dove-gray dress soaked with rain. She looked poetic; they both did. A perfect pair. And Rhys was barreling toward them like a bull.

I elbowed my way forward through a sea of lumpy dark coats, the thick mud sucking at my shoes. I caught snatches of what was happening through breaks in the crowd: Father was still reading, although I heard him faltering over some words. Rhys reached his destination and tried to embrace Arthur. I lost sight of them, and when I looked up again, Rhys and Luma were arguing, Rhys jabbing his pointer finger at her sternum, while she dragged Arthur behind her by his wrist. The people closest to them were pulling away, and I slipped in the mud as someone backed into me. I caught myself on his coat and used him to drag myself out. When I broke free of the mourners, Luma and Rhys were shoving each other.

"What are you two *doing*?" I said.

Rhys glanced instantly toward me, and Luma followed his gaze. I felt hot with rage.

"Rhys, leave them alone. Luma, stop slinging Arthur around," I hissed. "And both of you, show some respect for once. You're embarrassing us."

Luma rolled her eyes at me, but Rhys began to shake; he looked like he might hit me, or cry. Instead, he turned on his heel and flung himself through the crowd, elbowing people aside, and disappeared into the trees. When he took off, people relaxed, although a few of them watched the woods for signs he might be coming back. I glanced up triumphantly, trying to make eye contact with Father, but he glared at me without pausing in his speech.

Arthur, standing behind Luma, was looking at me with his head tilted to one side, his mouth open a little. When our gazes met, he smiled and shook his head a little. He slipped away from us through the throng. Luma didn't seem to notice he'd gone.

"Why'd you say that?" she said. "You really hurt Rhys's feelings."

"He was attacking you!"

"I can handle him."

I thought about Rhys's look when he'd fallen out of the closet, the murderous grin on his face. "I'm not sure Arthur can. We have to keep him safe."

What did Rhys even want with Arthur? Half the time he acted like a girl with a crush, which made no sense to me. The other half the time it seemed like he wanted to kill Arthur. I thought of the fingerprints on the sides of Rhys's neck. The closing door. None of it made sense, or lined up in the way that I wanted it to. And thinking about it made me feel like I was standing on the edge of a cliff.

"I don't know," Luma said. "Maybe I should just go talk to him. See how he is."

"No!" I said. "Can't you see that's just what he wants you to do?"

"Yes," she said sadly.

I was incredulous. I wanted to ask her what she'd expected me to do, how I, the one who'd broken up the fight, was suddenly the villain. Rhys was dangerous. Even if his intentions were good, he was too impulsive and rough to be safe. Arthur needed our help. He was already so frail. His poor leg. His weak eyes. But some worm was eating at the back of my brain, telling me that I was missing something, that I was leaving something out.

Father finished his speech, crumpling his paper up in his hands as Father Thomas stepped up to meet him. They shook hands, and then Father Thomas was standing at the grave, his head bowed. I focused my attention on him, trying to ignore Luma beside me, her body radiating warmth. I didn't like knowing she was mad at me. It was like having a stone in my shoe.

Father Thomas bent to pick up a handful of ashy brown mud, then straightened and cleared his throat. The villagers shifted their weight and turned their attention toward him, although they still darted nervous glances over their shoulders.

A shiver ran through me as he turned his face upward. The lenses of his spectacles were dappled with rain, and his thin gray hair was plastered flat against his head. He was more composed than he had been in the churchyard the other day, but his nose was still swollen and pink.

"We gather here to commend our sister Persephone Palaiológos Zarrin to God our Father," he said. "And to commit her body to the earth."

When he said that, Grandpa Miklos burst into sobs. They reminded me of the ones that Father Thomas had been wracked with outside the church a few days before. Father Thomas stopped and waited. After a long moment, Miklos looked up at him. Their eyes met; Miklos nodded, and Father Thomas continued.

After the rites, after everyone who wanted had thrown a handful of gritty mud onto the coffin, we shuffled out through the iron gate. Aunt Margaret stayed behind, shoveling with grim determination, doing the real work as always. When we returned to the house there was cold food in the dining room: funeral meats, pickles, saltine-crackers-and-cheese plates brought by village women, and strange jiggly custards; they were fruit colored, but underneath even my weak nose could smell horse. I skirted around awkwardly, shaking hands and smiling in a way I hoped was reassuring, until I found myself in the hall and realized suddenly that I was alone there. Not quite alone, though; Arthur was arranging villagers' umbrellas by the door.

"How are you?" I asked.

"You sound like Miles," he said. "How I am isn't really that interesting."

I bristled a little at that. "Then tell me something that is."

A smile flickered on his face.

"Lusitania is searching the house," he said. "I believe she's looking for your grandmother's tarot cards. All families are the same."

"I thought it was *all happy families*."

He quirked an eyebrow. "You're right, of course."

"It looks like Father Thomas isn't taking it well," I said. "He said he and Grandma Persephone were friends, but I don't remember him ever coming to the house."

Arthur turned his head slightly. I followed his gaze and saw Father Thomas standing by Miklos's side. They had their arms slung around each other's shoulders. Father Thomas had a drink in his hand. As I watched, he took a big slug of it.

"He and Grandpa seem close, though," I said. "I didn't know they even knew each other."

Some little tic disturbed the calm of Arthur's face. I was beginning to know what that meant: something he wasn't supposed to say. "What am I missing?" I asked.

"I don't know what you're talking about."

"You know you want to say it," I said. I felt exasperated, but also thrilled; it felt so much like chasing him that I could feel wind whipping past my face. "You wouldn't have made that face if you didn't. So why don't you stop playing with me, and just *tell me*?"

"The priest was your grandmother's lover," he said. "Lusitania is his daughter."

We both stood there in silence for a moment.

"Are you shocked?" he asked at last.

I dropped my voice to a whisper. "What are you saying? Does Grandpa know? How is Father Thomas even still alive?"

"I don't think Miklos has ever really known what jealousy is," Arthur said. "Lusitania was one of his favorites. I suspect that helped things."

I felt suddenly cold. For all his flaws, Miklos had clearly loved Grandma Persephone with every breath. And she'd betrayed him. I wondered what I could have done that made Grandma Persephone think *I* was the monster.

"Are you alright?" Arthur asked.

"I'm just—thinking."

He touched my shoulder, and for a moment his usually cool hand flared with a little heat. Then he limped away, leaning on his cane for support, to talk to my mother. Luma caught up to him and grabbed him by the elbow, which he let her take, and Mother swept over to Grandpa Miklos and wrapped him in a damp hug. Rhys flung open the front door, his clothes mud-streaked, a gamey smell hovering around him, his knuckles bloodied dark red, as though he'd been hitting something. He strode up the stairs and disappeared from sight.

Rhys climbing the stairs reminded me that I hadn't seen Aunt Lusitania in a while. If Arthur was right, and she was ransacking the house, I should find her quickly.

I looked everywhere I thought she might be searching—the parlor, Grandma's library, the greenhouse—hoping we could talk. Maybe I could convince her I needed the cards more.

Finally I came back to the front hall to find Charlie kneeling on the hall table, trying to lift the boar's head from the wall. I cornered him and glared until he turned around.

"Leave me alone," he said.

"The cards aren't behind that."

He sat down on the table next to the glass bowl of stale peppermints. I crossed my arms.

"Where's your mother?" I asked.

"She doesn't want to see you," he said. "She knows you're going to ask her to teach you."

I blinked. I'd only just thought of it. "How did she know?"

"Because we're witches and you're not."

He was giving up secrets just to taunt me, a mistake he would never have made if he'd been to preparatory school. He had no subtlety. I flicked him hard on the ear. "Ow!" he said.

"Why won't she teach me?" I asked.

"I'll scream if you hit me again."

"I'll say you're lying."

He huffed. "There's something wrong with you. There's something wrong with your mother, too. Everyone knows it, but no one would say anything because of Grandma."

"What's wrong with me?"

"You don't want me to tell you."

I ignored the knot of dread in my throat. "Yes, I do. Tell me."

"No."

"Tell me." I was shocked by the force in my words.

Charlie swallowed. His eyes unfocused, like Grandma Persephone's when she read the cards.

"You're not from here," he said, his voice suddenly vague and deep, as though coming from a long way off. "You're not of the wolf, and you're not a daughter of women. You're like something from the bottom of the ocean. A fish with a light on its forehead that lures other fish in and eats them. Not a real person at all, but you look like one. And that's why Mother doesn't like you. She knows you're not real."

My stomach churned.

"Well, I don't like her, either," I said. I got a little closer to him, put my nose inches from his. "Your mother is crazy, and so are you."

He picked up the cut-glass candy dish and swung it at me in a shower of peppermints. The dish smashed into my nose. Blood began pouring down my face. I flung up my hand to cover it. Charlie was right, I wasn't real, and my strange orangish blood confirmed it. I'd hid it in school, any time I got a cut or a scrape. I thought it meant I was like my family, secretly. But I wasn't like anyone.

I ran from him, my feet slipping on stray peppermints, reached the stairs and climbed up and up, hoping no one in the dining room had seen. I just had to get to the bathroom. Mother was downstairs with the guests. I could stop up my nose and no one would see my strange blood. I flung open the door.

Rhys was in the bathroom stripped to the waist, rinsing off in the sink. I paused in the door, not sure what to do. I wanted to run, but where? Back downstairs? To my room? Out into the rain? Blood was pooling in the hand I held under my nose.

Rhys splashed his face with water and shook his head wildly, making me jump. He caught a glimpse of me in the mirror and turned.

For a moment, he looked confused—horrified, even. Then he grabbed me by the shoulders, and I screamed.

"Who did this to you?" he demanded.

"Char—" I'd spoken reflexively. I stopped myself, but it was too late. "Wait, it's nothing!"

Rhys let me go, almost tossing me to one side as he flung himself out the door. He was barreling down the stairs by the time I got out of the bathroom. "I said wait!"

I slipped on the wet floor, got up, tried to stay on his heels. He'd had a violent look in his eyes. I had to stop him. Grandma Persephone had told me so.

As I came down the stairs, I realized I was too late. Charlie was still holding the bloodied candy dish, looking a little stunned, as Rhys flew down the stairs and pinned him to the wall with one hand.

"What did you just do?" Flecks of spittle flew from Rhys's mouth and spattered Charlie's glasses.

"Rhys, stop!" I said. "*Stop it now!*"

Rhys stopped stock-still, one hand holding Charlie to the wall.

"You moron," Charlie said calmly. "Now she's going to make us leave."

That was when Aunt Lusitania came in.

She saw Rhys holding Charlie, strode up to him, and smacked Rhys on the nose. Rhys cowered back. Charlie sank down again until he was huddled on the hall table with his arms around his knees. He looked at me. Aunt Lusitania saw me then, seemingly for the first time.

"Charlie hit me," I said, realizing how stupid it sounded.

Charlie glowered. "She called you crazy."

My father stumbled in through the doorway. "What's going on?"

Lusitania glanced at me, and there was something so cursory about the look that I shivered. She turned to my father.

"You need to get rid of her," she said, pointing to me. "Papa won't do it. Mama wouldn't do it. But now she's dead and he's in pieces because you let this thing back in your house. That leaves you in charge. So be a man for once, Miles, and get rid of her."

"Grandma Persephone left me in charge, actually," I said. "Well, she left me the business. And Rhys got the house. So you should really talk to us."

I didn't know where it came from; the words were out of my mouth before I could stop myself. My father's face went ashen. I knew he wasn't going to stand up for me. I just hoped he wouldn't listen to Lusitania.

"What did you say?" Lusitania's head swiveled slowly until she was looking at me.

"She said I'm supposed to take care of them," I said. My own voice sounded strange to me through my smashed nose. "I don't know how to do that. I need you to teach me magic. So I can protect them. Please."

I watched her expression change from disgust to rage. She strolled over slowly until she was very close to me.

"They should have buried you out back with the others," she said. "They should never have let your mother in this house. I will never teach you anything, and as long as you're here, I won't be."

"I don't understand," I said.

And then, from behind me, I heard footsteps.

Luma was coming down the hall toward us, growling softly under her breath. I glanced back and saw that her eyes had narrowed to slits. Her mouth was open to show her long teeth. And then from my other side, Rhys slunk into place behind me, growling, too.

For a moment I thought they were closing in on me, that they'd taken Lusitania up on her offer and now they were going to kill me. I turned back to my aunt, ready to tell her I'd get on a train, leave tonight, if she'd just tell them to let me live.

And then she stepped back. She pulled Charlie down from the table, pivoted on her black bootheel, and snatched up her hat from the coatrack.

"No need for the theatrics," she said to Rhys. "I'll go. But don't say I didn't warn you."

She slammed the door behind her. My father looked in the direction she had gone, and back at me, and shook his head.

"Really, Eleanor?" he said. Before I could say anything, he slunk out of the room. He had to elbow his way past the citizens of Winterport, who had crowded into the doorways of the parlor and the dining room. Worried faces looked out from all sides as silence descended.

"Sorry," I said to them feebly, trying to surreptitiously wipe the blood from my lip. "Sorry, everyone. Please, don't worry about that, it had nothing to do with you—"

One or two began edging toward the door, and the rest followed after. Soon ribbons of black streamed out of the house and down the hill, moving briskly, some sprinting ahead. Behind me, Luma and Rhys whined in my ears.

"They're running," Luma whispered to me. "That means they want us to chase them."

"Can I . . . go outside?" Rhys asked. "Just for a minute?"

"No," I said, and I placed a hand on his shoulder to make

sure he stayed. Under his sweater I could feel his muscles tensing. Had he threatened Lusitania to protect me? I wondered.
Or just because he'd smelled blood and wanted more of it? I
gripped his arm more tightly, hoping it would hide the shaking
in my hand.

That night, Father Thomas rang the church bells in the town. I
went into the front hall where the sound reverberated through
the empty space like the roar inside of a seashell. I brushed aside
the thought that the priest and my grandmother might have
been lovers and tried to just be content that at least the day was
over. I'd gotten through it, and no one had died. Today, that
was enough.

And then from the shadows of the hall, I spotted Grandpa
Miklos.

He stood stock still, with one hand raised in front of him—I
couldn't tell whether in self-defense, or to point, or to shield his
eyes from some invisible sun.

"Grandpa," I said, "what's wrong?"

He didn't seem to see me, even after I'd spoken. "The bells."

"They're for Grandma."

"No!" he said. "No, no . . ."

"Grandpa."

"Where I come from," he said, "the bells tell you it's time to
hide from the crows."

"Tell me about the crows."

He balked, saying nothing. "*Tell me*," I said again, insisting. I'd been insisting a lot today.

He didn't look at me. When he spoke again, it was in a quieter voice than before.

"It was in the silent country," he said. "The crows came sometimes. The flock was a cloud that blotted out the sun. We hid in the church and held the doors and they battered at them and at the windows. We waited and they left. But one day . . ." He paused and licked his dry lips. "One day I was late."

He slipped out of speech then. I watched his old body straighten before me until he was pantomiming young Miklos, no older than me, cracking his back and leaning on his pitchfork. And then staring up, and up, and up still, his eyes roaming the giant hollow hall. I realized he was seeing it again, a swarm of crows as big as the house.

"There were a lot of them," I said.

"I lost my hat, I ran so fast."

And my Grandpa Miklos, lost in his memories, pivoted away from me and sprinted for the front door.

He hit it, and began to beat on it wildly, slamming the heels of his hands against the black wood. I looked around for someone to help, but we were alone.

He yelled wordlessly, his mouth opening and shutting, tears streaming down his face, casting glances over his shoulder as the swarm of crows got closer and closer in his mind.

Why was he acting like this now?

Because of the bells.

There were no bells in the house. I remembered Luma had gotten a toy lamb with a bell once and Grandma Persephone had put her hand over the clapper and cut the ribbon, throwing the bell away without a word. There was no dinner bell, no chimes in the grandfather clock, no doorbells, no Christmas bells, no telephone.

"Grandpa!" I put my hand on his arm. "It's not real."

He whipped his head around, a wolf's head, lips curled back over sharp teeth. He lunged at me, and his teeth snapped shut inches from my face.

I fell backward, caught myself on the staircase, tore up the stairs to my room. I wasn't sure if he was behind me—my heart pounded so loudly that I couldn't hear him. I locked myself in my room and shoved the chair under the door. And then I stood there, too afraid to breathe. There was no one to yell, "Miklos! Stop it!" No one to protect me. I was alone.

Toenails clicked on the parquet. They stopped in front of my room.

For a while, he scratched and whined at the door. After he left, it was a long time before I could bring myself to breathe. When I did, it came out in heavy sobs that I tried to keep quiet. I collapsed onto the faded rag rug, clutching my head. I couldn't do this. Not by myself.

And that was when I realized I might not have to.

I thought about the letter I'd found, from my other grand-mother. The one who lived in France and who wrote about how she'd always love her daughter. The paper had smelled like lavender water. And she was Mother's mother, so she must know about some of this. She must understand something about monsters.

I thought about what Luma had said—that maybe she was like Mother, but all over. But I didn't care anymore. I needed help.

Eventually, I cried myself out and dragged myself into bed. But I was still too afraid to sleep. So instead I lay in bed with the covers pulled up to my chin, imagining my grandmother. When dawn was starting to break over the water, and I heard Luma singing as she padded around in the hallway outside, I finally felt strong enough to climb out of bed.

I stayed in my room with the door cracked, my face pressed to the opening, until Father left his room. When I heard the back door slam, I slunk in and opened Mother's trunk. The cigar box full of letters was just where I'd left it. I snatched it and I left the room feeling like I'd gotten away with it. And then as I rounded the gallery overlooking the front hall, I felt a cold wind whip over me. Panicked, I peered over the railing at the front hall below, wondering if someone had come in, if I was about to be caught. But the door was shut. No one stood on the parquet below. The only sound was the hollow clacking of the old clock, and the tinkling of the chandelier as the draft swept through it.

I breathed a sigh of relief, even as I wondered where the wind had come from. Old houses were like this, I told myself. There were always cracks.

Still, I felt nervous as I looked for a safe, quiet place to write the letter. There was Grandma Persephone's library, of course. But when I went in there and tried to sit down at her long worktable, I had the distinct impression that I was being watched. I abandoned the library and cut through the laundry, up the winding back servants' staircases to the third floor and its warren of small identical rooms and corridors. Some of them were furnished, others had single objects in them (a coin lying in the middle of the floor, a chess table with a kind of wooden mannequin seated behind it), and others were completely empty. I chose an empty one with a window I could pry open, and settled in to write.

It took me a while to figure out what I was going to say, and longer to remember how to translate it into my clumsy French:

> *Dear Grandmere,*
>
> *I am sorry that I do not know your name. This is Eleanor, your granddaughter. I am writing to you because I do not know what else to do. I am sure my mother has told you about our family and what they are like. Well, I have returned home from school, and shortly afterward my father's mother died. She left me responsible. Our business is failing. My grandfather is sick. My father is angry at me. I would*

*like your help if you can give it to me. I want to invite you
to come to visit if it's not any trouble for you. Or if not, can
I write to you for advice?*

*I am sorry to bother you. I am sure you are very busy. But
I read your letters to my mother and it sounds like you miss
her. If you do visit, please do not tell her I asked you to come.
I don't know why but she's against it.*

Sincerely,

Eleanor

I mailed it the next day, saying I wanted a walk down to
the village. The letter to our other grandmother was expensive
to post, and Mrs. Hannafin behind the counter looked at me
warily. But I was a Zarrin, so she said nothing.

I waited through a tense few weeks: checking our post office
box in town as often as I dared, walking past houses where cold-
eyed women stared at me out of their windows until I felt like
the girl I'd seen in my dream. And then one day, there was a letter
for me. *To Miss Eleanor Zarrin,* it said in flowing script on the
envelope. I snuck it down to the cove and sat barefoot in the sand
to open it. The letter inside smelled like honey and lavender. It
was written in the same lyrical French as the letters to my mother:

My dear heart,
*I was touched by your letter. From what you have told me, I
can see that you need a friend. Please take courage and know*

that I am coming to you as quickly as I can. We can keep it between us that you invited me. I am sure I can find a way to explain my visit to your mother.

I am beside myself with happiness that you have written to me, my treasure. I have longed for the day I could come to you for some time.

All my love,

Your Grand-mère

I sniffed it and held it close for a long time. And then I took it down to the waterline and tore it into pieces. I was almost crying, but I told myself it would be alright. She was coming. She loved me, and she was on her way.

And a few days after that, Mother got a letter of her own. I brought it upstairs to her, and she opened it in the bathtub. The human half of her face contorted into an expression of deep concern.

"It's your grandmere," she said at last. "She says she's coming to visit for a while."

SIX

WEEKS WENT BY WITH NO WORD: NO TELEGRAMS or letters or phone calls to the post office in town about when Grandmere was coming. In that time, I was delirious with impatience. I tried talking to Mother again, I was so desperate to know anything at all about her.

"France," she said, when I asked where she was from. She was scrubbing at her skin as though angry at it.

"I know that," I said. "I want to know what she's like."

"Honestly, I barely remember."

"But you write to her. You must know something."

She frowned. "How do you know I write to her?"

Oops. "Well, you must write to her," I said. "How else would she have our address?"

"Believe me, she'll come soon enough," she said. "In the meantime, just go about your life."

"I do need to check on the drakondia," I said.

"So do that," Mother snapped.

I jumped; she'd never been testy with me before. She sighed, then sank into her bath until all that was visible was the top of her head, and the little bubbles that came from the side of her face that wasn't human.

I left her alone and took myself, along with a book on exotic plants, down to the greenhouse. I wondered what Grandmere would be like, when she came—just another sensible old woman in black, an immigrant from the French countryside with a headscarf and a battered horsehair suitcase? Or something like Mother, a living reef? I thought sadly of little Junia. No, surely this grandmother had eyes. How else would she see to write a letter? How else would she have read mine? Lost in imagining, I didn't notice Rhys until he leaped on me out of the shadows in the portrait hallway.

He knocked the air out of me and for a moment I shut my eyes, not wanting to see my own death. I clung to the paneling, waiting for a blow to my head or chest that never came. After a moment, I opened my eyes.

He had straightened up and was bobbing up and down on his feet like a boxer while I struggled upright. I tried to collect my book from the ground, but then I realized I'd have to either bend over or break eye contact. I slowly lowered myself into a crouch, picked the book up by its spine, and stood up, my eyes darting from his hands to his eyes to his teeth.

"Be careful with me, please," I said. "I'm not as strong as you."

"Where's Arthur? Why haven't I seen him lately?"

"I don't know," I said, trying to sound dismissive. "Why don't we play cards?"

He ignored me and looked left and right, up to the balcony and down the long, dark hallway. "I haven't seen him," he said. "But I can smell him." He closed his eyes. "The whole house smells like him." The look on his face hurt me. Maybe it was like love, I thought, but twisted, violent. I would have felt sorry for him if I hadn't been so afraid.

"I'm going to go read," I said, and tried to edge past him. But he caught me by the arms. Close to him, I could smell the phenomenal stink of young man.

"If he comes by," Rhys said, "tell him I'm looking for him."

He let me go so abruptly that I nearly fell over, and then he was gone, disappearing into the shadows the way he always did, the clacking of claws on the floor the only evidence he'd been there at all.

He was getting more and more uneasy. For a while he'd been distracted by offers to play chess or cards, although we both played very badly. Well, at least I didn't have anything to hide from him. Arthur hadn't been to the house since the funeral. But sooner or later he would come back, and all of Rhys's pent-up anger would have to go somewhere.

In the greenhouse, the snake lilies were drooping, yellow leaves falling to the floor. I'd scoured the library for a book on their care, but all I could find was one guide to orchids, and I was doing everything the orchid book told me. I was going to ruin this family if I didn't figure something out soon.

In the meantime, I was trying to be sensible about things. I looked through the financial records of past years. They seemed more precarious than I'd expected, but then, I wasn't sure how much money it was supposed to take to run a business. And I'd found in the personal ledgers some money going to a woman named Katherine McCloud, who I thought might be Sister Katherine, but no matter how much I searched, I couldn't find any letters from her in the file boxes. I wondered if Grandma Persephone had burned them.

Arthur continued not to visit. I had a thought, one day, that maybe he was letting me ruin my family, maybe to get back at Miles. But I dismissed that as silliness. He was my grand-mother's accountant, my sister's boyfriend, my father's best friend—what reason could he possibly have to do that?

And I was having dreams.

In the first one, I had been cornered by a group of boys and had stabbed one of them with his own knife—a long one, like the one Margaret used to fillet fish. I fled up a hill into a scrubby forest, and the dream went on for hours: walking, tripping on rocks, none of the smoothing that dreams, or memories, usu-ally give to the passage of time. Heart pounding in my chest, I stumbled out of the forest and into a ring of standing stones. As I entered the ring, I realized too late that the ground was teeming with snakes, except for the narrow path leading me to a flat slab at the center.

I tiptoed along the path, clambered up onto the stone slab. And all at once I was ringed in darkness, and voices, asking me over and over again what I wanted. And I wasn't sure if it was me, or the girl I was, who thought, just to understand, all I want is to know why—

And then, I woke up, and tried to have a day where I didn't think about what I'd seen in the dream, where I stumbled around exhausted, and then went back to bed. And it happened again and again.

In most of them, I was not myself. I was some other young woman, living in places I'd never seen. None of them made any sense or resembled anything that had ever happened to me. I was placidly chopping the heads off of fish for hours while women around me yelled in a language I didn't understand, or rocking a baby in a house that looked like ours but cavernous and unfurnished. I started dreading going to sleep at night—the dreams were miserable, like being trapped in someone else's life, just behind her eyes, powerless to do anything but watch as time slipped past me.

And even those were better than the night I dreamed about being me.

It started out normally enough. *Somewhere in the night*

forest—I was young, I had a new ribbon tied in my hair that bounced while I ran. My feet were bare in the pine needles. To my left was Rhys, all sleek and dark. To my right, Luma, a blur of white. Up ahead, the boy. He smelled so good, his heart beat so fast in his chest, and I was happy, and hungry—

I sat up in bed and forced my eyes open, willing myself awake to make it stop. I'd been having this dream ever since I'd decided to come home—first on the train, and at least once a week since. Always the same, if I let it go long enough. Running between the trees, catching up to the boy, the terror in his eyes.

I looked out my window at the sky. Predawn, but just barely. I might as well get up, I decided. If I fell back asleep now, I'd sleep all day. I wanted to sleep all day. I'd felt sick and tired almost every day since Father had hit me: it was the first thing I remembered when I woke up. What had I ever done to him? I didn't want to be in the same room as him, watching him act like everything was normal. So I decided not to be in any room. I'd go spend the day elsewhere.

The morning grass was cool under my bare feet as I made my way across the backyard to the rickety wooden steps that hugged the cliff and then down to the water. It was fifty feet from the cliff to the shore, and the staircase had to double back on itself twice to bridge the distance in the narrow little spit we owned. Our beach was only maybe twenty-five or thirty feet wide, and about as deep, although slightly longer at low tide. It was bordered on all sides by big boulders that, when we were younger, I liked to use to jump into the water.

A part of me wanted to scramble up one of those boulders and throw myself in. But as much as I wanted to, my legs wouldn't obey me. I sat in the sand far above the lapping waves, watching the sun struggle up over the horizon, fat and red.

The nuns had always discouraged us from swimming. Too revealing, too dangerous. Currents and riptides and the rise of the two-piece swimsuit were their enemies. I imagined that they'd be better at it than they thought, though: that if a nun fell over the side of a boat, her habit would spread like a manta ray, and she would jet through the water, made new. I moved up into the wet sand near the water, my feet in it, but still not ready to dive in.

I'd missed this. When I was in school, I'd felt like a different person, and so I hadn't known what I'd missed, or what I'd loved, but now the sorrow was catching up with me and making up for lost time. It felt like having my heart restored to me just to feel it breaking. Eventually it became too much and I retreated up the steps, disappointed in myself.

When I returned to the house I stood for a moment, scraping sand off my feet on the back porch. Margaret flung open the top half of the back door, nearly hitting me. She stuck her head out and jerked a finger inside.

"Wha—" I started, and then remembered. I tried a shrug.

She only pointed more insistently, and walked away grumbling under her breath. Something was happening.

I went through the kitchen into the front hall. There were suitcases there, propped up against one another: a new set, floral tapestry with leather trim. Two steamer trunks, three hatboxes, and an upright valet trunk with wheels. She must be rich, I thought. Rich beyond even the Zarrins, who might not actually be rich for much longer.

Mother stood up from a chair in the parlor. She was fully dressed, which surprised me, and completely dried off. She came out into the hall, looking nervous.

"Eleanor," she said.

"What's going on?" Luma asked, sailing down from upstairs, dressed in a nightgown of yellowed lace. She flicked her hair back and then picked her nose. "What's all the fuss about?"

Mother looked at Luma, and her eyebrow went up, and her mouth turned down. Was she sad? Embarrassed, maybe?

"Girls," Mother said. "Come meet your grandmere."

In the front parlor was a dim shape sitting in one of the wingback chairs.

Luma hung back, slouching against the stairs. She was nervous, I realized. I resolved not to be. Whatever Grandmere turned out to be, even if she was an eyeless horror, I would meet her head on.

When I saw the woman in the chair, I nearly gasped.

She was dressed in pale gray, with pink gloves. Her gray hair was swept up in victory rolls. She was short and plump, her face full and youthful, her only two wrinkles a pair of smile lines. As I came up to her she rose up out of the chair, tilted her head, and smiled warmly.

"Eleanor," she said, "after all these years, how wonderful to finally meet you." She spoke English, but with a lilting and light French accent.

"You know about me?" I asked.

"Of course!" she said. "Your mother wrote me years ago to tell me she had a child with my mouth!"

She did have the same mouth as me: wide and thin-lipped, accentuated with bright lipstick. When she smiled it almost split her face. She looked so friendly, so open. I felt a little surge of pride. My face wasn't in the portraits in the front hall, but it was here.

"I'm so glad to see you," I said.

"I've heard a good deal about you." She lowered her eyes. "But I never thought we would have an opportunity to meet."

"You must have been busy overseas."

"Oh, not as much since the War. Terrible thing." Her accent was so beautiful that I had to work to look sad. "I am so lucky to have survived. The things that happened in that war were simply . . . unbelievable."

"I'm sorry," I said. "I didn't mean to bring up bad memories."

"Don't worry, child," she said. "Come here and give me a kiss."

I gave her a peck on the cheek, and she pulled me into a warm little hug that smelled of talcum powder, and something briny that I liked. She put her hands on my shoulders and turned me around to face Mother. Behind her, in the hall, Margaret was trudging up the stairs, laboring like an ant under the weight of all of those suitcases.

"What a beautiful child, dear," Grandmere said to Mother. "I love her already."

And then she caught sight of Luma in the doorway.

"And who is this?" she asked.

"This is . . . Luma," Mother said. Although I could tell she was trying to be cheerful, she sounded dismayed. "Your other granddaughter. I wrote to you about her, too."

"Of course."

"She's twenty-one," Mother said, "and quite the beauty."

I couldn't see Grandmere's face, but I felt her hands dig into my shoulders a little, as though pulling me close to protect me.

"Do you speak, my dear?" Grandmere asked.

Luma nodded sullenly.

"Then please speak to me," she said. "I do want to hear your pretty voice. Do you always . . . dress like that?"

Luma glowered. "I don't see how it's any of your business. I'm not a child."

I was surprised. I widened my eyes at Luma, trying to insinuate to her that I needed her to mind her manners. If she frightened Grandmere off, I was going to kill her.

"Very true," Grandmere said. "You're a young lady. I am surprised that you are playing dress-up."

Luma opened her mouth, and then shut it. She'd lost but she didn't quite know how. Instead of saying anything else, she growled.

Grandmere tilted her head at her. "I'm sorry," she said. "I don't understand why you are so upset with me."

Luma looked as though she was going to cry. She shoved my mother out of her way and took off down the hall, out the back door the way Rhys had gone not that long before. We heard the door slam behind her. Mother stood there, shocked, unmoving.

"Interesting," Grandmere said. "And there's a . . . boy living here also?"

"Their cousin Rhys," Mother said. "He's probably outside."

"Well, I assume we'll all have dinner together?"

"Yes," Mother said. She sounded relieved. "Of course, Mère."

"Well, hopefully I can undo that terrible first impression," Grandmere said. "I do feel bad that I spoke so strongly to her. I just know how important it is, as a young lady, to be taken seriously. It helps to avoid so much unpleasantness."

"I'll talk to her, Mère," Mother said hurriedly. "I'm sure it will be alright."

It was amazing to me to watch this woman cow my mother, and my sister, too. I couldn't imagine her being able to hold her own against Grandpa Miklos, but perhaps that, too, was possible. She took up so much space for such an ordinary person. It was hard to imagine Rhys doing anything to Arthur with her here. She was a steadying presence, and I reached out my hands to the hands wrapped around my shoulders, and held them. I felt her head tilt down toward me, her warm breath on my forehead smelling like peppermint.

But something dug at me, in the back of my mind. She hadn't needed to be so cruel to Luma, had she? I thought about what I'd said to Rhys at the funeral, how he'd looked at me like I'd bitten him.

"Why don't we go upstairs?" Grandmere asked me. "I'm very tired, and all my things are still packed."

"I can ask Margaret," Mother said. She stumbled forward a little. "Or . . . I can help you."

"No, no," Grandmere said. "I want to get to know my grand-daughter. We've lost so much time already."

I led her out of the parlor, edging past Mother, trying not to meet her eyes. I could tell that she was disappointed with me, that something about this wasn't sitting right with her, but I wasn't sorry. What had she ever done for me? All she did was soak herself and moon about after Father, who didn't even seem to care about her anymore—if he ever had. She'd never seemed to take much interest in me, or told me I was a beautiful child. She hadn't even tried to find me when Grandma Persephone sent me away. Grandmere wanted to be my friend.

I helped Grandmere up the staircase by the arm. Her movements were graceful but stiff, like a tightrope walker or a ballerina. I wondered if she liked to dance. I wanted to know everything about her.

As I went up the stairs, a howl went up from the woods. Luma's voice. And then Rhys's. It sounded strange, particular. And then I realized that they were calling to me, beckoning me to the woods. But I had never been able to respond to their call. I didn't have the voice. They'd all kept saying it would come in, like the teeth, but it never did.

"Are the others upset?" Grandmere asked. "Should you go see to them?"

"They'll be fine," I said. "Let's get you settled in."

We went looking for where Margaret could have put Grandmere's things. We finally found them in a tiny bedroom near the front of the house, with few windows and a bed that hadn't been used in probably centuries. I patted it and a cloud of dust rose up.

"Oh," I said. "I'm really sorry. I don't think anyone knew when you were coming."

"It's no trouble!" Grandmere said. "I believe, though, that having the spare bedroom always ready is one of the secrets of the perfect host. It is such a comfort to know that it is prepared."

I nodded. I imagined what it would be like to be a family that was ready for company, or that even turned in our taxes on time.

"Well," she said, "I brought my own bedding, as a provision. Will you help me? It should be in the trunk that says two."

I opened the trunk with the two on its luggage tag. The

smell of lavender wafted out. Inside, in neat compartments, were quilts, bedding, and a nightstand set in a wooden box inlaid with silver. I helped Grandmere strip the sheets off the bed, and when a giant cloud of dust engulfed us, I ran laughing to open the window and let in the breeze. She shut her eyes and breathed in, just the way I had when I first came here.

"What a beautiful view," she said. "I love the sea air."

"Me, too!"

She caught my hand and squeezed it.

We went through the trunk, putting sheets on the bed. Underneath were even more sheets, satin ones and ones trimmed with lace.

"Do you like them?" Grandmere asked.

"They're beautiful."

"They're for you."

She went to the upright trunk, which was tied shut with twine, and deftly plucked out the knots. She pulled open the top drawer, which was full of white linen underthings. The drawer underneath was larger and held clothes.

"And these are for you as well," she said. "I thought just a few nice pieces from France—a skirt suit we can have tailored, a few dresses—might be the right present for a young woman. I hope it's to your taste?"

"This is so kind of you," I said. I took out one of the dresses and held it up. It wasn't like Luma's airy little things, the ones that made me look like a little girl. It was black silk, high-necked, long-sleeved, but with little gestures and tucks that made me suspect it wouldn't look stuffy at all. "I haven't had new clothes in . . . a long time."

"My poor thing," Grandmere said. "Has your family fallen on hard times?"

"No, just . . . well, maybe now." I was mesmerized by the sway of the dress. I swished it through the air, wondering what shoes—what stockings—you wore with something like this. "There wasn't much call for me to have clothes of my own. I went to school, so all my clothes are uniforms."

"And you've been home for weeks," she said, "and no one's thought to get you anything new."

"How did you even know what to bring?" I asked.

She smiled. "You're just the size I was at your age," she said.

It was all too much. The dress, black and rustling and smelling of lavender. The box of clean white underclothes. The beaming woman with rosy cheeks and wrinkled crepe-paper skin, a storybook grandmother. I sat down on the edge of the bed. My throat felt tight. I realized I was crying. I never cried, not in front of people. I covered my face.

"Shhh," she said, sitting down beside me. She cupped my shoulder in her hand. "It's alright, my dear."

I cried silently, the way I'd learned in boarding school, and she sat beside me, rubbing my back. When I could catch my breath again I wiped my face with the heel of my hand.

"I'm sorry," I said.

"My poor thing," she said. "Well, I came at the right time. I'll do what I can to help. I am worried about that sister of yours."

"Luma?" I said, feeling a little jealous. "She's fine. She's just a bit . . ." I stopped myself, not sure what I wanted to say next.

"She's certainly . . ." She hesitated. "Pretty."

"I—yes," I said. "She is. And so I think she doesn't try very hard." It was a relief to say it to someone. But at the same time, I felt my chest tighten, as though Luma might hear me.

"Your mother tells me you're very clever, though," Grandmere said. "Why don't you tell me everything that's been happening?"

I told her about Grandma Persephone dying, about Grandpa and the funeral and what Lusitania had said. I told her about my father getting angry with me for trying to run the business, and about him hitting me, and she winced in shock. It poured out of me so fluidly that at first, I didn't realize what I was trimming out. I didn't mention the strange card on the night of Grandma's death, and I didn't mention Rhys's obsession with Arthur. Or Luma's. Or mine.

I felt guilty about that, at first. But she thought I was sweet. I didn't want her to know anything that would make her think badly of me. Maybe when we were closer, I'd be braver, but not just yet. It was better to test the waters, to not let everything go at once.

"And then I wrote to you," I said. "I thought you'd be . . . I didn't think you'd be so . . ."

"Normal?" she said.

I laughed a little. "Yes."

She patted me.

"Well, I assure you, I have my moments," she said. "I am your mother's mother."

"Grandmere," I said, "can I ask you something?"

"Of course!"

"Why is Mother like she is?"

She looked away and gave a long sigh.

"Poor girl," she said. "She was born looking like that; I tried everything to help her, but she refused me. She told me later that when she met your father, it wasn't that he was particularly kind, or particularly drawn to her—it was just that he didn't see her as strange. I think that was what she liked about him."

I thought about my father, standing so close to Arthur in the front hall but shrinking from my mother when she'd tried to comfort him after Grandma Persephone had died. I couldn't imagine spending my life with someone who didn't love me. I'd rather be alone, I thought, but a part of me questioned that. After all, I was here now, wasn't I?

"Your family does seem to revel in strangeness, after all," Grandmere said. "I think she felt at home. But do you?"

"I think I'm not strange enough for them," I said. "Or too strange for them. I can't tell."

She reached out to cup my cheek in one pink suede glove.

"You are not strange to me," she said. "I don't see anything that is not right about you."

I helped Grandmere sort and put away her beautiful things until the late afternoon, when she finally insisted on a nap.

"Do you want me to bring you anything?" I asked. "A glass of water? Something to eat?"

She patted my hand. "No, my dear," she said. "Just rest. We'll talk over dinner. Why don't you take your new things to your room?"

I left with the trunk she'd brought for me. I was in the third-floor hallway, rolling it toward my own door, when Luma sprang at me out of the shadows.

"We have to talk," she hissed.

She pulled me into her room, trunk and all, and shut the door behind her.

"What's all that?" she said.

"Presents," I said. "For me."

Her eyes narrowed.

"She's brought you a lot of stuff," she said. "Why didn't she bring me anything?"

I laughed.

"What's wrong with you?" she said. "Why are you laughing?"

"I've been wearing my school uniform since I got here," I said. "I don't have anything. You've got plenty of stuff. Look at this place!" I waved a hand around at the piles of antique lace dresses, faded silk underwear, chokers and jewels and pearl combs tossed around like garbage.

"I just take what I want," Luma said. "There's more stuff in the attic. Lusitania used to have stuff sent here by mistake, too, you can have some of those. Why didn't you say you wanted clothes?"

"That's not the point," I said. "I didn't have anything, and she's the only one who noticed."

"But how could she know that?" Luma said. "She just got here."

That made me pause. First I thought of the letter, and that I'd have to be sure to tell Grandmere not to mention it to anyone. Then I realized that in my letter I'd said nothing about clothes.

"There's something wrong here," Luma said. "I can feel it."

"You feel a lot of things," I said, regathering the trunk. "It's a good thing I'm here to do the thinking."

"What do you mean?"

"Grandmere is here to help," I said. "Right before she died, Grandma Persephone said that you all don't know how to take care of yourselves. And from what I've seen, she's right. I need someone who knows how to run a house."

"I could help you," Luma said. "Or Mother."

"You haven't been."

"I'm just saying we don't need this mean old lady to tell us what to do."

"Is she mean?" I said. "Or does she just say things you don't like?"

"What's the difference?"

I sighed.

"Luma," I said, "she's an old woman. We're, well, we're Zarrins. Why are you letting her get to you?"

She leaned toward me, and looked at me very seriously.

"If she says one more thing to me about my clothes," she said, "I'm going to rip her throat out."

"No, you won't," I said. "She's your grandmother, too. Treat her with some respect."

Luma slunk back to her dressing table and started brushing out her hair. Silver strands caught in the brush as she ripped out big tangles.

After I left her, I tried to rest like Grandmere had suggested. I should have been tired; we'd unpacked trunks for hours. But I felt too alert to lie down, too jittery to sit quietly and read a book. Finally, I couldn't stand it any longer. I slipped down the back stairs and out the kitchen door, past a mumbling Margaret, and out to the backyard. I went to the cliff's edge and followed the rickety staircase down to the beach below. I had to finish what I'd started.

I looked around to make sure no stray village children or fishermen had made it out here, and then I stripped out of my skirt and my worn school uniform shirt, my drawers and my camisole, took my shoes off and tucked my socks inside them. I picked my way along the rocks, clambered up one of the boulders, and looked at the water below. I knew it would be freezing, which was always Rhys and Luma's excuse for not swimming. For a moment I stood paralyzed. What if I couldn't swim anymore? What if that was one more thing that I'd forgotten?

But something about Grandmere being here had made me feel a little bolder. And I'd survived everything else this place had thrown at me. I took a deep breath and lifted my arms above my head. I brought them together, pointed like an arrow, and flung myself off of the rocks.

My body knew what to do, mostly. I slid into the water. The cold electrified me, but it didn't hurt, exactly—not the way Luma and Rhys used to complain about. It felt like turning over, like the sensation I'd felt while tumbling down the stairs at school—like being someone else, someone for whom the cold was restorative, pure. The water was shallower than I'd remembered, and I was almost immediately brushing the bottom with the tips of my fingers. I swam along it for a little bit, my eyes open underwater, keeping my nose tilted down so my nostrils wouldn't fill with brine. Other people always complained that salt water stung their eyes, but I didn't feel it. I could look around, see the schools of fish that darted in loose formation. I could watch crabs crawl along the bottom, see bits of shells pulverized by the waves as they floated past my outstretched hands.

I remembered a trick from when I was younger and sucked my nostrils shut. I turned over onto my back, looking up at the last little bit of sunlight that filtered down through the water. The waves here were harsh and crashed up against the shore, but this far down they were gentled by the weight of the water, and barely moved me at all. I was too skinny for my age and dense like a rock, so I could sit on the bottom without much effort and just look up, the sky over my head a murky green dappled with gold.

Eventually, though, I ran out of air and had to struggle to the surface to breathe through my open mouth. I gasped again and again, my lungs arguing with the rest of me about where we really belonged.

I didn't think Grandmere would approve of this, a girl swimming by herself, swimming naked. But something about being in a room with her had made me want some air. I liked her, but being with her felt like being watched. Like being in the same room as a good teacher who expected me to do well. That was it, I told myself, and I felt guilty that I still wanted to sneak away from her.

When the sun had dropped behind the cliffs, I lingered a moment more, floating on my back in the water while the fading light turned everything murky. Then I started back toward the shore. I was wading through the breakers, up to my waist, when I saw a dark shape on the sand. It resolved into Arthur, leaning on a folded umbrella, its point buried in the sand. He was beside my pile of clothes. I hadn't seen him in weeks, and now here he was, as though by magic.

At first I felt embarrassed, but as I swam closer, as my feet started to brush the bottom, I didn't crouch down. I let myself emerge from the water a little at a time, flicking my hair forward to cover my chest. He was always putting me at a disadvantage—knowing more than me, keeping it all to himself. A part of me wanted to see if I could shock him. I stepped up out of the breakers. I couldn't believe myself. The nuns would have strangled me with their bare hands.

"Your mother asked me to fetch you to dinner," he said.

"Thank you," I said. "I wouldn't have thought I'd see you here."

"I do look out of place on a beach."

We were standing closer to each other now. He still wore his jacket, his antique celluloid collar, his shiny shoes. His smoked glasses revealed nothing as I stared into them. I felt like I was playing with him, asking him whether he was going to look away, and maybe he was playing back. It was hard to tell exactly, but I felt like he was looking right into my eyes. Out of the dim light of the house, I could see things about him that I couldn't usually. The deep lines on his lips were not wrinkles, but pearlescent scars. There were others of those on his body, little raised ridges that looked almost like embroidery, as though someone had very carefully sewn up rends in his skin. Maybe he'd been in a war, I thought. My father had been in the War. Shelling, gas, shrapnel. Maybe that was what had happened to him.

"I have heard the mermaids singing, each to each," I said, the words sliding out of my mouth unbidden. And for a moment I saw myself that way: not as a gawky teenage girl, but a creature of the waves. I felt imperious, commanding. He could not resist my power.

For a moment I thought he seemed incredulous, stunned. And then he turned his head away, pointedly looking out over the ocean.

"I do not think that they will sing to me," he said, and took a few steps away from my clothes.

And like that, the ethereal creature was gone, and I was a girl again. I dove for my clothes with a fervor that surprised me. I scrambled into my shirt and drew it around me without buttoning it up. Instantly, it made me feel safer, but it also made me feel like someone who needed safety. It was a bad trade.

"You know your Eliot," he said. He was still looking away. I was sure he'd never look at me again.

"I thought I read him at school," I said. "But when I came home I found his poems tacked up all over my room."

"So that's what happened to my book. I wondered where it had gotten to."

I froze.

"Oh no," I said. "I cut it up. I'm so sorry."

He laughed, a dry, raspy sound. "It's hardly the worst thing a Zarrin's ever done to me."

The way he said it made me think of seeing that secret door

under the stairs; a thing I hadn't known existed, opening just long enough for me to see it slam shut.

"What have they done to you?" I asked.

I realized I'd stepped closer to him without meaning to. We were as close as he and my father had been in the hall the day of the funeral, so close that I was surprised I couldn't feel his breath on my face. For a moment I thought he was going to speak. But then I heard the click of his jaw locking up. I knew this by now: something was keeping him from speaking, something beyond him.

"Arthur," I said. But he shook his head and held up a hand.

"You're going to catch a cold," he said, when he managed to speak again.

I flushed, reached down for my skirt, and started tugging it up over my waist. He turned his back entirely, leaning on his umbrella and looking out at the surf. The sun was red on the water, hovering just above the lip of the world.

"Your grandmother was the one who insisted on this beach," Arthur said. He spoke slowly, as though picking his way across the rocks, choosing each word with care. "Your grandfather never cared much for water, since he was raised in a landlocked country. But your grandma told me once that she liked the high cliff. She said it reminded her of her mother's village in Crete."

Crete. I thought of the blinding white town on the dark

ocean. Was that what I'd dreamed of? Those steep hills, those old women in black?

"Do you miss her?" I asked.

He turned toward me abruptly, me with my shirt half buttoned. I suspected he wasn't looking at my body, such as it was. It was the question that got his attention.

"What happened between you two?" I asked. "You seem to be so angry at her sometimes. But sometimes it sounds like you liked her."

"I don't know if I liked her," he said. "I think I just knew her very well."

"But you must have forgiven her." I felt suddenly bold. "For the worst thing the Zarrins did to you, I mean."

"What makes you say that?"

"You still come to dinner."

Another pause. And then: "I suppose I do."

It was too much: the last rays of sunlight breaking into fragments on the waves, the light reflecting across his face giving him a strange bloom. My heart was breaking. I wanted to know everything about him, but I knew it wouldn't happen. Not with Luma after him, to say nothing of Rhys. And not with that something else, whatever it was, that I didn't yet understand.

I was the head of this household, even with Grandmere here. I had to handle this with dignity.

"I know you're seeing my sister," I said. "I think you two might make each other very happy. I know things have been strange, and I've been rude to you. But I hope you can forgive that. I hope we can be friends. And as friends, I think I should warn you about something."

"Yes?"

"Rhys has been looking for you," I said. "I'm not sure exactly why, but he seems obsessed." My face flushed as I said it, not wanting to say much more than that. "It would probably be better if you weren't alone with him."

His scarred lips stretched back over his smooth, perfect teeth.

"I'm not worried about Rhys," he said.

"Maybe you should be. I know you're used to us, but he's being . . . strange."

"You mean he's in love with me."

I'd expected him to recoil from the idea, but he said it so calmly. I was stunned. "I mean, you could call it that."

"Don't worry about it," he said. "You all go through a phase like that." I thought about Lucy Spencer, but he went on. "I'm familiar, but I'm not family. I'm friendly enough. I'm around but not too often. It doesn't have anything to do with me at all."

"But what if he hurts you?" I asked.

"I've been hurt before."

"But what if he kills you?"

He laughed, more harshly than I'd thought he was capable

of. His voice bounced off the cliffs. The sun had already sunk below the tree line, but improbably, some red light seemed to strike him, making his papery skin glow.

I knew that I loved him, and I knew that he'd never believe me if I told him that. He'd think I was just like my sister and my cousin: liking him just because it was easy, because he was there. Not because of who he really was. As his laughter died away, he seemed to notice the dismay on my face.

"I do like you, Eleanor," he said. "But you remind me very strongly of your grandmother, and that's . . . difficult."

Maybe he did miss her, then. I could see them sitting in front of the fire together, the way they'd played chess, their dry humor. Maybe this was his apology. I could be his new her, if that was what he wanted from me.

"Well, we can start slowly," I said. "Maybe you could play chess with me sometime."

"If that's what you want," he said. "But I should warn you: I always win."

We turned toward the house on the hill. From here, we could just see the top of the central tower, its windows ablaze with the setting sun. I stuffed my socks hastily into one shoe and my underwear into the other, and we climbed up the staircase together. Arthur took each step first with his good leg, and then brought his other one up to meet it. It was a mystery to me why he seemed so feeble sometimes and so strong at others. I found myself looking at his face for signs of age, trying to guess whether he was as old as my father. Younger? Older, maybe? But he gave nothing away, not even that.

At the top of the stairs, I told Arthur I was going to sneak in the back and change. He grinned at that. His teeth glinted in his skull.

"I'll stall your grandmere," he said.

"Thank you."

I started for the back garden, and he started to turn away, but at the last second he swung back and caught my wrist. His hand was so cool, but his grip felt impossibly strong. I imagined him lifting up my father and swinging him around.

"You're going to want to be careful," he said. And before I could ask him what he meant, he strode away. He moved quickly on the even ground, disappearing almost immediately around the side of the house toward the front door.

I let myself in through the garden gate and skirted around the rows of shoots and leaves that were starting to come up. Nobody had touched the garden since Grandmother Persephone had died, but she had worked on the soil for years, and the plants kept coming up without any help, at least for now. There were weeds, too, and I thought maybe tomorrow I'd come down and tend the garden, do a little watering and weeding, make sure I could keep it up. Maybe I could practice on these easier plants, figure out the snake lilies, and things would go on as they always had. Maybe with Grandmere to help me find my way, I could still turn things around.

Upstairs in my room, I tried to dry out my hair, but it was crusted with salt and started curling around my shoulders. I opened the window to let the breeze in as I scrambled out of my wet clothes. I wiped salt water off of my arms and legs, and looked at the black dress draped over the trunk.

I laid my uniform over the back of a chair to dry. It looked so strange without me in it. I shimmied into the black dress. In the trunk I found black silk stockings and shoes with a small heel. I slipped them on, and turned to the mirror to examine myself.

I looked like a stranger. I brushed out my hair and let it fall over my shoulder, like Luma's. No, that was no good. I piled it all on top of my head and pinned it into place. That was better. I looked older, sterner. I looked . . .

I jumped. There in the mirror, for just a second, I'd seen another face. Young, white-haired, but not my own. When I looked again, the other face was gone.

I forced myself to take a few deep breaths. I was thinking about Luma, I reasoned. Her bad mood had infected me, and now I was seeing things. But the more I thought about it, the more that idea seemed flimsy. I'd felt the cold breeze. I'd seen the pots rattle in the kitchen.

But I couldn't deal with it tonight, because it frightened me, and I couldn't be frightened right now. Grandmere was here, and I had to be at my best if I was going to convince her to stay.

The breeze from the window fluttered the poems I'd tacked

to the wall. I went into my suitcase and fetched my copy of Eliot's poems. At least I could make this small thing right.

When I went down to the front hall, I found Arthur and Grandmere standing in the front parlor. They were speaking quietly, their heads bent close together. They both glanced up when they saw me. I had to hold on to the banister to walk down the stairs, the little heels of the shoes tripping me up.

"There she is!" Grandmere said. I had never seen anyone smile so widely for me.

I held my skirt with one hand and concentrated on feeling for each step with my shoe. They watched me, Grandmere's face proud, Arthur smiling faintly. But the toe of one of the shoes caught on one of the stairs, and my foot came out, and I took a wild step forward into the air. As smoothly as a machine, Arthur stepped forward and put his hands out to catch mine and steady me. The book clattered to the floor between us. I clung on fiercely, and as I did, I heard Grandmere give a little startled "Ah!"

I gathered myself up, got the shoe back on, and gave both of them a winning smile. "I'm fine," I said. "I just need a little practice."

"What's this?" Arthur asked, bending to pick it up.

"It's for you," I said. "It's not the same one I cut up. But it's . . ."

He wasn't looking at me, but holding it and staring down at the cover, his mouth moving without speaking. I trailed off, and in the silence, Grandmere stepped forward and embraced me.

"Eleanor, dear," she said into my ear, "you look so lovely tonight. We really must work on your balance, though." And she let me go, and swept on ahead of me into the dining room.

Arthur turned to me. "Thank you," he said.

I realized I was blushing. "It's nothing," I said. "Are you hungry?"

"As always," he said, and I almost laughed at the joke. He offered me his arm to walk into the dining room. I took it gratefully; I was still wobbly on the shoes.

Mother and Father were already waiting at the table, standing behind their chairs. Mother had dried herself off and was fully dressed, the water barrel gone. Her polyps, shriveled, clung close to her skin, but she smiled wanly when she saw me. I'd never seen her out of the tub for this long. I'd assumed it was impossible.

"Where are the children?" Grandmere asked when she entered. She bustled to the foot of the table and sat down. "The boy and the girl?"

Rhys and Luma came stumbling in from the front hall, dressed for dinner but hair askew. Grandmere glanced up at them, and so did I. Rhys had a spreading red-purple bruise around his eye, and Luma kept poking her tongue around in her mouth as though testing a loose tooth. They must have been scrapping silently, maybe in the corridor between the music room and the library. I wondered who had started it. I'd have to ask Luma after dinner, make sure she was alright. Arthur didn't seem to notice her. He seated himself next to me.

And at last, Grandpa Miklos came in. He was tying his tie, his face bearing a fresh scratch from the woods. He wandered in half aware, and then stopped and stared at Grandmere. His whole body went rigid, his face filled with anger.

"Ah, you must be Miklos," Grandmere said. "How nice to finally meet you after all this time."

Grandpa Miklos took a halting step forward, and then froze in place. He looked like he was straining against something.

"Grandpa," I said, "Grandmere is here to visit us for a while. She's a *visitor*."

He nodded in a dreamy sort of way. He took his seat at the head of the table, looking pained and confused. I wondered what was wrong with him. He'd let Father Thomas come to our house, but he was enraged at the presence of this old lady?

"*Let's have a pleasant dinner,*" Grandmere said. Grandpa seemed to relax at that. He settled back in his chair. I looked at her in awe. She already seemed to know exactly the right things to say.

Margaret came in, carrying a tray with an enormous roast fowl on it. She set it down in the center of the table while I tried not to think about the vulture from a week ago.

"Oh, Margaret," Grandmere said, without looking up. "*Please carve that for us.*"

I braced myself. Any minute now, the low moan would start up, would rise to a shriek, would threaten to bring the house down around us—

It never came. Instead, I heard the sound of clinking cutlery, and then Margaret was cutting the duck into slices.

I looked up at Grandmere, trying to read anything on her face. She was beatific. Calm, patient, an elderly woman waiting for dinner. But there had to be more to it than that, I thought. She'd done in a sentence what Grandma Persephone hadn't been able to do in a lifetime: she'd pacified Aunt Margaret.

Maybe she was a witch, too, I thought. It would explain some things: how she'd known what to bring me, how she'd showed up without any help with all those trunks. But I'd need to know more to be sure.

Grandmere talked during dinner, pausing between bites to lay her fork down.

"It's so wonderful to be here," she said. "I must say, Paris has lost some of its charm for me. Maybe I stayed too long."

"I wish I could have gone to Paris," Arthur said. "By Miles's account, it is a charming city."

Father glanced up sharply. He mouthed something at Arthur that I couldn't discern.

"Oh?" Grandmere said. "I knew Miles was in France, but I didn't know you had not gone as well. Were you exempt?"

Arthur's jaw made a clicking noise, faint enough that I wasn't sure anyone else could hear it. He shook his head and tapped the side of his face. His teeth were grinding together, almost inaudibly. Now that I recognized the signs, it seemed impossible to ignore. I couldn't see how Rhys and Luma could sit there snarling over duck legs while he struggled to open his mouth. What was it that was stopping him from speaking?

"I see," Grandmere said. "I've asked too much. My apologies."

"Let's talk about more pleasant things," he said, through gritted teeth.

"But of course."

The conversation moved on, mostly between Arthur and Grandmere. Mother jumped in now and then, but as dinner wore on, her voice got scratchier, until finally she excused herself early. Grandpa didn't speak at all, just chewed the same mouthful of duck. Finally, he got up from the table without excusing himself and slipped out to the kitchen. I heard scratching at the back door, and then a creak as Margaret opened it for him.

"I hope I haven't offended him," Grandmere said.

"He can be like that," I said. "He's a little impulsive."

"Strange, in an older gentleman," she said.

"Not at all," said Arthur. "The old have less to gain from denying themselves. I've often noticed that the older you are, the more you become yourself."

Grandmere smiled. "By your measure, I must be very young."

"Ever-youthful," he said.

After dinner, Father said, "Arthur, may I have a word? We should discuss our finances."

Grandmere's head snapped around to look at Father. She looked like she wanted to kill him. I almost regretted telling her about the slap.

"We should all talk," I said. "Father—"

"Oh, *business can wait*," Grandmere said. "Since I am imposing on your hospitality, I intend to supply you with all the funds you need to entertain me. As long as I am here, you shouldn't fret over such petty things. Let's sit in the parlor and enjoy one another's company."

A silence descended on the table.

"Mère," my mother said at last, "that's too generous of you. How long are you planning to stay with us?"

"Well, as long as you need me," Grandmere said. "You have just suffered such a loss, I will let you all tell me when you need to be alone again. Until you send me away, I will stay and do my very best to help you all get settled once again."

I felt a little in awe. She had said it so perfectly: that she was here to stay, but only as long as we wanted her here.

"I know we could use some help getting back on our feet," I said. "Thank you, Grandmere."

My mother gave me a worried look. I refused to meet her gaze.

"That is generous, Madame," Father said.

"Oh please, do call me Mère," she said. "I am your wife's mother, after all."

"That's very kind of you."

"Girls," Grandmere said, "why don't you sing us something? I understand Eleanor plays piano."

"Luma's a fantastic singer," I said.

"We'll see!" she said.

Grandmere and Father and Arthur stood around in the dining room talking while Margaret laid out Arthur's coffee. Glancing over my shoulder, I saw Grandmere say something I couldn't quite hear, and then Father laughed. At least she was being cordial to him.

The grand piano that Miklos had bought for Persephone had been draped with black since her death, and the parlor, unused since the funeral, smelled faintly of dust. I started to pull the drapes off of the piano, but Luma caught my wrist and began to dig her nails in. I could feel them changing, growing downward into my arm.

"Stop that!" I said.

"I saw you look at Arthur," she said. "Do you like him?"

"What?"

"Is he your Mr. Rochester?"

"Luma, not everything is a gothic novel," I said. "And no, I don't like him. He's your, I don't know, Heathcliff."

She retracted her claws and yanked her hand away. I looked down at the red marks on my wrist.

"Well," she said, "you should be more careful around Grandmere. You know Grandpa's afraid of her. I can smell it on him."

"That's ridiculous." I couldn't imagine Grandpa Miklos being afraid of anything. "You can't possibly smell that."

"I can smell a lot," she said. "For example, you stink of fish right now." She took in another breath. "And something else, too. Are you sure you don't like him? You smell strange."

I felt suddenly hot and panicked.

"I was thinking about a boy from school during dinner. Do you really need to know that?"

"You'd better not be lying to me," she said.

I steadied my voice like I learned to in boarding school and said, "Well, I'm not." Her sense of smell was going to be a problem. How was I supposed to protect her from the way I felt if she insisted on sniffing it out?

"Good," Luma said, and I fought the urge to sigh with relief. She flicked the light switch on and off a few times until the shaky electricity kicked in. The man who had done the wiring for the house hadn't been very good. I had a sudden memory of him running out of the house and into the woods, and Grandpa Miklos following after. I shook my head to clear it. There were too many of these kinds of memories for me to get upset about just one. And anyway, Grandmere was in the house now. Together we were going to change things.

I opened the lid of the piano. Luma stepped closer to me, still sniffing.

"Didn't you go to an all-girls' school?" she asked.

"It was someone I met at winter formal. Not that it's any of your business."

Winter formal last year had been a disaster; I'd stood in the corner in a borrowed dress while other girls twirled around with boys. But I looked right into her eyes and willed my lie to work. I knew with her the trick was to be shameless; she was not particularly clever, but she could smell sweat and she could hear heartbeats. I breathed in deeply and held it to slow my heart down. It was part of a set of skills that felt dangerous to use, foreign from what the rest of the family had. But it gave me an edge with Luma; she didn't really understand lying. She'd never really needed to lie. She'd always just gotten what she wanted.

I wished I could tell her about all of this. I didn't like having to be the mature one, the one who sacrificed. I wanted to be a little girl again, have her hug me and tell me I was silly and everything would be alright. But Grandma Persephone had told me to take care of her, along with everyone else. She was innocent, in a way. If she lost that, I'd failed. Must be nice, I supposed, to live in a big house away from the world, where everyone you saw was someone who loved you.

We called in Grandmere and Grandpa Miklos and Arthur. Rhys came sulking in, too, and stood in the corner with his arms folded over his chest. I sat down at the piano and played a few chords experimentally, testing my fingers. My piano teacher at school had said my webbed thumb made my span too short, and if I ever wanted to be a professional I would have to get it operated on. In response I'd developed a way of leaping along that gave my playing a little bit of a lilt. I won a prize for a song I performed, a Bible with real gold on the edges of the pages. Where was that now? Probably still in my dormitory room where I'd left it when I fled. Or taken by the police as evidence, if things had gone that far.

I wished I'd been practicing, suddenly. I wanted Arthur to see me at my best. I sat up straighter on the piano bench, arching my back, bending my head toward the keys. I tried to remember songs I was good at playing that weren't in Luma's range. If I was going to be bad, I at least wanted to be better than her.

There weren't many songs like that, though—she had a good clear voice that went from alto to soprano. So I settled for a song I liked, a song about love, something Father had played for us when we were younger. It was a translation of a song Grandma Persephone used to sing in Greek, something she'd learned on Crete. I struck up the chords, and Luma nodded her head in time with my playing.

Luma's voice sounded high and clear, and then Rhys came in on the low part and I felt something resonate in my chest. We should have played together more often when we were younger, I realized, now that I heard us all together. We were good at it, and although usually at school I didn't sing, the words rose unbidden and came tumbling out of my mouth:

"Let me be ground to crumbs or dust
My shattered bones would still have strength
To run to you!
When you've made up your mind
No use lagging behind
And no relenting
Let your youth have free rein
It will not come again
So no repenting!"

It was a giggly song, one Grandma Persephone liked to sing to Miklos. I suddenly remembered being little and watching her in the garden, humming the tune while she worked. Grandpa Miklos had come up behind her and uprooted her like a carrot from the ground, and both of them fell over backward laughing like children. No wonder he could barely stand the sight of a new person in the house.

How could she have had an affair? Grandpa had loved her more than anything, and it still hadn't been good enough for her. I hated her more than ever. I'd never be loved like that, not if I lived a hundred years, I was sure of it. Who had she been, that woman who had run our lives for so long, pruning us like plants, lying to us, keeping secrets?

"Tell me with a laugh
Tell me with a cry

Tell me you don't love me—
What care I?"

I glanced up and saw that Arthur was watching me. I looked away as I sang "What care I?"

When I looked back, Grandmere caught my eye. She was watching me, her head tilted to the side, brow furrowed. Something had troubled her, or maybe she was having a hard time following the song in English. But when we stopped, she applauded. "Beautiful!" she said. "Absolutely beautiful." She stood up to catch me by the hands and beamed.

"My accomplished granddaughter," she said softly to me. "So lovely and so talented."

Luma scoffed. She was jealous, I told myself. Jealous of how much Grandmere liked me.

"But I'm sure your Mr. Knox is tired," Grandmere said. "We should say good night."

That didn't seem right somehow. Everyone in this house stayed up until all hours, working or sleeping or playing when they pleased, and when Arthur visited, he and whoever wanted to would sit in the parlor, sometimes until the sun came up if they felt like it. But Grandmere seemed to know how a household was run. This must be how real people lived; certainly that was how it had been at school. Maybe it was time we tried being normal.

Luma glared, and her shoulders started to go up. But she looked at Arthur and tried to relax. That was unexpected. She was trying to behave in front of him. She turned, glaring at Rhys on her way through the door. He slunk out after her, keeping his distance.

Grandmere and I ushered Arthur into the hallway. "Thank you for coming," Grandmere said. "I do hope you'll call again."

"If it suits you," he said, stepping out onto the porch. Grandmere closed the door behind him once he had made it down the stairs.

Luma emerged from the shadows in the hallway. I'd thought she'd left, but she'd just gone into the kitchen. She was eating a duck leg left over from dinner. Fat dribbled down her hand.

"Luma, *go to bed*," Grandmere said. Something in her inflection seemed familiar to me, and then I realized that it was how I talked sometimes. A certain emphasis.

Luma took a big bite of duck. "No."

Grandmere's brow furrowed, as though she were concentrating on something.

"I asked you to *go*," she said again, a little more insistently.

"And I said no."

Grandmere glared, but only for a moment. Then she composed herself.

"Very well, then," she said. "Do what you like."

Luma stuck the duck leg between her teeth and stomped off down the hall. Halfway down she dropped to all fours and turned beast, then disappeared around the corner as a blur of white fur. Grandmere watched her go before turning to me.

"Eleanor," she said, "may we speak privately?"

Grandmere led me down the hall to the door to Grandma Persephone's library and put her hand on the knob. And then there was a chill in the air and a sharp noise, and a shudder ran through her. For a moment her face contorted into something that looked like rage.

"Perhaps outside," she said.

Outside, we walked around the house until we came to the cliff staircase. Grandmere stopped at the top landing and leaned against the railing, looking out at the water that roared against the sand below.

"Oh, that sea breeze," she said. "What an absolutely lovely, perfect night."

"Now that I'm back here," I said, "I can't believe I stayed away for so long."

Grandmere raised her eyebrows.

"Well I do hope you will still consider traveling with me someday," she said. "I love this place, but there are so many other parts of the world."

"Travel?" The idea thrilled me. "Do you think you could take me to France?"

"Someday I will go back to France, yes," she said. "And when I do you will come with me, of course. For now, though, I want to see what America has to offer me. It is so big and so full of possibility."

"I'd like to go anywhere," I said.

"It's good to hear you say that," she said. "I want you to say what it is you want, Eleanor. It's important to me. I do not think anyone has asked you what you want in a long time."

It was true. Nobody had really asked me what I wanted, not when they sent me to school, and not since I had been back.

"So tell me," she said. "What is it you want?"

"I can't have what I want."

She laughed.

"So young to be so cynical!" she said. "You are a lovely young woman, and talented, and hardworking. You could have anything. So just name one thing. And I will make it yours."

I thought about all the things I could ask her for. She had money, didn't she? And had traveled all over the world? I could ask her for clothes, books, lessons, a trip to anywhere I could think of. And then I realized what I wanted was nothing she could give me, because it wasn't anything that could be given. I thought of Arthur. Of the way I'd felt when we stood together in the crowd at the funeral, when it felt like we were alone together among all these people, and he told me things. There were so many things I still wanted him to tell me.

"You're very kind," I said. "But I don't think anyone can give me what I want." And I told her about Arthur and Luma. About what he'd said about it being a phase, although I didn't mention Rhys. As I told her, she put her hand to her cheek in astonishment.

"My!" she said. "You are selfless, to give all that up for your sister when they are so clearly a bad match. I thought I saw you watching him. He is a trifle, a nothing. But we can start there and perhaps later you will want more."

She wouldn't say that if she knew him like I did. But all I said was, "But he's with Luma."

"For how long? They aren't married, are they? They have no children?" She tilted her face into the night breeze and smiled serenely. "You can have him. All you have to do is be bold."

I thought about it. Maybe she was right. But then what about Rhys? Luma was strong enough to fight him, but was I? I tried not to think about how his teeth would feel in my throat. And there was something else, too. I hated the feeling of being cruel to Luma. I thought of us singing in the parlor, how relieved I'd been when I realized I couldn't ruin her singing, how beautiful our voices had sounded together. I wished we were younger again, when I hadn't felt like we had to fight to get what we needed, because all we needed was each other.

"Well, I don't know," I said. "I don't want Luma to be unhappy."

"Well, it might be that another man will suit her," Grandmere said. "We just have to find her someone else. You work on your Arthur, and I will think about who she might like instead."

"I don't want to work on him," I said. "I mean, not until she doesn't want him anymore."

"That's very noble of you," she said. "But I want you to know that you are every bit as important as she is. She's had her way for far too long. So if you want something . . ."

I wanted to be back in the ocean, floating just under the surface, staring up at that great glowing moon. But I didn't say that. Instead I watched Grandmere's face, waiting for her to reveal what she wanted from me. She was hoping I'd show her I was powerful enough to take what I wanted. And if I did, she'd be impressed. Was it so bad to want that?

"Have I upset you?" she asked. "Please tell me what I've done, and I'll make it right."

"No," I said. "It's just . . . nothing. It just feels like things are so easy for Luma."

"You can't want to be like that," Grandmere said. "She's lazy and spoiled. Once her looks fade she will be nothing special."

I was stunned. It was crueler than anything I'd dared to think. But at the same time, was it so far from the truth? Luma did spend a lot of time lying around. Playing. What did she know about hard work? Not like me. Grandmere must have seen my incredulity, because she reached out and patted me on the hand.

"Don't worry," she said. "Your sister will be happy enough. We will find her some man she will like, and she will get married and have a lovely, simple life. Really, she is the lucky one. People like you and me suffer more for our rewards." She smiled. "But I have seen the way Arthur looks at you. I think you can have everything you desire."

"Really?"

"Really."

She took my hand then in her small gloved one and led me back toward the house.

"Thank you," she said. "It makes me so happy to be here with you, to spend time with you. I've always wanted a daughter like you, and now, I feel that I have one."

No one had held my hand in so long; it was hard to figure out how to respond, whether I should squeeze her hand back, or simply let her hold onto me. She pulled me along with her, and I let myself be led. I wanted this walk to go on forever—me and my grandmother who loved me, who wanted me. Her daughter, she'd called me. Over my mother, over my sister, over everyone else. Me.

But I knew the noise I'd heard when she opened the library door. It was the icy sound of a slap. Between that, the face in the mirror, and the strange dreams, I could no longer deny it. Grandma Persephone was haunting the house. She had been here since the night she'd died.

I had to get back into that library.

When we got to the house, Grandmere stretched theatrically and yawned.

"I am quite tired," she said. "Why don't we go to bed?"

"I think I'll spend some time looking over the finances," I said, and started for the library door.

"Eleanor," Grandmere said, "*that can wait until tomorrow.*"

There was that tone again, the one that sounded like me. I found myself stopping short. I looked back at her, trying to figure out what she was trying to tell me.

"I'll leave it for now," I said.

"That's a good girl."

I said good night to Grandmere at the door to her room. As soon as it had shut behind her, I went up to my floor and into my own room. I waited for a while, reading snatches of a paperback novel. I told myself I just wanted to wait until everyone had gone to bed, but even after the house was still, I stayed in my room. I found myself checking the little alarm clock on my nightstand. Why was it so important to me, I wondered, that I follow Grandmere's ruling to the letter? It felt so childish. Finally, the little clock said midnight, and downstairs the chimeless grandfather clock clacked, and I stood up. It was tomorrow.

I took the servant stairs. I'd never used them to sneak around before, and so one of them surprised me when it creaked loudly underfoot. I held very still. No sounds came from anywhere else in the house. I breathed out slowly.

I wasn't sure exactly why I felt the need to sneak. It wasn't like Grandmere would do anything if she saw me climbing around in the dark, not exactly. But I didn't want to disappoint her. She'd made it clear that she didn't want me in the library, although she hadn't made it clear *why*. Better that she didn't know, then, if it was only going to upset her. From the laundry, it was easy enough to pick my way along in the dark to the library. Nobody stopped me. I was fairly sure no one else was home and awake.

At the door, I paused. I had the wild thought that maybe there was no ghost—maybe Grandma Persephone had been hiding in the attic this whole time. She'd controlled everything else so tightly that I could almost believe she could have gotten everyone to go along with it. So when I opened the door to the library, I half-expected to find her sitting in her usual chair, reading a book. "You've failed the first test, girl," she'd say. "I'll just have to find someone else before I actually die." It would be a relief.

Even in the faint light, I could tell the room was empty.

I shut the door behind me and leaned against it. I wanted to cry, but I didn't want anyone to hear me, to know I was in here. I couldn't say why just yet, only that it felt like there was no one I could trust. And then I felt a cold rush of air on my face. In the dark room I felt the hairs prickle on the back of my neck.

The windows were shut. I crossed to the fireplace and checked the flue; it was closed. And then, out of the corner of my eye, I saw a little flicker of movement.

On top of Grandma Persephone's glass-fronted cabinet, high over my head, was a box. As I watched, it moved again. In tiny bursts it inched forward, and I stood mesmerized like a rabbit, watching it. It moved with painful slowness, like someone was pushing it with just the tip of a broken finger. At last, it teetered on the edge, and with one more little movement, it fell.

It hit the floor with a crash. Panic welled up in me, threatening to drown out my other senses. I stepped back and back, toward the door, felt for the knob with my hand, stumbled out into the hall—

And ran into something cool and solid.

I spun around. Arthur stood there, in the dark. For a long moment, we both stood in silence. Then I whispered, "What are you doing here?"

"I never left."

Luma must have let him back in after Grandmere showed him to the door. They'd probably been upstairs, doing who knew what. For a moment, I was angry. And then I was just glad to see him.

"Please don't think I'm crazy," I said. "I think there's a ghost."

"I believe you."

"So you've felt it, too?"

"You might say that."

"Will you come with me?"

I felt like a coward, needing someone there, but I did feel safer as I stepped back over the threshold. Arthur walked past me into the room. I noticed he wasn't wearing shoes. His black socks were threadbare; I could see the white of his heel showing through on one side. It made me feel tender toward him.

"It's cold," he said. It was still dark in the room, but he tugged aside the curtain, and in the moonlight, everything came into focus.

The box lay on the floor, its contents strewn all around it. So it was real. I caught my breath. Arthur stared at it with no expression on his face.

"Is she trying to tell me something?" I asked.

"I wouldn't say."

"Come on," I said. "You knew her better than me. Help me."

When I said that, I thought I caught him scowling. Then Arthur took a step toward the mess, and I moved quickly to join him. I spotted the tarot cards first: the pack had come open in the fall and some of the cards had escaped. I hadn't seen them since the night Grandma Persephone died. How had they gotten in here?

"Those are her work materials," he said. "Things she used to do magic."

Aside from the cards, nothing else in the box looked special. There was a pair of scissors, a pincushion full of needles and different colors of thread, a heavy snow globe, taper candles wrapped in colored strings in various stages of decay, a book of matches, a pair of spectacles without the arms, a few yellow Kodak canisters with lids. The box itself was just a crate of rough wood with a sliding lid. I bent to gather everything up. When I got to the cards, I couldn't bring myself to put them away.

"This means she wants me to use them, right?" I asked.

He shrugged.

"Do you think she's here now?"

"I think she's close," he said.

"Why do you think she doesn't want Grandmere in here?"

"I wouldn't say," he said.

"Wait," I said. "Couldn't or wouldn't?"

"Are you going to make me tell you?"

I thought about telling him he had to tell me, but the idea made me uneasy. I remembered last time he'd done exactly what I'd wanted, and then he had disappeared for a while. And this last time, I'd known what I was doing, a little. Not entirely, but enough to count. I shook my head.

"Thank you for helping me," I said. "You scared me at first, but I'm glad you were here."

"I'm only doing my job."

"You don't have to stay if you want to go."

"Don't do that," he said. "You're saying I can go, but you want me to stay."

I closed my eyes, and swallowed, and thought.

"I do want you to stay with me," I said. "But I want you to do—what you want."

"Then I'm leaving."

He stood for a moment longer, as though he were waiting for

something. When he left, he cast a glance backward at me, and I gave him a little smile, hoping I looked brave. As soon as he shut the door, though, fear crept back in. Without Arthur here, I was alone with a ghost.

Well, if she could try to communicate, so could I.

"I know you're here," I said, feeling both silly and terrified. "Are you giving me these things? Do you want me to learn magic?"

A thump came from behind me. I spun around. On the floor was a slim volume. I picked it up.

"Sheep Husbandry," I read. "I don't think this is—"

I glanced up. Next to the place where *Sheep Husbandry* had been on the shelf was a large leather-bound book. Something about it looked familiar.

I had to stand on a stool to reach it; Grandma had been a tall woman. When I pulled it out, the weight of it in my hands felt familiar. I'd felt that weight before. It was the journal I'd had in the dream, the one where the woman had tried to kill me.

"This was yours," I said.

A breeze blew on the deck of cards, scattering them. I clambered off the chair to pick them up, and then I froze.

The one that had blown face-up was the same card I had seen the night that Grandma Persephone died. The curling, swirling vague shapes, the pair of yellow eyes. There was no text on the card, no hint of what it represented.

I held it up, perplexed, and tipped it left and right. It never seemed to change when I was looking at it, but if I looked away, it seemed different when I glanced back. It seemed closer.

I heard footsteps on the stairs outside and held very still. I thought about the thing on the cards, imagined it oozing down the stairs, and the hairs stood up on the back of my neck—

"Eleanor?"

I sighed with relief: it was just Grandmere. Still, I didn't want her to know I was up this late. I held still and waited.

"I thought I heard you calling me," she said. "Are you in there?"

I didn't answer. She must have heard my voice, I told myself. I must have said *grandma*, and she must have heard it, and thought I meant her. That was all. I felt a chill run down my back and wondered if it was just the ghost, or something inside me.

"Hmm," she said, as if to herself. "Strange."

Her footsteps receded up the stairs, and I waited in the dark, holding the book to my chest, until she was gone.

The room had gotten warmer, and somehow I knew that meant that Grandma Persephone was gone. I grabbed the journal and the tarot cards and fled up the stairs with them as quietly as I could.

SEVEN

I'D PLANNED TO SPEND THE ENTIRE NIGHT reading the journal and learning its secrets. But when I got back to my room my fear had dissipated, and I was exhausted. I curled up on my side and fell asleep almost immediately, and when I woke up, someone was knocking at my door.

"Eleanor, darling?" Grandmere. I shoved the book and the cards under the covers, feeling a little guilty, and went to answer her. She was wearing a sky blue dress and a white sweater, and her soft gray hair was piled on top of her head like a little cloud. She looked like a grandmother from a catalog.

"You slept later than usual this morning," she said. "I hope you don't plan to miss breakfast."

"I'm sorry. I had a hard time getting to sleep last night."

Her face clouded. "I'm sorry to have bothered you," she said.

"I know you have your own life and your own plans, but I hoped to spend the morning with you."

I gave her a smile. The ghost might not like her, but what did I care what Grandma Persephone thought, anyway? She could be wrong about things. She'd been wrong about me.

"I'll be right down," I said. "I just want to get dressed."

I took my time picking out clothes and heading downstairs. I didn't know why: I was excited to spend more time with Grandmere. But I kept returning to my mirror, arranging my hair, smoothing the collar of my blouse, wondering if I looked perfect, too. And I kept waiting, also, to see if anything would appear in the mirror. But there was nothing but my own worried face.

Before I left, I tucked the journal and the tarot cards into the drawer of my nightstand. No sense leaving them lying around, I thought, although I wasn't sure exactly who I was hiding them from, or why.

"I'd like us to have a dinner party," Grandmere said, when we were eating breakfast with Mother and Luma. Father and Rhys had retreated into the woods to check on Grandpa Miklos, who had not been back to the house since the night before. And Luma and Mother were mostly silent. Mother picked at her food in between dabbing at her face with a damp handkerchief, and Luma worked at the same piece of bacon fat indefinitely, staring moodily out the window.

"A dinner party?" Mother asked.

"Just a small one," Grandmere said. "I want to invite the woman who is the most important in the village and her husband. Who is that? And perhaps your Arthur?"

I blushed at the "your Arthur." "I think it's Mrs. Hannafin," I said. "She runs the post office. Her husband owns the general store."

"Is there no mayor? No elders?"

"It's too small for that," I said. "Mrs. Hannafin is the only person I've seen tell anyone else what to do. Other than Grandma Persephone."

Grandmere looked sad.

"I know I should not speak ill of someone who has passed," she said. "But it troubles me so, the way she treated you. It makes me angry to think of you alone like that."

Luma growled in the back of her throat.

"It doesn't matter now," I said. "I hope wherever she is, she's happy."

"Well, the house cannot stay closed to company forever."

"Miklos isn't well," my mother said. Her throat sounded scratchy. "I'm not sure he's ready for company. He can be a little hasty around people he doesn't know."

Grandmere sighed.

"I had noticed that," she said. "I barely see him, and when I do, he seems upset with me. Maybe I should have a word with him and find out where we stand." She stretched and shimmied her shoulders a little in anticipation; for a moment she reminded me of Luma, and I remembered that she was her grandmother, too. "We can get that arranged, and then we can have people over. Maybe someone for Luma to meet."

"I have a boyfriend," said Luma. Grandmere speared a piece of fruit with her fork.

"You know," she said to me, as though Luma hadn't spoken at all, "all my daughters met their husbands at my salons. All except for your mother."

"You have other daughters?" I asked. I had aunts! Aunts who didn't already hate me. I imagined them, different, older versions of me. But Grandmere looked downcast.

"Lost, now," she said. "The War took so much from us all."

"They died?"

She nodded. "Excuse me," she said, and stood up. "I need a little time to be alone."

She left the table, her long skirts swishing behind her.

I glanced over at Mother.

"Did I upset her?" I asked.

Mother looked bewildered. I realized that she had tuned out the whole conversation, and I was summoning her from far away.

"What? Oh, no," she said. "You didn't do anything wrong."

"I didn't know you had sisters," I said.

"It was a long time ago."

I wanted to ask her more, but she stood up from the table, took her cup of water, and splashed it over the side of her face.

Her polyps quickly sucked up the water, and strained down toward her empty cup.

"I'm going to take a bath," she said. She stumbled from her chair and dragged herself along the picture rail toward the door.

"She's scared of Grandmere," Luma said glumly, when Mother had reached the stairs. "I can smell it."

"That's silly," I said. "She's her mother."

"She's not staying wet," Luma said. "She's dressed up. And she doesn't talk much anymore."

"Maybe she's just worried," I said.

"About what?"

"About embarrassing us."

Luma frowned. "That sounds like something *she* would say."

"Grandmere's not cruel," I said. "She's a long way from home and out of her element. We can try to make her comfortable."

"By making Mother miserable?"

"Since when do you care who's miserable?" I said. "You know I found all the letters that I sent to you? Grandma Persephone was stealing them."

"Why would she do that?"

"I don't know, but why wouldn't you even check? You just gave up. All of you gave up."

She flipped her hair over one shoulder. So much hair, the color of white gold. She looked good when she was angry, imperious. It was annoying.

"Well, I'm sorry," she said. "But how was I supposed to

know? You've always just done what you wanted to do. How was I supposed to guess you were writing to me?"

"Because you're my sister," I said. "And you didn't even try."

"That's not what we're talking about. You're here now."

"I'm supposed to be happy you all forgot about me?"

"You don't really care if I say I'm sorry, you just want to be angry. Why?"

"You're imagining things," I said. "Now, I need to go do some work in the greenhouse, so if you'll excuse me—"

"'If I'll excuse you'? You even sound like her."

Her eyes tunneled holes into my back as I left. It felt like she wanted me to do something. But what? Throw out our only living grandmother because Mother seemed a little nervous? I didn't have time to worry about Luma's every whim, I told myself. If she wanted to be in charge, she could make an effort. Like me. I was doing everything I could to save this family. Could Luma say the same? No.

When we were little, Luma and I had been inseparable. We'd looked the same when we were small: the two of us floating around the house in matching nightgowns, sitting on Grandpa Miklos's knees, begging him to show us his other face to make us jump and scream. And then one day Luma did it back.

The next morning she'd woken up and showed me her bed littered with her baby teeth, her pillowcase streaked with blood, and her new bright wolf's teeth gleaming in her mouth like pearls. And then I'd bitten her, hadn't I? Grabbed her arm and sank my dull flat teeth as deep into her flesh as I could, hoping that if I bit down deep enough, my teeth would fall out and my real ones would come in.

When they pried me off of her, Grandma Persephone had taken her to one side, cradling her, shushing her. And Grandpa Miklos, I remembered, had taken me and hoisted me up by the armpits. He'd looked proud, almost.

"My girl," he'd said quietly, "your time will come. She is older. Someday, you too will become the wolf. I can feel it. You are as powerful as my firstborn son."

And he'd put me down and clapped me on the back.

"Do not bite your sister," he'd said. "You are lucky to have each other. In my country, I was the only one of my kind."

And then, all at once, I was not in my own memory anymore. I was watching myself and Grandpa Miklos from a distance. My arms were wrapped around something. I looked down and saw Luma looking up at me, a handkerchief clamped over her arm, blood soaking through it in a ring. Looking back up, there was my husband, tousling Eleanor's hair—

I shook my head to clear it. At once, I was myself again, and everyone else was gone. I was alone in the hall of portraits. I wondered if I'd somehow dozed off on my feet. That had felt like one of those strange dreams I'd been having, but I'd never had one during the day. I looked around warily. The ground felt unstable now, as though at any moment I might find myself in the past. Feeling unsettled, I fled to the greenhouse.

It was bright and hot inside, with birds chirping up in the girders over my head. I breathed in the smell of the soil—it felt like clearing my head, like escaping.

Grandma Persephone was somewhere in this house. She was trying to tell me something—after all, she'd given me the journal. I had better find out what, and soon. I sat down in one of the battered armchairs, opened the journal, and started in.

It opened with tight, crabbed handwriting I didn't recognize in a language I couldn't read. I flipped through that, and came to Grandma Persephone's familiar loopy handwriting, but still in another language. Italian, maybe? I squinted at it. Between French and Latin, I could pick through it, getting every other word. Something about picking herbs, something about doing laundry. Her mother was sick. I thought about the woman I'd seen in my dream, her foul breath, the hatred in her eyes. That didn't seem quite like sickness to me. But why should that surprise me? Persephone was a liar.

I skipped ahead to the pages she'd dog-eared, and eventually came to a drawing of the drakondia plant: I instantly recognized its long black tongue and frilled leaves. Next to it were a series of notes about where it grew. Rocky hillsides. Something about the soil not holding any water. Dry earth. For the first time in my life, I was grateful for my years of Latin grammar drills.

I went over to the long row of plants and looked down at their roots. The soil was dark and damp to the touch, not at all how it should be, according to the book. I'd overwatered them;

the flowers had fallen off of the stems and littered the floor, and the leaves were yellowing. I'd been treating them like orchids, when they were really something else. I almost wanted to laugh. I'd been trying to take care of them, and what I should have done was leave them be. I just hoped it wasn't too late.

I skimmed through the instructions for preparing the extracts of drakondia: the poison came from the oil in the leaves when distilled down, and the love potion from the flowers' nectar. That sounded easy enough, once the plants recovered. Absorbed in reading, I must not have heard the door from the house open. I glanced up when I heard a cough.

Grandpa walked in slowly on two legs, dressed in his smoking jacket and trousers. He seated himself in the chair across the card table from me. He didn't speak at first, just watched me. He had his hands folded in his lap. He looked as though he was trying to be on his best behavior.

"Yes?" I asked.

"I have something bad to tell you, my child," he said. "This woman who has come here is not what she seems."

I furrowed my brow. "What do you mean?"

"She has come for me at last," he said. "She means to kill me."

I almost laughed. Come to kill Grandpa Miklos? I'd like to see anyone try.

"No," I said. "Grandpa, you're confused. She's Mother's mother. She came to visit us."

"You are wrong about that," he said. "She is the reason I came here. She almost caught me once. She is here to catch me again."

The door behind us opened, and Grandmere waved cheerily at me from the doorway. Without turning around, Grandpa began to growl.

"Oh, I'm sorry," Grandmere said. "Eleanor, come find me when you have a chance. Apologies, Miklos."

She left, but the growl persisted even after she'd gone. I was getting frightened that he'd lash out at me like he'd done the night of Grandma Persephone's funeral.

"Grandpa," I said. "Grandpa! *Stop it.*" I must have said it in a firm enough voice, because he stopped growling. He looked up at me and gave a little whine.

"You don't understand," he said. "You must let me chase her away."

"I know you're upset," I said. "I know you miss Grandma Persephone and that everything feels strange right now. But Grandmere is here to help. Please don't drive her away."

He shook his head at me, uncomprehending. "Don't ask me that, please," he said.

"I'm telling you," I said. "*Don't ruin this for me.*"

He stood up, and left. A few minutes later, the howling started again from the woods, and the kitchen door banged open and shut as Rhys ran out to meet him. They had each other, I thought. Must be nice.

Well, I wasn't alone anymore. I had Grandmere. I should go find her.

I found her on a settee in the parlor with a notebook on her lap and a stack of catalogs spread out on a side table. When I came in, she positively beamed at me.

"I am starting to plan our little party," she said. "Tell me about the Hannafins. What are they like?"

"I don't know," I said. "Do you really want to have them to dinner? Mrs. Hannafin is a little . . . mean."

"Oh, the Hannafins do not matter," she said. "This is a chance for us to practice having guests. Eventually I want to start entertaining more important people. In France I was quite the hostess. Everyone came to my parties, even minor royalty."

"Really?"

"Really."

"And you think we could do something like that here?" I asked.

"Of course! It's a lovely little town, and a beautiful large house with many rooms. We could set up some of the ones upstairs for visitors. It would be no trouble. And we could start your introduction into American society. Those kinds of connections are very valuable to people like you and me."

"Like you and me?" I asked.

She furrowed her brow, perplexed. "Yes," she said. "It is essential to be well connected. It makes your life so much easier."

"I've never been good at making friends."

"I cannot believe that," she said. "You are so charming! Here, come sit by me. Look at this menu."

She patted the spot next to her on the settee. When I sat down, she draped an arm around my shoulders. I almost flinched at it. It was so cozy, and so foreign to me.

"We will have to get into the kitchen, you and I," she said. "Margaret is excellent at meat, but I have never seen her prepare a dough."

"We don't eat a lot of that here."

"Well, it will go a long way toward making guests happy," she said. "I was also thinking that the house needs to be brought into this century if we are going to entertain. You know I could not find a radio? Or a record player?"

"There's a Victrola in the library."

She waved her hand dismissively. "How about this one here?" she said, pointing to the catalog with the tip of her pen. "And while I am ordering things, what else are we missing?"

We spent about an hour going through the catalog, making up a list of things to get from the market in town, and writing out an invitation to the Hannafins. When we'd finished, Grandmere bundled up all the outgoing mail and handed it to me. "Will you tell Margaret to take all this to town?" she asked.

She must have seen me wince; her eyes filled with concern. "What is it?"

"Margaret doesn't like to be talked to," I said. "You can't tell her anything. Or at least, I can't. I don't know why she listens to you."

"Oh, that won't do," she said. "You are the head of this house, are you not?"

"No one seems to think so."

"Is that not why you asked me to come here?" she said. "You know, we haven't yet spoken about that."

"You just got here. I didn't want to impose. You're our guest."

"I am here for you, Eleanor," she said. She cupped my cheek in one gloved hand. "You cannot possibly impose upon me."

I couldn't help but flush with pride.

"Do you want me to teach you how to do what I do?" she asked.

I nodded happily.

"The most important thing," Grandmere said, "is that you have to learn how to feel every part of the place as though it is a part of you. Every room in the house is your body. Every being in the house is a finger on your hand. You have to learn how to feel them if you want to learn how to move them." She flexed her own fingers a little. "Here is the first lesson. I want you to sit quietly and listen to the sounds."

She took my hands in her hands, and settled herself a little farther onto the settee, and closed her eyes. I watched her face for a moment as she frowned, and the corners of her mouth twitched, and sometimes her eyebrows shot up. It was clear that she was hearing things I couldn't. I shut my eyes, too, and strained to hear.

There was a faint clanging sound, I realized. Banging pots. I could hear the kitchen from here. From upstairs I could hear splashing water: Mother, taking her bath. I relaxed and tried to hear more. I could feel, too: a faint current of slightly colder air was coming from the hall, which meant that someone had opened a door to the outside. The clicking on the floor meant that someone had come in on four legs. Grandpa Miklos, by the weight of his footsteps. I opened my eyes.

"Tell me what you know now," Grandmere said.

"Margaret's washing pans," I said. "Grandpa just came in—through the front door, which means he didn't catch anything in the woods. Mother's running water right now."

"Good," she said. "Very good. Eventually you will learn to always be listening at the back of your mind, and you will hear more, and know more. And eventually you will learn how to make things happen without ever lifting your hands."

"Like . . . magic?" I asked.

"Exactly like magic. The kind of magic that you use to make a party—or a household—work perfectly. Now, I want to rest, so why don't you go practice? You can tell Margaret to post these. If she won't, or if she makes a fuss, come to me and I will help you."

I took them and headed for Margaret. But when I stepped into the kitchen, I balked. Margaret was plucking a wild turkey, its head in the sink, a bucket of feathers on the floor beside her. She looked up when she saw me come in. She made a low droning noise in her throat, almost a growl.

I cleared my throat, but I couldn't bring myself to speak. For one thing, the idea of upsetting Margaret frightened me. But that wasn't the only reason I hesitated. I didn't like the idea of telling her to do anything, even if it worked. Margaret was always working; she was working right now. And anyway, I had feet, didn't I? I could take the mail to town.

I held up the invitations and waved my hand toward the back door: *I'm going out.* Margaret frowned, but she turned back to her work.

As I slipped out through the back door, I instantly felt like I'd done something wrong. But why? I'd felt guilty about the idea of bothering her, and now I felt guilty about doing it myself. Or at least, worried about what Grandmere would think. I found myself sneaking around the house, hugging the edge of the woods, hoping she wouldn't see me setting out for Winterport.

The walk was longer than I'd remembered; I hadn't made the trip on foot since that first day, and I'd been buzzing with nerves then. My feet slid on the gravel road. And then I came around a bend and I could suddenly see the town curled below me, following the edge of the land, the spars of its docks jutting out into the harbor. Boats bobbed at their moorings. Red brick buildings caught the afternoon sunlight. It was so peaceful here. I wondered, for a moment, what it would be like to be any one of these people. To not be feared. And of course, I could see the church from here. I realized I was tempted to stop in, to see if Father Thomas would receive me.

Errands first. I passed the church and made straight for the post office, where I dropped off the catalog order forms and the invitation. Mrs. Hannafin spotted her name on the envelope and gave me a suspicious look before ripping it open in front of me. Her lips moved while she read it.

"GRAND-meer?" she asked.

"Gran-mare."

She read on. "Well, I suppose we could. We need to bring anything?"

"Just the pleasure of your company."

"No wine or nothing?"

"We'll take care of that."

She nodded, and eyed me appraisingly. "Alright, then."

I put in an order for delivery at the store in town, and the man behind the counter shook his head. "We don't go up there," he said.

Well, here was a chance to practice what Grandmere wanted me to learn. At least it wasn't Margaret; that was too hard. "It says on your sign that you do deliveries twice a week. Our address says Winterport. Why can't you deliver to us?"

"We don't go up there," he repeated. He was gripping the edge of the counter, and I wondered if he was imagining me springing across it, sinking my teeth into his throat.

I took a deep breath. I remembered that tone that Grandmere used sometimes. I mouthed a little to myself, trying to
imitate it.

"What're you doing?" he asked.

"*I need you to make that delivery,*" I said.

He nodded. "Hey, alright, then," he said. "Didn't realize it
mattered so much to you."

I smiled. "Good," I said. "We'd like it on Friday."

As I left the shop, I felt elated. I'd stood up for myself and
gotten what I wanted. But on my way out of town, a creep-
ing doubt set in: that what I'd done wasn't just talking. And
more than that: it had been familiar. I'd heard my voice do that
before. But when?

It had been warm the last few days, but the road was shaded
over and cold, and I found myself shivering in my light sweater.
Father Thomas's rectory was the last house on the way out of
town. I felt a sudden nervousness. I didn't know why I felt so
guilty about it. After all, hadn't Grandmere told me to go after
what I wanted? Maybe I wanted to save the plants. And to do
that, I needed to find out how to care for them. I'd asked everyone in the house except Margaret, and nobody seemed to know.

Father Thomas answered the door holding a cup of tea in his
liver-spotted hands.

"Can I come in?" I asked.

He looked at me, starting with my feet and ending on my
hair.

"We'd better go into the sanctuary," he said.

He led me up the path that connected his cottage to the church. It was a small one, capable of seating maybe a hundred people. In the nave, he sat down on the steps to the altar and gestured me toward the front pew.

"Is this where you talk to people?" I asked.

"It is where I like to talk to Zarrins." He must have seen the dismay on my face, because he added, "Your grandmother came here, at times. Weekdays, when it was empty. She said that God lived in empty places. That if you could empty a place out, something would move in to occupy that nothingness." He pushed his glasses up his nose. "Not sure if that was a superstition, or more of a metaphor."

"You two were close," I said.

He shook his head. "Maybe when we were younger. Later on, she mostly wanted to be with her family. We still saw each other a good deal, though, at births and deaths." His voice told me something different than his words. He sounded hopeful, even now, after she was buried in the ground.

"You were in love with her."

His neck turned pink above his clerical collar. "Well, yes," he said. "I suppose there's no point in denying it. But we stayed— well, loyal to our own lives."

I knew he was lying. Arthur had told me, after I'd pressed him. Had I asked him in the same way I'd asked the shopkeeper? With emphasis, with intention?

"But why don't you tell me why you came to call on me today?" he asked. "I haven't seen you at Mass since you arrived."

"I'm sorry, Father," I said. "Things have been very busy since the funeral. But there's something I wanted to ask you about."

"And what's that?"

"Did Grandma Persephone ever tell you why she sent me away?"

He sighed and put a hand to his forehead. "She said you might ask me that."

"Did she tell you not to tell me?"

"I'm afraid she didn't tell me anything, really," he said. "She said that if you asked, I should say that you know why."

I shook my head. "I'm sorry," I said. "I really don't. She never told me, and I was just a child. Maybe I did something, but I can't remember."

He looked pained, like he wasn't sure whether he felt wary or sympathetic.

"I wish I could help you," he said. "You know, she had a journal she carried everywhere."

"I have it."

"She wrote everything down," he said. "I'm sure she wrote something about her decision. Maybe that will give you some clarity. But, um . . ." He hesitated. "Be careful. I am sure she wrote down a good deal about her practices. And I hope you won't be tempted to engage in any of them."

I pretended to be surprised. "Practices?" I said. "Like fortune telling and that sort of thing?"

He laughed in my face.

"That was a good try," he said. "But I know Zarrins too well for that to work on me. You've done something already, haven't you?"

I thought about the vulture. About feeling around in the dark, knowing that somewhere in those teeming slimy guts was a secret. I looked him in the eyes. "I don't know what you're talking about," I said.

He chuckled again and planted his hands on his knees to rise shakily to his feet.

"Well, young Eleanor," he said. "I feel obligated, as a professional courtesy, to remind you that dabbling in witchcraft may be detrimental to your immortal soul."

"Do you think my grandmother lost her soul?"

"Well, no," he said. He smiled, the wrinkles deepening around his eyes. "I don't. But I can't trust myself when it comes to her."

He walked me to the door. On the threshold, I could not resist any longer. I turned to him and said, "I think she's still here. In the house."

He nodded. "That wouldn't surprise me one bit."

"What should I do?"

"There isn't much you can do," he said. "She has to find her own way to heaven. I could never lead her there. I suspect that neither can you."

The day was still clear and bright, but I barely saw it as I trudged up the hill out of town, through the birch forest. I realized I was nervous. I'd done nothing wrong, I told myself. But I hadn't asked Margaret to do the errands, as Grandmere had asked me to.

I was being silly. I'd just say I'd wanted the walk. I'd tell her about talking to the shopkeeper. Everything would be fine. And why was I so afraid? She'd been nothing but kind to me. Still, I'd rather not have that conversation. And so I skulked through the edge of the birch wood and let myself in through the back door, feeling like a fool and a coward and wondering why that didn't make me feel any less worried.

When I slipped into the kitchen, Margaret was waiting for me. She grabbed me by the arm and yanked me along the passageway into the scullery. Through there to the little door that led to the corridor that led to the library. She pointed through the open door.

The room was a mess. Books were strewn everywhere, some piled up, some flung facedown. The box of magic implements, too, was overturned again, spilling its pincushions and film canisters. Nothing was where it should have been; even the chair was upside down. The inkwell had been tipped over onto the desk, and the word LEAVE was spelled out in spilled ink across the blotter.

Margaret pointed at the mess again, and then jerked her hand at me. Was she telling *me* to leave? Asking me to explain myself? I shook my head. Tears sprang to my eyes. None of this made sense. Did Grandma Persephone want me to leave, after she'd given me her book? And how had she torn the room apart like this, when last night she could barely move a box? Was she getting stronger?

I tried to back away, but Margaret caught me by the shoulders. She stared into my eyes as though trying to see something inside me. Her eyes were green, I realized, and more wild than any creature's I'd ever seen. It was worse than staring down Grandpa Miklos.

"Eleanor?" came a voice from upstairs. "Was that you coming in? Where have you been, darling?"

Grandmere. Margaret let go of me, almost flinging me away, and stalked off back down the corridor that led to the scullery. She slammed the door behind her as Grandmere swept down the stairs.

"Ah, my dear," she said. "I was wondering where you got to!"

I was so relieved that I ended up telling her everything. About taking the mail to town, about the shopkeeper, about Father Thomas. She didn't seem concerned until I told her about Margaret, and the library.

"I thought I heard banging from upstairs," she said. "This is why I want you to be able to speak to her. She could have hurt you!"

"You don't think Margaret did this?" It certainly made more sense than Grandma Persephone. And I was afraid of her. But I had a hard time picturing Margaret making a mess.

She sighed. "I do not know," she said. "I am afraid it is possible. She seems suspicious of you. I want you to be careful not to be alone with her for now, my dear."

"I want to clean this up," I said. "I don't like seeing the place like this."

She smiled. "You have such a good heart. I wish that everyone saw it as clearly as me."

She cupped my cheek and kissed me on the forehead.

"I am going to go speak to Margaret," she said. "Thank you for going to town."

As she swept away, I wondered why I had ever been afraid. She was so gentle with me. She'd never hurt me. She loved me more than anyone else ever had. She'd all but said so herself.

Alone in the library, I made piles of the books, smoothing out bent pages before closing them and tucking them back onto their shelves. I was up on a stool putting one back when I heard something fall off the desk. The spilled inkwell. A cold breeze blew against my legs.

"Hello?" I said.

The inkwell, leaving a trail of black ink behind it, had rolled under the desk. I got down on my hands and knees and crawled into the footwell to pick it up. As I did, the breeze came again, and a few little wisps of something lifted off of the carpet. They blew toward my face. I grabbed at one, clambered back from under the desk, held it up to the light.

It was a little plume of black down, a feather of some kind. For a moment I thought it must have come from the inkwell, but it was the wrong kind of feather for a quill: too small, too fine. Black as night all over. Something was wrong here.

What was she telling me? Was this from Margaret, who was always plucking birds? But this couldn't have come from the turkey. The vulture, maybe?

I retreated upstairs, as quietly as I could, with the feather tucked into the palm of my hand. I knew Grandma and Margaret both did divination with bird guts. Maybe I'd find a list of the types of birds they used. Maybe I'd learn something. I locked my door and crawled behind the bed to read.

The journal was a mess: hard to look through, entries written crammed in the margins of older entries. I flipped through it looking for pictures that would give me clues. She drew about half as much as she wrote: pictures of plant anatomy, diagrams of interlocking circles and lines that I couldn't interpret and that made me remember Father Thomas's warning. When I eventually found a page with a bird on it, it was a drawing of a pigeon with its guts arranged on the ground in a bed of pine needles. Beside it in cramped handwriting, it said, *May 11. Got off the train in Ohio. I am close. The man I am supposed to marry is in this town. I will find him by sunset.*

I am afraid.

I flipped through, looking for more birds. There were a few more drawings like this, of patterns of guts. But no black birds. They were as absent from the journal as bells were from our house. I wondered if that was because of Grandpa Miklos and his fear of crows.

"Eleanor?" Grandmere called from downstairs. "Have you finished in the library? It's dinnertime."

"I'm up here," I called. I tucked the feather into the pages of the journal, shoved the book between the mattress and the bed frame, and scrambled for the stairs.

The next few days were a flurry of cooking and cleaning, led by Grandmere, with me as her assistant. The meat from the woods was fine, she said, but people from town wanted vegetables, dinner rolls, casseroles, and desserts with their deer haunch, and they wanted it less bloody. Grandmere stepped into the kitchen herself, evicting Margaret, with me at her side. She showed me how to make puff pastry dough, and how to efficiently chop vegetables. She produced aprons for both of us, although hers never seemed to get dirty.

"I have not cooked in a long time," she said. "I never thought, after the War, that I would ever cook with one of my family again. You have no idea what this means to me."

Through the door to the dining room, I could see Margaret at work taking down the curtains and putting them into a laundry basket. She hadn't come near me since the day before, and when I had tried to come to her, she'd scurried away. I was sure now that she hadn't been the one to overturn the library, although I still had no idea who, or what, had done it. I wished I could speak to her, ask her what she had seen.

"Where have you gone, mon coeur?" Grandmere asked me.

"Sorry," I said. "I was just thinking. So if I had aunts, did I have a grandfather?"

"He has been gone for some time," she said. "Luckily, you still have your Grandpa Miklos. He seems to have been kinder to me recently, as well. Did you have some hand in that?"

I blushed and nodded. "I talked to him about you."

"Good, good!" She was rolling out dough, her gloves put off to the side for once. I noticed that she did not have the same webs between her fingers that I did. Had I gotten mine from my lost grandfather? I didn't dare ask. Grandmere got so sad when I talked about the past.

"I've been wondering how to invite Arthur," I said. "I don't have an address for him. And we don't have a telephone."

Grandmere raised her eyebrows. "I will ask Margaret," she said. "Unless you are feeling ready to . . ."

"No," I said. "No, that's fine."

The groceries were delivered, along with several bottles of wine. Grandmere poured us little glasses and we tasted them, with water in between. She asked me what I liked. She lamented that we wouldn't have the record player in time to put it on for the party.

In the afternoon, she took a nap, and I snuck back upstairs to read more of the journal. The page I had bookmarked had been calling to me since I had left it.

Grandma Persephone's entries were sparse. The one that followed *I am afraid* just read *We have been married.* The one after that was a list of household items she planned to buy, and so on. The day after that, she wrote, *When I was on the hill of serpents they told me I would take a demon lover, and that our love would consume my life. I am not in love with this beast. He is shorter than I am, he is a brute, and he is afraid of me like everyone else. I woke up last night and he was gone.*

And then, a line down: *I woke up this morning and he was sleeping across my feet in the bed. His mouth and the sheets were covered in blood. The air was full of black feathers. When he woke up I asked him why he had killed so many crows. He told me, because they remind me of her. Because you remind me of her, but you are not her, and I do not want to kill you. I think this man will murder me someday. And I cannot bring myself to leave his side.*

I shut the book. Grandma Persephone had gone by train to meet my grandfather. She'd been afraid—terrified that he would kill her, angry that he seemed to think she was the dangerous one. It felt so familiar. I liked the girl she'd been a lot more than I liked her. How had she gone from one to the other? I kept reading, hoping for more glimpses into her life. But the next several pages were all recipes and scribbled lists, names and addresses and ailments. The scared girl was gone, and the witch was back. And I still was no closer to understanding anything.

At last, the evening came, and so did the Hannafins. They'd brought a car, along with a skinny girl who I didn't recognize at first. Luma and I watched them from the window.

"Who's that?" I asked.

"Oh, Jane Hannafin," Luma said. "I bit off one of her toes when we were younger."

I stared, aghast. "Why?"

"She said she didn't think I could do it," she said. And sure enough, the girl looked around nervously as they got out of the car, taking little steps, like she was scrunching her feet up inside her shoes.

"Why'd they bring her?" I asked, mostly to myself.

"Maybe she wants me to even them out. Do the other side."

"Don't say that in front of her."

"Why not?"

I gave her my best stern look. She, as usual, looked perfect. I'd spent the afternoon fussing over my one good dress, trying to put my hair up on my own. I didn't trust Luma not to ruin it if she knew I wanted to look nice. I was starting to think she was onto me.

"I'm going to go check on the food," I said. Luma didn't look up from her vanity. She was smudging pink powder onto her cheeks, frowning at her own reflection. I slipped out of her room and down the stairs.

In the front hall, Grandmere was ushering the Hannafins inside. They looked up at the cavernous darkness all around them, at the wall of portraits, at the pile of briefcases by the door. And then Grandmere said something softly to them, and they relaxed, and I did, too. She waved them past her into the parlor, and then beckoned to someone in the doorway of the dining room across the way. After a moment, Margaret stepped from the shadows. Grandmere said something to her and then swept off to join the Hannafins in the parlor.

I hung back from the railing a little as Margaret scuttled across the hall below. She stopped in front of the black front door and knocked on the inside of it: *one, two, three*. And then she stood and waited. I didn't move, or even breathe, although I didn't know why.

A full minute passed. Just when I was feeling stupid and trying to convince myself to start moving again, an answering knock came from outside. *One, two, three*. Margaret opened the door, and Arthur stepped in.

He was wearing a new-looking suit, a shirt that was clean and freshly pressed. He nodded to Margaret, who scurried away. And then he tipped his head back. With his eyes covered, it was hard to be sure, but it felt as though he was looking right at me.

I forced myself into movement, as though I'd only stopped at the top for a moment. He looked almost translucent in a way that made me think of the pages of books, how they sometimes glowed with lamplight when you turned them.

"Good evening," he said as I swept down the stairs, holding my skirt back, the way Grandmere had showed me. "You look lovely."

I thrilled a little. But I couldn't quite forget what I'd just seen. "Were you waiting outside?" I asked.

He smiled at me but gave his head a tight little shake. "So many questions."

"If you get here early, you can always just come in," I said. "You're like family."

His grin was wide, and again, I got the impression of light, flickering from some unseen source. His lips closed, and it was instantly doused. He offered me his arm.

"Let's go in," he said.

I took his arm as Luma emerged from her bedroom upstairs. We both glanced up at the same time. Whatever she'd done since I left, she was radiant in a white dress, her white hair gleaming gold where the lamplight hit it. As she stepped off the last stair, she stretched out her hand to him.

"You have to walk *me* in!" she said, laughing.

With the crook of his elbow, Arthur gave my arm a tiny squeeze. But then he extricated himself from me and took Luma by the hand. "If you insist," he said, smiling.

"I do," she said, and giggling, caught him around the waist and walked with him into the parlor.

From behind me in the hallway, I heard a soft growl. Rhys stood in the shadows on the far side of the stairs, his eyes following the two of them into the parlor.

"Shush," I said. "We are going to have a nice evening." But I heard the sharpness in my own voice as I spoke, my own little bit of growl.

"I don't like it," he said. "Ellie, why are we doing this?"

"We're trying to help Grandmere feel at home. And we need to keep the people of Winterport happy. I don't know if Grandma Persephone ever told you this, but a lot of what she did was make sure they didn't turn on us."

He looked horrified. "Really? Why?"

I sighed. Sometimes I wanted to strangle him.

"Because we're strange and dangerous," I said. "So please, if you can, try not to be too strange and dangerous tonight? Please?"

He sighed. "Okay," he said. "I'll try."

I offered him my arm, the way Arthur had done, and he linked up, and for a moment I remembered us playing together as children. He'd been bigger than me, but he'd been gentler, then. Always willing to do what I thought sounded fun, even if he didn't like it. I remembered us breaking my dollhouse one afternoon by stacking heavier and heavier things on it, the glorious moment when the roof finally buckled and crushed the dolls under a cascade of knickknacks. I smiled up at him, and he grinned back at me. He was almost a brother.

When we got to the parlor, Mrs. Hannafin was in the middle of a long story of some kind about how her father had worked on building this house.

"More money than he'd ever made before or after," she said. "How much did the whole house cost, do you know?"

"About a hundred thousand, if I recall," Arthur said. He was sitting in the armchair by the chessboard. Luma perched on his knee. Jane, the Hannafins, and I all couldn't look directly at him. Beside me, I felt Rhys's whole body go taut, like he was pulling on a leash. I gave his foot a little kick with my toe.

"And lots of disappearances around this house," Mr. Hannafin said. "My ma used to tell me about a schoolteacher disappeared here in 'eleven. She used to tell me, 'Now, George, don't ever take money to go up to that house'—"

"*Let's talk about more pleasant things,*" Grandmere said.

Mrs. Hannafin tilted her head to one side. "My," she said, pointing to a picture on the wall. "Is that an Impressionist?"

We chatted along for a while, mostly Grandmere and the Hannafins. Jane sat jammed into a chair in the corner farthest from Luma, her feet tucked up under the chair as far as they would go, silent and sullen. She had little horn-rimmed glasses and a sour expression. Grandmere kept trying to get Rhys to go talk to her, but he stayed close to me, silent and wary. I could hear his heart pounding in his chest. What about this was so frightening to him? Was it just watching Luma petting Arthur?

At last, Grandmere said, "Ah, I think dinner is ready. Shall we go to the dining room? *Rhys, please escort Miss Jane.*"

Jane stood and let Rhys take her by the arm. Grandmere hung back, and I stayed with her.

"Isn't she fetching?" she asked, tipping her chin after Jane.

I flushed. "She seems alright," I said. I hadn't expected the Hannafins to come up in our conversation, or to be asked to evaluate the quality of a girl. The question made me nervous, like I'd done something wrong.

"For Rhys, I mean!" Grandmere said.

"I don't know. Rhys seems . . ." I hesitated, not wanting to tell Grandmere what I knew. "Fine on his own."

She sighed.

"I want to take you into my confidence," she said. "He is not showing a proper interest in girls for his age. A young man from such a fine family should have prospects." Prospects, I thought. It sounded like such an old-fashioned term, something from one of Luma's books. "She has a certain something that I think he might like. She almost looks like a boy."

Oh, no. She knew about Rhys. As long as she didn't say it, though, I didn't have to deny it. She frowned and studied my face. I made sure that it was blank, perplexed.

"You mean to tell me you haven't noticed?" she asked.

"Noticed what?" I already knew, of course.

"That Rhys is a little strange," she said. "I see you look shocked. You're too well-behaved to think about such things, I know, but you should not be naive about this, Eleanor. It draws unwanted attention. And it is only a matter of time before he does something unspeakable."

I was angry, but also confused. I hadn't liked that weird violent grin I'd seen on Rhys's face, the night he fell out of the wall. But I didn't like the way she talked about him, either. As though it would be evil of me to even have noticed how he was around Arthur. As though there were something poisonous about the very idea.

She must have seen the look on my face, because she said, "This is too much for right now, I see. We can talk about it later. Shall we go eat?"

When we got to the dining room, Mother was already there in a long veil, and Grandpa Miklos was slumped at the head of the table, Father at the foot with a half-full glass of brandy in front of him.

"I am so glad we could all be here tonight," said Grandmere, settling into her place at the table. She picked up a small silver bell beside her wineglass, lifted it, and rang it, and Margaret came in, bearing a tray.

I watched Miklos's face as Margaret set down trays on the table and ferried choice dishes from the kitchen to the buffet and from the buffet to our places. He was as rigid as he had been the night that the bells rang in town, but he didn't bolt from the table. He sat there as though he'd been glued into his chair. I wondered what he was thinking.

"Since we have company," Grandmere said, "*let's all eat politely tonight.*"

I was beginning to recognize that tone of voice; it was like the one I had used on the shopkeeper. Grandmere had already used it a few times this evening, I realized. That thought made me uneasy, especially as the family began to eat. My father's hand went to his fork, and he picked it up, staring at it strangely as he did. He took up a bite of a salad laden with cucumbers and ate it off of the end of his fork with great curiosity. He looked like someone having a difficult thought for the first time.

Luma was the only one who seemed unaffected. She picked through her salad with her hands, eating the cucumber slices by tossing them into the air and catching them in her mouth. Grandmere squinted at her, perplexed. Father emptied his glass of brandy quickly. Mother kept pressing a damp handkerchief against her cheek, hiding it in her lap when Grandmere glanced at her.

It seemed wrong to me, but dinner was certainly pleasant. Mrs. Hannafin gossiped about people in town, and Grandmere egged her on until the stories became increasingly wild: affairs, fistfights in front of gravestones, unpaid debts. I began encouraging her, too, teasing out details, thinking it would be useful to know these secrets if I was going to keep our own safe.

And the Hannafins seemed to like us. At one point, Mr. Hannafin even clapped a red and chapped hand on my father's shoulder. Surely, none of that would have happened if Grandmere hadn't insisted we eat politely. The difference was obvious in Luma's case. The older Hannafins wouldn't look at her, and Jane kept casting sideways glances at her as though she expected to be eaten right up. I imagined her scuffing her foot under the table, her sock rubbing up against the stump of the toe Luma had bitten off.

Grandmere got increasingly annoyed as Luma continued to slosh her wine and lean her weight on Arthur's shoulder. When Margaret brought out a meat pie and cut slices, and Luma made to pick hers up with her hands, Grandmere finally said, "*Luma, control yourself!*"

Luma contorted her face into a hideous scowl. She reached over and dug her hands directly into the pie, and stuffed handfuls of it into her mouth. Juices streamed down her face as she chewed with her mouth wide open.

"Miles, *take her away from the table,*" Grandmere said. Father stood up and wordlessly put a hand on Luma's shoulder.

"Come on," he said. "Let's go."

She tilted her head back to look at him. Whatever she saw in his face, she stood up, and followed him out of the room. Father came back after a few minutes and sat down, flushed, and poured himself a glass of wine.

"Miles?" Mother said. "So much?"

His face got rigid, and he took a long sip.

Rhys got up from the table. "I'm going outside," he said.

"Miklos," Grandmere said, "*You can be excused, too.*"

Grandpa Miklos stood up, looking like he'd woken from a dream. He shuffled out of the room after Rhys. As the kitchen door swung behind them, I saw flashes of dark fur, and then the back door slammed.

"*Please forgive them,*" Grandmere said. "They have had a difficult time since Persephone passed."

The Hannafins nodded. "Of course," Mr. Hannafin said.

"Understandable," said Mrs. Hannafin. They looked at one another uneasily, but then turned back to us and smiled. "A wonderful evening," she added.

I glanced at Arthur. He looked blandly back at me. I smiled back, hoping the Hannafins didn't notice that my hands were shaking. None of this felt right.

When dinner was done and Margaret had laid out Arthur's coffee, I glanced at Grandmere, and mouthed, "Can I talk to you?" She shook her head and raised her eyebrows toward our guests. She didn't want to leave them unattended. That made some sense. But I didn't like the way the Hannafins had looked after they'd so quickly forgiven Luma.

Father poured himself more wine, and the company moved from the dining room across the hall to the parlor. "Shall we play some music, Eleanor?" Arthur asked. He seemed unfazed by any of it, as though this were his usual evening. I supposed in some ways it was.

"What a lovely suggestion!" Grandmere said.

We sat down at the bench together. Outside, Luma was howling in the night, but in here, Arthur had asked me to play piano with him. I suddenly remembered being younger, sitting with him at the bench.

And then suddenly I felt a cold hand on my back, and for a second I was transported.

It felt like the dream I'd had, the dream of being Grandma Persephone, except that I was awake. Dimly, I felt my body sitting at the piano, but I was in another time, another body, even. I was standing in the doorway of the parlor, watching Arthur teach young Eleanor how to play piano.

He looked exactly as he did now, not a day younger. His thin hands moved on the keys. Little Eleanor was kneeling on the bench to be tall enough to reach the keys. She had a look of fierce concentration on her face as she hit wrong note after wrong note.

"Maybe that's enough for today," Arthur said quietly.

Her head whipped around, making her short white hair bounce. "I'm not done yet," she said. "*Keep teaching me.*"

"Arthur!" I said. Or rather, I felt myself say it, but it wasn't my voice: it was Persephone's. "What are you doing?"

He regarded me coolly. Little Eleanor turned toward me.

"I told him to teach me," she said. "I'm good at it already. Listen."

"Eleanor, go play outside. I mean it."

She scrambled down off the bench, glowering at me. "When I'm the grandma, you won't be able to tell me what to do," she said.

"Well, it's a good thing that day hasn't come yet."

She ran past me, disappearing.

"I'll never understand why they like you," I felt myself say. But of course, it was not me, it was Grandma Persephone.

Arthur smiled tightly. "Perhaps they get it from their grandfather."

And all at once, I was back in the parlor. Grandmere was looking at me strangely.

"Are you alright?" she asked.

"I'm fine," I said. "Just a strange feeling."

And then I glanced at Arthur. I knew at once that he'd felt it, too. I gave him a quick little nod. We opened the book of sheet music and picked out a song.

We played beautifully together: he compensated well for my narrow span, and added little flourishes, and sang a slightly flat accompaniment. I felt a sense of loss. Could we have been doing this before, without Grandmere here? Could we have been doing this from the first night I arrived in the house, if I hadn't felt so small and shabby and unworthy, if I hadn't shoved

Luma in front of him? If I'd only just asked instead of telling? A few times I met my own eyes in his smoked lenses, and I quickly looked away.

It was in the middle of our second song that Rhys came banging in through the front door. He was disheveled from the forest, shirtless, twigs in his hair and scratches on his face and chest. I leaped to my feet, not sure whether to help him or block his way into the parlor. He was looking past me, to Arthur, who was also rising to his feet. I wasn't sure what he was going to do next, and maybe, neither was he.

"Rhys," I said. "What's wrong?"

I saw a flicker of movement from out in the hall. Luma was watching from the staircase landing. She had wolf eyes, and they caught the light and reflected back two perfect green discs. In that dim light I could see her long teeth bared. They'd chased each other in here, and now he was cornered. I sighed and stood up to calm him down. But Grandmere was already rising from her chair to meet Rhys.

"*You will stop this at once,*" she said, and midstride, he froze, his hands dropping to his sides. "*Go to your room and stay there,*" she said to Rhys.

And then he went. He walked mechanically up the stairs, past Luma, whose wild eyes bored into mine from the darkness. And then she slipped away into the shadows, and I lost sight of her.

The Hannafins had stood up and were moving toward the

hall, gathering coats and hats, mumbling about what a nice time they'd all had. Grandmere was slumped back into her chair. She seemed tired, I thought; maybe making Rhys do something so against his nature had worn her out. Father poured himself another glass of wine. Mother looked so faint on the settee that I thought she might lose consciousness. So with no one else to do it, I walked the Hannafins to the front door. Arthur followed a little behind me. When they'd gone, I turned to him.

"You felt that, too," I said.

He started to nod, but his head froze on his neck. At last, he shook it free.

"Persephone did something to you," I said. "You don't have to say anything."

He scowled. "You shouldn't assume you know what's going on," he said.

"Don't be cruel."

As soon as I said it, I regretted it. His face all at once became neutral.

"Alright," he said. "Good night, Eleanor. It's been a pleasure."

He slipped out into the night.

I wanted a moment to myself to parse what I'd seen: Margaret, knocking on the door. The cold hand on my back. The vision I'd had earlier that night. But Grandmere was beckoning me languidly from the parlor, so I went.

"I think that went well," she said. "But your cousin . . . he continues to behave quite badly." I raised an eyebrow, waiting for her to go on. "None of this is your fault, of course. Your father, or your grandfather, should have said something to him by now—explained to him how a young man must behave. But of course, they baby him because he is their beloved heir."

That much was true; Rhys *was* babied. He did get away with everything. I hated that, and I always had. But I thought about that night he'd fallen out of the closet in the hall. The bruises on his neck. The look of wounded joy on his face, like he was about to sink his teeth into something wonderful. I thought for a moment of Lucy Spencer, and my whole body filled up with shame. After all, I'd gotten away with something, too.

Still. I didn't want him around Arthur. He could find someone else to . . .

"What if we sent him abroad for the summer?" I asked. "Send him to Europe?"

She scoffed.

"I doubt he could manage that," she said. "Outside of our protection I'm sure trouble would find him."

"He's not exactly vulnerable."

"He is young and impulsive. He might hurt someone. He might get arrested. And if that happens we won't be able to protect him, not without revealing ourselves. No, we should find him someone to marry. Someone trustworthy, who can keep him out of trouble. I would like this town to like us, not merely tolerate us. I think the Hannafin girl might help with that."

"I don't know," I said. "She seems a little frail. What if he hurts her? Grandmere, do you know anyone who's like us?"

She looked at me quizzically, as though she didn't quite understand.

"Oh," she said at last. "You mean, like them. You know, I think I might—let me write to some, and see if there are any eligible ladies who might visit. And maybe I can find someone for Luma, while we are looking for Rhys." She stroked my cheek. "I'm sorry, my darling. I thought you meant like you and me." Her hand lingered on my face. "And there is no one else like us in the whole world."

"I'm tired," I said.

"Of course you are, my dear," she said. "Why don't you go get some sleep?"

I nodded and stumbled up the stairs. Rhys was pacing in his room down the hall, stomping around, slamming against the walls. I tried to ignore him, but the sound carried all the way to my room, so at last I got out of bed and flung his door open. He was gnawing on one of his bedposts and looked up abruptly at me.

"What are you doing?" I asked. "Why are you making such a racket?"

"I can't leave," he said. He ran toward me, and then doubled back and ran toward the opposite wall. "I can't leave. I can't leave."

"Oh, calm down," I said. "You can."

He looked up at me hopefully, and then ran toward the open

doorway, but then doubled back again. "I can't!" he said, and slammed his fists into the wall opposite.

"Why are you doing this?" I asked. "If you're going to be so noisy, *go outside*. Grandmere is sleeping."

He walked toward the door and stepped through it. And then he looked at me, confused.

"I can leave," he said. "I'm going outside."

"Yes? Just go!"

He took off down the stairs and disappeared around the corner. The kitchen door slammed open, then shut.

It was a week later when the first suitor arrived.

We'd had a quiet week at the house. Arthur hadn't been back. In his absence, I'd fallen into a routine: a late breakfast with Grandmere, some chatting in the parlor, tending to the plants in the afternoon, trying to parse the journal while Grandmere napped, whenever she napped. Then dinner with the family: Luma wasn't speaking to me, and Father was drinking more than he used to. I tried my best to make good conversation, to invite people to play chess or sing with me in the parlor. Some days were better than others.

And then, at night, I dreamed about being Persephone.

It had started on that first night after she died, when I'd dreamed about walking uphill through that unfamiliar town under that bright blue sky. Every few nights, it happened again.

Sometimes the visions were only flashes: I was crushing herbs with a mortar and pestle, or squeezing a cheesecloth while acid-green fluid wept from it, staining my leather gloves. At other times, the dreams were more detailed: whole afternoons or days. The strangest, so far, had been a long argument with Grandpa Miklos, where I insisted that he not tell the children about—something, it was difficult to understand exactly what. That dream was what had woken me up early on that particular morning, leaving me feeling unsettled and unable to go back to sleep. Maybe, I thought, it had something to do with why Grandma Persephone had sent me away. So I took the journal from my bedside table and carried it down to the greenhouse.

The drakondia were recovering. Their leaves had gone from yellow to deep green, and some of them had new, tight buds at the ends of their long stems. I sang at them as I passed—*Tell me with a laugh, tell me with a cry, that you do not love me, what care I?*—and felt them bob and sway behind me while I sat down with Grandma Persephone's journal.

I was trying to find any reference to myself, but everything was out of order. The first few pages were clearly written by someone else, someone with immaculate Italian and a number of detailed drawings of local ruins. Then followed several in a large, childish hand that got smaller and smaller until Grandma Persephone's distinct handwriting emerged like a moth from a chrysalis. Then, when she'd reached the end of the book she had clearly started back at the beginning, filling in any available space on earlier pages with entries wherever they'd fit, in tiny penmanship. So next to a childhood drawing of a goat I found her note *Lusitania born June 3,* with no year listed, just some details about inducing afterbirth.

I tried to skim, looking for any notes about me. But the main text kept catching my eye. Here she was, running from a mob of villagers after she stabbed a boy in the gut, although she didn't say why. Here she was waking up in a stone circle in a bobbing sea of snake lilies that had grown while she slept. And here, fleeing to America on a ship, and an inventory of what she'd brought with her. It was covered in little pencil ticks, as though every day she had emptied out her bag, noted that everything was present, and stuffed it all back in.

I wished I could talk to her about this. I'd never thought much about what her life was like when she was young. To me she had always been old, and then those years had gone by when I hadn't thought much about her at all.

And she hadn't been making her presence known, not since the *leave* written on her desk in spilled ink. Every night I got frightened, expecting her to fling things around my room. But her silence was its own kind of frightening.

I glanced back down at the page and saw a note in the margin that caught my eye, mostly because the page was dog-eared, and the little point of the page pointed right to it:

To summon: three knocks on the door.
To admonish: three knocks on the floor.
To banish: three knocks on the wall.

I stared at that for a long time, chewing on my nails. Margaret had knocked on the door, and a minute later, Arthur arrived. As if he'd been called.

I'd come to think of Persephone's witchcraft as a pretty tame thing, even the grotesque parts that involved rummaging around in dead things, feeling their guts. Asking questions about the future and brewing little potions out of flowers seemed innocent enough. This looked simple in a way that felt ruthless. This felt like evil.

It was bright and hot in the greenhouse, too hot to think about these things. I put the book away upstairs, in the drawer of the bedside table with the tarot cards, and decided it was time for a swim.

I left through the door at the back of the greenhouse and went down the wooden steps that led to the ocean. I undressed and threw myself into the water. All at once I felt blissful. The plants were recovering. In a week there would be new flowers and I could extract the nectar and distill it in the kitchen. I let the current sway me back and forth, losing all sense of time or space.

I was swimming facedown when Rhys came tearing down the wooden stairs. He reached the water and splashed in up to his knees to call out to me. I felt the splashing before I heard him, and popped my head up.

"What's going on?" I yelled to him.

"Someone's here!" His face was streaked with something; at first I thought it was tears, but when I got closer I realized it was just a bit of dried blood. I treaded water and kept myself submerged up to my neck. Rhys didn't seem to be looking at me, though; he was staring out across the water.

"Who is it?" I asked.

"I've never seen her before," he said. "But she's talking to *her*." He growled and started pacing. It's hard to pace in water; he looked so stupid that I started laughing.

"Stop it!" He lashed out at me, but I ducked underwater and swam easily away from him. He tried to follow me but fell off the edge of the sandbar and was suddenly forced to paddle. He scowled at me across the water.

"Why are you like this now?" he asked. "We used to be friends."

"No," I said. "*You* used to be able to bully me."

"I mean when we were little."

"Well, I don't remember that."

He gave me a withering look and began paddling for shallower water. I watched him stalk out, shaking himself dry. I thought about chasing after him, but it wasn't really my business if it upset him. However, I grew curious. Who had come to the house? I waded ashore, put my clothes on, and went to have a look for myself.

I peeked in through the front parlor windows and saw them all frozen in a tableau: Grandmere, standing with her hand on the arm of a young woman. The girl had auburn hair piled high on her head and wore an attractive blue dress. She laughed, flashing a mouthful of tiny pointed teeth, like a piranha's, arranged in a double row.

Grandmere had come through on her promise of a suitor for Rhys. She'd found him someone like us.

I was surprised, despite my talk with Grandmere. Before then, I hadn't realized there were other things like us, ones who weren't already related. I wanted to ask her questions. Where had she come from? How did Grandmere find her? But I couldn't imagine asking those kinds of things in front of Grandmere.

"I never smelled her," Rhys said.

I jumped. Rhys was beside me, squinting in through the window, still damp. I'd forgotten how quiet he could be.

"What do you mean?" I asked.

"She was just here. All of a sudden." He stood beside me with his hands on the sill, a low growl building in his throat.

"Calm down," I said. "It's just a guest. I think she's here to see you."

"Why?"

"So you can meet someone," I said.

He shook his head.

"I don't want to see anyone," he said. "I'm already in love."

It was shocking to me to hear him say it like that; I laughed a little in surprise. He turned on me, his jaw popping a little as his other teeth came in.

"Don't you laugh at me," he said. "You don't know what I feel."

"Rhys," I said. "Listen to me. This can't go on."

"Why not?"

"Because he doesn't love you!" I said. "He's with Luma." I felt my throat close up when I said it, and I forced myself to keep going. "And anyway, it's not for you. You're not some—I mean, look at you!"

"You don't understand," he said. "You'd never understand."

I felt my hands ball up into fists.

"You're right," I said. "I don't understand why you're so selfish. It's not enough that everyone fawns over you and does whatever you say? So you have to come up with new things to want because getting everything is just so *boring*, isn't it?"

He swiped at me, claws out, and I felt them brush past my face. Then he slammed his way up the porch steps and flung open the front door. I followed him, not really sure what he was going to do. He stormed into the parlor where Grandmere sat sipping tea with the girl.

"I'm never going to see any woman you bring here," he said to Grandmere. "So don't invite any more. I've made up my mind."

And all at once, as Grandma Persephone had predicted, my eyes adjusted, and I saw Rhys differently. His chest was heaving, his jaw set fiercely against Grandmere. He looked heroic.

I felt suddenly shabby and ashamed, embarrassed that I hadn't seen how serious he was. He might be a dangerous grinning animal, but he really was in love. He was willing to stake everything on that. When had I ever been that brave?

I glanced at the red-haired girl in the chair. The teacup in her hand had paused midway to her mouth. She hadn't lost her smile, though. It hovered around her face, exactly as natural and bright and sharp as it had been a second before.

Grandmere stared at Rhys coolly.

"*Stop what you're doing*," she said to him.

Midstride, he froze, his hands dropping to his sides. He looked around wildly, and found me.

"Eleanor," he said. "Do that thing you did. Let me go."

"What?" I said.

Grandmere didn't even glance sideways. "*Go to your room and stay there*," she said to Rhys. He turned and started walking out. "Eleanor," he yelled. "Eleanor, help me! Help me, Eleanor—"

"*Shut up*," I said, and then clapped my hands over my mouth. But it was done.

"I'm so sorry," Grandmere said to the young woman, glancing at me as she did. "I had no idea he would behave so shamefully."

The woman turned to her, and then to me.

"It's no problem," she said. "I like an honest man. We can catch up and then I will see myself out."

"He is a fool," Grandmere said. "Eleanor, would you go to my room and wait for me while I say good-bye to our guest? And then I want to talk to you about some things."

I nodded. Upstairs, I sat down on the bed, wondering what I could possibly say about any of this when Grandmere inevitably asked me.

It was strange, I thought, Rhys walking out of the room like that. He didn't *walk* anywhere, generally. He strode, or he stormed, banging open doors, bolting down hallways. His walk just now had been calm, almost mechanical.

After a few minutes, Grandmere swept in and sank onto the bed. She looked exhausted.

"Are you alright?" I asked.

"It's so hard to keep things running smoothly," she said. "Especially with your cousin. He is difficult. And Luma won't listen to me at all. I really need help from you, Eleanor. I need you to take charge more. I'm not as young as I once was."

"I know," I said. "I'm so sorry."

"It's not your fault. I just can't believe the way he treated that poor girl."

"Who was she?" I asked.

She paused and looked at me strangely.

"It is no matter," she said. "After the way he behaved, she will never return to this house."

I wanted to ask more, but she seemed devastated.

"Grandmere," I said, "forget Rhys. He's too stubborn. Why don't we start by finding someone for Luma?"

"So you can have your Arthur, of course. I see." She sighed and rubbed her temples. "I have a headache, child. I'm going to go make myself some tea."

"Do you want me to get it?" I asked.

"No," she said. "But do you know how you can help me? *Do not let Rhys out of his room again.* I know you meant well, but it's for his own good."

She patted me on the hand and glided away, out the door and down the stairs.

What a strange, nonsensical day it had been. I wished Grand-mere would talk about it. Maybe I should try reading the cards, I thought. Maybe I could make some sense of it.

At the door to my room, I paused. It was open just a crack, when I was sure I'd left it shut. I slid inside and felt so uneasy that I ducked down to check under the bed. Nothing was quite right: my wardrobe was open, my bed hastily remade, but without the hospital corners I'd learned at Saint Brigid's. Someone had been in here. Someone had gone through my things while I was out.

I knew before I looked that the journal was gone. And so were the tarot cards.

At first, I felt a chill, fragile calm. I must just not have looked properly. I glanced around the floor, anywhere they might have fallen by chance. I checked between the mattress and the bed frame, under the pillows, behind the broken dollhouse, and in every other corner I could think of. Nothing. A bubble of panic started forming in my throat.

Margaret could have done this. I shut my eyes and listened, the way Grandmere had taught me. Margaret was downstairs in the scullery, washing clothes. Why had she opened up the vulture, if not to look for the cards? And she had never liked me. She'd called me a traitor.

I started down the hall, but as I passed Luma's room, her door opened and her hand shot out. She grabbed me by the wrist and pulled me inside.

"What's going on?" I asked.

"We need to talk to you."

I looked around. It took me a moment to spot Grandpa Miklos. He was under the bed, wrapped in Luma's comforter. There was a leaf stuck in his hair.

"Shut the door," Luma said. "And be quiet. Grandpa has something he needs you to hear."

"What, that he thinks Grandmere is here to kill him?"

Luma glowered. "You knew about this?"

"I told her," Grandpa Miklos said. "This is why I came to America."

"He's confused!" I said. "He's got Grandmere mixed up with something else. Something that happened to him a long time ago. It happened to him the night of Grandma Persephone's funeral, too—he thought the bells in town were the church bells back in the old country."

I looked at Luma as though to say, "See?" She rolled her eyes at me and turned to Grandpa.

"What is she?" Luma asked. "Not a wolf, like us? She doesn't smell like us."

He shook his head no.

"Grandpa," Luma said, "why don't you tell us what happened?"

Grandpa Miklos looked reluctant.

"Your grandma, she didn't like that story," he said. "She said it was in the past. She said not to tell the kids."

I could tell Luma thought I'd been hiding something from her. I hadn't, though, not really. I had to turn this around. Figure out what Grandpa was talking about. Not that I thought it was Grandmere. Just . . .

"Before she died, Grandma said I was supposed to take care of things," I said. "You remember me telling you that?"

Miklos nodded.

"So tell me what you saw," I said.

"You will believe me?" he said. "Do you promise?"

Luma glared at me until I said, "Alright, I promise."

Miklos sighed.

"When I was young, I lived in a silent country," he said. "We were afraid of a thing that lived in a castle near us, but we did not have words for that. All we had were the bells, to tell us when to run from the crows."

He told us about the day that he had run, the day he had been late. I sat paralyzed, terrified that he would become the wolf, that he would attack me out of fear. But Luma stroked his hand, and held him by the shoulder, and kept her eyes on him while he told us about being picked up by the crows and carried away. They tore at his clothes and his hair, flinging him between them to keep him airborne, while he remained terrified that at any moment they would drop him and he would die.

"They carried me away, over the fields," he said. "Over a forest so thick I could not see the ground. In the middle of that forest was a ruined castle. They flew with me through a hole in the roof, and dropped me. And then, all the birds flew backward."

"Backward?" I asked.

"Backward," he said. "Into the mouth of an old woman."

He stopped speaking and gazed at me solemnly, as though I should understand exactly what that meant.

"I don't understand what this has to do with Grandmere," I said.

"It was her," he said. "She told me to stand still, and I couldn't move. And then she opened up her mouth so wide, and inside it wasn't a mouth, it was a deep hole." He closed his eyes. I realized he was breathing hard, straining with the difficulty of describing. "She tried to swallow me. That was when I turned inside out. That was when I became the wolf the first time. The wolf could move when I could not. I ripped her in half, and she fell apart. And then"—he paused—"and then I left." He seemed surprised to have come to the end of his tale so easily. "I have told no one that but your grandmother in my whole life."

I tried to imagine that, a mouth like a deep hole. My jaw ached.

"Did she turn you into the wolf?" I asked.

He shook his head.

"I found the wolf," he said. "I went deep in me and found a way out."

I sat with that for a long time. I thought of every person I had met, wondering how many of them had wolves inside them and just had never pulled them out. Or perhaps more horrible: how many of them, in a moment of fear, reached inside themselves for something to save them, and came up empty.

"But Grandpa," I said, when I could shake the thought, "how could Grandmere be the same woman? That was a long time ago. And you killed her!"

"No," he said. "All I did was rip her in half."

"But she was old," I insisted. "You were a child then. Grandmere's old now."

He and Luma exchanged a look. Did they think I was stupid?

"Grandpa," I said calmly, "do you remember the night when the bells rang in town?" He nodded. "Do you remember how confused you got? How you thought they were the bells of your church in the old country?" He nodded again but more warily.

"What are you getting at?" Luma asked.

"I think you're confused now," I said. "I think that you're

very upset about Grandma Persephone, and it's bringing up old memories. You thought the church bells were the same as when you were young. And an old woman came to stay with us and you think she's the same old woman from when you were young." I felt like I'd solved a mystery; I felt almost giddy. "Don't you see? You're getting things mixed up."

"I believe him," Luma said. "I think we should get rid of her."

"Get rid of her?" I said. "Aunt Lusitania wanted you and Rhys to get rid of me. Is that what you think we should do with our grandmother?"

"Calm down," she said. "It's not the same. You're one of us."

"It doesn't always feel that way. Grandpa, you promised to leave this alone."

"You made me promise," he said.

Luma froze.

"You can't do that to him," she said.

"Can't do what?"

"Make people do things," she said. "You promised me you'd stop when we were little."

I felt suddenly very cold and grew very still, the way you might on a warm day when the wind sweeps a cloud in front of the sun. I wanted to tell her she was making things up, that I couldn't remember promising, but it felt familiar: I couldn't remember, but I could almost feel the place where the memory had been.

"I didn't mean to do anything," I said. "I don't know if I did anything at all."

"You have to fix it," Luma said. "Tell Grandpa he can do what he wants."

I looked at my grandpa, half under Luma's bed. His hair was sticking up at an odd angle where Luma had mussed it with her hand. He seemed young, looking up at me like that.

"Grandpa," I said. "You can do what you want. *You don't have to keep your promise to me.*" I turned to Luma. "There, are you—"

He shot past me, out from under the bed, and leaped up at the door. He grabbed Luma's dressing gown from the back of the door and ran down the steps and into the front hall. I followed after, stunned, with Luma right behind me. We reached the bottom of the stairs and I ran to the side table to get the candy dish. If things went badly, I wanted to have something heavy in my hands.

Grandmere was coming around the corner from the kitchen, holding a teacup. Grandpa Miklos planted himself in front of her.

"You get out of my house," he said. "Get out of my house!"

"Miklos," Grandmere said. "Surely, *we can*—"

I felt time slow as he leaped at her, changing into a wolf in midair. He was going to kill her.

"Grandpa!" I yelled. "*Stop that right now!*"

He twisted violently in the air, as though his back had been wrenched, and hit the floor at a bad angle. He scrambled to a four-legged stand, and looked at me, and looked at her.

"Now," Grandmere said. "Miklos, *I insist*—"

He bolted directly at me, and I screamed, drowning out Grandmere's words. As he came toward me, I thought dimly that I was not a Zarrin, because a real Zarrin would have fought tooth and nail, or at least hit him with the dish. And I just stood and let him rush me, shut my eyes against my impending death as his paws struck me in the chest hard enough to knock me to the floor.

He bolted down the hall into the kitchen, and I heard Margaret fling the back door open wide for him. And then he was gone.

My vision was red around the edges. I realized I couldn't breathe. Panicking, I gasped a few times. Slowly, the air came back into my lungs. I lay there on the hall carpet for a moment, stunned, staring up into the gloom. The chandelier was missing a strand of crystals. Strange.

Grandmere rushed to my side. She stooped and felt my cheeks, and touched my shoulders and hands.

"Can you feel this?" she asked. I nodded. "Are you hurt? Can you move your toes?"

"Yes," I said, or tried to. I coughed. "Yes, I'm fine."

She helped me sit up. My head hurt, and I was dizzy. My back hurt where I'd hit the floor. My chest hurt where Miklos had hit me. I felt like crying, but I couldn't get enough air in me to cry.

"You saved my life," she said. "I knew it, I knew you were one of my own. I knew I had to come back for you, after all these years."

She embraced me, more heartily and more carelessly than she ever had before, overwhelmed with emotion. And I felt something move, under her dress, under her skin.

It moved like an eel—started in her side and wound its way out into her arm, where it disappeared. I was still stunned, and that made it easier not to flinch. So she was hiding something, although I didn't know what. I didn't know what to think, or rather, I had so many thoughts all at once that they were turning into a kind of soup.

I pulled away from her embrace. She had a wound in her neck where Grandpa Miklos had attacked her. A long straight rip, like in fabric, but it wasn't bleeding. Instead, the edges were beaded with funny orange stuff, like tree sap. Like my blood, but thicker. Stranger.

"I'm very tired," I said. "I think I should lie down."

She helped me upstairs to my room, and folded back the sheets for me, and tucked me into bed. She kissed the top of my head.

"I cannot tell you how long I have waited for you," she said. "You aren't my granddaughter. You are my child, my only living child."

She shut the door behind me, and I was alone. Grandpa Miklos was afraid, and had fled into the night from her. And she was more than what she seemed. These two ideas chased each other around and around my head, while my chest got tighter and tighter, as though they were winding me up in rope.

Just because she wasn't a human grandmother didn't make her bad, I told myself. Luma wasn't bad. Grandpa wasn't, either, or at least, not completely. Maybe I could talk to her. She didn't have to hide, not with us. And maybe if she didn't have to hide, she wouldn't be so mean to Luma, so cruel to Mother.

I was exhausted to the bone; the fight, and the panic after, had taken something out of me. And so I slept.

I dreamed that Mother was standing over me, dripping from the tub, watching me sleep. A drop of water fell from her forehead and landed on mine, and I realized it wasn't a dream, and sat up. She started to leave.

"Wait," I said. "Why did you come here?"

Since Grandmere had arrived, I had barely spoken to Mother. When she wasn't demanded for dinner or an event, she spent more time than ever hiding in her bathroom.

"I just wanted to see you. I like looking at you." It sounded like an apology.

"Come back," I said. "I miss you."

She came and sat down on the bed beside me, a little damp spot spreading out around her. She was wrapped in a bathrobe, but it too was soaking wet. She looked better than she had in months, all her tendrils alert and waving. They were pretty.

"You can't be out of the water very long, can you?" I asked.

"Mère always hated that about me." She looked away from me, turning her eye and her polyps toward the floor.

"Grandmere hated you?"

Her expression changed. She looked afraid.

"No," she said, laughing nervously. "Not 'hated'! I mean she was sad for me. She wanted better for me. No, no, not hated. Goodness, Eleanor." She started to stand up. I caught her left arm and smoothed down the agitated polyps on the back of her hand.

"Shh, it's alright," I said. "I'm sorry, I didn't mean to say that, Mama. I'm sure Grandmere loves you very much. I was just surprised."

She sat and let me hold her hand for a moment, but she didn't say anything else for a long time. She kept taking little breaths, as though she were about to begin a sentence, and then letting them out again. Finally, she turned to me.

"I really love this house," she said at last.

"I know you do, Mama."

"And our family."

"Me, too." It wasn't a lie, I realized. I wasn't afraid of them anymore. "I think Grandmere helped me see that."

Mother stood up and smiled at me.

"I'm glad she's done that for you," she said. "I really am."

I understood something about Mother then that I hadn't before: that she was willing to give up just about anything about herself to make someone else happy. And with that, I understood that having Grandmere here was hurting her—in little ways, maybe, but hurting her nonetheless. I wanted to tell her, but I was terrified that if I started talking about it, I'd start crying and never stop, like Margaret, weeping until I wailed the house down. So instead I leaned against her damp side until the brush of the polyps through her dress didn't unsettle me quite so much.

After she left, I couldn't sleep for a while. I heard the kitchen door open, and Rhys's heavy tread climbing the stairs and slamming the door to his room. Outside, Grandpa Miklos was wailing in the woods. I wanted to run to him, to say—what, that I was sorry? But I wasn't sorry that I'd stopped him from killing Grandmere, and when I tried to sit up, my chest and back hurt more than I could bear. I wondered if this was how Grandma Persephone had felt when she'd sent me away. She must have thought she was protecting them from me, from what I could do. For the first time, I wondered if she was right.

EIGHT

THE NEXT MORNING, GRANDMERE BROUGHT
me breakfast in bed. She carried the tray up herself and sat next
to me on the edge of the bed while I ate. She couldn't stop looking at me, and sometimes she reached over to stroke my hand.

"I cannot believe what happened yesterday," she said. "What
nearly happened to me—terrible!"

I nodded. It was hard, in daylight, to believe what I'd seen
and felt the night before. She didn't seem like someone who
could scare Grandpa Miklos so badly that he would run from
his own house. She had a bandage over the wound on her neck,
and when I asked about it, she shook her head.

"Oh, it is hardly anything," she said. "A scratch."

"Are you alright? Maybe someone should look at it." I reached
for it. "I've been reading a little about medicine. I could—"

Her hands flew to the bandage, protective. "No, my dear," she said. "Please, do not trouble yourself. I am fine. More than fine, because I am with you. In fact, there is something I would like to talk to you about."

"What is it?" I asked.

"When you saved me from your grandfather the other night," she said. "Did you know how you did it?"

I did know. I'd spoken, in a particular way, and Grandpa Miklos had to obey me. I'd been doing it for a while now, pretending that I didn't really know what I was doing, but sure of it all the same. I thought about the vision I'd seen of myself as a child; I'd used it then, too, hadn't I? How often had I forced people to do something they didn't want to? I thought of the shopkeeper in Winterport. I thought of Rhys.

Grandmere saw the look on my face, and she rushed to press my hands in hers.

"Don't be so worried!" she said. "What you have is a gift, a natural talent. You should be proud."

"I feel . . ." I said. "Is it alright to do that? I mean, really?"

She looked suddenly serious.

"Anything that helps you to stay alive is permissible," she said. "It is a dangerous world for us."

I was beginning to know when she was putting on an emotion for my benefit and when she was sincere. When she said this, she looked down at her hands, folded and unmoving inside their lavender gloves. She always became very still when she was upset, not wanting anyone to see her in pain. I did the same thing.

"Please talk to me," I said.

She looked up at me with a sad little half smile.

"I had three other daughters," she said. "Angelica played the violin. Marietta was always falling in love with boys; she was a flirt, but clever, too. She took up with a German officer at one point and I was so angry with her. I wish I had been kinder. And Ofelia was my youngest, practically still a child. I lost all of them over the course of the War. Ofelia was the last." She said it with a mournful calm. "I wish I could say more. I don't even like to think about them. How I wish you could have known them."

I wanted to hug her, to pull her close to me and lean her against my shoulder. But I knew if I tried, she would tense up, and then politely excuse herself. So I sat next to her in silence for a long time. I couldn't believe what she'd been through. I couldn't believe that after all that, she'd come here, to find me. She was one of us; she was just looking for a home. Why couldn't Grandpa understand that?

"Ofelia wasn't old enough to use her gifts yet," Grandmere said at last. "And your mother refused to. I cannot help but think that if we had all remained strong together, I might not be the only one who survived."

That did explain why Grandmere was so cold to Mother. She'd wanted help, and Mother had refused. I thought of Ofelia, who didn't know how to use her gifts. I wondered what Grandmere meant when she said Ofelia had been practically a child. Had she been my age?

"So you want me to control people so that I can be safe," I said.

"So that we together can go anywhere," she said. "Live wherever we please without having to worry."

I felt a twinge of doubt. Not everything Grandmere did seemed necessary—it wasn't all just to survive. But maybe after years and years alone, it had gotten hard for her to tell the difference. She was alone, and she was afraid. Maybe I could teach her not to be afraid anymore.

"Then I'll practice," I said.

She nodded.

"Can you leave me for a little while, my dear?" she asked. "I want to be alone with my thoughts."

I wanted to be there for her, but I got up quietly and closed the door behind me on the way out. Without her, I felt abandoned.

I didn't want to practice this gift. The idea that I'd made Grandpa twist like that in midair made me feel sick. But I'd saved Grandmere's life with it. Maybe if she felt like she could depend on me to protect her, she could relax. Maybe we could all be a family together. After all, wasn't there room for strangeness in this house? I could make them see that she meant us no harm, that she wouldn't need to harm anyone if she felt safe. Maybe she'd stop worrying about Rhys.

And surely, just because Grandpa Miklos was afraid of her didn't mean that she was the old woman he'd seen all those years ago. She would have been young then. There must be a mistake. There must be an explanation.

After Grandmere left, I tried to sit up and read, but my chest still hurt from the fall, and I felt strangely tired. I napped through most of the afternoon, and when I woke up, it was dark out, and someone had left a tray of supper. I eased myself up and ate slowly. It was hard to swallow.

I kept thinking about what Grandmere had said, about practicing my talent. Maybe someone would let me try it on them, if I promised not to make them do anything they'd hate. But who was home? I shut my eyes and listened to the heartbeat of the house. Upstairs: Mother, splashing in her tub. No, she was too upset still. No sounds of Grandpa anywhere; I hoped he was alright, that he'd be back from the woods soon, so that we could talk. Margaret in the kitchen, a scraping sound that told me she was scrubbing down the flagstones. And a faint sound from down the hall, in Grandma Persephone's old study. Music, I realized. The record player, turned nearly all the way down. I didn't know who was playing it.

I limped down the stairs as quietly as I could. The door to the library was closed, so I knelt down and pressed my ear up against the door. The record scratching away on the Victrola. And shoes scuffing on the rug. And my father's voice.

"We don't have to stay here," he said. "I could leave. You could leave with me."

"I don't think that's possible." Arthur's voice. What was he doing here? Their footsteps were rhythmic, in time with the music. I realized they were dancing. I imagined the way that Arthur must dance, stiffly, lightly. I imagined resting my hands on his fingertips, the two of us gliding like air, graceful as marionettes. My father's footsteps were heavier, stumbling. I wondered who led, when they danced. I couldn't picture what it would look like.

"I know you say she made you stay," my father said. "But she's dead. She can't be why you're still here. It must be something else."

"Maybe it's Rhys."

"Don't say that."

"If you insist."

I wondered if Arthur was afraid of my father. I didn't like that stiffness in his voice, in the movement of his feet. I increasingly had the feeling that he didn't want to be here, that it was one more thing he was forbidden to say.

Well, my father couldn't hate me any more than he already did. I stood up, took a few steps back, and strode toward the door. I opened it lightly and casually, as though I were just coming in to get something.

I thought I would have to pretend to look startled, but it

was easy when I saw my father frozen, one hand on Arthur's waist, the other on Arthur's hand. Arthur looked perfect, with impeccable posture; he paused midstep. I was shocked by the ordinary intimacy of it. I thought of girls at school practicing dance steps together and the feeling that had always given me, the same feeling I had now: that I was seeing something I wasn't quite supposed to see, something that gave me a sharp pain under my sternum.

"I—Father," I said. "I wanted to look over the books. I . . ."

Father let go of Arthur, almost flinging him away. He pushed his way past me out the door, slamming it behind him. Arthur didn't look after him, I noticed. He looked at me.

"You did that on purpose," he said. I was suddenly embarrassed.

"You sounded—" I shook my head, not sure how to explain what I'd heard. "You didn't sound happy."

His smile vanished. "I wish you wouldn't pretend to rescue me. It's disingenuous."

"Why does he make you dance with him?" I asked.

"He asks, and I say yes."

"Why do you say yes to everything?"

"Because I"—he paused, working his jaw—"don't say no."

"Why?"

He came and took me by the arms. His mouth twitched in what was almost a smile.

"You'll give up soon," he said. "Soon you won't care. Soon

you'll just love that I say yes. And maybe then you can relax, and stop asking so many questions that you don't want answered."

The record was still spinning. My father had fled. The door was closed. Luma wasn't in the house, or I would have heard her. It was just the two of us.

"Do you like to dance?" I asked.

"I dance."

"Would you want to dance with me?"

"I would dance if you asked me."

He'd said so little, but I could tell he was saying more. I thought carefully before I answered.

"I'm not asking you to," I said. "It was only a question of interest."

His mouth was open but he didn't speak. I felt like we were groping toward something, together, blindly. That we were almost there, wherever 'there' was. For a long moment Arthur was silent.

"Then no," he said at last. "I would rather not."

My face burned red. I felt ashamed; he'd seen through me. He knew now how much I liked him, and he didn't like me. I felt like a fool. No amount of help from Grandmere would ever make him love me. No pretty dress or anything else. He didn't like me, or anything about me.

Maybe I had misunderstood that night in the hall, too, when Rhys had fallen out of the door in the wall. Maybe Rhys meant something to him, something I didn't. Something I could never mean. Maybe Father had, too, once. Arthur was . . . I didn't know what Arthur was. But we didn't have the secret kinship I kept thinking we did. It was all in my imagination.

"Don't look so sad," Arthur said. He stepped toward me, lightly, his movements still lithe. "I don't mean to hurt you. I mean to be . . ." He gritted his teeth as though biting back words. Or having something bite them back for him. "Honest," he said at last, with much effort.

There was so much I wanted to ask him—was he in love with Luma, then, or Rhys? Or my father? Was being with Luma a kind of disguise? How long had this been going on? I had so many questions. But the idea of staying and pressing him on any of it made me uneasy—I wasn't sure if he could tell me, or if I could survive understanding. I looked up at him. He was so close to me again, always getting so close, in a way that made me want to grab him and cling on for dear life.

"Eleanor," he said, his teeth grinding with every word. "Do you remember talking to me about your friend from school? You said her name was Lucy?"

I didn't want to think about Lucy Spencer. This was about him, not about me. "Maybe you should go," I said.

"You didn't say you want me to go," he said. "Why did you bite her? If you really want to understand, it's right in your reach."

I didn't want to think about Lucy. I wanted him to leave me alone, for this whole awful scene to be over. And then I thought about banishing.

Without thinking, I reached out and thumped the wall.

One, two, three. As soon as I'd done it, I knew I'd done something unforgivable.

Arthur pivoted on his heel and strode from the room. I tried to follow him. "Wait," I said. "Wait." I caught the back of his jacket. "Arthur, I'm sorry. What did I do?"

He shrugged me off and kept going. We passed the front parlor, where Father looked up from the book he was ignoring. Across the parquet of the front hall I followed Arthur, until he flung open the front door. "Arthur, wait!" I said.

He turned and looked at me.

"Good-bye, Eleanor," he said.

He stepped out into the night. The wind sucked the door shut with a slam. I stood, panting, wild-eyed.

"Proud of yourself?"

Father stood up from the darkness of the parlor. He was holding a glass of brandy. It sloshed as he started toward me and stumbled.

"He's not going to fall in love with you," Father said. "It's not part of his nature. I tried to warn you."

"What is he?"

"Something your grandmother made," he said. "To look after the children." He laughed.

"I don't understand."

"Of course not. How could you?"

"Why are you like this with Arthur?" I asked. "You're married. Don't you ever think about what this is doing to Mother?"

Father growled low. "Drop it."

That made me angry.

"Why should I?" I said. "All I want is to understand, and to be a part of things, and all you ever tell me is no. Why? What are you so afraid of?" I took another step toward him, and he backed away, a spill of brandy sloshing to the edge of the glass and onto the floor. "What are you afraid I'll find out? That you're in love with him? That you wouldn't let him leave after Grandma died, even though he wanted to go?"

He backed up, stumbled, caught himself against the front door.

"You know, my sister was right about you," he said. "You're trouble. You should never have come back."

"Papa," I said, stepping back. My eyes filled with tears. "You don't mean that."

He looked down, and I knew that he didn't mean it. He was afraid. He was ashamed. He was like me. Suddenly, I understood.

"You didn't want anyone to know," I said. "But you didn't want to lose him."

"I didn't know how to help him," Father said. And he started to cry.

I wanted to run to him, hug him. We could figure this out, I realized. This wasn't the kind of fight fathers and daughters usually had, but then, we were different. We were Zarrins.

"I have something I need to tell you," I said. "About why I left school."

But my father's gaze shifted upward, to somewhere behind and above me.

"Goodness, Miles," Grandmere said, from the top of the stairs. "Are you drunk?"

He looked down at the glass in his hand, as though seeing it for the first time.

"*Go to bed*," she said. My father started up the stairs. He cast a look backward at me as he went. A look that said *help me*. But now it was my turn to wonder how.

"I am so sorry," she said to me, when he was gone. "I cannot believe he would speak to you that way. The things he said!"

"It's alright," I said. "He was just upset."

She frowned and shook her head.

"It was unacceptable," she said. "Simply unacceptable." Something about the way she said it unsettled me, as though she'd arrived at a decision.

"I'll talk to him about it in the morning," I said. "After he sleeps it off, I'll handle it."

"Eleanor, dear," she said. "If you're feeling better, could you go fetch me something from the kitchen? Maybe some bread and butter?"

"You'll let me talk to him?" I asked.

"Of course. In the morning."

I went into the kitchen. Margaret was standing by the sink. As I came up she started groaning, her tone escalating.

"*Don't,*" I said. She fell silent. I cut a slice of bread from the loaf in the kitchen and buttered it. When I brought it up to Grandmere, she was back in her bed, tucked in under the blankets.

"Did Father get to bed?" I asked.

"He went." Grandmere gestured into her room. "Won't you come in, my dear?"

"I'm . . . very upset," I said. I realized I was crying. "I think I'm just going to go get some sleep."

"My lovely girl. I hope you know I'll always protect you from people who just don't understand."

"He's not so bad," I said, the tears still falling. "I'm sure you convinced him. He won't do anything like that again. Please don't be too hard on him."

"You're generous," she said. "I like that about you. Sleep well, my dear."

The next day my father was not at breakfast.

I checked the woods, and the beach, and finally went to town to ask after him at the post office.

When I came back, my father was in the parlor, sitting in a low chair behind a newspaper.

"Father," I said, coming in. "I'm sorry about last night. We both said things we shouldn't have, and I—"

"Nonsense," he said, from behind the paper. "I just want you to be happy."

"But . . ." I glanced left and right before kneeling on the floor in front of his chair. "I want to know what you were telling me. Please, what is Arthur? You said he was something Grandma made. What did you mean?"

"It does not matter, as long as you're happy."

"But I'm not happy. I'm . . ." I realized I was looking over my shoulder with every fifth word. "I'm scared, Papa."

"Nonsense."

"But—"

"I just want you to be happy."

I grabbed the newspaper and ripped it out of his hands. I stared into my father's blank face.

I expected to be able to see what was wrong. His eyes would be different, or his coloring. But he looked exactly like my father.

"Papa," I said. "Tell me what's wrong. Please, Papa."

"Nonsense," he said.

NINE

FOR A WHILE, I WAS AFRAID. THEN, I WAS ANGRY.

I went upstairs and banged on Grandmere's door. She didn't answer right away. "Eleanor, dear," she said. "I am so fatigued. Can you come back another time?"

I rattled the knob. Locked. "I need to speak with you," I said.

She sighed and, with a surprisingly loud thump, rolled out of bed. I heard a shuffling and skittering behind the door, and then the lock clicked open. "Alright, come in," she said.

When I opened the door, she had gotten back into bed. The room looked more disheveled than usual for her. I spotted something on the floor out of the corner of my eye, something black and shiny against the bright carpet under the edge of the bed. What was it?

"What did you want to talk to me about, dear?" She reached

for a cup on her bedside table and sipped from it. "I am feeling a little sick."

"I need you to undo what you did to Father," I said.

She snaked out a hand and patted the covers beside her. I didn't move.

"My darling," she said. "I cannot undo what I have done. And if I could, I would not. I have done so little, after all."

"What do you mean?" I asked.

"All I did was change him a little," she said. "He can still walk around and speak to you, and he is very friendly. He can do everything he did before."

"He's just sitting in the living room," I said. "He's not moving. I tried to talk to him and he just said the same things over and over again. That's not the same. What did you do?"

"Nothing you cannot do," she said. "Would you like me to show you how to do it? Would that make you feel better?"

"No," I said. "I want to know how to fix him. I want him to be able to do whatever he wants."

"Whatever he wants?" she said. "Whatever he *wants*? He cannot be trusted, Eleanor. I heard the way that he spoke to you last night."

"He was sorry!"

"He didn't seem sorry to me." She was upset, I could tell. "I could not bear to hear anyone speak to you like that. Telling you that you do not belong, that you are the one who is wrong, when he himself has—" She shuddered, and a ripple ran under the skin of her neck, as though some other shape swam beneath it. "When he himself has done such hideous things. He and your cousin are things that should never have been. There is no place in the world for men like them. What purpose do they serve?"

Why did people have to have a purpose? Weren't they enough? I nodded along, though; I felt ashamed of it, but I had to buy myself time to think. What was I going to do about her?

"I did not want for you to have to see this so soon," she said. "But I suppose you have to grow up sometime. I am glad you finally understand why I did what I must."

I nodded again, swallowed hard. I remembered what Grandma Persephone had said. My eyes had adjusted; it was like looking at one of those pictures that can either be two young women or a skull. Grandmere had become something else now, in my eyes. And I was afraid of her.

"So, how often do you have to . . . do that?" I asked. "To keep him this way?" I hoped I sounded helpful, eager to learn.

"Oh, it is done," she said. "He will never again be as he was. He is a good father now. Obedient and friendly. I think in time you will get quite used to him this way. And . . ." She watched my face tentatively as she went on. "I thought perhaps you and I could practice, and in a little while, you may be ready to help your cousin in the same way."

I forced a smile onto my face. I was a good liar; I hoped it bore up against someone who had known me so well, whose arms I'd cried in.

"Thank you, Grandmere," I said. "I'm glad I understand now."

She beckoned me closer. I took a slow step toward her, and she reached up and stroked my cheek with her hand.

"We will start tomorrow," she said. "Today, I am tired from my efforts. Please, *leave me alone to rest*."

I felt my body turn to leave. "Sleep well, Grandmere," I said, as my legs walked me to the hall.

Downstairs in the empty kitchen, I grabbed a knife from the block. I started back up the stairs, moving faster and faster as I climbed. I had to get this over with. I had to do it now, while she was tired.

When I reached her door I stopped. I didn't mean to. I swung my arm as hard as I could toward the knob, but it stopped short. I couldn't even bring myself to knock. I lifted my foot to kick at the door. Nothing. Nothing at all. I wanted to scream, but the sound died in my throat. I laughed a little. Of course I couldn't scream. She'd told me to let her rest.

I needed help, I realized. I needed someone who could act when I couldn't.

And then I thought of Luma, of all the times she'd disobeyed Grandmere. She was impervious where I was not. She was, after all, Grandmere's granddaughter, too.

I ran to Luma's door and threw it open. It looked as though a bomb had gone off in it; makeup tubes lay strewn everywhere, and her dresser drawers had been ripped out. Things were missing, I realized. Had she run away, like Lusitania? Was she gone for good?

And then I heard the howl from the woods. Luma's high pure cry, and Grandpa Miklos's. They were calling for Rhys. But he couldn't call back. Grandmere had told him to stay put and be quiet, after all.

Well, she'd said to stay put. I'd told him to shut up. My face burned just thinking about it.

He was scratching at the wall. I was forbidden to let him out, I knew that much. But then I looked at the dresser. Grandmere had said nothing about going in.

It took some shoving to get the dresser out of the way. But when I moved it, there was the hole: torn wallpaper, crumbling plaster, and Rhys's face as he crouched on the other side, snarling, his mouth full of long yellow teeth.

"Shh," I said. "Rhys, it's me. It's just me. *You can talk to me.*"

"You did this to us," he hissed under his breath.

"I didn't!" I said. The words stung; I knew they were at least half true. "I didn't want it to end up like this!"

"Come in here so I can tear you in half."

"No," I said. "You can't do that. You need me to get rid of her."

"How?"

"I can make you do things, remember? Maybe I can help you fight her."

"Then let me out," he said.

"I can't," I said. "She told me not to."

"Then what good are you?"

"I have to come in," I said. "I have to whisper so she doesn't hear. But I'm not going to tell you not to hurt me, because I want you to decide. I'm trusting you. So maybe you can trust me."

He tilted his head to one side but didn't try to lunge at me. I climbed through the hole into his room. Crouched half inside the wall, I pulled his head close to mine. It turned into a wolf's head in my hands. I flinched, but I didn't pull away. I leaned close to his ear.

"She's done something to my father," I said. "I think she killed him. He's not himself anymore. He acts like . . . a puppet."

The mouth of the wolf that was my cousin growled in my ear. I could feel his rancid breath on my neck. I held as still as I could. He took after Miklos; I knew if I flinched, he'd tear me to pieces. But then I felt his head change in my hands, and he whispered back.

"She's made him like that thing she brought to the house," he said. "She looked like a person but she smelled like nothing."

As soon as he said it, I realized he was right. I'd never seen the woman with the sharp teeth arrive or leave. And she hadn't said anything that Grandmere would have disapproved of. She'd felt like nobody at all.

"How does she do it?" I asked.

"I don't know. Maybe the way you did it."

"What do you mean?"

"The way you did to that boy," Rhys said. "In the woods. Before Grandma sent you away."

I froze.

"I didn't do anything," I said. "I didn't. He disappeared."

"No, you swallowed him." Rhys looked at me. "Is that what she did to Uncle Miles?"

"No! I don't know." I found myself scrambling backward out of the hole.

"Wait," he said. "Wait, is she going to do it to me? You won't let her, right?"

"Of course not," I said. I knew at least that much, even though right now it felt like I knew nothing at all. What had I done? "I have to go think. I'll be back."

"Promise?" he asked, but I was already pushing the dresser back over the hole in the wall. I leaned against it, panting.

He was wrong, I told myself. I couldn't possibly have done that. That boy had gotten lost in the woods, or Rhys or Luma had killed him by mistake, or maybe I wasn't remembering right. Maybe he'd gotten away from us and run out of the woods and into his father's arms.

Maybe, maybe. I had to be sure, though. I sat down on the floor and sobbed into my hands, straining to remember. I cried quietly, not sure whether I was doing it out of habit or because I couldn't wake up Grandmere.

The moon had been shining through the birch trees that night. I remembered my cousin Charlie and his shiny black dress shoes. When had Charlie lived with us? Had he been there for the summer? No, this was back before Lusitania had left. She'd left that night. It was all coming back to me now.

I made myself remember the banker's boy. Fast, but unsure on the rough terrain. Gasping with the exertion, his breath so loud we could have followed that sound alone, even if he hadn't been crashing through the undergrowth like a truck. And the cool wind whipping at my face, the brightness of the moon, and the ecstatic joy as Rhys and Luma and I sprang onto him in a single motion.

I didn't like remembering this. I didn't want to remember. But there I was, bright and happy and very, very hungry. I tipped my head down toward the boy, feeling like if only I could kiss him, I could engulf him, and he'd be with me forever, and I would always feel this way.

I'd fallen through the place he had been and landed in the bed of pine needles that had been under him. And he was nowhere. And I'd felt tired, a heavy ache lingering in my jaw.

"You're going to get in trouble," Charlie had said, from just behind my left shoulder. And I'd turned and screamed at him, because I knew it was true, and I deserved it, and at the same time, I hadn't done anything. At least, nothing I'd meant to do.

Back in the bedroom, I realized I wasn't breathing. I gasped a few times, catching up. I crawled into Luma's bed and bundled myself up in her blankets, just to hold on to something real. Anything was better than this. And so I let myself think about Lucy.

When I was twelve, Lucy Spencer was the most beautiful girl I'd ever seen. She had red bouncy hair she pulled back with a headband. Her skin was starred with freckles. She moved gracefully and slowly, except when she played sports or got in fights, when she was suddenly animated with fury. Looking at her felt complete. She was all one piece of art.

She had come from another school so, at first, we were friends. She didn't yet know where she fell in the order, so she fell in with me. I had given up on having real friends and had been waiting like the dead, seeing only what was in front of me and doing only what I was told.

She changed that for a while.

We told jokes. I learned how to comb her curly hair. I went to her parents' house one Christmas and met her family: her older brother, who teased her about our constant studying for spring exams; her mother, who did embroidery; her father, who was the vice president of a bank. Her grandmother, who stared in shock when I asked her if she read tarot.

One night in her room I told her that I loved her. It came out so suddenly that it surprised me. I thought about ways to take it back: to say "like a sister," or to say "I mean, you're my best friend." But I didn't. I let it float out over the darkness, and in response, she climbed across the gap between our twin beds and wrapped her arms around me from behind and slept next to me like that. I stayed awake the whole night, my body stiff as cordwood, not daring to breathe in case she woke up and changed her mind.

When we went back to school in January, people started to make fun of how much she liked me. At first, she said we just couldn't be friends in front of other people. Then she started making jokes about me. Soon it was like we had never been friends at all.

She grew two inches over the summer and was suddenly tall. When she came back to school she wore lipstick. She started talking about how in love with her I was. How the one time she tried to be nice to me and have me over to her house, I'd tried to sleep in bed with her, and how she couldn't tell if it was because I was trying something, or if my family was so poor we only had one bed.

"My family's richer than yours," I said, which was a stupid thing to say.

The way it blew over was like this: on the day I punched her in the stomach, while she was staring at me in shock and pain, I realized that the only way to escape the trap I was in was to stop existing, to become someone else.

So I turned myself inside out, and that was who I stayed until the day Lucy tripped me on the stairs. On that day I snapped back in midair, although my body stayed the same. There was more than one way to perform my family's trick, the inversion of selves, the different skin.

I was a wild, unthinking thing when I tripped her and brought her down as easily as Luma would fell a deer in the forest. When I wrapped my arms and legs around her body it had felt like coming home, the way she smelled like Christmas spices, and when I sank my teeth into her soft freckled neck it was like that calm, empty-headed joy that comes sometimes when falling asleep.

I woke up in Luma's bed in the middle of the night. I sat up, not knowing at first where I was. In the dark, the familiar shapes of Luma's dresser and makeup table looked like wild beasts. I got to my feet and startled myself by kicking something across the floor: a tube of lipstick. I reached for the light, and then thought better of it. I wasn't sure I wanted anyone to know where I was.

I crept down through a house as still as a stopped clock. I didn't know what time of night it was, or where anyone was, or, I realized, if any of them were still alive. The only sound I could hear was the creak of the stair treads under my feet.

I glanced into the parlor, where an odd shape startled me— and then I realized it was Father, sitting in an armchair, a newspaper blocking his face and body. His hands didn't move, but I watched them intently. I didn't want him to lower the newspaper; I didn't want to look into his blank eyes and wonder if Grandmere was watching me through them.

I slipped around to the kitchen door. Margaret wasn't there. I told myself that she was probably just in bed. Through the kitchen, past the closed door to the laundry, and down the hall to the greenhouse. I knew something bad was waiting there, but I wasn't sure yet. I wanted to be wrong.

I found the snake lilies trampled.

They were scattered around the ground, their bodies ripped from the soil, their flowers broken off and torn to ribbons, their leaves ground up and oozing the sap that I was supposed to harvest in only a few days. The door to the greenhouse stood wide open, blowing back and forth a little in the wind.

I felt numb. Had Luma done this, on the way out, to spite me? I got down on the ground and started picking up pieces, cleaning up. I gathered up the long stalks and started laying them in a pile.

It was then that I spotted it, half buried in dirt. A large black feather, gleaming with a blue sheen when I held it up in the faint moonlight. I realized that it was the same thing that had been on Grandmere's floor earlier.

The crows flew backward, Grandpa Miklos had said, into the mouth of a woman.

I had to be sure. I stood up, and that was when I saw that the floor was littered with paper.

The tarot cards and the journal had both been ripped to tiny shreds, scattered across the floor of the greenhouse, buried under bits of dirt, but I felt I'd recognize them anywhere. She'd destroyed them so I couldn't use them, and she wanted me to blame it on someone else. Maybe Margaret, maybe Luma. She wanted me to distrust everyone but her.

I felt like crying. I picked up little bits of cards, holding them up to one another, trying to see if there was enough left that I could piece them back together. Nothing. I sank to my knees.

And then, I felt a breeze on my back, the one that blew colder than the air outside.

"Help me," I whispered. "I need to know what she is."

And the little bits of paper began to slide and jostle across the floor, skittering on some invisible breath. They came from every corner of the room, until they were piled in a heap: little bits of colored paper, fragments of words or images. When they came together, they stopped. I stared at them, tears welling in the corners of my eyes.

"What do I do?" I asked. "They're all ripped up."

Silence. Nothing moved.

I bit my lip. What had Grandma Persephone said? Meta-phors. The cards didn't have to be cards, did they? They could be stones. They could be guts. They could be scraps.

I shut my eyes and picked through the pile. I tried to hold

my question in my mind. What is she? Rough torn edges caught at my fingers and I pushed them around, and ripped them up smaller, until I knew they were where they should be, until at last I opened my eyes.

The little bits of cards overlapped to make a new picture. A picture that was hard to look at, that seemed to move in the little breeze coming through the open greenhouse door. Arms and outstretched hands from the Ace of Blood, the circling dogs from The Moon, fish tails and wings and in the middle, eyes torn from every card in the deck, and then in the center of that every little bit of black paper, piled up on itself until it looked deeper and denser than black. A swirling hole of nothing. A mouth that could swallow the world.

I stared at it until I became aware of a sound from somewhere in the house. The creak of the great main staircase. I froze. The footsteps reached the bottom and turned toward the kitchen.

"Eleanor?"

Through the kitchen into the laundry. Then it would only be a matter of time until she found me here. "Eleanor, did you call me?"

With a whoosh, the bits of cards scattered, strewing themselves across the floor, back to wherever they'd been thrown before. I felt an icy hand push at the small of my back, and I ran out the back door of the greenhouse, still open, still creaking back and forth in the wind. Down the little steps until I was in the grass. And then I realized if I sprinted across the lawn now, she'd see me. I huddled up against the foundation of the greenhouse, in the shadow between the wall and the stone steps.

I could hear her then, up there, treading on the floorboards of the greenhouse. I pressed myself more tightly into the shadowy corner and held my breath, and willed my heart to stop beating so loudly, and squeezed my eyes shut. In the quiet dark I could feel everything: the damp from the grass seeping into my clothes, every ridge of the brick foundation, every shift of the wind.

"Hm," Grandmere said. "I was so sure."

She turned; I heard the rustle of her skirts. The greenhouse door banged shut behind her.

When I was sure she was long gone, I sighed. And that was when I spotted the shape speeding toward me across the lawn.

Luma was a white wolf, her eyes glowing, her teeth gleaming. While I got out of my crouch the ground between us vanished like it was nothing. By the time I opened my mouth she'd knocked me sideways into the grass and put her mouth around my neck. I could feel her teeth gripping the base of my skull. A warning not to scream, but my mouth was already full of grass and dirt. Another set of paws thudded overhead. Grandpa Miklos, I thought. I hoped he wouldn't just decide to rip my throat out.

I felt hands on my shoulders, and then one of them slipped

around to cover my mouth, pressing the dirt harder into my mouth and nose. The hand smelled like rosewater perfume. Luma.

"Crawl," she hissed in my ear. "Quietly. Or Grandpa kills you."

We crawled across the lawn in the dark. The grass was cold against my hands. Luma changed back to the wolf and kept pace with me, slinking low, with Grandpa Miklos just behind me. What would happen when we reached the tree line? I wondered.

"Please," I whispered. "I can explain." Luma answered with a low growl.

We moved across the lawn and into the trees. Pine needles embedded themselves in my knees. Finally, Luma grabbed me by the collar of my dress and dragged me up against a tree. She changed and crouched in front of me, her long hair draped over her like a cloak. She gripped my face with one hand. Her fingernails were caked with dirt and blood.

"Tell me what you did," she said.

I spat out grass and turf. "I never meant for it to happen like this—" But she sank her fingernails into my face, and I realized they were growing into claws, piercing my skin.

"I'll pull your face off," she said. "Grandpa says if we take you apart you'll look like her on the inside."

I looked over at Grandpa. He was hunched low, still in wolf form. He was growling at me. He'd lost one of his big canine teeth, and some of his other teeth were broken. His coat was ragged, too, his fur missing in spots on his sides. His ribs heaved with the effort of staying crouched to spring at me.

"What's happened to Grandpa?" I asked. "He looks really sick."

Luma glanced at him, and then back to me. "Don't look at him! What do you care?"

"I'm your sister."

"You killed our grandmother."

"I didn't!" I said. "*She* did."

"She wasn't even here yet."

"There was a card, a card that showed her Grandmere's—real face," I said. "Grandmere tore up the cards, but I saw her real face again just now. In the scraps."

She sniffed at me. "You're not lying," she said. "But what aren't you telling me?"

I looked away. She grabbed me and wrenched my face back toward hers. I could feel blood trickling down my cheek where her claws had sunk in.

"I wrote her a letter," I said. "After Grandma died. Asking her to come help me."

"Why?"

"Because I didn't know what to do."

She let go of my face; I clapped my hands to my cheeks, not sure what to do to stop my strange, wrong-colored blood from spreading down onto my neck, my clothes.

"You've ruined everything about our family," she said.

That made me angry.

"No, I didn't," I said. "Grandma Persephone wasn't that much better. Think about what she did to Arthur." When he heard the name, Grandpa Miklos began to growl.

"What did she do to Arthur?"

"I—" I realized I didn't know. "Father said she made him to be our servant, I think—"

"Where's Father?" Luma demanded. "I'll ask him."

"He's—I think he's dead—"

"Liar!" She slammed her hand into the tree just above my head. Her jaw contorted, her face expanding and shrinking from wolf to girl and back again. Her body snapped just as rapidly between shapes; it was like looking into a spinning door. She threw herself against the ground, against trees, scrabbling at the dirt, trying not to look at me. I sat paralyzed until I realized that she was trying to keep herself from killing me. Which meant she didn't want me dead. Not yet, anyway.

"Luma, listen to me," I said. She glanced up but kept striking the ground with her fists. "Grandmere can control me. She can make me do things. But she can't control you. If we work together, maybe we can stop her." Something dripped past my eye, and I realized I was bleeding from my forehead. I swiped at it. "Please. *I need you to help me.*"

"No," she said, crawling toward me, still crying. "You can't trick me. Not anymore. My sister is dead. You're one of her now. Maybe you always were."

Her mouth got long, and her big teeth got bigger, and she opened her mouth and wrapped it around my neck. I squeezed my eyes shut. I could let her end this, I thought. My body relaxed. I wondered if this was how a rabbit felt when she had it by the throat. It would be so easy to sigh and let her kill me. But what about Rhys, trapped upstairs with Grandmere? What about Margaret, or Mother? What about Grandpa, old and sick in the woods? What about Arthur?

And what about me?

My eyes snapped open.

"Grandpa," I said. *"Distract Luma 'til I get away."*

He threw himself at her and knocked her over, and the two wolves went rolling across the bed of pine needles. I scrambled and ran, first using my hands, and then on two feet. I kicked off my shoes. My feet scuffed across the pine needles.

I broke through the tree line and onto the lawn, my arms waving, my heart pounding. It was almost dawn. Behind me Luma and Grandpa were fighting, but soon they stopped. I was *away*, and now they were both coming for me. I could hear them, just barely, a whisper-soft padding that got louder as they got closer. Luma and Grandpa swung around so that they were between me and the house, driving me toward the cliff. They moved together, closing in on me. I wanted to yell out to Grandpa to stop, but I could barely catch my breath. I looked around, dizzily, for some way out. Behind me was the cliff, and beyond that, the ocean. It wasn't a straight drop. But maybe if I was lucky, I could hit the water.

Luma leaped at me, but I leaped farther, and she stopped short at the last second to avoid the edge of the cliff. For a moment, my feet kicked in the air as I tried to run on nothing at all. I looked down and realized I'd made a mistake. The beach was narrow, but not that narrow. Beneath me were sharp black rocks. I was going to die.

And then, suddenly, there were crows.

They descended from the red-streaked dawn sky in a torrent, a curtain of black that plunged down around me. They battered at me with heavy wings, but they broke my fall, and I tumbled and slid on a carpet of crows. More of them, above me, snatched at my collar and hair and the skin of my arms, trying to get hold of me. We soared up, and turning in the air, I could see Grandmere striding across the grass below. Grandpa Miklos tried to growl at her, but Luma screamed at him and they took off at a run for the trees, before she could say anything that might call them back.

She was saving me, I realized, the only way she knew how. She might do anything she wanted to anyone else, but she wouldn't let me get hurt. I was hers.

She opened her mouth, and the crows began to recede backward, carrying me with them. She was reeling me in. And when she had me, she'd fawn over me and tell me she loved me. And then she'd make me kill Rhys. For my own good.

But she couldn't make me if she couldn't catch me.

I tore at the birds holding me and leaped forward, taking big, running steps. Crows rose to meet my feet, not letting me fall. When I ran out of birds, I made my body into an arrow and pointed the arrow at the water.

Crows swarmed around me as I dove. They tried to grab me with their talons. But they were too late. I plunged, headfirst, into a wave, and all around me heard the smacking sounds of their bodies breaking against the water and the rocks.

TEN

EVENTUALLY, I HAD TO COME UP FOR AIR. I WAS afraid that the crows would still be circling overhead, looking for me. But when I came up to the surface and gasped out a few breaths, they were gone. Grandmere must be tired, I thought. These displays seemed to wear her out quickly. That meant I should do something now, while I had the chance. But what? I couldn't just walk back in, not without a plan. Not without help. And Luma and Grandpa weren't going to do anything to help me now, I was sure of it.

The sunlight was breaking over the water. I had to figure out how I was going to get my family back their house. And I had to do it without Grandmere seeing me, either through her own eyes or the eyes of the thing in the parlor that used to be my father. But I was so tired I could barely see straight.

I crawled out of the water. The air was chilly, my clothes clinging to me. I crept along the beach to the rickety stairs and climbed up them on hands and knees. When I got to the top, I hesitated. The woods were to my right. Up ahead, I could see Grandmere's bedroom window, the sunlight gleaming off of it so brightly that I couldn't see in. Was she awake in there? Was she watching me right now? I had to risk it. I gathered myself, and then sprang across the lawn. I kept expecting to see shapes sprinting after me from the woods, to feel claws on my back, but I vaulted the back garden gate and tore up the steps to the kitchen door.

Margaret stood inside, staring at me. She had been chopping up meat for stew and had a cleaver in one hand. As I watched, a little rivulet of blood ran off of the cleaver and onto the butcher block.

I could command her to silence, I thought. All I had to do was say the word. But I didn't want to. I didn't want to be any more like Grandmere than I already was. So I held my hands up in surrender, and then slowly, I put one finger to cross my lips.

She lowered the cleaver.

I put one of my hands over the other, and lifted them both up together. She tilted her head to one side, and then mimed lifting something herself. I nodded. Help me. Please, help me.

She stared at me for a long minute, and then nodded. She went to the cupboard and got down the silver coffee service.

I almost laughed. Coffee might actually help. The nuns had cautioned us against it, even as they drank steaming vats of it.

I looked out at the garden. The iron tub had been emptied and turned upside down, but the table was still out there, the bunting tattered to almost nothing. It seemed like years ago that they'd poured champagne for me in the garden. Had they been happy to welcome me home, or trying to placate me? I kept hearing Grandma Persephone saying I was powerful. She'd known what I was. She'd tried to keep me away from her family because she knew I'd bring Grandmere here, or perhaps become just as bad as she was. She thought I'd make the whole family into my toys.

Margaret set something down and I jumped. The coffee was done, thick and oily-looking as ever. I poured myself a cup and sipped it.

Poison flooded my tongue. I spat it out and rushed to the sink to rinse out my mouth under the running water, elbowing Margaret out of the way. I spat until I could no longer taste it, and then looked at Margaret.

She shrugged. Had she tried to kill me?

I went back to the cup and stared into it. It was thick and sludgy at the bottom. I tipped it out onto the tray. The bottom layer was all dirt—mud, really. The rest was a kind of shiny, foul-smelling broth. If it wasn't coffee, what was it?

I pointed back to the cup. She gestured to the things laid out on the counter, her preparations. A big glass jar of clear fluid. A brown paper bag. A smaller jar full of . . .

I examined the ingredients. The big jar was the source of that ungodly stink. It said FORMALDEHYDE in pharmaceutical type. The bag was full of dirt. The smaller jar was fingernails, and mats of black-and-white hair. From Zarrins, maybe? And finally, there was a small brown vial. Extract of the drakondia, labeled in Grandma Persephone's tiny, spidery handwriting. I shuddered. Was it the poison, or the love potion? Either way, what Arthur had been drinking wasn't coffee. It was a spell, and more importantly, something no living person should be drinking.

Margaret was trying to tell me something. She knew everything that had happened in this house. But it was all inside her, where I couldn't get to it. It was like she was privately living in Grandpa's silent country.

I could always summon him, I thought. Three sharp knocks on the door and he would be here. But I didn't want to summon him. I wanted to know where he was summoned from.

I clapped my hands to get her attention. She turned to me. I straightened myself out as tall as I could, pressed my lips together tightly, mimed putting on a pair of smoked glasses. I thought myself long and lean and strangely delicate, almost womanly, yet also brittle and sharp. I sipped an invisible cup of coffee. And then I let myself drop the act, and was back to being

Eleanor again. I raised my arms in a shrug, and looked around me—*Where is he?*

Margaret frowned, and then she nodded. She pointed at the floor.

I shrugged again. She pointed again, more insistently. Two sharp jabs at the ground beneath our feet.

The cellar.

Margaret saw my eyes widen. She got down a kerosene lantern from a high shelf and handed it to me. I nodded to her, and then realized that wasn't enough. I hugged her, and to my surprise, she stood still and let me do it. She was warm and smelled like sage.

I left through the back garden and went around the side of the house to the cellar door.

It wasn't locked on the outside, but when I tried it, somehow it wouldn't lift more than a few inches. I got down on my knees, pried it up, and saw an interior latch. *Strange.* I jammed my fingers in through the gap and after a few tries, I managed to flick the latch open.

The cellar steps were steep, and when I reached the bottom it was almost pitch dark. I fumbled with the valve of the lantern, turning it until the flame was bright enough to see by.

The walls of the cellar were lined with dusty jars of pickles and preserves that gleamed a little in the lantern light. But there was also a hole in the dirt floor of the cellar, dug roughly. The hole had a ladder stuck in it. I crept to the edge and peered over with the lantern.

Down the hole was a second room, low-ceilinged, dug out of the earth, with walls of packed dirt. There was a long, lidded box made of cedar, a box long enough to bury someone in. And lying on the ground beside the box was Arthur's old jacket.

I scrambled down the ladder, into the hole. On the floor lay my copy of Eliot's poems, and on top of them, a pair of dark glasses, the old-fashioned kind with lenses on the sides.

I set down the lantern and crept over to the box. I was sure of what I'd find on the inside, when I lifted the lid. But I had to look. I got my fingers under the lip of it, dragged it to one side. Another latch that I had to scrape at with my fingers. Latches where they shouldn't be, on the inside of things. I finally pulled the lid off. I wasn't ready for what I saw.

Arthur lay in the box, but he didn't look like the Arthur I knew. Arthur was graceful, animated, a body in motion. What lay in the box was a corpse. His eyes were hollows, the eyelids stitched shut over empty sockets. His arms lay folded across his chest. I wanted to cry. He wasn't moving at all, not breathing. I put my hand to his hands. They weren't just cool. They were as cold as the earthen walls around us.

I took a deep breath. There had to be a trick to this. I'd banished him, hadn't I? And that had left him like this. So to bring him back, I had to summon him.

I crawled back up the ladder. The journal had said *the door*, but I couldn't risk going to the front door. I got to the top of the cellar stairs and gave three little tentative knocks on the wood, hoping no one outside would hear me.

When I turned back to the pit, the coffin was empty.

"Looking for something?" said the shadows on the other side of the hole.

"Arthur?" I whispered.

His hands gripped the edge of the hole. They were long spidery hands, hands that spanned an octave and a half on the piano keys. In the dark of the cellar they became something else. Strangler's hands.

"Well, you summoned me," he said. "What do you want?"

Upstairs I heard footsteps. Both of us tilted our heads up toward the ceiling. I wasn't sure whose they were, but they reminded me of Grandmere.

"Listen to me," I said. "Everything's gone wrong. Father's . . . dead, I think." I choked on the words a little bit. "Luma and Grandpa are in the woods. Rhys is trapped upstairs and Grandmere wants me to—to eat him. Will you help me save him?"

"I don't see why you think I would be interested."

"Because the two of you . . ." I hesitated. "I heard you tell my father you were staying for Rhys."

"Do you really think that's true?"

"I don't know. I don't know anything."

"You don't like to know," he said. "None of you do. I spent years trying to figure out how to use that against you. And now you've done all my work for me."

"You want to hurt us?"

He grinned at me humorlessly. "You don't know anything about me."

Crablike, he crawled across the hole toward me, his long arms and legs bridging it easily. I fell and started to scramble backward, away from him. But he caught up and loomed over me. He couldn't hurt me, I told myself. I could stop him whenever I wanted to. But it didn't make me any less afraid. I'd thought he was annoyed with us, amused by us, resigned to us. He wasn't. He was full of rage, and that rage alone was terrifying.

"You don't know what I've suffered," he said. "You don't know what I've lost."

"So tell me." It came out small and weak. I tried again. *"Tell me."* He stopped moving, stunned, while his jaw clicked with the effort of staying shut. Something was keeping him from talking, but I was stronger than it. I sat upright and grabbed his face with both hands. *"Tell me!"*

He collapsed into my arms. The light from below went out, and in the dark around us I could feel Grandma Persephone, cold and electric, pressing in on all sides, while in a slow leaden voice he began to speak. This is what he told me.

"Arthur Knox came to Winterport in the fall of 1908, to be a schoolteacher, and to escape some trouble in his hometown. The Zarrins had moved there shortly before, and he—I—learned of them because they'd donated the new stove to the schoolhouse. I saw their name for the first time on a plaque they had installed on the stove.

"I didn't know much about them, except that they had bought some land on top of the hill, an old abandoned hunting lodge, and on its skeleton they were building some kind of palace, or fortress. It was half done already. The shape of the new wings loomed amid a clearing of felled trees. The workers were milling the boards on-site as they cleared the land.

"The Zarrins had no children yet, although the woman was expecting. She had white hair that made her look much older than she was. The man's hair was black and thick, and he was short but strong. He had a habit of standing with his legs spread and his hands planted on his hips, like a king surveying his lands.

"Dogs and cats disappeared often from the village, and some people said there was a cougar or a wolf hunting in the woods at night, but no one seemed to mind so much, with the money rolling in as the young Mr. Zarrin ordered all kinds of supplies and goods from the town. There was talk that he had been a gentleman in Europe, and that he had fled from persecution, or from something he himself had done. Whatever the case, he was rich, and he had no accent that they could make out.

"The young missus was a nurse, maybe. She grew herbs in big pots in the windows of the old wing while they built the new, and she kept the fire going at all times for the sake of her plants. Sometimes she brought gifts to women in town: baked breads, things in bottles. The man was different. He kept to himself except for sudden bursts of generosity. But whenever he saw me, I got the impression he was staring at me. I told myself that I was imagining things and that I shouldn't stare back. I didn't want to get myself in trouble, I suppose.

"Then one night he came to the schoolhouse. He knocked on the door persistently. When it opened he stared at me again. He picked me up by the arms and carried me clear to the back wall of the schoolhouse until my back was pressed against it. I thought he was going to beat me. I'd been beaten before. As a child, and later, by other men. But no beating came. Just Miklos, staring, and waiting. He'd caught me, and he wanted to see what I would do.

"I don't know what impulse made me kiss him. Maybe I wanted to make him angry, to make him kill me. But I didn't die. It was what he'd wanted. I don't know if he knew it was what he wanted, but it was.

"And then: passion, I suppose. It's strange to think now of how I loved Miklos then, now that I have hated him for so long. You understand. But Arthur Knox, the man I was, did love him, to distraction.

"I was happier, after that. Kinder to students, friendlier with parents. Waiting for the young Mr. Zarrin to knock again. But then . . . the missus came to visit me.

"I was terrified that she would be furious. But she didn't seem that way. She didn't seem to know anything; she just said she had seen me, and admired me. She wanted to . . . be with me. And so it was."

He seemed to hesitate, the way someone else might pause for breath, but I knew that wasn't it.

"Is it hard to remember?" I asked.

"No," he said. "But it's like I'm watching it happen again. As though it happened to someone else. That boy doesn't feel like me."

A part of me wanted to silence him again. I knew I could. I didn't want to hear what had happened next. But I quieted myself. I wouldn't be like my father. Whatever my family had done to Arthur, it was my business.

"The Zarrins started to invite Arthur . . . me . . . to dinner. They supplemented their food from town with wild game, which raised eyebrows—most men were afraid to hunt in the woods, ever since they'd started hearing a wolf, seeing mangled animals. People in town asked me all kinds of questions: About the house. About the furniture, the food. What they wore at home. How they were with each other. I can remember pulling up my collar to hide the scratches on my neck. Indentations from teeth, from fingernails.

"I liked them both. Or maybe I only liked the feeling of being wanted. I'd been alone for most of my life. I didn't know how to say no to the feeling. I remember sitting across from the both of them in their home in a cold sweat, wondering what they knew. I lied to both of them while they stroked my legs under the table. But it was also exciting. They were both so important to the town, so beautiful and, seemingly, so happy. But I was stealing from both of them and neither of them knew. Maybe that made me powerful, too.

"But then, Mrs. Zarrin had her baby.

"They both stopped coming to see me after that, for a while. Arthur Knox, the man who had been for a moment so powerful, was alone again. They didn't need me. I'd just been a moment's distraction. So I went back to doing what I had done before. I taught sums. I went to bed early. The snow fell, and melted, and fell again, as I waited to grow old alone."

This was what it was. This was the secret. In the dark I could feel my face getting hot. I thought about the way Grandma Persephone had looked at Arthur, or Grandpa Miklos, trying to parse if I'd seen any flicker of that passion they used to feel. I didn't think so. They'd left him behind.

"After a year had passed, they invited me to the house again. It was different. There were three of them now: Miklos, Persephone, and a baby. But the baby wasn't right. It was too big, too strong, already running around on hands and feet. I knew about Miklos, but the baby was wild. It had no control. A few times I saw Persephone scoop it up to hide it from me while it changed shape.

"About a year after that first visit, one of the girls from town disappeared in the woods by her house. It was one of Andy Haywood's little girls. She turned up a few days later, disoriented, with bites on her arms and legs like she'd been gnawed at. She had to be sent to a hospital in Boston to be treated and didn't speak for weeks. The wolves, people in town said.

"The next time I went to dinner, there were bolts on the insides of the doors. High up, where a child couldn't reach them. Before the Zarrins sat down to dinner, the missus put the baby to bed.

"While we ate rabbit stew, I decided what must be done. I decided that it had nothing to do with them abandoning me. That it was the right thing to do. That it was what anyone would do."

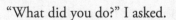

"What did you do?" I asked.

"I waited until they'd put the baby to bed," he said. He tilted his face down, almost looking ashamed, if that were a thing he

318 • ROSE SZABO

318 • ROSE SZABO

318 • ROSE SZABO

318 • ROSE SZABO

318 • ROSE SZABO

318 • ROSE SZABO

could feel. "The second floor was still under construction, so the baby was sleeping in a crib by the hearth in the kitchen. I excused myself—I forget what I said. I went into the kitchen, while the Zarrins chatted and held hands across the table. I told myself that it was the only thing that I could do. But when I did it, I knew I was doing it for myself."

"You killed him," I said.

"I hated them," he said. "For letting me know what it felt like to be happy, and then taking that away."

My chest ached. I thought about Lucy.

"I choked him to death," Arthur said. He put a hand to his lips. "He fought hard. He scratched me here. But he was a child. And he died."

In the cold of the cellar, I stopped breathing.

"When Mrs. Zarrin saw me walk out of the kitchen she knew right away that something was wrong. I hadn't been planning to hide it; I assumed they'd kill me. But when she shoved past me into the kitchen, and Miklos followed her, some part of me still wanted to live. And so I ran.

"I made it halfway across the lawn before Miklos hit me. The weight of his body felt familiar. I didn't realize he was hurting me at first. The pain, when I felt it, was welcome. I was ready to hurt for what I'd done. My vision went dark. I was sure I would die. And I almost did. But then I heard Persephone yelling from across the lawn, and I felt Miklos's jaws open, and he dropped me."

He stopped and held his chest. He looked like he was in pain, like he was dredging up all of this from somewhere deep inside himself.

"She grabbed me," he said. "And started to drag me. And when I woke up again, I was like this."

"What did she do to you?" I whispered.

He laughed, but without anything like joy. "I can't remember," he said.

The shadows around us felt thick and sticky, like cobwebs, and the air grew so, so cold. And in that darkness, I felt my own mouth open, and a voice came out that was not mine. There was something in me, sharing my body. And that voice said, "I remember."

I forced my own voice forward. *"So tell me."*

And she did.

Trapped in this house since the moment of my death, all I can do is remember. Memory feels as real to me as the present, and I am forced to watch it all happen over and over again. Fleeing my home. Coming to America to find Miklos. I live it all again.

When I was a little girl, I lived in the fishing village of Agia Galini. I killed a man by mistake. I fled into the hills and walked until it got dark. Eventually I came to a ring of stones. The grass around my feet was moving and rippling, and I realized it was teeming with snakes. I was frightened of the snakes, and of what was behind me, so I let them lead me to the middle of the ring, to a large flat stone, and I climbed up onto it. I was suddenly shrouded in heavy shadow that clung and stuck to me like cobwebs. And then I heard the voices.

They asked me what I wanted. I tried to ask them anything else, get them to tell me what they were, but they refused. And so I said the only thing I could think of: that I wanted to understand. I wanted to know things. And so they began to tell me. In guts, in cards. Sometimes in invisible signs that I could not name. Sometimes they told me things I wished I could unknow.

What I saw told me of a life I could have in another world, with a man who was like me. A monster. They led me across an ocean to find him. But on my wedding night, when Miklos looked at me, I suddenly saw past and under his lust for me, and through to something else, something I would never understand. I got so angry. All at once I was ringed in sticky black shadow, the kind that had pressed close around me atop that hill. I screamed at him so loudly that he, great grinning monster that he was, fled in terror from my rage and into the night. He always took refuge in being a wolf, in that part of him that would never, ever belong to me.

The next morning I woke up with a weight on my legs. When I looked down I saw a wolf curled up with his head on my thighs. His muzzle was smudged with blood, and the sheets were flecked with blood and black feathers.

I stroked his head while he slept, watching dust and feathers float down in the beam of sunlight from the open window he'd climbed through. And I thought: I will try to love all the parts of him, even the parts I will not see. I will try to let this go. And mostly I do. He will tell me little about his life before he came to America: I forgive him. He does not like to speak when he is angry: I forgive him. He disappears sometimes at night and comes back without saying a word, and I forgive that, too, or so I think.

We make money, off of my poisons and off of investments: it is easy to be rich when you can tell the future. We flee many towns, many suspicions, before at last we find a town so small and so poor that we know they will need our money. We settle in. I get pregnant with our first child. Miklos, though, becomes distant. He begins spending time in town. He's met Winterport's new schoolmaster and they've become friends. Or so he says. But he cannot lie to the guts.

I decide to investigate: I brew tinctures and teas and go to town to make myself useful. As I tend to the cough of young Betty Hannafin, her mother gossips to me about the new schoolteacher, whom I've only met once. Apparently all the young ladies love his green eyes, but he's showed no interest in any of them. Something about that makes my ears prick up. I go to investigate, and to give him something to stave off the cough, which will inevitably make it into the village schoolroom.

When I find him, he is watching the children run around a muddy yard next to the school at lunchtime. He is pretty: tall and thin, with high cheekbones ruddy from the wind, wearing a threadbare brown coat. So this is the man my husband has been sneaking off to see. I know it the way I know everything: metaphors, invisible signs.

"You must be Mr. Knox," I say, in my rough English. "From away, like us." And he smiles at me.

"Not quite as away, just a few states down. And you must be Mrs. Zarrin." His eyes are lovely: dazzlingly green in a face like a Renaissance saint's. I feel plain and ugly compared to him. He makes me jealous, and he makes me hungry. And more than that, he overwhelms me with a question: Who was my lover before he was mine? Who is he, when he is not with me?

For years, I have tried to tell myself that his other self is a curse, that he is a victim who wakes up after his nighttime journeys frightened and confused, as though from a nightmare. But looking into the worried green eyes of the village schoolteacher, I, too, begin to feel like a victim of his curse. And that makes me spiteful.

"Do you have a minute?" I ask him. "To step inside and talk to me?"

I tell myself that I only want to know what Miklos sees in him. I will seduce him, and therefore I will understand Miklos, and if I can do that, I can love him. I can forgive him. The edges of my vision go red. I imagine claws erupting from the tips of my fingers as I dig nails into the teacher's back, covered in scratches Miklos has left there. My nails find them and rake, reopening them, and when I leave I have blood caked in the quicks. But when I am leaving, for a second, I glance over my shoulder, and I see . . . Arthur.

Not the young schoolteacher he was, although there he is, disheveled and confused in the doorway, watching my retreat. No, a ghost

behind his eyes, trapped in his past, as I am trapped in mine. A
ghost like me, watching it unfold over and over again.

I want to talk to him, but then he vanishes, as though he was
never here. I wonder if he is flickering, too, trapped between the past
and the present. If he is . . .

It was my idea that we have Mr. Knox to dinner. I remember I
wanted to see if Miklos noticed, if he could smell me on the young
schoolmaster, if he ever noticed the triumph in my eyes. Miklos
thought he was stronger than me. He thought I was his possession,
to love or not love as he saw fit. He had no idea what I was capable
of. I liked making the young schoolmaster squirm, too, letting him
sit across the table from us wondering who knew what. It made me
feel like a lord of life. After so long working so hard to protect myself
from men, I was their master. I would have both of them until I
decided it was time to stop.

But then the baby was born.

And Miklos and I changed.

Suddenly he didn't want to go anywhere. Suddenly, I didn't want
to go anywhere. We could sit for hours playing with our baby, whom
we named Rhys. We could spend forever watching him sleep. We all
slept together in front of the fireplace, in a dreamy haze. Miklos
brought us food from the woods and roasted it over the fire. I nursed
our baby. We ordered him toys from the Sears catalog. We stopped
working on the house and did nothing and wanted nothing more
than to be next to each other, next to Rhys. We were invincible and
perfect bodies.

And then I began to feel magnanimous. It was a shame that the young schoolmaster should be left out of this. He should see how happy we were.

My younger self can't see it from here, but I can: how charity can be just another kind of spite.

And soon, young me is sitting across the table from young Arthur, and I spot him again, inside himself. Arthur and I are looking out at each other through the prisons that we used to call our bodies. I cannot say how I know, but he is there with me. Trapped, too. Watching.

Watching it happen again, watching our hands move to the plates and lift food and drink to our lips. Eating dinner together, something we did before, something we have done hundreds of times since. I want to whisper to him across the table, but I am bound tightly inside my younger self. She is rigid in her triumph. She has a husband, a beautiful baby, a big fine house. And he has nothing anymore.

I did this. I made Arthur. As surely as I have ever known anything I know this. And now my punishment: from inside myself I must watch him stand up from the table, brush the crumbs from his shabby jacket, and leave the room while my unsuspecting idiot younger self laughs and whispers to my unsuspecting idiot husband and kisses him across the table in the presence of my enemy.

When he comes back into the dining room, walking quickly, young Persephone knows something is wrong. She shoves past him through the door to the kitchen, and as she does so, Arthur and I are suddenly touching.

And then we switch bodies.

It happens so fast that at first I don't realize I am running the wrong way: not toward my baby, dead in his crib, his throat lined with black bruises. I, instead, am sprinting out my front door, across the lawn. I feel something strike me hard from behind; I recognize Miklos's weight on my body—Arthur's body, I remind myself, as Miklos knocks me to the ground. His jaws clamp around my leg, and he drags himself up my body with his claws raking through my jacket and into my back. The pain is enormous. It's like being hit with a wave, and then he grabs me by the neck and shakes, and I feel almost nothing.

I am rolled onto my back as Miklos yelps and falls away in fear. And then, towering over me, I see a woman bearing down. Tall and clad in black with white hair. Black sticky shadows cling to her. She does not so much walk as glide along the ground. Her hands, like talons, grab hold of me by my clothes. It's me, of course, whom I'm seeing. But it doesn't feel that way; not right now. The wind blows the way she wants it to, and it whips and snaps around us as she pulls me across the grass and up the steps. She reminds me of . . . no. I'm not quite like the creature that's taken over my house. But seeing myself from outside of myself, I am terrified.

When she adjusts her grip, grabbing Arthur by the wrist, I am sucked back into her. But I cannot lose what I have seen. Looking around I can feel the thick cobwebby shadows hanging over everything she does.

She drags Arthur into the kitchen, where the body of her son still lies in its crib. She screams for Miklos until he appears, cowering, and makes him help her lift the body onto the table. She wants to torture Arthur, but he can feel nothing; his neck is broken. So in frustration she slits him open and starts pulling out his guts, determined that she will augur in them the way to bring back her son.

She doesn't see it, the one thing she wants to know. She searches frantically through intestines and organs looking for truth. She's panicking. But I am studying his entrails. I have no magic left in me, no body, no hope, no luck I have not spent. It is the only thing left that I can do.

There is far more to read in Arthur than that one single thing, the only thing my younger self can care about in this moment. In him, I see the whole history of my family: secrets I never knew the answers to, no matter how hard I searched. Why Margaret never speaks. Where Lusitania went when she ran away. How my son first fell in love with Arthur, and how he convinced himself to marry someone else. What Luma fears the most.

And I see Eleanor. Fifty years before her birth, here she is, written in Arthur's body. What she will do to that boy, that night in the woods. What she will do for us, before it is all over.

I see all of us, the past and the present and the future, unspooled inside his guts. And I see Arthur, too. That he loved us. That before we shut him out, he would have done anything for us. That if we had found a way to welcome him in, we would have become a three-bodied creature of impossible size and power. An invincible rolling ball of monsters we would have become, if only we'd had the truths Arthur has inside of him. I see it all, and then my younger self, in impotent rage, screams and scrapes it all onto the floor.

"Oh, my friend," *I whisper to him, across the gap between our younger selves.* "What have I done to you?"

For young Persephone will not let him die. She has decided that his pain was over too quickly, that he must stay and suffer for what he has done.

She begins to chant. She asked for knowledge on that hill, and sometimes when she wants it, it rises into her, unbidden. Her voice is a dark and rolling sea. I scream at her in her mind, "Girl, stop this nonsense, let him go, we don't need to do this, can't you read the entrails?" *But in this moment she has a body, and she has the power. Shadows creep in closer, gaining mass and shape. They cling to her body and her hair. They cling to Arthur as she begins to cut him up into something she can preserve.*

She cuts out his eyes, which she has envied. She whispers into his ear commands: he will not leave this place, he will not hurt any Zarrin again, he will obey no others, he will serve them and give them, and be, whatever they require, whatever they desire—hah, what a mistake to make. She takes his heart from his chest and puts it into a wooden box. She stuffs his chest with rags and stitches him shut roughly. She takes his heart, in its box, and pries up the floorboards in the front hall, and lets it drop down into the foundations of the house with a heavy thud.

When she is done with Arthur, he is her thing to command. When she tells him to sit up, he sits up. When she tells him to stand, he stands, although one leg is twisted and bent, although his head dangles precariously from his broken neck. She makes him walk out of the house, to the cellar, and climb down into the earth. She tells him to dig, and to not stop digging until she says he can. She ignores him for a month, although she can hear him every night: digging, always digging. She orders him to build his own coffin. She orders him to lie down in it. She writes commands that he must follow: he must come when she calls, and do what she wants, and when she is done with him he must go back to his box and lie perfectly still in the ground until she needs him again.

I had forgotten this. I'd told myself that I would never do any magic like this again, and I didn't, for as long as I lived. And I thought that meant I had left it behind me. But how could I, when doing it made me who I am, when Arthur has been with me ever since? How many days, in fifty years, did I summon him from the ground, or send him away to lie in his grave? Whole years had gone by where I hadn't called him forth at all, where he must have lain still, trapped in his own dead flesh. I wonder how I could have ever for a moment joked with him, or had him help me with my taxes, or let him teach my children, and not thought about what I had done.

For a long time I lay still in the dark. And then, after what felt like forever, the lamp below us fizzled and came on, lighting the cellar with a faint glow. Arthur was beside me. I reached over to his shoulders. My heart felt like a cup poured up to the brim. If it tipped over, I knew I would cry.

"I'm sorry," I said. "I didn't know."

"Of course not. You've been preoccupied with feeling *all alone*. You don't know what alone is." He pulled back from me. "You're lucky to have been born into a family that loved you."

"I can't believe she did this to you."

He waved a hand.

"I killed her child. But later, she promised that she'd release me when she died. She said it wouldn't have to be forever."

I could see now how it had gone. He was their thing, their wonderful, eternal plaything.

"Do we all fall in love with you?" I asked.

"For a time. Usually it passes."

I felt sick. Was that all I'd felt for him? Some ghost of a feeling, handed down from my family? I didn't want Arthur to be a thing to me.

"It's funny," he said. "Persephone wouldn't let me talk about any of it. Some part of the magic. I suppose she didn't want anyone to know what she had done. I've never been able to tell anyone until you."

The way his mouth had tightened at the dinner table, not letting him say certain words. He could joke with us, laugh with us, sit at our table and pretend to eat our food. But he could never tell us what he really wanted, what he really meant.

"You deserve better," I said.

He scoffed and looked away.

"I mean it!" I reached out and pulled his face back toward me, looked into the places where his eyes should have been. "I'm going to get you out of here."

"You'll do nothing. You want to keep me here as badly as any of them."

"I do," I said. "But I won't."

I gritted my teeth. How did I say it? It usually happened by mistake.

"*You're free, Arthur,*" I said.

For a moment, we both waited, anticipating. The darkness felt thick around us. But at last, he shook his head.

"I'm so sorry," I said.

"Well," he said. "I have tried many things, over the years, to free myself, or to ruin the family. When you came, I thought perhaps you were my answer, since you seemed determined to ruin the business." He smiled humorlessly. "But you did better than that. Soon your grandmere will kill everyone here. And then maybe I'll be free. Or at the least, I'll be alone."

"You can't let that happen to us," I said.

"You're wrong," he said. "I can't hurt anyone in your family. But the beauty of this plan is that I don't have to do anything at all."

"I could make you help me."

"I know you won't."

"Does that mean you trust me?"

That made him smile a little, although I saw him try to hide it.

"I'm going to kill her," I said. "I'll poison her while she's sleeping. The drakondia is strong enough to kill anything. But I need to get upstairs without anyone seeing me come in. There's another way into the house, isn't there?"

He nodded and pointed into a shadowed corner. At first, I saw nothing, and then I realized that the dark stain on the wall was actually a hole. And inside that hole was a steep little flight of steps.

"Those used to come out in the kitchen," he said. "But now, there's a little hollow space, and they come out—"

"Under the staircase," I said. "I know."

He grabbed my hand. "It's a bad idea to go up there," he said. "She's very dangerous."

I looked down at the hand that had killed Miklos and Persephone's baby, wrapped around mine. Cool to the touch, but gripping me with surprising strength. I looked back up at him, and he let go as though I'd burned him. In spite of everything he'd said, he didn't want me getting hurt. That was something I could warm myself with.

"I'm going to find a way to get rid of her," I said. "And once she's gone I'm going to break the spell on you."

"Nothing will be different." He moved back and away from me, further into shadow. "Nothing is ever going to change for me."

"It will be," I said. "Because I'm different."

"I don't believe you."

I scrambled forward on my hands, feeling the damp cellar floor staining my skirt at the knees. I looked into his lovely, mutilated face.

"You don't have to believe me," I said. "Because I'm going to show you."

I wanted to kiss him, or to bite into his neck. But I didn't. I grinned at him in the dark instead, baring all my teeth.

"If I need your help," I asked, "can I count on you?"

"I am yours."

"Not for long!"

I thought I heard him laugh. But I was already scrambling through the hole on my hands and knees, into the crumbling ruins of an older basement with a half-rotted set of stairs.

I climbed up it carefully in the dark, testing each stair to see if it would hold my weight. And then, I was inside the walls. Wires hung down here and there and smacked me across the face. But I picked my way along slowly, feeling with my hands for the panel I knew was here, somewhere. Then, under my fingers, the latch that had stopped me last time.

The half light of the hallway was blinding after the darkness of the cellar. At first, I did not see Father crouched in front of me.

He was growling low, under his breath, little more than a dim shape on the carpet. I found myself wondering: How quickly could I get back into the wall? Would the panel hold him, if he tried to come after me?

"*Don't hurt me,*" I said, feeling sick doing it. "*Be quiet.*" It wasn't really him, so maybe it wasn't so wrong. But the growling didn't stop.

"That will not work, my dear," said Grandmere, from above us.

She came down the stairs and swept around the corner. She was wearing a long day dress of pale green, and she had her lavender gloves on, her hair perfectly coiffed. I hated her, but at the same time, I felt embarrassed to stand in front of her looking so dirty.

"Miles is a part of me, and you cannot possibly expect to command me," she said. She didn't sound angry, I realized. She was brisk, matter-of-fact. "But it is good that you have returned."

Father had not stopped growling and was advancing toward me.

"Now," Grandmere said. "*Shut that door, and do not leave this house again until I say you may.*"

I squeezed my eyes shut and poured every ounce of my concentration into holding my hands at my sides. But they lifted, and I turned around, and without looking, without wanting to, I closed the door. Grandmere smiled at me.

"At last," she said, "we can begin to talk seriously about your future."

When I finish speaking, Eleanor's body expels me. Without her to anchor me I float between the present and the past, as I have done since I died. I can show her snatches of it in dreams, but I cannot explain to a living girl what it is like to be dead: to be reliving everything that happened to you, all at once. I cannot leave the house; I have tried, and have found that if I try to leave by the back door, I come in through the front. High enough in the attic and I find myself down in the bottom of Arthur's pit in the cellar. My world is circumscribed by these walls.

I float through lonely years, when I could barely stand to be in the house: after Rhys died, after Lusitania vanished in her teens, after she left for good the day I sent Eleanor to school. I watch myself lie in bed for nearly a year after the death of Rhys, Miklos stalking the hills like a wild animal. Briefcases and suitcases piled up in the hall during those years I waited for Miklos to die. Margaret was born in those years, my strange child who spoke in single words before the age of one, and never spoke any more than that in her entire life.

I linger here, through the pain of reliving this grief, because I want to see Margaret again. After all, I was barely awake for it the first time around. As it goes, I only catch glimpses: when she toddles to my bedside to nurse, when she first brings us something: a glass of water, and my younger self drinks it, and holds her, and cries for the mother she was, once, to Rhys.

It is not anything he does that rouses her from her torpor. It is the visit at their door from a little group of women from town. They come in a huddle up the hill, carrying sticks and barely concealed boning knives. The woman at the head has a pistol. They knock on her door. We drag ourselves out of bed to answer it.

So sorry to bother you, *they say.* It's no trouble, *she replies with automatic politeness. When she talks to these women from town she sounds just like them.* My, what a surprise. Please, come in.

They crowd into her parlor and let her make them tea. She can feel them looking around the place. Miklos has an eye for architecture—or did, before we lost Rhys and he took to the woods. But he never cared much for furniture, so all we have is what she bought before she lost everything, including her interest in picking out chairs. The parlor has one chair in it and one low table. The women stand. Little Margaret comes and carries in the sugar bowl proudly in both hands. I look at her through the greasy hair that falls over my younger self's eyes. She must be three or four. She looks like I did as a child, if you had poured everything I was into a short squared-off body like Miklos's. Large eyes, dark hair, that good Cretan nose. I want to snatch her up from the past and bring her forward to a time when she could be loved properly, rather than being the goblin of my grief.

"We wanted to tell you," *says the elder Hannafin woman, the unspoken leader of the group.* "Your . . . dog has been getting closer and closer to town." *She uses the word dog with care, to avoid another word, but my younger self can't tell that right now.*

"I don't understand," she says. "We don't have a dog. Dogs don't like Miklos."

I want to slap her—is she asleep, or was I actually this stupid once?

"Well," says the old Mrs. Hannafin, "There is a . . . big dog . . . that comes from your lands. It's been seen a few times in the street at night. Maybe it's a wild dog." She will not say wolf. It has become the unspoken obscenity of this conversation. "Maybe your . . . husband could take care of it. If he doesn't, then we will have to do something about it."

Bless them. They didn't have to be this polite. They're showing gratitude for the love potions, the loaves of bread, the words whispered over their bellies in better times.

"We know you lost your boy," says a smaller woman from near the back, very young.

The others ease to the sides to let her forward. She is thin and dark-haired, with a deep crease in her forehead despite her youth. She could be a daughter of Agia Galini, one of the Cretan fishwives' children that Persephone had played with. She purses her lips together to wet them before she speaks again.

"I felt like you did once. Everything looks dark, you look at your family and you don't know them. But you've got a little girl now, Mrs. Zarrin. I know it's not the same. But she needs you the same. Time to adjust."

My younger self stirs a little inside her grief. Waking up.

"I'll talk to my husband," she says. "He's a hunter. He'll take care of the dog. I'm glad you told me."

That night when Miklos comes in, she is waiting for him. She has bathed, dressed, and combed her hair. Margaret has a clean dress on and sits on her lap, silent as always, pensively thumbing a silver spoon.

"You can't kill anyone in town, Miklos," she says. I help her along by mouthing the words. "And not their cows, their chickens, their pets. Stay away from the town."

"You can't tell me what to do," he says. I can see that he is trembling; he is afraid of me, after what he saw me do to Arthur. "I did not come to America to have another witch in a castle rule me."

This may be the first time she has ever heard him speak of this. She's angry. Why did he marry a witch and build her a castle if he was only going to hate her for it?

"You'll stay away from town, and you won't kill people, because if you do they'll kill you," she says. "That's why our son is dead. It's what happens when people are angry."

"I'm ready this time. They won't kill me."

"Miklos, you're not a god. If they cut you into a hundred pieces you will die. And I will die. And our daughter will die."

"So?" he says, meaning he doesn't care what happens to him, or to me. But Margaret, in her lap, begins to groan. He trembles.

"Little one, I didn't mean that," he says. Margaret's voice is *escalating in pitch. She is like her father, born without words. But she is not content to be silent. He shrinks back from us, growling as he goes.*

"Listen to me." Persephone has to raise her voice higher and higher to be heard over Margaret. "You can hate me. You can live in the woods. I don't care if I never see you again. But if you kill anyone from town or their animals, you will be killing our child. So promise me right now. Promise me, or we will leave and you will never see us again. And when they come to kill you and burn down your beautiful house—"

And then she feels Margaret go limp in her arms. Persephone lays her on the floor and puts a hand over Margaret's nose. She's breathing. My younger self and Miklos hunch over her for a long time, watching her with furious concentration, until her eyelids flutter open. Then she picks her daughter up, and he changes shape, and we scatter: Persephone to put her daughter to bed, Miklos to the woods, and my current self through the floorboards and down, until with a kind of splash I emerge into the cellar. I push through the dirt and cobwebs, slip around the rotted wooden box where Arthur's heart still glows like a hot coal, and go down into the present.

Eleanor and Arthur are there still. I'd felt years of my life peel away while they'd barely finished their conversation. I watch them curiously. Eleanor is promising Arthur that she'll help him. She'll be the one to set him free, to keep my broken promise. She doesn't want to. Like her father, she'd like to wrap up this strange man in her arms, keep him tucked into her bed like a hot water bottle, play piano with him in the dusty parlor, live and die with him by her side.

I don't understand it. But then again, I never saw the appeal of him. I only wanted to be with him because I thought it would answer my questions, but what I learned from him instead is that no one you love is ever fully yours. Not your lover, not your husband, not your child. No wonder I hated Arthur so, for introducing me to that truth. No wonder I made him stay and serve me, just to prove to myself that I had absolute control, if I wanted it. But understanding has come for me and has me in its grip. It hurts.

I believe Eleanor when she says she'll save him—she doesn't have any reason to love the rest of us, but he's different. Eleanor looks into the place where his eyes should be, and her expression is familiar. There's exasperation there, and pain and wonder and hope. Her feeling is real, even if the object of the feeling is not. Arthur died on that hill; whatever she is looking at isn't the man I knew, the man he pretends to be because I demanded it.

But there's something else. I've watched Arthur for years. I have a sense of how he feels about us: pity and loathing when someone takes an interest in him, and bitter rejection when they eventually abandon him, all without ever seeming to want anything from anyone. He doesn't even long for Miklos, not now that he's seen who Miklos really is: someone who would rip him up and leave him for dead. But this is different. He leans toward Eleanor like he's cold and she could warm him. When she eventually retreats up the steps, he flinches when she slips on a broken step. When we are alone again, I tell him, "I should never have done what I did."

"You had your reasons," he says. He clambers face-first into the pit in which he lives, and picks up his book, ignoring me and the sounds from upstairs alike. "Luckily she forgot to put me away. At least I can do some reading while I wait to find out if she dies."

I whisper to him in the darkness, "You sound almost melancholy."

"I don't love her, if that's what you mean," he says. "I just want her love to save me."

I don't tell him that that's how it always begins: in selfishness, in ambition, in lust or desperation. That love starts out as something you want to bite into and ends as something that swallows you up.

ELEVEN

FOR A MOMENT, I WAS NOT MYSELF. I WAS IN the past, watching a group of nervous women cluster in the empty hall, clutching one another's arms tightly in terror as they tried to explain something to me. But then I was myself again, in the present, the same hallway now lined with paintings. Grandma Persephone was telling me that she was here. That she hadn't abandoned me.

I took a deep breath as Grandmere gestured me toward the dining room.

"Will you come and sit down with me?" she asked. I didn't move. "I would rather not have to tell you."

I followed her into the dining room, Father padding along behind us. She seated herself, and when I'd done the same, she folded her hands together and beamed at me from across the table.

"Why did you do this to him?" I asked her.

"Because it was necessary," she said. "He was too useful to ignore or get rid of, but he was not behaving as he should. I did what I had to do."

"He wasn't something for you to use," I said. "He was my father."

"Oh, these things come and go," she said. "When you are as old as I am, you can take a longer view. I believe you will understand eventually."

"How old are you?"

She shrugged. "I do not keep track of these things."

"How old is Mother?"

"Oh, she is quite young. Perhaps two hundred. Does that help you?"

That meant Grandmere very old indeed.

"So," she said, "I think we can both see that this went badly."

"You've done this before."

She nodded. "I have to, from time to time, to stay alive. But it's useful in other ways, too."

I imagined her doing this over centuries. Turning up places and then managing them, commanding some, devouring others, laughing and joking and throwing parties all the while. The ruse could last for a long time, I imagined, if she was careful.

"Grandpa said you tried to eat him when he was young," I said. "Have you been after him all this time?"

"I certainly never forgot him. What an interesting specimen! But I had no idea that he was here until your mother wrote to me. And then I came and found all of you. So many of you, and all so . . . useful."

"Are you going to kill me now?" I asked.

She looked shocked.

"Eleanor," she said, "why would you say such a thing? No, of course not." She reached out to touch my hand; I snatched it back. "You are one of mine, and I want only the best for you."

"Then leave me alone."

"Oh, I cannot do that," she said. "You are still very young, and you do not have very much. I have an army inside of me." She touched her throat with one gloved hand. Her neck was still bandaged. "You do not. You need some strong creatures to help you get started in the world. When you wrote to me, you asked me to help you. This is the help that I can give you, my love. You are your mother's greatest achievement. You are my only heir. I cannot let you go."

"You killed my father."

"I should have saved him for you," she said. "I meant for you to have all of them. To take with you, so you could keep them forever. But, sadly, it is too late for that."

I looked around wildly. "Wait. Where's Mother? Is she still here?"

"You think I would hurt her?"

"I'm going to go find her now."

She waved a hand. "Be my guest. I would not restrict you in your own house."

I stood up, looking at her warily. She shrugged. I went past her, past Father, and up the stairs to the bathroom on the second floor. I knocked. "Mother?"

A wary voice inside said, "Yes?"

"It's me. Eleanor."

I opened the door. Mother sat in the tub, submerged up to her chin. She looked like she had been crying.

"Is it you?" I asked. "Tell me something only you would know."

She studied me cautiously.

"When you were little, I knew what you were," she said. "I saw you telling Rhys what to do, and Charlie. I told you to stop, that if you did that, you would never know who your friends were. And then you cried."

I shut the door behind me and ran to the tub. I reached in and hugged her as hard as I could. When I pulled back, I'd stained her face with dirt from the cellar.

And then I reached over and turned on the tap. The room filled with the sound of rushing water. I leaned in close, so I could whisper.

"Mama," I said. "We can't let her do this. You have to tell me how we can stop her."

"I can't tell you," she whispered. She started to say something, stopped, tried again. "She asked me not to. I can't. Do you see? I can't."

She clung to me with her damp hands. I forced myself to look at her face.

"You can't," I said. "Because she won't let you?"

She nodded.

"Well," I said, "*you can tell me now.*"

She opened her mouth, and then put a hand to it in astonishment.

"She is very weak when she has just taken in a new person," she said. "And she gets tired when she tries to control more than a few people at a time." She saw my face fall. "I don't know if I can tell you much more than that. Other than . . ."

"What is it?"

"She loves you," Mother said. "That's real."

"Are you defending her?"

"No," she said. "I'm helping you."

There was a knock on the door. "Eleanor?" Grandmere said from outside.

Mother slid down under the water as I opened the door.

"Are you satisfied?" Grandmere said.

I glanced back over my shoulder. "Yes."

"That's enough, then," she said. "Will you come back downstairs with me?" She phrased it as a question, I noticed. I followed her.

"If you really want to leave this place," she said, when we

were back downstairs, "we can. But you should come with me. And I will compromise with you. You can leave the rest of your family, if you want. I doubt they will pursue us. *But before you leave this house, you will take one of them.* For protection. I think the boy is best."

"Rhys?"

She nodded. "He is strong and fast. He will represent you well, when you need him to—you can even wear him, once you are more practiced. It's useful to have a man with you, for traveling. You and I can even go our own ways, if you want. I will not make you stay with me."

I hesitated.

"Once we leave, the rest of your family can do what they please," she said. "Your sister and your grandfather will come back from the woods, your mother can stay in her bath for as long as she wants, your aunt can cook and clean in peace. They will be happy. And I doubt they will miss you very much." She frowned. "They have never understood you like I do."

She could make me do it. But Mother had said that Grandmere loved me. She wanted me to choose to do things her way. I had the most power if I could make her believe I was still like her. More power to save my family, to save Rhys.

"You're right," I said. "They don't understand me. They never even liked me."

I made myself cry, then. It wasn't very hard; I just looked at my father, sitting on the floor at Grandmere's feet, waiting for her next command. I thought of my grandpa in the woods. Of Arthur, somewhere in the dark below me.

"Oh," she said. "Oh, my dear."

She stepped forward and folded me up in her arms. I forced myself not to pull away. While she held me, I could feel shapes swimming under her skin. I imagined birds, fish, men-at-arms, and things I couldn't name.

There was no way out now, I thought. I couldn't leave until I ate someone. But maybe I could distract her long enough to get everyone else out. She'd told me not to let Rhys out of his room. But what if he was already out?

The idea began to form in my mind, but I didn't act on it right away. I cried in Grandmere's arms until I exhausted myself. She sent me upstairs to bed, and then sent Margaret up with a bowl of soup. I ate what I could, and then Grandmere came in to talk to me some more, to tell me about all the wonderful places we could go when it was just her and me. I listened, and leaned against her shoulder, and she stroked my hair.

"I think I would like to see California," I said at last.

"That is nothing," she said. "You still ask for so little. I wish you would ask for more. You deserve so much."

"I don't know how to ask," I said. "Can I have some time to think about it? About all of this? I want to come with you." I kept my eyes on her, even though they wanted to dart toward the door. "I want to see the world with you. But I need a little time to let go of this place. Of who I used to be."

"Of course," she said. "We have all the time in the world."

She kissed me on the forehead, and tucked the covers in around me, as though I were little. And she left, shutting the door behind her.

For a week, I came to her whenever I thought of anything I might want, or whenever I could pretend to be sad or lonely—which was not so hard to pretend, rattling around that empty house. Arthur didn't come upstairs. I wondered if he'd told Grandmere about the door, or if she had figured it out on her own. Either way, I wasn't sure he could help me. I was cold to Margaret and ignored Mother if Grandmere was out and about.

She started talking to me about her past. A lot of what she told me was jumbled. She didn't seem to have a clear understanding of time, and some details seemed to be from the wrong stories. But what I learned was that she had been doing this for centuries. This was her way of living: enter a castle, or a great house, and eat it from the inside. She had to eat, she told me. It kept her fresh and renewed over the centuries—a new body for her outside, new creatures to call upon. It didn't have to be people, but that was what she preferred.

She didn't seem to sleep at normal hours, but whenever she took a nap, I roamed the house. Sometimes I tried the doors, to see if her powers had worn off over time. I couldn't even touch the doorknobs. And always I had to stay out of sight of the thing that used to be my father, which stalked the house while Grandmere slept, moving silently from room to room.

And then one day, she said to me, "I think it's time to practice."

She sent Father out into the woods. He came back that evening carrying a struggling, kicking sack.

"Now," she said, "I will show you what you can do, if you only try."

She nodded to Father, and he opened the sack and pulled out a young rabbit by the ears. He held it down on the table while it struggled. Grandmere picked it up around its midsection with both hands and opened her mouth.

It got wider and wider, until it seemed to be splitting her face, until her jaw creaked and strained. Inside was darkness: not a mouth, just black nothing. She slid the rabbit in, and it vanished, down to its kicking hindpaws. She shut her mouth, and swallowed, and smiled at me, all at once a grandmother again.

And then she opened her mouth and let it fall back out.

The rabbit that emerged was not afraid. It ambled over to me, looked up at me, regarded me out of cool yellow eyes.

"It's mine now," she said. "Do you see?"

The rabbit returned to her and allowed itself to be swallowed again. I suddenly had a sense of enormity, of scale. I imagined ships. Villages. Forests. Creatures from the bottom of the sea.

Father pulled out a second rabbit from the bag. One of its legs was broken, so when he put it on the table, it was oddly still, although I could hear its heart beating wildly.

"Somewhere inside of you is a crack," she said. "Why don't you try to open it?"

I could feel something in the back of my throat. It was the feeling I got when I was angry, when I was lonely. The feeling that I was a pit and that I could swallow anything if I tried. I looked at the rabbit. I knew exactly what she meant. It had been in me for as long as I could remember.

I grabbed the rabbit with both hands and opened my mouth wide.

It was gone before I knew what had happened. It was so easy. My throat ached, and I felt sick to my stomach.

Grandmere was elated.

"Very good!" she said. "And on your first try. You know, your mother couldn't do it, even when I insisted. She tried, but she doesn't have it." She clapped her hands together. "Oh, I am so proud, my darling. Can you let it back out? I want to see you do it."

"I'm very tired," I said.

"Oh, of course. I am sorry. Please, get some rest."

I went to my room and shut the door. Sitting in the rocking chair, I tried to let the rabbit out. It slipped out of my mouth and into my lap and sat there calmly. I could feel it, in the same way I could feel my hand on my leg. I had it walk around the room. Its leg was healed, its body made perfect, but it wasn't alive. It was just me. Just more of me.

I had it get in my arms. I picked it up and carried it into

Luma's room. And then I pushed aside the dresser and had it crawl through the hole into Rhys's room. I made it hold still, in the middle of the room. I could see Rhys through its eyes. He sniffed at it, and then snapped it up in his jaws and broke its neck. It hurt, but only for a second, and then I couldn't feel it anymore.

I huddled up on my side of the wall and cried. Eventually, Rhys crept over to the hole.

"Wait," he said. "Should I not have done that?"

"No, I wanted you to."

"Ellie," he said. "Why did you do this to us?"

"I didn't mean to." I sniffled. "I'm sorry."

A long pause. And then: "It's okay."

I crawled through the hole and into his room. He had blood on his face. He wiped at it with his sleeve.

"I'm going to get you out of here," I said. "But you have to trust me."

"What are you going to do?" he asked.

"I can't tell you," I said. "But I promise, I won't mess it up this time."

At breakfast the next morning, I waited until Grandmere had settled in, and then coughed.

"Grandmere," I said. "Can I ask you for something?"

Her eyebrows shot up. "Of course," she said. "Anything."

"I feel a little silly."

"Nothing you could say is silly to me."

"I'd like to have a party," I said. "Before I . . . take Rhys. I'd like to have a party, like a normal girl. With guests, and music. And dancing. And flowers, and maybe someone other than Margaret to do some of the cooking. I've just never felt wanted here, not with Rhys and Luma always getting the best of everything." I made myself choke up. "I'd like to feel special, for one day."

I looked up at her, through the little haze of tears I was calling up by thinking of Grandpa in the woods, his broken teeth, his sad yellow eyes. Grandmere's brow furrowed in sympathy.

"I can give you that," she said. "If that is what you want. Tell me just how you would like it to be, and it will be."

I began to lay it out for her, a little at a time, over the next few days. First, we had to have as many real people as possible, and as few of Grandmere's pawns as I could get away with, so I said I wanted to invite the whole town. Fill the house with bodies, too many of them for her to control entirely. She made suggestions about guests she could call forth from her collection, but I rejected as many as I could, saying they were too odd, or not fun enough. I insisted on a live band for another ten people. And I said I wanted Rhys and Mother there; I wanted them to see me at my best, I said. I wanted them to understand just who they'd thrown away.

"And I want Arthur to come."

She smiled. "Of course."

She wouldn't let me go to town to post the invitations; she sent Father instead. But of course she didn't know that I wasn't trying to escape anymore. I threw myself into the details of the party: the decorations, the food. And in the meantime, I scoured the house for a way of setting a fire.

There is so much I want to tell them all. I have made so many mistakes. Things I cannot undo from where I am now.

I cannot go and find my husband in the woods, not that I think he could hear me if I did. He has always been a simple man. It is madness to love someone: there is no greater feeling of estrangement than the ways in which they are different from you.

I go to Margaret. She is the one who has always been the greatest mystery to me. I want to tell her I'm still here. I want to explain to her what has happened.

She is in the kitchen, looking out the window. She has always known I was here, since the night she opened up the vulture. When she feels me get close to her, she does something surprising. She steps backward, into me, and suddenly the two of us are together in the past. Margaret, how talented you are! I don't think I ever noticed. You were born when I was sick with grief, and so I never saw how you watched me, how you watched Miklos, how you gave up words and silently learned perfection in other things. She has brought me into her past, into her memory. She has brought me to a moment I did not know she saw.

She is small, standing on a chair to wash dishes in the sink. She is looking out the open window to the back garden, where I have gone to speak to Miklos.

Rhys was several years dead, Margaret old enough to be left on her own, and Miklos and I had barely spoken in years. And so I'd taken up with Tom. He was so young then, bad at sermons, a nervous stammerer, and I'd loved him for being normal after so much pain. And this was the day that I had read the guts and learned I was pregnant.

My younger self stands in front of him, trembling, until he glances up to see what kind of narrow shadow has fallen across him. She touches her stomach with a hand still bloodstained from augury.

"I'm sorry, Miklos," she says.

He changes so that he can stand on two legs as a man should when confronting his wife. She thinks with regret that he is lovely. Not lovely like a spindly fair boy, but lovely like a shark or a wave, the thing that is going to kill her. She hopes he will take good care of their daughter when she is dead.

"I should have belonged only to you," she said. "But I didn't." There's reproach in the way she says it, as well as regret—why didn't he want to keep her? "And now there's a child."

I remember young Miklos as a creature who never had a com-

WHAT BIG TEETH • 355

*plicated feeling in his life. His anger, his grief, have all had space in
them only for him. Now for the first time I watch as he feels a mixed
emotion. Anger certainly, but at what? She is not his, he is not hers,
and they have not been for some time. Except that they are glued
together by the ghost of Rhys. Miklos is not good at speaking. And so
he opens his mouth and puts together a few slow, faltering sentences.*

*"I left a place," he says, "where kings and princes owned us.
Where a witch in a high castle owned us. Where priests and work
owned us." He takes a step toward her, and she is transfixed like a
rabbit before a wolf. "You do not belong to me, and I do not belong
to you." Her heart falls through the floor. He sees this and tries again
to explain what he means: "I do not own the woman I love."*

"What should we do?" she asks. "About the child?"

He shrugs.

"Your children are my children," he said. "This is our family."

*She descends the steps and throws her arms around him. Together
they collapse to their knees among her cabbages. Her hand, still
bloody, caresses his cheeks and hair, leaves him streaked with red.
His fingers wrap around her fingers. This is the moment, I realize,
when I loved my husband for the first time. When I forgave him for
having parts of himself that did not belong to me, as I had parts of
myself that he would never know.*

*Margaret tips her head forward and I slide from the envelope
of her body. She has always been my greatest mystery, the child I
understood the least. And now I see that she is the answer to my
old question. Who was my lover before he was mine? He was like*

this. Silent and cunning, hardworking, savage, strange. Preparing a den for animals he hadn't met yet. I think suddenly of Margaret's teenage years, when she would disappear from the house for long stretches of time to the village and would come back looking like a contented cat. She is not secretive, not deceitful—she just does not ask and does not tell, because nothing she is must be said. We never explained ourselves to her; she learned how we loved her, and each other, by watching what we did. You care for people and you give them tasks. You leave them and you come back. You bite and you kiss, and there is nothing words can say more eloquently than gestures.

And then when she had a child, he looked so much like my boy that I took him from her and named him Rhys. I used her silence, her acceptance, against her.

Did I bring this other grandmother to our house? Maybe she didn't kill me by appearing to me in the cards. Maybe I was about to die, and the empty space I was leaving found something to fill itself. Some other monster of domination and control. A different skin, a different method. But a monster all the same.

But Margaret doesn't look at me like I'm a monster. She reaches out to stroke my ghostly cheek, and her hand slides through me. She smiles, and her smile is Miklos's, wicked and noble and all teeth. She reaches deep down into her throat and pulls out a single little-used word. "Mother," she says.

"I'm here," I say to her. "I'm going to fix this."

She shakes her head vigorously, then nods toward the doorway.

She grins at me before picking up a broom. Her whole demeanor changes, and she shifts from a wild, lovely thing to a shapeless drudge in a single motion, and begins sweeping and muttering to herself. Then the shape appears in the doorway.

The other grandmother looks less like an old woman with each passing day. The skin is still there, but the shape bulges oddly and occasionally wriggles like a sackful of cats. I can see that the shape has a hand clamped over its neck, and that something inside of its throat is struggling against the surface. It loses its grip for a moment, and a fat crow tumbles out onto the floor. She makes a grab for it, but Margaret, sweeping and muttering, knocks it away from her with the broom. It goes skittering across the floor, wings flapping in indignation. I'd laugh, if I had lungs.

I watch in horror as the creature advances on Margaret. It takes its hands off of the gash in its neck, and a few more birds slip out and orbit its body. It grabs for my daughter with both hands, and—

"Grandmere?"

It turns, clamping down on its neck.

Eleanor stands in the doorway. She looks different. Older, somehow, than when I saw her last. She wears a dress of gray silk. Her hair is held up by pearl combs. She looks like snow falling on the sea. She looks like a witch. The creature has changed her; she's become stronger, more substantial, more aware of what she can do. I spent so long hoping to keep that from her. Now I feel afraid of what she will do with it.

"My dear," the creature says, "I'm a little busy."

"Grandmere, your neck still hasn't healed," Eleanor says. "Please, let me help you."

The creature relaxes visibly. It is warmed by Eleanor's presence. I think, in horror, that it loves her.

"Oh, my dear," it says. "I am fine, please do not worry."

"What do you need? Tell me, and I'll fetch it. You should go upstairs and lie down."

Eleanor is controlling her, I think. Not with force. But she is angling her into a position.

"Very well," it says. It shoots Margaret one last evil look, and then turns for the door. Clutching the hole in its neck, it uses its other hand to take Eleanor's arm.

They've killed my son. They've driven my husband from his house. But when I look at Margaret, I see that she looks untroubled as they leave the room. She's humming. I recognize the song I used to sing to her when she was little, the song about bones ground into dust, as she finishes her sweeping and starts preparing dinner. I see her reach up to a high shelf and take down a bottle of snake lily extract, prepared as poison. She dilutes it and pours a little bit onto a square of bandage, and when Eleanor comes back downstairs, she hands it to her, still humming. Eleanor nods to her and puts her finger to her lips. Shh.

"Grandmere," Eleanor calls up, "I'm going to come change your bandage."

Margaret glances at the empty air I inhabit.

"Traitor," she says, raising her eyebrows and jerking her head in Eleanor's direction.

Traitor, yes. Our *traitor. I wish I could give her some sign that she is not alone.*

I wait until the creature has gone to sleep, then creep through the house, through ever unfolding layers of past and present, to Eleanor's room. She is holding a book of matches and looking serious. I dim the lamp beside her bed, just for a moment. She shivers and looks up.

"I think I know why you sent me away," she says. "You thought I was like her."

I realize that I can speak to her. I bring the lights up a little. She nods.

"Did you miss me?" she asks. "While I was away?"

There isn't enough light in the whole house to answer.

To stay quiet, she writes down questions in a notebook and points to them. And I make the lights go. On for yes, off for no.

At last, of course, she asks me about Arthur. Whether he is a dead creature (yes). Whether he has any other names, whether he was bound to the grounds (no and yes—why does she want to know that?). Some of her questions I cannot answer—how can I tell her how far he can travel with yes and no?

How can I break the curse on him, *she writes.*

I had honestly never planned for it. I'd promised him I'd let him go before I died, but I never really thought it would happen, so I had never worked to figure it out. I feel so foolish. I put the lights out entirely, and we sit in dark silence for a while.

WHY DID YOU DO THIS TO HIM *she writes, so forcefully that the tip of the pencil goes through the paper. There is no way for me to answer this as a yes or a no. She knows. She just wants me to know she's angry.*

I make the lamp flicker. It's the only answer I can give her. Because I was alone in a country not my own with a man I didn't know very well. Because I could. Because I didn't yet know what love was. Because my power had its own desire to be used. There is so much I cannot say to her, and so I slip my soul behind her eyes for just a moment, and open her mouth, and hear the ghost of my own voice say, "I'm sorry. Eleanor, I am so, so sorry."

TWELVE

IN THE DAYS LEADING UP TO THE PARTY, MRS.
Hannafin had done her part and drummed up most of the people in the village to come to the house to celebrate. Rhys and I were going to Europe with our grandmere to study in Paris, it was said. Mrs. Hannafin had talked about how much our hospitality had improved with Grandmere here, how good the food was, how polite and respectful we'd all become.

And so, right on time, about a hundred of Winterport's finest came pouring up the hillside. The musicians we'd hired from a few towns over were tuning up in the parlor. Grandmere swept in, looked outside, and gestured to them. "Go on," she said. "Start playing!"

They shrugged and looked at her. "We're not quite ready yet."

I'd told them earlier to take their time tuning up. "I've got good pitch," I'd said. "And I don't want to have a headache while my guests are here. Even if people come in, don't start until you're sure."

She waved at them impatiently. "*Start playing,*" she said, and the conductor began waving his hands, and she turned to me. Her cheek bulged for a moment, and she gave it a swat with her hand to quiet whatever was moving beneath her skin.

"It is going to be lovely, just lovely," she said. "I will see to every detail. You enjoy yourself."

I had already seen to every detail. I'd told Grandmere that I wanted white frosting, and then had crept into the kitchen and put a few drops of coloring into the mixture when no one was looking. I'd hired a photographer and had given him the wrong start time for the party. And I'd insisted that Rhys come to the party, his last party, and that he behave himself. By the time the day was over, Grandmere was going to be exhausted from managing every little detail I could throw at her.

Meanwhile, I'd sent Margaret to the cellar for a jug of kerosene and put it in the hall closet behind a curtain of dusty winter coats. Margaret, when she'd seen what I was doing, had given me a wicked grin and a sack of flour to really get the blaze going. I was starting to like her.

People whispered about the flower garlands on the stairs, the cleanliness of the hall, darting nervous glances at me the whole time. I smiled tightly back at them.

"Big day!" Mrs. Hannafin said next to me.

I turned. She looked the same as she had the last time I had seen her, perhaps a little better dressed. But something about the way she'd said it made me uneasy. I'd seen her and Grandmere talking only a minute before, and Mrs. Hannafin had seemed flustered then, not calm the way she was now. I had to test it.

"I thought you'd be disappointed we're leaving," I said. "I know you wanted your daughter to marry a Zarrin and get rich."

She exhaled and leaned back on her heels. "Big day."

Her eyes looked vacant. I wondered if Grandmere was behind them, watching me.

"Well," I said, "I can see that we have nothing to talk about." And I moved on, through the party. I was looking for Arthur. There was something I needed to tell him. But I couldn't find him anywhere: not in the parlor, or the dining room, or even the library, which had filled with village women drinking wine and oohing over the books. Where was he?

I ran into Rhys instead. He was dressed up and smiling wildly. I didn't know exactly what Grandmere had told him to do, but I could see the rage bubbling just behind his eyes. He was holding a champagne flute so tightly that it had cracked a little, and drops of it had beaded on his hand. But he was out of his room, and that was what mattered.

"Rhys," I said, "listen to me very carefully."

I ordered him to do nothing at all out of line until I said his name again. And even if he didn't hear it or see it, even if he'd been told to do something else, when I said his name he should run upstairs, get Mother from the tub, carry her down the back stairs and out to the woods. He should go find Luma and Grandpa, and tell them that Eleanor said she was sorry, that she loved them. He should tell them that she couldn't promise the house would be safe again, but that at least they would be free. Tell them they should run and not look back. Tell them Eleanor was going to end Grandmere once and for all.

"Do you understand?" I asked.

He nodded, his eyes filling with tears. Sentimental creature. Good thing he had me to look after him.

I threw my arms around his neck then. I kissed him on the cheek. And then I melted back into the crowd, before Grandmere could see me.

Everything after that became a kind of blur. The feast was, of course, spectacular, and thronged with well-wishers. Grandmere had supplied some of them from her collection: charming men and women and a few children who rounded out the party and made it feel like a real occasion, full of real and happy celebrants. The villagers believed it. Women who ordinarily frowned at me in the street came to tell me what a good time they were having. Men shook my hand. Mrs. Hannafin appeared periodically to tell me what a big, big day it was.

And then the door opened one last time, and Arthur came in.

My breath caught when I saw him. I'd forgotten how it felt to look at him, the giddy ache. I wanted to cry and run into his arms. I wanted him to take me away from this place and never look back. He wore the black silk jacket that Grandmere had ordered for him, his dark glasses reflecting the faces gathered in the room. And then he spotted me and gave me an almost imperceptible smile.

"Will you dance with me?" he asked.

With everything that was happening, it surprised me that I could still feel shy.

"Don't worry," he said. "I asked you."

I let him take my arm and walk me into the parlor, where a few other couples were swaying to the music. Arthur put a hand on my waist, twining his other hand in mine and pointing them together toward the sky. He twirled me and then guided me by the waist closer to him until I felt like I was floating along the ground to the tune of a slow violin waltz. I couldn't breathe.

"What's your plan?" he asked.

"I'm going to burn down the house. The family will leave after that and not come back. You'll be alone, and have the run of whatever's left, the grounds. I know it's not the same as being free, exactly, but at least there won't be any Zarrins here anymore. It's the best I can do."

He looked irritated; his chin flicked up and away from me, his head moving slightly as he scanned the room. I wondered what his empty eyes saw in this dim room lit with candles, filled with nervously dancing bodies. The villagers seemed to bumble aside every time they got too close to us, wrinkling their noses at the smell of embalming fluid and mothballs.

"I am still not free," he said. "You, like every other Zarrin before you, have broken your promise to me. I suppose I should not be surprised."

"But you're angry."

"What do you care how I feel?"

"I . . ."

I felt silly. The home I had once loved was stitched up in Grandmere's plans. Luma and Grandpa Miklos hated me and were living off of squirrels in the woods. My father was dead, my mother a prisoner. Everything that mattered was lost. But still when I looked at Arthur I felt some little warm point of hope.

"Because I love you," I said.

He shook his head.

"That's an empty sentiment," he said. "I'm yours, inherited along with the house, so I suppose you can do what you want with me. If you say you love me, all you mean is that you like that I belong to you."

"It's not like that."

He spun and dipped me, bending me back until our spines were parallel to the floor. Close to me now, I could see the stitches that held him together, little threads shoring up rips in the fabric of his thin body.

"If I could kill you, do you think I would?" he asked.

I stared past my own reflection in his dark glasses. I could see the sunken sockets of his eyes through them; I'd just never bothered to look before. I forced myself to really look.

Yes, I thought he would kill me if he could. For months I'd studied him, wondering what kind of man he was. But he wasn't a man. The schoolteacher of Winterport had been vacated, a series of empty rooms leading only to other empty rooms. In trying to know him, in trying to solve him, I'd only ever seen what was left from the disaster. And meanwhile, he'd been elsewhere; maybe I'd never seen him. Or maybe only in moments: the part of him that had taught me piano when Grandma Persephone wasn't looking, or sat with me in the dining room after everyone else had left. He was that anger I'd seen in the cellar. He was the question he'd just asked me. He was a carefully nurtured spark of defiance. He was what happened when you cornered someone, when they had nowhere left to go. I remembered Grandpa Miklos saying, "The wolf could move when I could not."

How could I help Arthur? There *was* no Arthur. When I'd said, "You're free, Arthur," I'd been talking to no one at all.

"You're not Arthur Knox," I said.

He paused for a moment. "Don't play games with me."

"No, really," I said. "You're what was born when he died. Arthur is just a name for your body."

What had Luma said about changing shape? That it was like

turning yourself inside out. Underneath yourself, another self. As close as skin, always there, whether you used it or not. I took a deep breath.

"Somewhere inside of you there's someone else," I said. "You just have to reach in and pull it out."

He stopped stock still, as though listening for a distant sound. Around us, I felt the villagers grind to a halt, too. I reached up and touched his face; it twitched under my fingertips. It felt warm—soon, almost hot.

"You aren't the man who died on this hill," I said. "You're something else. *And that something is already free.*"

A shiver ran through him. Dimly, I was aware that we were being watched. Arthur reached up to his face and took off his glasses.

Where his eyes had once been, now there was a red glow along the line of stitches, a sourceless bright light that seemed to press outward. He gleamed and burned from the inside, as though his body were a paper lantern. He opened his mouth and grinned at me, and light poured out from the gaps in his teeth. A gleaming clear spirit, wearing his body loosely, like a skin that might be shed.

"I see now," he said.

He turned and the crowd gasped.

He began wading through them, toward the door. Some of them screamed and jostled. People fainted. Father Thomas stepped between Arthur and the doorway and put up a hand.

Arthur picked him up by the waist, as though waltzing with him, twirled him lightly through the air, and set him aside. The man who had been Arthur leaped out of the house and into the night. His outline shone through the spaces between the trees as he ran.

I wanted to watch him until I couldn't see him anymore. But I didn't have time. I needed to make my move.

I pushed my way upstream through the crowd. Grandmere was on the other side of the hall, in the dining room, pushing her way toward the center, too. She sounded weary and irritable. Good, I thought. I started making my way toward her. "*Rhys,*" I said, just before she reached me.

"Grandmere," I said, when she got close, "Arthur's gone! He turned into a monster!"

She rushed to my side and grabbed me in her arms. Her whole body rippled, as though something very large had just passed beneath her skin. "I'll keep you safe," she said. "*Everyone stay put!*"

Behind me, I heard the back door slam. Rhys had made it outside.

I looked up to the ceiling. I wondered if Grandma Persephone was here. "Help me," I whispered. And I felt the air around me grow cold.

When I manage to climb my way back to my family, the house is full of people—a party, from the looks of it. In the kitchen, Margaret is

weaving in and out of the cooks who have been hired to cater. She is keeping them busy, undoing parts of their work, staying underfoot. Then Eleanor appears in the doorway, and I see a look pass between them. Margaret hugs her. There are tears in her eyes. Eleanor disappears back into the party.

I follow Margaret into the recesses of the kitchen. She's staring out the back door. At the tree line, I can see the wolves. The bright white of my granddaughter's fur points them out to me, and only then can I make out Miklos's shaggy gray coat.

They're waiting.

Margaret starts packing up her set of kitchen knives. She casts a long look back toward the parlor as she clicks the lid shut on a suitcase stamped with the letter Z. Her eyes flick to the tree line, back to the parlor.

They're going to abandon her, then. Eleanor is alone. Why should she not be, I think briefly. Was I ever not alone at her age?

But why should she have to be, when she has us?

When Margaret opens the door, I shove it shut. Only an inch or two, but it's enough. She looks up at the empty air, touches the doorknob gingerly again. I shut it again.

She nods. She puts on her boots, but she leaves the suitcase behind. Soon she is striding across the lawn, her hands raised as she pantomimes a story about a girl who wants to save her family.

A dark shape rushes through me and follows her out the door. Rhys! He bounds across the lawn to catch up to them. Eleanor is working hard tonight. Maybe there's something I can do for her.

I flit into the main hall. It's a teeming crowd, re-expanding after parting to let Rhys through. It's a riot about to happen. How can I make this worse? The front door is gaping open; I fling it shut on some poor fisherman's fingers. I rattle the windowpanes. I turn off the lights.

THIRTEEN

THERE WERE ENOUGH GUESTS THAT THEY couldn't all be controlled. Some of them stood stock-still in the front hall in whatever poses they were in when Grandmere told us not to move. But others were bolting for the doors. And I realized that I could help the chaos. She'd told me not to move, but she had said nothing about speaking.

"*Everybody panic!*" I yelled, and the air filled with screaming. People were running, trampling. Someone grabbed the coat rack from the front hall and charged at Grandmere with it. It happened in slow motion, while she was screaming at me, and I had time to wish I panicked like that. The prongs of the coat rack went into her, and I watched them come out her front, bent and distorted. "*Run,*" I whispered at the man, and he bolted into the night. I hoped he would stop running eventually.

Grandmere stared down at her chest for a moment. Then, arms bending backward, she reached behind her and grabbed the coat rack. She yanked it from her back, and a little torrent of creatures came out of her: the rabbit, a pair of spotted hunting dogs, a fistful of snakes. Eventually, she was ringed by a ragged cadre of animals, growling and snapping at anyone who came near her. From the other room, I could see the red-haired girl with the double row of teeth, pushing her way toward us.

And then the lights went out. People running past jostled me, but I couldn't move from the spot. I tried to keep my eyes focused on the dim shape in front of me that was Grandmere.

"Listen to me," she said. "I am not angry with you. But I am very disappointed. Don't you love me? Don't you care what happens to me?"

I felt like crying. "I do love you," I said. "But I can't let you keep doing this to people. They don't belong to you."

It was suddenly quiet and echoey around us. I realized the guests had fled. It was just Grandmere and me, and her cadre, a gathered assembly that looked almost like one mass in the dark.

"I don't want to fight you," she said. "You would be utterly destroyed."

I tried again to move. I still couldn't. The matches were tucked in the palm of my hand. The hall closet was not so far away, if I could only have made a run for it. But I was glued to the spot.

"I must remind myself that you are young," Grandmere said.

"That you may someday not be as hopeless as you are now. We will have to leave this place, of course. I will have to find us another household."

This was how it ended. She wouldn't even kill me. She was going to take me away somewhere and make me eat someone else. At least my family was safe, what was left of them. They shouldn't have sent me away to school, I thought. Lusitania was right. They should have killed me the night I ate the banker's boy.

And then, I had an idea.

"Grandmere," I said. "Please." I was already on the edge of tears. It wasn't hard to cry. Her face softened a little, and she took a step toward me. I opened my mouth.

The boy's body slid out onto the floor with a thud. It was my body. I could steer it as easily as my own. I let go of the book of matches, and he caught them as easily as if I'd passed them from one hand to another.

"What?" Grandmere shouted.

I got him scrambling to his feet. He was small, maybe eight or nine, and quick. He darted easily around Grandmere's pile of bodies. She was tired and wounded. The snakes lunged for him, the hunting dogs sprang up and trotted after him, but he was fast. It was too dark to see, but I knew the way. I got him to the closet, threw open the door, struck a match, and tossed it in. It blazed for a second. And then, I felt that second body of mine erupt into fire. The pain was indescribable. I screamed, and I would have fallen down if I could.

The staircase was burning now, a great waterfall of fire at our sides. Grandmere and her creatures were illuminated by the flames.

"That was clever," she said. "I admire that. I was wrong to call you hopeless. But you must come to see the futility of fighting me. There is too much of me. And I suspect," she said, "that that was your last trick. Unless you want to throw a rabbit at me—"

It took me a second to hear it, over the roar of the fire. A steady growl coming from the kitchen.

And then, the pack lunged.

Grandpa Miklos fell on the hunting dogs, while Rhys leaped at Father. Luma, on two legs, took a run at the girl with her piranhalike teeth, and then slashed a handful of dagger claws across her throat.

It was seamless, beautiful, like a dance. Luma dropped to the ground, and by the time she landed she was a white wolf of enormous size. She snarled at Grandmere, sprang up lightly on her paws, and leaped through the air and into Grandmere's face. Luma tore Grandmere's dress, her skin, her flesh on her way past. She landed and turned, ready to strike again.

Grandmere stood suddenly still. She clutched at her neck and face. A gash on her cheek split open. A hard ridge of black bone came out, and slick, oily pinfeathers, and a red-black eye. The crow wriggled out of her cheek, tearing as it went, and when it burst forth, it uncorked the wound and a torrent of black birds flew screaming into the burning hall. The beating of their wings turned the room into a black cacophony, until I couldn't see more than a few feet in front of me.

Grandmere reached up to her ruined face and took the edges of the wound in her lavender gloves. She grabbed and pulled.

And darkness poured out.

The room filled with crows, more than I could possibly count. Wings and beaks and eyes, shrieking, tearing at my face and hands. When they cleared, I saw what Grandmere really was.

The soft old woman who smelled of violets lay crumpled in a heap on the floor, and the thing that lived inside that body had poured out into the hall. There were tentacles and beaks and fins and human arms and legs, the paws of a lion, and those malicious slit eyes I'd seen on the card. But all of this was just a corona circling a purple-black hole in the air. I felt my feet slip on the carpet, dragged in by the magnetic pull of that rip in the world.

"I've done this more often than you have," she said. "If you want to learn, I can help you."

Scattering crows in his wake, Rhys lunged at her. "*Stop!*" I yelled, but it was too late. His momentum carried him forward even as he turned to try to obey me. Grandmere lashed out a tentacle, snatched him up, and flung him toward the maw.

Without thinking, I opened my mouth and breathed in.

He hung, for a moment, suspended between us. And then

Grandmere let go, and Rhys was flung backward. Before I knew what had happened, he disappeared.

I yelped and spat him back out. He lay on the floor unmoving. I was still rooted to the spot; I couldn't run to him. I couldn't tell if he was still Rhys, or a thing.

"See?" Grandmere said. "That wasn't so bad, was it?"

My whole body was shaking. I stared at her with all the fury I could manage.

"Oh, don't be sad," she said. "What would he ever have done with his life? You'll make better use of him than he ever would have."

Luma and Grandpa were still here somewhere, buried under the torrent of crows. "*Don't touch her*," I said, not knowing where to direct my voice. "She'll pull you in."

"Why help them?" she asked. "What have they ever done for you?"

It was then that I saw the torches appearing in the yard.

The townspeople of Winterport had panicked. And they'd done what townspeople did, in a panic. They'd gone home, and prepared, and gathered their forces. The torches bobbed and swayed as they got closer to the house. Their flickering light gleamed off of scythes and the barrels of hunting rifles. And in the midst of them was a strange shape, like a moving pillar of flame. I squinted at it, not understanding what I saw.

Grandmere noticed it at the same time as I did. "Oh,

foolishness," she said. She bubbled and writhed past me toward the door.

Luma darted out of the cloud of crows and grabbed Rhys under the arms. As she did, she looked up at me. "You can do it," she said. "I love you, Ellie." And then she was gone, dragging Rhys's body away into the shadows.

"Grandmere," I said. "*Forget the townspeople.* Talk to me."

She turned, and a thousand mouths opened and showed teeth.

"Do you really think you can command me so easily?" she said. "I have business to attend to. I'll deal with you later."

"*Leave us,*" I said. "This is your last warning."

Her many voices cackled.

"We're leaving together," Grandmere said. "And only after you help me eat this awful little mob."

"That's not happening."

"But why?" she asked. "Why be alone when you could be with someone who loves you?"

I knew she meant it. I couldn't move toward her, but I held out my hands.

"I love you, too, Grandmere," I said. "I mean it. I hope you know that."

I was crying as I opened my mouth wide.

First a crow flew backward into my mouth, struggling and flapping its wings. Then, from somewhere in her mass, a handful of mice broke loose, and they too careened across the space between us and disappeared. Grandmere seemed to feel it and turned the bulk of her body toward me.

"You think you're clever," she said. "I—"

I pulled harder. She pulled back. But she'd been spreading herself thin all day, and she'd lost the skin that usually held her together. I yanked, and a pile of soldiers in brown uniforms spilled out onto the floor, stumbling backward into the black hole in the middle of me. Grandmere howled and screamed and sent a torrent of crows toward me. They pecked me, tore at me, and I couldn't move to stop them. But eventually, they too were swallowed, and as they began to vanish into me I could see that we were ringed with fire. There was nowhere to go.

It was horrible, the feeling as I devoured her—exactly as horrible as it would have been to do it at a table with a knife and fork. The hundreds of twisting limbs stretched and contorted as they were dragged toward me, and she screamed and begged and fought. As I worked my way through the limbs of all those creatures, I felt the void at her center begin to tug at me. But it was just nothing, I told myself, vast empty nothing. There was room inside of nothing for more nothing.

And so my nothing devoured her nothing and then it was over, and I felt heavy, and expansive, like I'd been swollen up with things that were not me. And I wondered briefly if this was what she'd been pushing me toward, what she'd wanted to happen.

And then I fainted.

When I opened my eyes again, the house was burning down.

I could see people from Winterport running back and forth across the floor. They were stomping around, throwing things for the sheer joy of throwing them. They knocked down the cut glass candy dish and it smashed to pieces, scattering peppermints. The stairs still blazed, and people were lighting smaller fires in the dining room and the parlor. Others ran past me into the night with beautiful things from the house. They grabbed our silver coffee service, our dining chairs, and any paintings that weren't of us. The portraits of the family made their own bonfire just a few feet from me.

I started trying to crawl, and then saw the shiny shoes of Father Thomas. I lay very still and played dead. He did a hasty anointing of the sick, and then a blazing chunk of wood fell between us from the upstairs, and he jumped back and ran out of the house.

I tried to lift my head, but the air was filled with smoke, and I could barely see. My skin felt hot and ragged, blistery. I didn't want to burn to death, but it didn't seem like I could do much else. At least my family was safe. I wondered what would become of Rhys, if he would ever get better. I felt to see if I could control him, wherever he was now, and found nothing. That seemed like a good sign. I let my head sink down and imagined the cool cellar beneath me. Imagined lying still in the dark. I could die like this.

And then I felt hands lift me up, hands that burned to the touch.

"You do like feeling sorry for yourself," a voice said beside my head. I thought I recognized it, but then I wasn't so sure.

I woke up with cool grass pressed against my face and the sting of burns all over my body. I sat up, and all around me was my family.

Luma and Grandpa Miklos sat on their haunches, their heads tipped to the side, watching me. Mother was a little ways off, but when she saw me sit up, she dragged herself across the grass and threw her arms around me. Her damp skin hurt and soothed my burns at the same time. Margaret squatted a few feet away, holding a frying pan in one hand and a butcher knife in the other, looking furious. But when she saw me awake, she nodded soberly.

Beside me on the ground was Rhys. He was breathing, I could see, but only shallowly. And his open eyes seemed to stare up at nothing.

"I swallowed him," I said. "Luma, I'm so sorry."

"I saw what happened. You tried to protect him."

She looked sad and glanced from Rhys to me and back again.

"He'll be alright," she said. "I know he will."

I could feel the heat on my legs, but it took me a few minutes before I could bear to look forward. I knew what I'd see.

The house had gone up quickly: it was late summer and the air was dry. The place we'd called home was now a skeleton, or a drawing, spindly lines that climbed toward the sky, blazing. The carvings, the shingles, the baroque trim were all gone. It was now just a house of flames under a sky filled with billowing clouds of smoke. A wall fell down and suddenly I could see in, as though it were a dollhouse. A family of flames seated at the dining room table, flickering children racing up and down the stairs.

We heard a noise like a gunshot, and I realized the roof of the greenhouse must have fallen in. That was when I started to cry, thinking of all the drakondia dead, the snake lily that had come all the way from Crete to be here, and all the things inside me that were useless to smother the flames. Luma reached out her arms and pulled me in, and I sobbed until I couldn't breathe anymore.

"We lost everything," I said, and I had to say it again, because I was muffled by her lap.

"We didn't lose everything," she said. "We've got Mama, and Grandpa, and Rhys, and Margaret, and you and me. And you know Arthur won't let anything too terrible happen to us."

I started crying harder.

"I let him go," I said. "I let him go, and now we're never going to see him again."

She rubbed her palm along my back in circles.

"Silly," she said. "He's the one who carried you out."

She pointed to something standing closer to the house, hard

to see against the flames, because it burned so brightly itself. A man made of wildfire.

I tried to walk to him, but all I could do was crawl. So I crawled to him. When I got closer, I reached out to touch his leg, and yanked my hand back—he was too hot to touch, too bright to look at.

"Wait," he said. A little ways away, on the lawn, I could see a body. It looked like nothing without him inside of it, barely a skeleton. But he bent over it, and the fire curled around it, and he slipped it on. He stood up, Arthur again, but different. The creature inside of him still burned, but more faintly.

I forced my legs under me. When I got up, he held out his arms. I took them to keep from falling. I still felt like I was made of lead, heavy with all that mass and nothingness. He was warm from the inside out, and all the burns on my arms and legs seared in response to that heat.

"You came back," I said. And then I thought about the procession of torches. "Did you bring the mob?"

He pointed to the house. The column of smoke was the color of Grandma Persephone's old dress. "The house had to go," he said. "Persephone didn't deserve to stay trapped there." He looked down at me, and the light that blazed from his eyes was so bright that it hurt my eyes.

"You know what it's like," I said. "So you let her go."

"And you, too," he said. "This is too much house for anyone."

I laughed. I was weak, but the tension in my muscles built, the feeling of wanting to leap onto him and tear into him, rip him to shreds, bury my face in his chest. The feeling overwhelmed me. I laughed and cried and couldn't wipe my eyes, because my hands on his arms were the only thing keeping me upright.

"I'm going to leave your family," he said.

"That's fine!" I said, laughing, crying.

"I haven't been alone in fifty years. There is so much I want to do and see."

"Then you should go."

"You could stop me."

"But I won't." Why would I? I'd already let him go. My reward was this: to see him remade. To see him, one last time.

He smiled, light streaming out from his mouth.

"This was real," I said. "You really—"

"Yes, I did."

"Then no matter what else happens, that will never not be true," I said. "And if we never meet again, that will be a happy thing."

"And it will be happy if we do."

I realized I was crying. He wasn't. I don't know if he is something that can cry. I don't know what he is; he is nothing I have ever heard of.

My love is a haunted house, a ghost possessing his own body, a fire that burns itself alive. A light almost too bright to look at, but I forced myself to look as long as I could.

I kissed him. He was startled at first, but he held on. I bit him a little; it was like biting into the sun. I felt the void in me open up and panicked for a moment. But it couldn't devour what he was.

When he put me down and walked away down the hill and into the dark, I crumpled to the ground and stayed there.

I am on fire.

It doesn't hurt, or it does hurt but I don't care, because I can feel myself breaking into pieces. As I rise into the air, I can see my family on the ground below.

As I look at Eleanor, I can remember—not see, not live, but remember—a time when she was six, sitting on my husband's knee, and he held out the watch that he loved so much, the one that gave him his name. She snatched it up, held it in her hands, and looked at me with her ordinary little girl face, and said, "I lived here before, but then you were my mother, not my grandmother."

I had laughed at her then, thinking I knew where my son was—my son was the child Margaret had made me, the one who looked just like my Rhys. But knowledge twists and bends in your hands all the more when you hold it tightly. Does that mean that Eleanor is kissing her murderer on this hilltop while the house they both died in burns behind them? Or was that just something a child said once, a game? What power do I have, or what authority or reason, to say what should or should not be?

And that thought breaks something, some last connection between me and the earth. Beneath me, I hear a tremendous crash and a shudder as the house collapses in on itself: all those high towers and empty attic rooms, all those scratched floors and lovely rugs, the piano, the books, the ledgers and the joists and the walls and, somewhere, the box that held Arthur's heart back before my first dead son taught him my family's oldest trick, how to let yourself turn inside out and become something else. And now I am inside out, too, spilling out in all directions in curling entrails of smoke that I have no desire to read, spiraling into the sky, little shreds of who I was raining down on my husband, on my children and grandchildren, on the village below, and into the wine-dark sea.

EPILOGUE

LOVE IS HARD FOR THINGS LIKE US. LUMA SAYS love feels like carrying an egg in your mouth. I know what she means: it is holding someone between your teeth and knowing how sweet it would feel to bite down, and not biting down, and letting that be sweeter.

After the fire burned out, we picked through the still-hot ashes of the house, looking for anything of value we might sell. There wasn't much. We found a handful of fire-softened gold coins here and there, and a blackened tintype of Margaret as a young woman, hugely pregnant, looking pleased. And we found the pocket watch, glowing almost red, the face cracked and broken, the hands stopped. We pulled it out anyway. We put it around Miklos's neck, once it had cooled down. He thumped his tail on the ground and yawned at us.

Margaret killed a pheasant with a frying pan and slit open its belly, and together we put our hands inside and felt for what we should do next. The only answer we could get was *Go somewhere else.* So at first light, we gathered ourselves up. We walked together down the long road through the birch forest in the pink light: Grandpa Miklos on four legs, Luma and me on two with Mother between us, an arm around each of our necks. Margaret bundled Rhys up into a singed blanket and carried him like a child in her arms.

Nobody in Winterport had gone to bed. When we reached the edge of town, they were milling around in clumps up and down the street. They stopped what they were doing to watch us.

"It's alright," I said, as loud as I could; my throat hurt from the smoke. "We're leaving."

Grandpa went through first, on all fours, the creature they'd heard and sensed in the woods but never seen. Whatever they had imagined, in the light coming off the water he was nothing more than a large, old dog with bad teeth and a lame leg. They parted to let him pass. Babes in arms stretched out their chubby hands to try to reach his fur, unafraid.

We followed the roads until we got to a place where we were unrecognizable enough that we could hitchhike, and then we caught a truck heading south. Four women, a boy, and a ragged dog.

We will eat and find shelter and sleep. We will protect Rhys until we see if there is anything left of him to protect. We will hunt in the forests and barter in the towns, until someday we come to a place where we can stop moving, where we can plant ourselves. Maybe then I will go back to school. Maybe I will learn how to be a witch. Or maybe I'll be something else, something I can't even imagine yet. Maybe that something will see Arthur again. But first, I want to be with my family. I have been away too long, and we need each other now.

We are Zarrins, I tell myself. *We will be fine. We have always been fine.* If I say it this way, I can make it true.

ACKNOWLEDGMENTS

A book is not written by one person, no matter what I might tell myself while looking in the mirror and crooning softly to my warped and shifting reflection. A book is cowritten in two ways: by the people who shape the print material, and the people who shape the writer's experience.

I owe a good deal to Jennifer Azantian, who read an early draft and rejected it so kindly that I sent it to her again three years later. She has since become my agent and has been instrumental to making *What Big Teeth* a book other people would want to read. Thank you, Jen, for not deleting my second email. I would also like to thank my editor, Trisha de Guzman, for believing in this book and for championing this project at every stage of the process. And a thank-you as well to the members of VCU's Novel Workshop, who read this book over the course of a year, especially Cade Varnado. Cade, you helped me diagram my plot in an empty classroom after-hours and let me talk you into ordering a cocktail called Those Damn Witches. You are so loved and so very missed.

More personally: I owe a lot to my parents, who showed me Edward Gorey and *The Addams Family* and who suggested that I might try writing some stories down instead of shouting them, to the state of Maine (especially Anthony Elkins), and to my Hungarian great-grandparents who found each other in America by chance because they both had the same last name, Anglicized in the same way: Sabo. And finally: thank you to Anna, and Jake, and Khan. With you, all things are possible.

Turn the page for an excerpt from
We All Fall Down

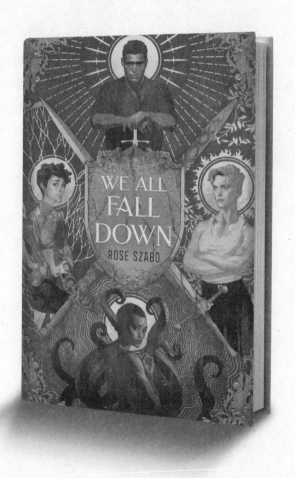

The first book in the River City duology

WE ALL
FALL
DOWN

BEING AN ACCOUNT OF
THE LIVES OF FOUR YOUNG PEOPLE
OF RIVER CITY

As told to R. L. Emblem

In the Year of Queen Zara 42.

PROLOGUE

In the secret city at the hub of the world, the revolution was over. King Nathan the Giant was locked in his own dungeon, waiting to stand trial. But the heavy rains would not stop falling in cold sheets as Astrid made her way to the palace.

People wanted to be in the streets, but the pounding rain drove them back, and so they huddled in archways and under awnings. Yellow squares of light stained the water that pattered ankle-deep in the street as Astrid scurried along. On a wide porch, teenagers in palace livery sang the city anthem in four-part harmony. They stopped as she passed, and some of the boys gave her ragged salutes. She dipped her umbrella forward, a kind of nod, and kept going. No matter who saluted her, she was alone out here in the middle of the street, as she sloshed her way through the puddles. Nobody else had any reason to venture forth tonight. Nobody else's life was coming apart in their hands.

At last, she came to the palace. Its front gateway was unguarded, and the iron gates lay crumpled in a slag heap on the cobbles, so she traveled uninterrupted through the sentryless double doors into the atrium with its great mural of Otiotan fighting the serpent with his flaming sword. Here there was a party. And when they saw who stood in the atrium shaking the rain from her umbrella, the crowd let up a cheer. Astrid, the small brown witch they'd known since they were children, who was now their champion. Astrid, who had blown the gates off the palace with her powerful witch-craft. Astrid, with a sprig of wild mint pinned to her coat, to signify that she was one of the people. Astrid, whose pager was always on to answer the calls of the sick and the needy.

She had to be careful. This was supposed to be a people's revolution. She didn't want to draw too much attention to herself. Didn't want to risk becoming a Hero. She almost laughed at the thought: a flaming sword in one small hand. Any blushing Maiden would have to bend down to cling to Astrid.

Still, it was useful that no one would stop her. Why would they? She was on their side. They'd let her go wherever she pleased.

Where she wanted to go, of course, was the dungeon.

She picked her way through the clusters of revolutionaries who cluttered the halls and vaulted rooms of the palace, stripped to their underwear or wrapped in towels made from torn-down banners. They'd broken into the vintage, and now they were getting smashed on wine older than their grandparents. She made her way down through the winding levels of the palace, past the kitchens, where a bunch of drunk ten-year-olds were trying to roast a pig on a spit under the direction of the palace's old cook, who winked and grinned at her as she passed.

The guards at the edge of the dungeon saluted her. Kyle and Pete, of course. They'd joined the revolution for the same reasons they'd joined baseball games and bar fights: They liked to feel part of something. They were sloshed, too, but trying to hide it behind good posture.

"What of the prisoner?" she said.

"He hasn't spoken or taken food this past day."

"I'll try to get him to eat," she said. "We need him to be strong enough to stand trial."

They nodded fervently.

"Will you execute him, Astrid?" Kyle asked. "It would be fitting."

"No, dummy," Pete said. "It has to be all of us. We'll throw rocks at him or something."

She tossed her head. "Leave me."

They glanced at each other briefly, and then hurried out of the corridor and up the stairs. She knew she'd find them in the kitchen when she was done, drinking with the kids.

The king was in the last cell at the far end of the hallway. Of course he was. It was almost laughable, how things always went exactly the way you would expect. On the table just outside the cell was a dented plate with a few slices of stale bread on it; no wonder he hadn't eaten. She slid back the iron partition that covered the little barred window. "Nathan," she said.

He stood up perfectly straight, his arms folded behind his back as though he were examining a piece of art. His red beard was streaked with blood from his chin, and more blood was crusted on his eyebrow. He smiled when he saw her. Oh, they'd broken his front teeth. She winced, and tried to hide it.

"Astrid," he said. "It's good to see you."

Astrid's heart swelled in her chest. Her king, now and forever. A great thinker, an inventor, big like a tree. Thirty now, with wrinkles blooming at the corners of his eyes. A man with a voice that could lead armies. She had to steady herself against the door to stop her knees from buckling, seeing him like this.

"There's no need for your bluster, tyrant," she said. "We're alone." She hoped he would take her meaning: that they were alone, but to still be careful.

"My apologies, old friend."

"Hardly friend to you these days."

He shook his head. She knew what he meant, so he didn't have to risk saying it out loud. They'd always been like this, even after Marla. Always knew the other's mind.

"Where's Marla?" he asked.

"The people blame her," she said. "They are saying that without her, your excesses would not have been possible. She has fled."

Nathan's brow furrowed. "Is she hurt?"

"Rest assured," Astrid said. "She'll be found."

He put a hand to his mouth.

"Please," he said. "You have to do something about the baby."

"That's up to me now, isn't it?"

He managed a smile. She smiled back.

He mouthed to her through the bars: *Come here.* She took a step closer to the grate, and he approached it from his side. Then: *Shut your eyes.*

In the darkness behind her eyelids, Astrid stood close to King Nathan the Giant. She took her hands off the cold door so that she could pretend there was nothing between them but air. He was right in front of her, so tall that her head only came up to his chest. She could smell his cologne from here, and behind it his breath, sour from hunger and tinged with blood. And something else, too: a metallic smell.

He'd been standing when she approached, she realized, because he'd been standing all day.

She opened her eyes.

"It's getting worse, isn't it?" she said.

He laughed a little, and she could see him flinch when the air hit his broken teeth. "It's bad today. I can't bend my knees."

Astrid's stomach dropped. "But you're not king anymore."

"We knew there was a chance it wouldn't work that way."

Astrid's heart sank. Everything they'd done to make things different, and it still wasn't enough.

Astrid tried not to let her fear show on her face, although they both knew what would happen to him soon; what happened to every king. She'd need to do something about that, and soon, but she wasn't sure yet what. She had no plan. She—

"I really thought it could be different," he said. "I thought *I* could be different. But I'm like all of them, aren't I? I can feel myself going mad. And now—" He looked down at his legs.

"Stop that," Astrid snapped. "This isn't over yet."

He was looking at her again with those clear eyes. Astrid had a hard time with his eyes these days. He was right. He was entering his madness. But he wasn't there yet.

She'd been working on this spell without telling him for some time. He wouldn't have approved, would have told her that they should focus on their plan, that if it worked, they'd both be free. But Astrid was never one to count on a single plan. And now she was frightened, but relieved.

She quietly said a word or two, and felt a little ping on her scalp as one of her braids undid itself. It would take a few minutes to work, if she'd done it right. And by then she'd be long gone. She looked at Nathan, trying not to cry.

"You should eat something," she said.

He nodded, looking weary. "I will," he said. "Just make sure this is over."

She fled from the dungeon. In the kitchen, she told the spit-turning guards to fix the prisoner a plate, a good one this time. And then she went upstairs, through mazes of corridors, stole a raincoat, and let herself out through a side door into the rainy night.

As soon as she was out of sight of the palace, she said the four words that would release another spell she'd braided earlier. It came undone, and she was no longer walking but skimming low across the ground. It was faster this way, and she needed to be fast. She needed to get to Marla before it was too late. Luckily, she knew the queen well. She knew exactly where she'd go in a crisis.

She slid over the wet streets, the rain quickly soaking her skirt, and over the edge of the hill that led down to the riverbank. When she reached the river, her heels dipped just below the surface, soaking through her worn-out boots. She swore and skidded on. The water was raging tonight, and the magic that kept her just above it could barely keep up with it. She stuttered along the waves, picking up her feet to avoid logs that were tossed as easily as kindling in the torrent. She kept her eyes ahead as she ran, on the island that loomed ahead, and the crude stone castle built directly into the island's cliffside. The summer palace. No light came from it that she could see. Good. Marla had enough sense to hide.

When she reached the island, she found herself running sideways up a wall of debris: churning logs and branches that battered against the palace's battlements with every surge of the river. Her foot got caught and she heard something snap. Before she could feel it, she unleashed another spell she'd saved in a braid, the one that killed pain completely. This was too important for her to be distracted. She cleared the wall and floated down into the courtyard beyond. She glanced down only briefly before deciding that pain or no pain, she didn't want to look at her foot just yet.

When Astrid opened one side of the great double doors, she spotted the heap in the corner immediately. A Black woman was huddled under a plaid blanket against the far wall of the great feast hall, next to a battery-powered lantern draped with a scarf. Her legs were splayed out in front of her and she clutched her belly with both hands. As Astrid got closer, Marla looked up at her with those wide, lovely eyes that swayed everyone who saw them.

She was beautiful, Astrid had to admit. Even with rivulets of sweat running down her forehead, even with her mouth locked in a grimace, she was the most beautiful woman who had ever lived. And more than that, she glowed from the inside, a font of living magic. It drew people to her; everyone wanted a little bit of what she had.

"You came," Marla said.

"Of course I did," Astrid snapped. She didn't like the implication that she might not. "Them turning on you was a surprise. What happened here?"

"I was running, and I fell," Marla said. "I think something's broken. And they're not coming."

Astrid let go of the spell that held her aloft, and even with the numbing, she instantly regretted putting weight on her foot. "Let me see," she said, and dropped to her knees. She realized the floor wasn't slick with water, as she'd thought, but with blood. A lot of it. Oh no. "Are you in pain?" she asked.

"Not anymore," Marla said. And then, seeing the look on Astrid's face, "That can't be good, can it?"

"It's not." Astrid put her hand on Marla's thigh, and it came back red. "How long have you been bleeding like this?"

"I don't know. A while."

Marla was a problem, Astrid thought as she worked. The most beautiful woman who had ever lived, a living fountain of love and magic, wife of the king, and she was so—so passive. How long had she been lying there while her life ebbed away, without doing anything, without tearing rags, without trying to save herself? Maybe that was why people lined up to do what Marla wanted. Maybe that was—

It was then that Astrid felt what Marla had already known. There wasn't one baby. There were two. And something else was wrong, too.

"Marla," Astrid said. "They're twins."

Marla smiled patiently. "I know."

"One of them is . . . wrapped around the other. It doesn't feel like the cord. It feels like—"

"One of them is special."

"I'm not sure—"

"Do whatever you need to do."

She made Astrid feel stupid. Damn her. Astrid worked by the light of the lantern until time grew hazy. She talked to Marla the way she'd talk to any laboring mother: making jokes, getting her to tell stories, keeping her awake. She undid spell after spell, feeling the braids burst loose on her aching head: a spell for more blood, a spell for a weak heart.

Everyone loved Marla. Even Astrid, who could barely stand her, loved her. It was impossible not to love her. Astrid fought back tears; she had to work.

"What do you think about names?" she asked when Marla fell silent for too long, when her breathing got too shallow.

"I don't know about the girl," Marla said. "But the boy's name is David."

"David," Astrid said. "That's a good name. How'd you think of that?"

She felt Marla's breathing change, and then stop. "Shit," Astrid said. She hated this. She undid a braid she'd been saving, one that was probably a bad idea: a spell to separate things that were stuck.

And then, all at once, there was a bundle of sticky flesh in her arms. One baby, and one tangle of boneless red snakes wrapped around it. She should have saved the spell. The baby wasn't crying, and his—his!—face was turning blue. Astrid screamed and dug her fingernails into the shape that wrapped around the baby's neck, and the thing made of snakes hissed and fell backward onto the floor in a heap. And then in the light from the lantern, Astrid saw it plainly.

It had a body like a child: two arms, two legs, a head of dark hair. A face that already looked like Marla's, wide-eyed and innocent. But it also had eight horrible long arms like an octopus, longer than its body, growing out of its back and sides, lined on the underside with rows of red suckers. Its hissing mouth was filled with rows of tiny teeth like a piranha. Astrid clutched the wailing baby to her chest and stared down at the thing lying on the floor in the puddle of Marla's blood.

It was horrible. Horrible, horrible. And Marla—Astrid looked down.

Whatever force had animated Marla, that had drawn witches and street sweepers and kings to her, had deserted her. She was dead. And Astrid's heart sank. If Marla was dead, they had no Maiden. And without a Maiden, no magic.

Astrid could feel it receding already, that current that she had always dipped into to make order in her world. To heal and to hurt. With Marla gone, it was like the tide had gone out and left her stranded.

There was nobody here to see her cry, so she let herself cry while she wrapped the baby in Marla's old scarf. David. He looked so much like Nathan. Beautiful. What would he become without parents?

The other thing was trying to drag itself onto its belly. Astrid hated to look at it. She shuddered, and limped away. She had to do something with this baby. She had to keep him safe.

For a moment, she had a vision of keeping him. Astrid the revolutionary and her beautiful son. But she shook the thought from her head. It would raise too many questions, her going off into the night and coming back with a baby. She swallowed the lump in her throat. He wouldn't be safe anywhere in this city, not with his mother dead and his father locked up. They'd want to kill him, too, just to make sure that the whole business didn't start up again. The son of a dethroned king and a dead queen was a good bet for a Hero.

A tiny, desperate hope bloomed in Astrid. She tried not to think of Nathan saying *You have to do something about the baby.* Surely, he didn't mean it like that. And even if he did, he was in his madness. And Marla was gone. There was no one here to make a decision but her.

So she had to get him out of here. She'd need to get him to the mainland, somewhere no one would recognize him. And maybe if she was lucky, he'd be back before Nathan was dead. Before the last of the magic had ebbed from the world like blood from a wound. Heroes always came just in time.

She staggered from the summer palace, into the driving rain. She undid one last braid. She hoped it would be enough. She tried not to think of Marla dead. There would be plenty of time in the coming days and weeks to feel the losses of tonight.

The baby in her arms wriggled, and for a moment, she thought of the other thing, the thing she had left on the floor. But between the pain blooming in her foot, the driving rain, and the warm baby sleeping in her arms and breaking her heart, Astrid blotted it from her mind.

THE
FALL

ONE

It was still August when Jesse ran away.

He'd been a good son, stopped asking questions about where he was allowed to go or when, looked down when Paul called him faggot, and mumbled *yes, sir, yes, ma'am* at the dinner table. He'd given his paychecks to Paul, and had hidden an envelope of tips, skimmed a dollar or two at a time, in the gap between the floor and the baseboard where he'd kept the postcard his best friend had sent him when he was eleven. He'd turned eighteen and sat quietly through the argument where his mom said he was just a kid and Paul said he was a man and should be fending for himself, and he'd waited for them to go camping for their anniversary, and he'd bought a ticket to the place on the postcard: a gleaming jeweled island city, like the Mont-Saint-Michel, with a great iron suspension bridge connecting it to the mainland. *Greetings from River City*, said the postcard. And on the back, in crabbed tiny boy handwriting, a note.

One by one, all Jesse's other secret places had been found: the shoebox in the back of his closet where he kept a girl's black T-shirt and a pair of soccer socks. The loose floorboard under the bed where he'd hid a magazine or two for a while. One at a time, like fortresses under siege, those hiding places had fallen. But the gap in the baseboard hadn't let him down yet. It had saved him $200 and that postcard. And so that was what he had when he left his house at 11:45 p.m. on a clear night, right at the end of summer when the heat was starting to break. He walked to the bus station, his big backpack heavy with packed sandwiches, clean underwear, and library books he felt a little guilty about planning to never return.

He'd done some research on the internet about River City. It wasn't supposed to be real; he'd only found it on old message boards, most of which were full of random nonsense about ghosts and games you could play with elevators and time travel. They'd said that to get a ticket, you had to go to a bus station at midnight on a clear night with a breeze in one of a handful of towns, and get on the bus that pulled up, and pay them whatever they asked for. Some of the older stories said that they'd ask for weird things, like blood, or hair, or a sigh, or the name of your true love. Other people said that was bullshit, that they'd been on the bus this year even, and all they'd wanted was cash. Jesse wasn't sure, but he was ready to give them whatever they asked for. It couldn't be worse than staying where he was.

The bus station was closed, so he huddled outside against the wall, hiding in his sweatshirt. He hoped that nobody would see him; Paul drank with cops, and they'd ratted Jesse out before. He pulled his hood over his face and folded his arms across his chest, hoping he looked tough. Tough was hard for him. He was too skinny, his face too soft and round for it to really carry off well.

From outside of him, we can see how beautiful he is. A little bit lanky and awkward, but with a good gentle face. A scar on his forehead, usually hidden by a soft shock of hair, that he got from Paul, with some help from the sharp edge of a coffee table. Until he was fifteen, he'd told people it was a witch's mark.

He checked his watch. Midnight. No bus. He waited. Buses were late, right? But minutes wore past, and he started to feel like an idiot. Maybe he should just come back in the morning, get on a bus to New York, or wherever it was that kids like him went when they ran away from home. Not that he was a kid anymore. Paul said it often enough.

He was about to shoulder his backpack and go home when he saw a bus coming down the road.

It wasn't a bus like the kind he was used to. It looked like a silver bullet trailer, with red trim, and windows set on an angle, giving the impression of speed, and big wide headlights and a wide front fender that looked like a cartoon mouth. He laughed out loud when he saw it. This was more like it. This was a magic bus to a city that only people on the internet knew about. One hundred percent.

It came to a halt, and the shadowy bus driver pulled a lever to hinge open the doors, and Jesse shouldered his backpack and stumbled up the steps. "Hi," he said. He looked around. There were only a few other people on the bus. A mother sitting near two girls wrapped in a blanket, falling over each other to press their faces to the window. A middle-aged couple and a dog. Jesse grinned wildly at all of them. And then the bus driver, an impossibly jowly and warty man, stuck out his hand.

"What do you need?" Jesse asked.

"What you got?"

Jesse rummaged around in his wad of cash. "I can do . . . fifty?" he said.

"Looks like more than fifty."

"What's the price? Is there a price?"

"Give me all of that."

"You've gotta be kidding me."

"Do you want on the bus or not?"

Jesse felt a stab of fear. Every bit of money he had seemed like a little too much, even for a journey into a magical world. But what choice did he have?

"Or I'll take that postcard," the bus driver said.

Jesse wondered for a second, fearful, how the man had known about the postcard. And then he realized he'd gotten it out with the money. It wobbled in his trembling hands.

"Uh," Jesse said. "Why?"

"Maybe it's valuable."

Jesse swallowed. "I'll give you the cash," he said.

The driver took the wad from him. "Sit wherever."

Jesse stumbled to a seat and fell into it, dazed and panicking. This wasn't at all what he'd planned for. Now he was on a bus with no money. He clutched the postcard for a while before stuffing it into his backpack. Nobody was taking that from him.

The bus rumbled along for hours, through small towns. Jesse wondered vaguely why the lore said the bus came at midnight, when it was clear that it was on a regular damn bus schedule, picking people up between something like 11 p.m. and 4 a.m., and late to each stop by the impatient, desperate looks of the people getting on board. The bus driver extorted all of them, although some people managed to talk him down to something reasonable. One guy didn't have any money, and Jesse watched the driver barter with him for his hat and his jacket and eventually his pocket square. The man sat down in the row opposite Jesse, looking lost and bereft. He kept putting his hand to something under his sweater that jerked periodically. Jesse watched, fascinated, until they stopped in another small town and a woman got on with a scarf wrapped so tightly around her throat that it almost hid the lump bulging from the side of her face.

As the bus filled up, Jesse realized that about half the people who got on had something they were hiding. He started scoping out the people who'd been on when he'd boarded, and realized that the girls sitting by the window were fused at the hip: two girls, one pair of legs. They were fighting over whether the window was going to be cracked open or shut.

Eventually, Jesse drifted off to sleep in the warm darkness of the bus, knocked out by the hissing of the hydraulic brakes and the rumble of the engine. He rocked from side to side, his legs tucked up and braced against the seat in front of him, his head propped on his knees for a pillow. The murmur of voices talking quietly entered his dream in dribs and drabs. *What if it doesn't work? This hospital is the best—they'll know what to do. Girls, stop hitting. I'm hungry.* Snores. The sound of the girls hitting each other and giggling while their mother shushed them angrily. He felt a kind of vague kinship with all of them. After all, there was something wrong with him, too.

He had to go now because he had to get away. He had a feeling that if he stayed, he was going to die. Not of sickness or accident, but because he would get himself killed. Maybe wanted to get himself killed. That feeling had been building in him for months.

It'd hit a peak in the last few days of junior year, when a kid he kind of knew—a starter on the football team—had been in the bathroom at the same time as him. Jesse usually got out of the way of guys like that; he was skinny, they were big. But for some reason he'd stared at him, and the guy had seen him staring, and before Jesse knew what was up, he'd been against the wall, the guy's palms grinding his shoulders into the cinderblocks, the guy's hips against him, too. Jesse wasn't sure in that moment if he was about to kiss him or murder him in cold blood, but the bathroom door had started to open, and the guy had let him go, and he'd escaped, for now, the fate he seemed to be courting. He had to fix himself, before something worse happened.

The sun slanting through the window woke him up at last. It was morning, and they were rumbling along an empty, straight country road, corn on both sides, waving in the breeze, as far as he could see. Trees behind the corn. It was like a corridor of nothing, a long, empty drive.

The man sitting opposite him saw that he was awake, and winked at him. Jesse realized it wasn't pocket square guy, who had moved several seats back and was eyeing them warily. This was a massive white guy wearing a greasy black raincoat, with a wild white beard like a feral Santa Claus. He was younger, though, than most of the men Jesse had seen who had beards like that. He also had a milky right eye, like a cataract, under which his pupil swam, just barely visible. Something about the guy looked familiar to Jesse, but he couldn't place him.

The man fished around in his pocket, and Jesse winced, until the man pulled out a hard candy in a crinkled yellow wrapper. "Want one?" he asked.

"No," Jesse said. "Thanks."

"This bus used to be faster."

"You taken it a lot?"

"Not in a long time," the man said. Jesse realized he smelled vaguely of piss, and also something else: a coppery smell like corroded metal. The guy took out a bottle from somewhere inside his coat, and uncapped it, and took a swig. He was missing a few teeth in the front. "I like to ride it now and then. Scope out what's going on."

"Huh."

"Here's a history lesson," the man said. "People used to come to River City because it was where they could be the way they are without attracting much attention. Then the hospital opened. Now they come here to get themselves cut up and put back together in the shape of ordinary people." He tipped the bottle in Jesse's direction; Jesse shook his head. "Is that what you're here for, girl? To get yourself cut up and sewn into something that makes sense?"

Jesse looked around to see if anyone else had heard. No one else appeared to be listening at all. The mother with the twin girls was checking her phone, over and over again, while the twin girls slept tangled in each other's arms. The middle-aged couple was petting their increasingly nervous dog. He'd sometimes had this happen before, people mistaking him for a girl. He didn't like how happy it made him.

"I don't know what you're talking about," he said to the old man.

"I don't have time for your feelings," the man said. "I got on here to warn you about something."

Jesse felt a prickle, like he might have to sneeze, or like he might be about to explode. And something else, too. The thrill of impending adventure.

"Tell me," Jesse said.

The man looked somber, like he was about to say something. And then he twitched, and his expression buckled. "Oh, shit," he said, groaning. His voice changed, and so did his demeanor, and all at once he looked stupid, helpless. He looked down at the bottle in his hand. "Fuck," he said, and took a big gulp of it, spilling some of it into his beard. Jesse had thought earlier that it was all white, but now he saw it was streaked through with red. The big man swallowed, wiped the back of his mouth with one hand, and tried to focus his one good eye on Jesse.

"I have a hard time," the old man said. "I have a hard time staying present."

Ah, okay. This was the kind of guy who always tried to talk to Jesse. It was something about his open face, he guessed. He had one of those faces that said, *Please, tell me everything bad that's ever happened to you.*

Jesse sighed. "It's okay," he said. "You called me a girl. How did you know?"

"I said that?" Jesse started to give up, but the man chewed on a fingernail. "No, I wouldn't call you *a* girl. I would've said *the* girl."

"What's that mean?"

"Ugh." The old man clutched his head. "Fuck. Okay. Important question. What time are we upon?"

"What?"

"Have y'all killed the monster already?"

"What monster?"

"How about the Hero? Have you met him?"

"Uh . . . no? I don't think so?"

"Do you know you're the girl?"

"You just told me."

"Jesus." The man shut his eyes, and took a big sniff, like he was trying to swallow a booger. He popped his eyes open and the milky one rolled around in his head. "You got anything I could eat? That helps."

"You've got some hard candies."

"Right on." The man dug around in his own pocket. "Huh, maybe I don't have them yet . . ."

"River City ahoy," the bus driver called out.

Jesse looked away from the old man, and up through the bus's bulging windshield. They must have been slowly climbing, because now they were cresting a hill, and below them, spread out, was a great and winding river.

It was called the Otiotan, he knew from the forums. They'd placed the river's origins somewhere in Virginia, or Tennessee, or Kentucky, but no one could say where it met the ocean. It lay across a valley, wider than any river he'd ever seen, like an unknown Mississippi. And in the middle of it was the island, shaped like a great teardrop, low at the upstream end, with a great hill on the downstream side. Gleaming with great silver buildings, and covered in trees. Jesse had never imagined a city could be so green.

"Wow," the old man across from him said.

"I thought you said you'd been there before."

"What are you talking about?" the man said. He glanced over

at Jesse, and smiled, showing a mouthful of perfect teeth. Jesse blinked, not sure what he was seeing, or what he had seen before. "You going there, too? Maybe we can seek our fortunes together."

"Uh," Jesse said. "Look, man, I—"

"Hey, don't worry about it," the man said. "More fortune for me." He propped his arms behind his head, flipped his hat down over his face, and appeared, to Jesse, to be getting ready for a quick nap.

Jesse studied the man. Even with his face covered, there really was something familiar about him that was hard to place. Something about his large square frame, the elasticity of his smile, even his weird way of talking, reminded Jesse of someone he'd known before, a long time ago. Or maybe it was just because they'd both called Jesse a girl without meaning it as an insult.

But Jesse lost the thread of that thought as the bus descended the hill and hit the bridge that led to the city. The wheels switched from a low rumble to a sharp staccato. The wind rushing through the metal bridge sounded almost like a harmonica, and below them in the river was a smaller island with a ruined castle on it, and Jesse lost himself in imagining being down among those rocks. And then, before he could breathe in to will it away, he felt that prickle again, and then a sharp *pop*.

It hurt, like having all your joints dislocated and jammed back in at new angles, like growing new organs, like a total bodyectomy, and the accompanying dizziness as his inner ear tried to compensate and the cramps, good god, the cramps. And Jesse sat there stunned. She knew without looking exactly what had happened to her, even though it was impossible, or at the very least, unlikely.

The old man in the seat glanced over at her. "Huh," he said. "I thought so."

Jesse widened her eyes at him. "Don't say anything," she hissed.

"I'll be quiet," the old man said. "But will you?"

They'd crossed the bridge, and were suddenly on a long boulevard with low old buildings on one side, and on the other, towering new ones. The bus was slowing. The old man jerked a thumb at the bus driver.

"He's gonna sell you to the hospital if you stay on this bus," he said, not bothering to keep his voice low. "They'd pay great for someone like you."

The bus driver turned in his chair as the bus stopped for a light. "Who said that?"

The old man winked his blind eye at Jesse. "Go find the baker's on God Street. Tell Astrid I say hello."

"Astrid," Jesse repeated.

"Yup. Watch your back."

The bus driver put on the hazard lights, and stood up. "Huh," the driver said, looking at Jesse. "Good tip, old man."

The old man stood up and blocked the bus driver's path. "Run," he said. And Jesse snatched up her backpack and ran for the back of the bus.

"Stop that kid!" the bus driver yelled. Stunned passengers stared, doing nothing, as Jesse sprinted past them. She ran for the back of the bus, found the emergency exit door, and flung it open. An alarm went off. Behind her, she saw the driver shove the old man out of the way. And she leaped.

Jesse had always been good at thinking on her feet, but now she was off of them, and careening toward the hood of an old Cadillac. She bent her knees, like they learned in track doing the high jump, and let them buckle under her as she rolled off the hood backward and hit the ground. It hurt, but adrenaline had her up in a second, backpack still on, sweatshirt hood flapping as she ducked through the next lane of traffic. Stunned, she noticed it was mostly bicycles and mopeds that flew around her, riders screaming at her, as she flung herself at the far sidewalk, where she scrambled away into a park on the far side. She glanced back just long enough to see the driver hanging out of the back door of the bus, yelling at her to get back there.

Jesse had always liked running. She wasn't the fastest in track, but she showed up and ran and liked the feeling of being alone, just her and her feet and the wind.

As she sprinted away, she thought briefly that this was the first time in her life she'd run quite like this. Running into the unknown, with no idea what was on the other side to catch her.